THE WESTERN GATE

HISTORICAL MYSTERIES COLLECTION

BARBARA GASKELL DENVIL

Cover design by
It' A Wrap

ALSO BY BARBARA GASKELL DENVIL

For Nick Lawson and Gill Trewick with much love and appreciation

CHAPTER ONE

NARRATIVE

The stench reeked of open sewers and of the unwashed as it oozed and slithered from every opening. The stink of misery, they called it. Misery carries its own vile flavour. Yet filth is equally vile and more tangible. The two putrid odours combined spelled Newgate.

They had all seen men hung from the gibbet, had watched as terror turned to pain, and knew that death could be instant, yet was more often slow. Arrest as the fastest road to the gallows was equally as individual as every criminal's fears.

Haldon knew his trial would bring the freedom he demanded. Bryce oozed the confidence of the man too clever to be caught, though if caught, would gain his freedom soon enough. Wyatt was content to stay living within the gaol where shelter and free food kept him warmer and fatter than living in the gutters of the city outside. Col took whatever came and thought the future a bore. Lewis desperately feared death yet Saul welcomed an ending, however unpleasant, that would finish his suffering. Some feared Purgatory, others sat shivering with thoughts of Hellfire.

Landry simply sat in the shadows, waited, and smiled.

Here the creeping stealth of Hell and the rage of knowing one hell would be replaced by the other more notorious still, encouraged the brutality of every emotion otherwise little seen.

Wyatt sat, legs spread, back against the wall, curls so thick his head felt cushions even against wet stone. The giant was more prominent than the man and he watched, waiting for whatever he could steal. He watched Haldon for Haldon's daughter brought him food and food was certainly worth stealing.

Once incarcerated amongst criminals unable to afford their own cells, most expected to die. The gibbet waited, yet death at the hands of other prisoners was also frequent. Gaol Fever, the plague and every disease known to man could infect prisoners and guards alike. Some surrendered. Others fought. Many were determined and desperation sometimes built hope instead.

Those who walked through the gate and past the gaol, leaving or entering London City through the fifth and western gate, held their noses and ignored the grubby fingers waving from the iron railed windows, and the voices begging for food, for coin, or for blankets.

Haldon yawned. When his mouth clamped shut again, he grinned. "Soon me daughter will bring me food what will last me till trial, and then I goes home to more food. She works in a pie shop. You hungry lot can just sit and watch me eat and dribble as I chews."

Until rain washed out the gutters, much of the city smelled of the collected debris from human and animal waste, but Newgate Gaol was the hurricane of decay and folk walking the pathway from the city through the old Roman wall by means of Newgate towards Tyburn Gallows, held their breath before sweeping onwards to the Strand's great houses, to freedom and the fresh air of the west with the hope of beauty, Westminster and the palace.

Yet those who wished to visit the prison itself, had no choice but to swallow it. Stopping before the archway out of the city and its gatekeeper half asleep, and with her hat pulled down over her eyes, Wren rang the large copper bell and waited for the face to pop into the barred opening high in the door.

"What's your business, wench?"

The rattle of the keys echoed, footsteps quickly down the

narrow stone stairs, and then the keys rattled again. Following the guard, she stumbled through the usual sickening smells and the swamp of black shadows. As the second door swung open the noise immediately crushed the reek. She kicked her way through the muck, the bodies, the squabbles and the fights.

Haldon saw her and jumped up, though his leg irons clanked, and he lost his balance, sitting again amongst the rushes. Wren bent down and flung her arms around her father's neck.

Pretending affection helped them both. "Dad, you look good. How do you feel?"

"As vile as always, girl. What else?"

Having expected the usual reply, Wren sat beside her father and began to unpack everything she had brought. The wicker basket held as much as she'd been able to afford. Bread rolls, dark with rough rye, but tasting of bliss to the half-starved. As she unwrapped the cheese, the tang momentarily overpowered the stink of the cell. Other faces looked up, hoping.

Apples too, one small slab of cooked bacon, and a kidney pie, cold now, but still rich in its filling. Haldon grabbed it all, shared nothing, and first ate the pie. He had always been well built but now the empty skin, deeply wrinkled, flapped around his neck and arms.

"I'd not say no, if some kind soul were to offer a scrap."

Wren turned to see who spoke. She shook her head. "It's for my father. I know you're hungry too, Bryce, but you know I can't afford to feed every man."

Nor could she afford to feed her father but didn't say it.

The dungeon was wide, buried beneath the roads above. Its windows were high for those imprisoned, but on the outside they sat in a row just above the street's cobbles. Each window was twice barred, although otherwise open. This brought air and a sliver of light to the men held within.

"Reckon you're a friend and I'm a good man." Haldon leaned forwards and tossed half a roll and a tiny wedge of cheese. Bryce scrambled for it, grabbed and stuffed it into his mouth before some other hand could steal the treasure.

Gulping, mouth full, Bryce said, "A good man indeed, Haldon. Save my life another day and I'll kiss your feet."

A dozen men laughed. "Bryce, maybe you'll live another day before you swing."

He caught the crumbs, spluttered, licking the lost scraps back from his palm. "I won't swing. Four more days till my trial and reckon I'll be back on the wherry."

"Or pushed off and drinking dirty river water 'stead of bread n' cheese." Col sniggered, knew he would swing and cared little.

"I told you," Bryce glowered, "I'm as innocent as the rising moon. I ain't killed no bugger."

"I'll swing. You'll swing too. I'll sing to you from the gibbet, my friend."

"Me?" Bryce demanded. "I'll not swing on rope nor rail, fool. I was set free last time, and the judge smiled as he said it, the purse I'd given him still hot in his hand."

"Then you'd best pray you gets the same judge."

"All of us are undoubtedly innocent," a soft voice spoke from the shadows. "Indeed, I am innocent of every theft I've ever committed."

Not recognising the voice, Wren turned back to her father. "Dad, your trial's the day after tomorrow. You know I'll be there."

"You'd better, girl," he told her. "I've every expectation of freedom. But if I swing, I don't want you there watching me piss meself."

"I'll prove your innocence, Dad."

"No judge will let you speak," shouted another man from his crumbled bed, the straw bundled into a flat heap beneath one blanket. "No trial will take long enough for other folks to have a say. Takes longer to stand up and speak the oath than time left before the judge yells for your ride to Tyburn."

"Piss off Nad."

Wren waited. She stared up through the nearest window and watched the feet marching past, Boots, wooden soled shoes that clopped, softer shoes, leather soled, tap-tapped. But outside it was

4

gloomy and cold, and so inside it was gloomy and cold. Autumn brought beauty elsewhere but not within the dungeons.

Most men in the dungeon were barefoot. If they had arrived wearing shoes, they had sold them for food and a blanket. Wren's father sat barefoot, and his ankles, iron shackled, were now bleeding.

Lowering her voice, she mumbled, "Dad, I've got to go."

"Girl, you only just got here."

"Yes, to bring you whatever I could. But the guard's waiting." She sighed. "And I have to get back to work, or there'll be no food next time."

"So when's next time?" He was smiling.

"I am wondering the same myself," said the soft voice from the shadows. "An interesting prospect."

Wren refused to look at anyone else. "I'll be there for the trial, and when they release you, there'll be good food ready cooked at home."

She saw nothing of the softly spoken man and he remained where he was, eaten by the darkness. The voice barely murmured, "He'll need no food at the gallows."

Newgate's dungeons had been dug deep but the roof, a little higher than street level, also echoed with vibration and the pounding of frustration and anger from cells above. Stone walls three foot thick, separated the cells below from those above, from those cells holding only one man or one woman, and from the further spread of rooms holding debtors who would stay incarcerated far longer, and sometimes even for life. While trapped in gaol it was impossible to earn and so without stealing, difficult to pay a debt. The women had only recently been separated from brutality and rape, and placed in their own wing. A disappointment for many of the men and also for some of the women.

Sitting on one of the long wooden benches, her sight now adapted to the deep gloom, Wren remained nervous. As always, she wanted out. Sitting in the hell of a prison when never arrested, was more nightmare than her dreams had ever forced on her. Behind her the freeze made her shiver where rain dripped from the high windows and traced the unplastered and unpainted walls. In summer the dampness sweated. In winter it turned to ice. Without the whitewash, common in the higher rooms, the bare stone teemed with lice hurrying to beds of straw, crevices and bare arms or legs. The fleas stayed cuddled in the warmer bodies, but spiders hung their webs where they discovered ceiling beams, cockroaches came out only at night and the mice and black rats kept to the shadows.

Sharing his fleas was inevitable when she hugged her father goodbye and could see the lice nesting on others crouching close. Easier then, to surrender to the guard's impatience and scuttle back to fresh air, however bitter the winds which blew through some of the stench.

"And my trial is also one day after tomorrow," the soft voice told her, "which might give me the chance to wave, noose to noose. But I doubt I shall still be here by then."

Wren did not recognise more than half those she saw and heard. Taken for trial, awaiting the gibbet, now dead, or perhaps released, the faces changed daily. Those she knew disappeared soon enough, and Wren never chose to ask whether set free. Or not.

A shrill shout. "You'll not escape alone, Landry. You'll explain it first, and take me with you."

The high ceiling and the damp stone composed distant echoes. Someone else howled like a wolf. The crash vibrated as he jumped. The shrill voiced man now sounded muffled. "Get off you bastard Or I'll have my teeth in your arse."

Now fighting, the chaos built, and the shrieks multiplied. Bryce leapt to grab the larger man, found him, and kicked. A bare foot kick can harm the toes more than the face beneath, but Bryce still wore boots.

Arms outstretched, Wren's escape was interrupted. Something huge whirled past her face and she cowered back. Haldon left her, scuttling to a darker corner. Wren did not follow. At just the breadth of a finger from her face, the largest in the

6

dungeon hauled at the hair of the smaller man nearby, wrenching him to his feet, then clutching at his neck. Scrawny and frightened, Lewis hung in Wyatt's hands, his feet dangling as he gurgled and choked, no longer able to shout or scream. Lewis saw most of his own hair in Wyatt's grasp.

"Let him go, you bastard." Someone hurtled, arms reaching. Tiny compared to Wyatt's giant frame, now the third man hung over the giant's back, hands to his shoulders. "He's not hurt you. You don't even know him."

Wyatt released the limp and half strangled body, falling heavily backwards, the other man smashed downwards beneath him. Wyatt, unhurt, sniggered. "Our great hero Francis. You reckon you saved a life? Reckon you feels happier now?"

Lewis, still choking, crawled off, rubbing at the blistered scarlet line around his throat. Francis cursed and swore, biting furiously at Wyatt's ear, which was all he could grab from behind. Wyatt yelped and rolled over, punching both fists to the writhing body below. Both hands missed as Francis escaped, and Wyatt was left punching the bare earth.

'Where you gone, you measly little flea?"

"I'm here and staying here till you calm yourself."

Wyatt sat. "Spoiled my fun, nasty little turd. Try it again, reckon I's ready to use yer face to wipe me cods after pissing."

Too close, now Wren followed her father. The rekindled noises sounded more fearsome than previously, and most had joined the fighting.

"What's we fighting for anyway?"

"Dunno. Don't matter none."

The giant's ear was bleeding. His sniff was an echoing snort as he plummeted himself onto the bench Wren had quickly left. With shoulders as wide as a ship's sail, muscles protruding from arms and chest, Wyatt's strength was a parade, his height took him almost as high as the windows. Yet, although of no concern to him, his calves were stick thin, barely holding the weight above, and when he wobbled he fell. His fall could break floors.

"Bastards, you done made a good day into a dumb 'un. There aint't naught wrong wiv a fight or two. It makes time speed a trot to a gallop."

"The gallop," said the soft voice though only to himself, "is the prerogative of the horse and the ox. It is somewhat ironic that you include yourself amongst them."

Col told Lewis, "You ain't bleeding. Lucky sod. But don't worry, the bastard will be off to Tyburn soon enough."

"Not true, shame though it is. That monster's been here for well nigh a month. Last time they dragged him off to trial, even when he was well shackled too, he broke one guard's leg and the other's nose. They left him here and he's not been called since."

"I got no other home." Wyatt was cackling. "Reckon this be as good as any."

Lewis had crawled to another wall. "If it's just a game," he sniffed from a distance, "why d'you pull out all me hair?"

Looking up and still grinning, the wide lips virtually dividing his face, Wyatt pointed to his own head. "That hair stuff be a right pain. Best have naught. Hundreds o' nasty little head crabs. One day when I cuts off me curls, reckon I'll have a head clean as a bathing tub."

Wren's father had not joined the fight, yet most had, and she was now used to it.

So once seeing the ground uncluttered before her, Wren stood, ignoring the soft voiced man, took a deep breath before kissing her father's cheek, promised to attend his trial, and strode hurriedly to the waiting guard who was once again rattling his keys. He had watched silently during the fight without any attempt to interfere, and was now impatient.

Jumping the central gutter which almost divided the cell, Wren held her breath. The gutter, since no other place was supplied, held urine and faeces, vomit, dead insects, rats, and the rich stench that accompanied them.

"I'm ready," she told the guard. He unlocked the door. Every man watched as the door was pulled open. Wren waved to Haldon and disappeared into the blackness of the staircase as the cell door was immediately slammed and locked behind her.

From the massive stone of the endless gaol, she walked east into the alleyways and the markets, through Cheapside and past the glitter of gold in the windows and the street washed clean, onwards to the clutter, the thrown rubbish and the stalls selling everything both vital and incidental. The sellers' calls proclaimed those goods, sometimes their prices, although barter was possible and bargaining was the usual way to buy. Beneath the legs of the shoppers and the stalls of the sellers, the stray dogs rummaged for anything partially edible.

Walking alongside the perfumes of food which made her feel she should be scavenging beside the dogs, she cut down Bread Street to the corner of Fish Street, dodged left into the Black Spoon Alleyway, and up the steps to the top floor of the small ash licked house over the cookery and eel soup shop below. More perfumes to aggravate hunger, but also a warm bed for a moment's rest before running back down the stairs to the shop where she worked.

Eel soup, eel stew, eel minced in red wine, and living eels squirming in water unaware of their inevitable end.

Wren hated eels cooked to any description but ate them when nothing else was available. When there were no customers, she cooked and cleaned. When customers came, she served them until her legs felt like lead.

The boxed iron oven was small but tucked indoors instead of out in the street, this was another luxury. It created a warmth that brought far more pleasure than simply cooking. Summer became exhausting and sweat dribbled from her face like oily tears, but in spring, autumn and winter the additional warmth was comforting.

Yet another stink, however, Eels enjoyed their own overpowering smells.

The day had already lapsed into twilight and the black shadows stood stark against a starless sky. Then absolute darkness leaked between the final flickers of vision, and Wren heard the first calls of the Watch.

Only living eels remained and what she had cooked, she had also sold. The street outside echoed empty and after locking the door, Wren sped wearily up the stairs to her own room. The other three rooms belonged to the shop owner, who Wren now heard snoring. As the church bell rang ten times, she accepted the hour which marked some peace at last and tumbled into bed. The straw base was partially controlled by a linen sheet, but straw pierced upwards and found her face to tickle. Yet tired enough, she was already in her sweet straw-free dreams.

CHAPTER TWO

NARRATIVE

The great hall where the Newgate trials were held, stood at the far end of the gaol and a bench was set for those relevant, solicitors, lawyers and those accused. The judge faced them from his high seat behind the table, where he leaned, scowled, and sometimes dozed.

It seemed strangely quiet. Here the stink drifted, less confident of its place amongst the titled. At the doorway stood another of the guards. Wren approached him. She was better dressed than usual and had discarded the flour dusted apron.

"I've come for Haldon Bennet's trial."

"Who? Give me that name again. It's not on my list."

She sighed. "Haldon Bennet."

"Not today," said the guard. He shook his head, tired of demands by those who couldn't even get the day correct. "Go ask Westwood over there – top of the steps. He'll know what's what." It was rare for anyone to know whatever was what, lists disappeared or were jumbled. The guards complained of an illiterate public, but the public also complained of lists muddled and misused, yesterday's today and today's next week.

Wren did as directed, but received little help.

"There was a break-out last night. Upset everything, it has. Who you looking for?"

Breakouts were rare. Wren frowned. "It's my father, so it's important to me," and she gave the name again.

"They've changed the list. Or given us the wrong lists, more likely. Chaos, mistress, chaos. Go ask one of the barristers in there."

"I can go in?"

He smiled. Wren was not accustomed to anyone here managing to smile at her. "But keep it quiet."

She stood at the back of the court, pushing between those already muttering, waiting for action. At the front, barristers were arguing. The judge leaned back in his chair as though utterly bored with the lack of proceedings, and no jury sat on their benches.

The brief words so often repeated, the eradication of man or woman, guilty or innocent, toiled its unravelling banality and could be miserably boring to judges, solicitors, and those in the public squash who had arrived on the wrong day. Wren wasn't sure whether to stay since no official appeared to know the list.

And then, startled, she saw her father. There was a queue of sorts, a shove of the impatient, waiting at the partially open doorway to one side. Four guards stood in front, glaring at anyone who caught their watchfulness. Haldon Bennet was shivering, face lowered. He hadn't shaved. The facilities for shaving and washing were difficult pleasures to find in Newgate.

"Gentlemen," the judge sat abruptly forward and roared at the scuffling and muffled murmuring before him, "is there anything at all likely to proceed this morning?"

"It's the escapee, my lord," one barrister bowed his head as he clutched his papers. "Landry Crawford, my lord, the thief and robber it took the king's men two long years to arrest, and now he's gone. He was first on our lists for this morning but gossip tells us he's been caught."

"Out in the countryside?"

"I believe so, my lord. But gossip doesn't always tell the same story."

"Then what the devil has that to do with us, Master Winston? Start with the next one on the list."

"As you say, sir." He bowed again, slammed down his parchment on another tabletop, and beckoned to the guards at the side door. "I call Haldon Bennet."

Wren ducked, finding the push easier from below. When she stood where she had wanted to stand, she saw her father pulled before the judge. Still barefoot and shackled, both arms forcibly held behind him by both chain and guards.

"You are accused of a wicked and unforgiveable murder," said the judge, studying his own fingernails. One had broken. "How do you plead, man?"

"I'm not guilty, it wasn't my fault, sir." Haldon shuffled his bare feet. The chains clanked and his voice trembled. "I did it, sir. But I got reasons, sir. And I couldn't help it. I never wanted to do it."

"You murdered your wife, man? Did you not approve of her cooking? And your daughter as well, I see. There's no excuse for that." The dutiful snigger amongst the crowd puzzled Haldon.

The barrister stepped forwards. "With your permission, my lord, I shall explain." Now Wren had escaped the standing crowd and stood behind the barrister. No one objected, as no one cared.

"Hurry up, my man," ordered the judge. He was anticipating dinner.

"I requested a trial by jury, my lord," the barrister continued. "This case is not straightforward. Master Bennet will tell your lordship how he did what he never intended to do. I ask that he take the oath."

"Carry on," sighed the judge with a deep sigh of reluctance.

The jury were called, clambered in, stared around with curiosity, grinned at each other and squashed themselves onto the long bench. "They've already been sworn in, my lord," one of the guards called.

"Then get on with it," roared the judge. He leaned back. The barrister leaned forwards. Haldon shivered with exaggerated eyes pleading towards the judge. He was shown a mighty leather-bound copy of the Holy Book, and swore to speak only the truth.

Wren pushed up behind him, folded her arms and copied the judge's scowl.

"My lord, this man has been accused of his wife's death, but the blame was hers, not his."

"An interesting declaration, sir," sneered the judge. "And can the dead woman testify to that?"

She kept the scowl. "No my lord," Wren said over the barrister's shoulder, "but I can."

The judge slammed his fist on the table and his small hammer, small pile of papers and his carefully placed cup, all bounced. He picked up the cup and drained it of whatever it once held. "What's this?" he roared at Wren. "The murderer's harlot?"

Henry Trackman, a barrister with less than the usual experience, bowed. "I – have no idea, my lord. Forgive me. I shall get rid of her."

"Oh no you won't," Wren said as loudly as she could over the muttering. "I'm Wren Bennet and I'm the accused man's daughter. I'll gladly take the oath and tell you the truth."

The judge's sigh was barely audible as he leaned back. "Very well, tell me your story and no doubt I shall wake at the end of it." He crossed his arms.

Wren stumbled over the oath as she clutched the bible. It was not an experience she ever hoped to repeat but nor was this a moment she wanted to think only of herself.

"Haldon Bennet's my father. He's a good man. I wouldn't be here in this horrible place without feeling strongly about it."

"My court, I'll have you know, mistress, is a place of justice and neither horrible nor unpleasant."

"It's terrifying, my lord, for anyone on a first visit like me." Wren tried to look taller than she was.

The barrister leaned towards her and whispered. "Not the best time to argue," he told her. "Get on with your story."

She did. "My lord, my father was happily married to my mother and he was good to her until she died. Years ago. I was just a child. He's looked after me ever since. But he's a sailor and served the king at sea and on land, so it was hard for him to be a father too. But he did it."

"Hurry up, girl," insisted the judge. "This judgement concerns the death of a Maggs Bennet. Is your story relevant or not?"

"Relevant, my lord." She grasped the rail that stopped her walking further towards the officials. "My father was unmarried all those years, he was a widower of course. Then he thought he wanted a wife again and he took a very young woman. Maggs. It was helping her more than him because her family was really poor. They were wed and both were very happy. I didn't like her, but my father did."

"So the man murdered the wife who made him happy?"

"He didn't mean to kill her. Honestly, he didn't. Anyway, after a few months she was carrying. But just a month or so before the baby was born, he was called back to sea. It was a carrack trading wool in Italy, so he was gone some time. He was excited, hoping he'd come home to see his new baby. Maggs had a little girl."

"So where's the child now? Do you have it?"

"No sir." Wren was feeling sick. She knew herself on the window ledge of tears. "I work in a shop nearby and I was busy. Before he sailed off, Dad asked the midwife Sara to look after Maggs and the baby. When I could, I tried to help but no one was there. Three times I tried, but I guessed Sara must have taken the child to her own home. I couldn't go again, I work all day, every day in the eel pie shop on Black Spoon Row. But Maggs was invited back to see her mother. The mother was sick. Maggs had to walk, and it was a long way outside the city, so she thought she couldn't take the baby."

"I remind you, girl, it's the proper thing for a daughter to take care of her sick mother." The judge continued to disapprove. He preferred to frown.

"But not to leave her new baby behind, my lord. She didn't want to carry a heavy parcel so far. Maggs said she'd often gone five days without food herself, so the baby could do the same. She wasn't very bright."

"My lord," interrupted the barrister, "this is a case of important questions." He turned hopefully to Wren. "The infant was left?"

Wren nodded. "Yes, and I wish I'd known. It's dreadful. I could have helped but I went on working and didn't realise. I thought Sara was there, but I haven't seen her for ages. That poor little mite was left on a blanket. Maggs got back home after six days. My father had already got home the same day and found his baby daughter dead on the floor."

The judge blanched. "Simply deserted? Starving?"

"Yes, my lord, for all that time. She must have cried her poor little head off, but the neighbours didn't hear or didn't care. Babies are always crying. Everyone just gets used to it. But when I visited, I never heard a thing."

The judge looked at Wren and Wren looked at her father. Haldon blew his nose on his sleeve. "Tis the truth, my lord. I rushed home to cuddle my new little baby girl Hanna. We'd already decided. Hanna for a girl and Richard for a boy. So, there I was cuddling little Hanna in my arms for the very first time but she were dead. Horrible it was. I broke down."

Wren looked back at the barrister and then at the judge. He was abruptly sympathetic. "Five or six bloody days without food nor drink for a new-born. Was that girl luna-ticked?"

"Perhaps, my lord." Wren spoke quickly, her hands shaking. "When my poor father came to the shop to see me, he held that poor little starved body, sobbing his eyes out. We arranged the funeral. He said it cost everything he'd just earned at sea. But my poor father couldn't be blamed for being angry when Maggs came running home."

"Her mother died," Haldon said, rubbing his eyes with the back of his chained fingers. The guard behind him had released the hold. "I didn't know how long Maggs had been away, so I felt sorry for the lass losing her mother. But then Maggs told me the truth. I was heartbroken. Any man would be. Said she couldn't carry such a weight so left her alone in the house. I was shocked. Then angry. Sad and furious."

Earnestly nodding, the barrister agreed. "Too true, my lord. So would you be, I'm sure."

"I'd never be fool enough to put myself in that position. But finish the story, Haldon." The judge still frowned.

Haldon now stared at the jury. One younger man was sobbing into his collar. "Right, my Maggs was proper simple. But when I knew exactly what she'd done, I was so angry. I couldn't help it. I lost my mind. You'd be angry too, I reckon."

Every man of the jury nodded fervently.

Wren nodded and wiped her eyes. At the funeral she had seen her starved half-sister and had wept for days. She had been furious too.

The judge shook his head. "What about the woman Sara. Where was she, then?"

Even Wren was confused. "I'm not sure, my lord."

"No more confusion, we need the story straight. Haldon Bennett was accused of murdering both his wife and his baby daughter. Now we see the accusation is mistaken." The barrister asked Haldon, "You beat the murderous wench?"

"I hit her," Haldon admitted. "Fisted her, maybe hard, I don't rightly remember, I was so upset. But I know I hit her. We stood at the top of the stairs in the tenement, high stone steps they are. And down she fell. Tumbled all the way down. Dead at the bottom. Well, now she's with her dead mother but I hope my little daughter don't speak to her."

"You threw her down those steps," the prosecuting barrister finally pushed with his accusation.

Haldon shook his head. "No. Well yes and no both. I never meant nothing. It was just anger it was. I hit her hard, but I never meant Maggs to fall all that way, I'm telling the truth. I swear it. Only the truth. She was running, getting away from me, but I caught her and punched her. I didn't make no notice of the stairs, blinded with tears as I was. I honestly never meant yet another death. Any man would beat his woman for such an act, but I never beat her. Just one punch. I spent my last pennies on her funeral."

"That'll do," sniffed the judge. He turned to the jury. "You know what to do," and he waved them away.

Scuffling off took two minutes. One minute more and they scuffled back. "Not guilty," said the older man. "Not the poor fellow's fault."

Haldon beamed. His sorrow for his daughter faded as he jumped, rattled his chains and thanked the jury and then his barrister. Finally, he thanked the judge. "Proper justice." The exclamation was spoken to a room of nodding heads. He held out his wrists and the guard unchained them, then bent and removed his shackles from his ankles.

"Free to go," the judge pointed directly at the open doorway. "But if I ever see you here again, Haldon, I'll not take your word for it without a witness. Your daughter calls herself a witness, but she saw none of it."

"She trusts my word, sir."

His voice disappeared behind the introduction of the next trial, the muttering and declarations. Wren grabbed her father's arm. "Quick, Dad. Let's get out of here."

Haldon stopped one moment to stare around. "That fellow Landry said his trial was the same day. Or maybe the next day. Do you remember?"

Wren shrugged. "Well, it's not him now. You called him Landry. Landry's the one they said escaped."

"If the bugger escaped that easy," Haldon grumbled as they edged towards the main doors, "why not take me? He talked with me all the bloody time over them last days. I wish he'd damn well told me how to get out."

"Don't complain, Dad. You're free now. Legally free. Not out there on the run."

"Landry's a clever sod," nodded Haldon. "Doubt if he's running anywhere. He'll be in a tavern getting cup-shotten."

"Someone said there was a rumour he's been caught. Probably back in Newgate."

Haldon grabbed his daughter's arm. "Never believe rumours, girl. There's not a single fellow's story ever turned out true," and he sniggered.

But it was a totally different voice that interrupted them as they headed towards fresh air. A woman, dragging her small child by the hand, came up behind them and dug one elbow into Wren's side.

"I heard," she muttered. "T'was you putting all the blame on the poor bloody woman and no blame on the bugger what killed her. As usual, tis always the poor suffering wench to blame, even when it's her wot's been murdered. Best not get born a lass, for you'll never get a fair deal."

Surprised, annoyed at first, Wren turned, rubbing her side where the woman's sharp elbow had slammed into her. "But," she started and then stopped. Perhaps, just perhaps she needed to think before speaking and she needed to change the subject, ironing away the thoughts of prejudice.

Wren had brought boots from the house. "Here, Dad. You can't walk all that way barefoot."

The angry woman pushed past and was gone. Squatting on one step, Haldon forced his toes into the boots. "Good lass."

"That woman said I was being mean to women," Wren sighed. "But Maggs was an idiot. I don't feel sorry for her, but I do for that poor sweet baby. It is the truth you told me, isn't it, Dad? Truly?"

Haldon hadn't heard a word, skipped down the steps, raised both arms and croaked, "Freedom for the innocent. Bloody gorgeous."

CHAPTER THREE

WREN

He had not paid his rent of course. Had no coin left and no way of getting more while peering through the gloom in Newgate. Now my father was free but also homeless and so trailed after me. He was delighted and smiling unlike the shakes and sobs on the day of his trial. There was still the occasional sniff when he told me how cold it would be to sleep in the gutter, but most of the time he danced. As always, his reactions depended on who watched him and who listened.

I'd held tiny Hanna only three times and the third time was when she was dead. You could see that she'd starved. Those poor little bones and sunken cheeks. I'd never really known her, but I still sobbed and sobbed until I felt it was all my fault. What a wicked experience. My little half-sister. I'd have pushed Maggs down the stairs myself if I'd been there. I really don't know if Dad did it on purpose or not, but he said he wasn't thinking and just went bang, one fisted.

I believed him though I can't be sure. *"She trusts me,"* Dad said, knowing perfectly well that I didn't and never had. No matter. It's all done now, though I cried until I was sick at the time.

But I only had one room and one bed, and I wasn't keen to have

Dad sleeping on the floor right beside me. He did anyway. Otherwise, it would have been the streets. I carried on working. Sometimes he helped serve but he wasn't any good at it and didn't know how to handle live eels. They kept slithering away and I spent ages kneeling on the wet floor trying to catch them. Not easy with eels. He agreed with me about their stink, though it was probably better than Newgate.

More important to me than smells, was waking up to my father early every morning. He snored. I didn't really care. He dribbled in his sleep. I didn't care about that either. But that bulk, mouth hanging open and empty skin like a sack of hessian without its contents, it wasn't easy as the first thing I saw and climbed over every morning.

I was wearing my shift in bed. I certainly wouldn't roll out of my skinny covers totally naked as usual. Nudity had been a problem for me as a growing child. No more, and definitely not now. However, I only had two thin shifts and they were constantly so badly creased, they looked more like rags.

Pulling on the dark blue working gown, flannel, beneath the large flapping apron, I could run downstairs to open the shop at around six chimes of the church bell. I had to start cooking early, although few customers turned up until eight chimes or later. Hard work I didn't mind – one of the few things I was good at. Funny to be good at cooking something I disliked, but I doubt I'm the only one doing that in London. It's a busy city. Good for sales. Pansy was the owner of this business and she got good profits, though she worked too. We did it between us, and she paid me well enough considering I had my bedchamber free.

"Your father?" With one look at his bulky shadow, she couldn't refuse though I heard a few muttered moans after the first couple of days. "Wren, warn him I'll not have a free lodger for too long."

"He helps in the shop and doesn't get a penny for it."

"He gets a bed. And he's a criminal. For all I know, he steals my takings." I denied that quickly, yet admitted to myself that it was probable.

I sold pies, counted pennies, cooked eel stews and spoke nicely to every customer. I even had a few favourites, like Jessy Ford and her youngest little boy, the midwife Sara, one of the wherrymen called Hob and another called Bill. There was a sweet natured whore called Julia who tramped the streets and bought an eel dumpling at half price if I had any left just before closing.

But it was my baby half-sister who refused to leave my thoughts.

I knew I was pretty. A little bit anyway. I'd seen myself looking down into bowls of clean water where my reflection bobbed, and some years past I'd worked as a cleaner in a grand mansion where there was a mirror. I was delighted when I saw I wasn't horribly twisted or frighteningly ugly. Anyway, I liked my eyes, and I didn't see any blotches or bits going in the wrong direction. I thought I was prettier than Maggs even though she was younger, but maybe that was just me because I never really liked her. Hard to speak to a stepmother who still looks like a child. But Hanna was so delicious.

When I told Dad, "You can't marry a girl younger than your daughter," he'd just cackled. I suppose he thought it was a compliment to him, that he could attract a wife not much more than a girl.

I stopped thinking about Maggs, even the baby, when I saw Wyatt in the old cheap.

He was leaning against a stone wall, shouting at a rather scrawny little man, who was shouting back even though he had to stare up so far, he was almost leaning backwards. There was no stall, no shop, not any noticeable form of work. Neither man attacked the other. Just shouted. But I was surprised to see Wyatt free of Newgate, less than three weeks after I'd seen him in there.

Hoping he wouldn't see me, I crept around the corner. I'd been shopping for flour and lard and wanted to hurry back home. When Pansy had started moaning more than ever about Dad, I'd told her I could make good pastry, and offered to make eel pies if she let my father stay a bit longer, so she pretended to accept with incredible magnanimity as though her angelic nature was the only reason.

I even ate some of those eel pies myself. I liked the pastry even if not the filling. Besides, I added in a tiny bit of onion and that helped the flavour.

When telling Dad I'd seen Wyatt, he blinked and sniffed and said I was wrong. "In all them crowds up the Cheap? You was muddled, girl. That bugger didn't even want to get free."

"It really was him," I'd insisted. "There's no one else can look anything like that man."

"No way he could have been found innocent. P'raps the bugger threatened the judge."

"Perhaps he escaped like that other man."

Dad had shaken his head over my pastry bowl, and it took me ages pulling out the bits of greying fluff. "Yes, Landry did, but Landry had a brain and Wyatt ain't got no brain at all." I wasn't sure that mattered when you had muscles the size of fifty eel pies.

I knew his temper, so hoped never to see him again. Pansy did most of the shopping and went down to the docks to buy the eels every afternoon. More fresh air, I suppose, so better than being stuck next to that oven all day. She usually kept me inside, so I only saw the customers.

After Newgate, Dad was refused back to any carrack, cob or even caravel but finally he got a job. From a thousand eels to ten thousand eels. He got a place on the docks just upriver from the outlet of The Fleet where the tiny port gathered the eels caught for sale. Dad still wasn't an eel lover, but he didn't say that to the men rowing the little flat wherries as they lurched to the quayside and unloaded their overflowing buckets. Dad was one of those who pulled it all on shore, stacked for sale. He finally learned to work a crane. He sold to Pansy almost every day when she trundled down there with her wheelbarrow.

She complained to me after each trip. "Seems happy enough, though I'm sure he tried to pinch my change. There's usually a penny missing. And now that crane, with its rope swinging out of the sky. He'll be unstuck if there's a bad wind."

There were so many eels I thought one day they had to disappear. How could so many live in one river, poor things. Just eaten day after day. One minute happily slithering and enjoying the warm water, and the next moment snatched up and cooked only for one person and one little meal. What a miserable reason for being born. The wheel of fortune is so often a wheel of misfortune. I'll die one day, but hopefully not just for one man's dinner.

And now Dad got paid enough. Bliss and heavenly thanks, Dad went off and rented a squashed up limewashed house behind the dock, two rooms, so better than mine. Upstairs there was just space for a pallet bed. Downstairs there was space for a fire on a slate on the floor, three stools around it, and a corner row of shelves for pots, pans, a platter with a spoon and anything else he wanted to keep.

He moved out and I walked with him all the way along Thames Street to the Ludgate and past it to his new home. We did not walk through Newgate. We stayed by the river.

So I had my tiny room back to myself. I invited Randle and my friend Jessy with their youngest son, and fed them eel pies. They never had any money as he worked in the northern quarry and earned half as much as I did, even though now he had two sons to feed. The older son, Martin who had just about reached his seventh year worked for a bakery nearby, but the younger son Peter at around four years hadn't yet been considered old enough for a job. He played on the streets most days, but Jessy still stayed at home to look after him, managing some poorly paid mending while sitting by her window.

Still Black Spoon Row, but ten houses along from mine, Jessy seemed happy there with her husband and sons. She had been my friend since we'd both played out on the streets about fifteen years gone. I liked her. I didn't have many friends – neighbours though, who waved and said hello – but not people I spent time with. Next door they had a sow, past the age of bacon, and the scruffy creature smelled the eels and sat on our doorstep, sniffing before waddling off to roll in the puddles. I can't call it a friend, but I was quite fond of it and called it Rappo. When Rappo's owner heard me call one day, and saw that the sow actually obeyed, she sniggered and said she just called the sow a sow. Then she copied me, and now Rappo is perhaps a friend too.

There's a few stray dogs, poor skinny things with their rib bones sticking out. Smelling food, they crowd the doorway before I even unlock the doors. They get all the bits of eel we don't want, like heads and bones and skins. Then, late in the evening if they come back, they get anything that hasn't sold for two days in summer and three days in winter, and a few scraps of pastry thrown in. Then Rappo comes hurtling along and skids to a stop, wobbling her belly and staring up hopefully at me. She usually gets something too.

Frankly my few friends come in very different shapes and sizes. Seeing less of Dad is a bonus, much as I tried hard to love him. He's a naive man in so many ways, bad tempered but sweet when he wants to show off. And besides, he makes me think of that poor baby. I still feel so wretchedly guilty. Dad sometimes seems like the most innocent out of us.

Scraps for the dogs, scraps for Rappo, and sadly, sometimes just scraps for Jessy. Free leftovers, even when stale, free pies if they'd been dropped on the tiles and then scooped up but broken. Once Bill, my wherry-boat friend, bought Jessy a big bowl of stew. I wondered if she ever got heartily sick of eels.

Then, I saw Wyatt again. That hulk was so huge and thrived on brutality. With little squashed eyes half hidden by his cheeks below, and then a mouth with a permanent sneering growl, he wasn't the sort of man I'd expect any woman to want. But I suppose power can be attractive. Now I kept seeing him with a whore I recognised. She worked our three streets at night and sometimes popped in for a pie when she got the first evening's pennies.

She was Ariana, or at least, that was the name she'd given herself. I think her real name was Eram, but she'd never liked it. Not a pretty whore – I think maybe I was prettier – but she wore such low-necked gowns with no shift beneath, I'm not surprised that Wyatt took her in. Of course, if she had a home, then she took him in. Then when she had her own customers, no doubt he'd go for a walk in the rain. Or sat and watched.

I'd got to know the girl enough to smile at her as I pulled pies from the oven. There were plenty of whores walking this part of London, and it was only Julia I thought sweet. As for Ariana I never bothered one way or the other until she hooked up with Wyatt. Then I decided I didn't like her.

She flounced in one evening with more coins than usual and told me she wanted three pies for the price of two. I'd laughed at first. It had to be a joke.

"This ain't no joke. One of these pies is for Wyatt. You know him I'd wager. Every bugger knows him now. He runs the Knife Gang and there ain't no one will cross him. So, he ain't gonna pay fer naught. Hand it over."

I glared back. "You want three? So you'll pay, and so will someone else. But Wyatt won't. That's his idea or yours?"

"Obvious, ain't it."

"I met him in Newgate. He knows me, more or less. And I know he's nothing special. Even if the king ever came for his supper, I'm damned sure he'd pay. Is Wyatt so poor or just greedy?"

I think she was attempting to spit at me, but she had no saliva to spare so she stood and puffed dryly. "You want him to set fire to the shop?"

"Ask him to visit. I'll talk to him myself."

She slammed down enough pennies for three pies, and I gave them to her, piping hot. She held them in the furl of her sleeves and tottered off. "I'll bring a knife next time," she screeched back at me as she left.

Naturally I told Pansy later, and she pulled a face. "You give any free pies to your friends," she pouted, "you'll still have to pay for them."

The face I pulled was probably worse. "They aren't friends, and I don't intend giving any free. But if I get a knife at my neck, I'll have to do it and I won't pay. It won't be my fault. I'm not a coward, but I don't intend getting my throat cut for the sake of six pennies."

"Any knives around here, I'll call for the sheriff," Pansy sniffed. "And don't you go acting all innocent. When I leave you in charge of my shop, I expect you to look after it." Fine by me. I didn't care as long as it wasn't me that got hauled off to Newgate. I'd seen enough of that vile place.

Two days – three days – four – and Wyatt still didn't turn up. Life just plodded along. I burned my fingers twice on the oven, but nothing more exciting.

I really don't think I'm a coward, but with Wyatt, I'd be a complete fool not to be nervous. He had a gang now. That meant he'd soon be back in gaol, but he'd wreck a few lives first. So, the next time Ariana swooped into the shop when unfortunately empty of any other customers, she didn't seem to have any coin at all.

"Not been a good couple o' nights' work fer me," she unexpectedly admitted. "But you know me, girl. So give us a few pies. Reckons I deserve it."

"You've left Wyatt?" I asked, not having the slightest intention of handing over free food.

But she shook her head. "I ain't gonna leave him, am I now! He's a good man. But the poor sod's sick."

"How?" I guessed someone had stuck a sword in when protecting themselves.

"Dunno," Ariana admitted. "He keeps spewing."

"Not the best moment for eating eels then."

"But I'm proper starving. Tis for me, not him."

I did it. In a moment of ludicrous sympathy while being fairly sure that living with Wyatt was probably a nightmare, I weakened and handed over a pie, one which had already gone cold. "Here," I said. "For you. But please, never ever come and expect free food here ever again. This is not the start of a habit and if you ask again, I'll chuck it."

She really grinned, didn't take offence, and grabbing the pie she started eating it before running from the shop.

When Jessy popped into the shop later, not wanting a pie but simply needing to talk, I gave her another of the shop's unsold suppers, a dumpling this time, full of minced eels.

"Go on," I said, knowing my lovely friend was always so hungry, and her family too. "It's a left-over and I've got three more." What a coincidence! Four very large unsold dumplings for my friend and her family of four, so one each, luckily.

"My sweet friend," she told me, her mouth watering as she smelled the food. "I know I'm a charity case, but I'll not be a beggar or leave you in trouble with Pansy."

She couldn't resist it and started eating. She scooped up all the crumbs too. "Jessy," I said, "when there's stuff left over, it's not right to throw it out, is it. And I don't like eels. So they're all yours."

It was a week later before anything else happened. Jessy managed to buy four pies from me one day, and I misjudged the change on purpose, which she shoved it into her purse without noticing that I hadn't charged for one. I served Julia a couple of times. Ariana did not return during those eight days, and I worked my usual routine, didn't have time to visit Dad, didn't see Jessy again, and flopped exhausted into bed each night, thankful to be alone.

August had been sunny but wet with chilly evenings. Then August slugged its path into September, and we were all hoping for a warmer autumn. The calendar mattered and the days made a difference. Easter was good for business, we celebrated the days when the church said no meat was allowed, so folk bought fish and beaver and eels.

One evening as I was cheerfully pulling hot pies from the oven, I felt something even though my back was to the shop door. I heard a scuffle. Then I heard heavy breathing, and immediately turned, almost dropping a pie. But there was nothing there, truly, absolutely nothing. Yet gradually, creeping to the back of the long table where

28

I mixed dough and pastry, I was sure I'd seen the top of a shadow. The breathing increased.

Not being a huge space, the shop was a mess of this here and that there. Our large window turned into the outer counter once the shutters were taken down each morning, the main door alongside. Most customers came inside, but they queued at the second counter, the chopping slab on its stand and the iron oven squatted in the far corner. On the far wall past that oven was another door, usually kept locked. That led both upstairs, and outside to the dismal back alley. Dismal indeed, but called itself Pot Lane.

That great stone slab was covered in flour and scraps of eels, pastry and beef dripping, I peered over the top of it, not bothered by everything which immediately attached itself to my apron.

Suddenly, the top of a head. Huffing and puffing with a faint growl forced me two steps backwards.

Wyatt appeared wearing a huge cheek splitting grin. "Come fer me pie."

My heart was beating fast and loud and I was furious with him and myself too. "No pies. Piss off."

He stared back. "That ain't playing the game."

"Not a game," I agreed, and my voice was gradually rising just as he had. "You frightened me."

"Codswallop," Wyatt growled. "I were playing a game. You done give Arry a pie when she were starvin' and I were sick. So tis a sort o' thanks."

"Terrifying me is like saying thank you?" I frowned back.

Then Wyatt plonked a small handful of pennies and ha'pennies on the little table and grinned again. "So's you still won't serve me?"

I was lost. Half guilty, but still angry, I counted the pennies. Enough for two pies. I mumbled a sort of apology and served him those two pies. I just wanted him gone. That cackle was more disgusting than the growl.

He was so huge, slumped shoulders the size of an average doorway, and his face like an ugly disease. So I didn't see the men entering behind him. They slipped in so quietly behind their leader,

I only noticed them when too late. I had handed Wyatt his two pies and looked up to find myself surrounded. I didn't know a single face, but they all sneered at me. Three held knives. Two thumped their fists on the counter. Wyatt shoved his way to the back of the crowd and stood there while stuffing his mouth full of pastry, spluttering and cackling. There were eight men leaning over me, swearing and cursing, threatening and waving weapons. I shrank back and my mind went blank. The oven was too heavy, but I had a skillet and a small spike for lifting the eels.

These monsters could kill me easily enough, but they didn't need to. They could just walk around me and help themselves to anything they wanted, including my little locked box where I kept the money. Yes, locked. When not being used, this was kept hidden under the long worktable against the wall. But smashed on the ground or kicked and stamped on, it would break. Whatever I tried to do to stop them would mean my death, or close to it.

They blocked me so I could see nothing beyond them. The shop wasn't large. I saw their rotten teeth. Furious greedy eyes glittered into me like steel darts. One leaned over the counter, pushing his fingers towards my neck, stretching as if to strangle me. So, shivering like an eel myself, I started to reach for every piece of food I'd produced. The eight members of Wyatt's gang were watching my every movement. Their stink was sickening and mingled with the smell of the eels.

Beyond the crush of their vile faces, a new voice interrupted, even more abrupt and even more unexpected.

CHAPTER FOUR

NARRATIVE

"You will stop immediately and you will leave," the deep soft voice from the doorway said, as though expecting instant obedience.

So soft, so kind, yet the underlying threat was clear.

Each man hesitated, pausing what he had been doing, and looked around. Wren stopped grabbing pies, stared but could only see the squashed bodies of those who had threatened her. Yet she thought she had recognised the voice.

"Stupid pissing swiver," one man said, raising his knife to the doorway. Wren still couldn't see. She hovered behind the counter and the crush of men on its other side were between that and the doorway. Suddenly she could hear the knife drop with a sudden clank to the floor, and could see the man himself collapse. For a moment his fall left a space for Wren to see past, but she saw only a tall slim shadow and the thin reflection of another knife.

Two men, fists forward, jumped the shadow. One toppled back, spurting blood, almost beheaded. The other fought on, shouting and thumping. Then he also fell and collapsed forwards onto his face.

Slipping quickly from danger, the men disappeared except three still too shocked. One said, plaintive, "You ain't the boss here. Nor does you bed the wench, cos I know she's always alone. So why?"

Since there was no answer, one of the other men asked, "What you gonna do now, Landry?"

Wren saw over the small man's head now. The tall shadow behind held his sword upright. She stared. It fascinated her and she wanted to look behind and see the man who held it. She now knew who he was, the soft voiced Landry who had escaped Newgate.

She said, even more softly, from shock this time and not from fear, "You're so so wonderfully kind. To put yourself at risk. Thank you."

The voice now filled the sudden quiet. "I thank you for your thank you, Wren." A small pause, then, "The rest of you, get out now, and take these bodies with you."

There was an instant shuffle of movement. Wyatt had previously wandered off but had now clearly returned. His voice squeezed past the door. "Hey, Landry, wot you saying to my lads?" Another pause. "They ain't hurt you, nor wouldn't."

"Then take the bodies, dead and living, and go back to your sodden alleys. Nor return, unless you have the coin to pay for whatever you want."

The shuffle and scuff faded as each man left. Wren gazed forwards with the hope of Landry staying to buy – to talk – or perhaps to advise on any future retaliation. Yet everyone had left in moments and not even Landry remained.

Wren sighed, trying to relax her shoulders and breathe deeply. The dead bodies were gone but the puddle of blood had not. Wren forced herself down onto her knees and cleaned. There was one candle lit and the flames from the oven, yet the light was little enough, and Wren hardly saw what she was cleaning. In the morning, she knew she'd have to wash the floor again. Eventually she stood, braced herself against the memories, and balanced for some moments beside the table. The sudden arrival of a customer made her blanch, but she served the woman, recognising her, and then the couple who arrived afterwards. In less than an hour her supplies had all sold, and she closed the shop with relief, locked the door and leaned back against it, finally blew out the candle, and staggered upstairs.

Avoiding the bed, Wren sat by her window and watched the stars discover new paths, brightening and scattering as all the tiny lights from the houses were snuffed, and the streets clung to a black as dark as pitch. She knew it beautiful, but her thoughts raced and endlessly repeated their circles. Hating to feel fear, she shrugged off the shivers. Yet she knew she wouldn't sleep.

Pulling her cape around her shoulders, she left by the back door, again locking it behind her. Two stray dogs were waiting.

She had nothing to give them and walked on. One very faint whimper stopped her. She looked behind. Both dogs sat, watching her leave. Each had pelvis and back bones jutting from skin without flesh, ribs like daggers pointing outwards, legs like splinters. One had been limping, and had lain back in bitter disappointment. The other still gazed, its large brown eyes clinging to hope.

Wren smiled, understanding, so returned and re-opened the shop. She ushered both dogs inside. They collapsed, drawn by the smells from the oven. One licked the blood still smeared across the floor tiles. She took the bowls of dead eels waiting for the morning's baking. She also took the pastry, half cooked and still warm. There was bread on a shelf, though stale and hard. Wren also gave them that soaked in water. As they buried their snouts and mouths in the food, she hurried upstairs and brought back her two blankets, folded each and lay them on the cold tiles for the animals to sleep in warmth. As every crumb of food had gone and the liquid lapped, both dogs hobbled to the soft new beds and curled for sleep.

Wren left them and left the shop once more, then walked down Black spoon Row and into the cheaps where folk were hurrying home, waving a goodbye to those they passed. She meandered, trying to clear her mind. Crying silently for the dogs she had almost ignored and remembered the horror of

Wyatt's gang. Yet the strange appearance of the soft-spoken man from Newgate, drifted through those same thoughts.

Her cape was somewhat waterproof though thin, and without comfort. Walking faster helped banish the freeze. Now she could hear her own footsteps echo in the dark emptiness. More confused still than tired, Wren walked in one large meandering circle and without intention, discovered herself back on Black spoon Row. No names of streets were written, no numbers and no directions, but even in such darkness, no one could misplace their own street. Not a street she loved, but the familiarity called.

Yet halfway along the lane's narrow inlaid gutter, Wren discovered a half-chewed apple at her foot, and picked it up for the dogs. Then she paused, wondering where she might find more scraps. Not the cheaps since now all shops and stalls were closed for the night. All city wildlife knew the times and places ripe for scavenging and begging. Children too of course, orphaned street brats or the youngest of poor families. They were fed first with whatever remained each dusk. Jessy's son Peter sometimes scurried to the eel shop with huge eyes and a runny nose.

"Mam's sewing a collar and Dad's got two buckets of limestone he can sell tomorrow. We'll have coin then, Mam says. Can we have four somethings and bring the money tomorrow evening."

Those four somethings were always supplied, and the next day the price was always paid. Yet this day not one of the family had been seen. Not so unusual, but Wren wondered if one of them had seen the gang and been too frightened to stop.

She could offer the shop's oven if Jessy had bread to bake. When Jessy's stock of logs and twigs slumped too low for a fire hot enough for cooking beneath her trivet, Wren's oven was always on offer. Then Jessy's fire, however tiny, would be just enough to warm her room. And more selfishly, she told herself but refused guilt, she needed to talk away the sickening memories. So she turned, and knocked on that family's door.

No light leaked out. No flickering candle. Bed, then. Wren sighed and walked on. Yet it was early for bed, and those without the money for candles could easily sit snug in the dark. Wren turned back, listened at the door and heard nothing, but knocked again.

The hinges squeaked a little and the door eased open.

Without light or sound, bed was the more likely but leaving the door open was unlikely indeed. Wren pushed her small nose into the blackness beyond and then crept inside. Not pressing further, since this was their only room below and one for sleeping upstairs, she stood and listened for the sound of breathing, a tiny gulp or snore.

Such silence seemed uncanny. Wren knew the family could never have wandered on a long walk in such cold, nor would ever put their few possessions at risk by leaving their door unlocked. Not wanting to knock over stools and wake those possibly sleeping, she stood and adapted her eyes to the darkness.

No sound, no sight, no idea and plenty of fear and worry, so finally Wren took one small step forward.

Something brushed against the top of her hair. Only a spider, hopefully, but she pulled hurriedly back. There was nothing else. Hand to her head, she stepped forward once more. When she felt the same light touch, she raised her hand again and stared upwards. Long dangling shadows stared back, shadows shapeless and threatening. Nothing of any kind should be hanging from Jessy's usually spotless ceilings, yet Wren felt the swish of a weightless yet hanging object. She now forced herself forwards.

Without light, Wren lifted her fingers higher and felt more carefully. Her touch slipped over and around and with the most panic she thought she'd ever known, she suddenly knew that she felt a small, lifeless bare foot.

Wren fell. In shock, she tumbled to the bare floorboards and stayed there, retching.

Wren rushed up to the single bedchamber. A misted moonlight crept through the unshuttered window. No one lay in bed and the covers, neatly pulled up to the bolster, were undisturbed.

She ran downstairs, struggled to find the tiny pile of twigs ready for fire, and reached for the tinderbox beside them. She built a bare flicker of flames, and stood again, looking around.

The fear and nausea pushed her backward like a brick to her throat. Once again, she fell, but this time stayed sitting while gazing upwards and around.

Four unmoving shadows hung from that ceiling, where two beams crossed, each serving as the base for hanging ropes. Each rope was short knotted, ending in a loop. Each loop held the head of a friend.

No movement, no sound, the bodies did not swing nor creak.

Randle hung lowest, almost to the ground. Within the loop, his head lay sideways as though relaxing on his shoulder. He wore boots, heavy soled, those of a quarry worker. His mouth and his eyes were tight shut but a dribble of liquid puke had dripped from his mouth and now shone from his chin. His hands were tied with wire behind his back. His ankles were also wired together. A thin streak of blood painted his neck beneath the rope.

It was not suicide.

Beside him, a shoulder's distance apart, hung the eldest son, the hard working boy Martin, whom everyone had loved. Although much shorter than his father, his death had been identical. The rope had crushed his neck, leaving no avenue for breath. He wore soft shoes on bare legs, his ankles tightly wired together. His short tunic shift of stained hessian reached to his stubby knees, and his tiny hands were roped behind his back.

It was the hanging remains of the youngest, Peter, that had tickled Wren's hair. Such a little child, yet he seemed now even smaller, strung up from the ceiling beam by a double strength of string. This had bitten into the child's neck so tightly that his throat was swollen and ripped, covered in blood now dark and dry. His ankles and wrists were also wired. The child was wide eyed with glassy blue staring pupils.

Jessy hung between those who had loved her.

The tears on her cheeks were still shining stripes in the small flickering firelight. Her hands, wired behind her back, were badly cut and her fingertips were blood encrusted. As with all hangings, bladders had opened and the pools of urine remained across the floor, sprinkled with blood, still liquid.

Wren curled on the hard floor beneath the four hanging bodies and wept. Another ugly smear of guilt jabbed. After feeding the dogs, she had wondered briefly if she might take free food to the Ford family, as much in need as the hounds. But then, she had taken nothing and locked the shop behind her, so had failed her friend. Yet had she done as she felt she should, now she saw why it would have helped no one.

Who had done this, why it had been done – or when, she could not know. But there had been a chance, perhaps, to help. The churning of her stomach prevented her from crawling away, she stayed, feeling as though the only help she could offer now was that of keeping company, and sending love through the chill of the night. Exhaustion eventually brought her sleep, but the sleep brought nightmares, and she woke after five hours with the bodies dark above her.

CHAPTER FIVE

NARRATIVE

Wren crept to the sheriff's office. He was not yet awake. She waited. The shop should be opened, and the cooking begun. The stray dogs should be shood from the premises to do their morning business. Yet the sheriff had to come first.

Wren waited at his door and then knocked again. He poked his head from the little window above. Wren stared up, shaking her head, yet struggled to explain. Her voice broke and she sobbed, unable to stop. Finally Sheriff Wilson, intrigued, and dressed, toppled downstairs, opened the door, and put his arm around Wren's shoulders.

"Tell me, m'dear," he murmured to her. And she did. She led him to Black Spoon Row, and pointed out Jessy's home, then stepped back.

"I stayed all night," Wren whispered, "because I had stupid thoughts and I couldn't leave even though it's a horror I'll never forget. But after that terrifying hell, they deserved comfort from someone. It sounds ridiculous but I desperately needed to help, and I couldn't think of anything else to do. Now of course – well - once I left, there's no way I can go back in. Not ever."

"You go back to the shop, I know where to find you," he told her. "I can deal with this, whatever it is."

Nodding with relief, Wren slowly plodded the few steps to her shop. She looked back once, and saw the sheriff violently puking in the gutter.

Although home, the eel shop seemed far from homely, as if she could recognise only ugliness. The two stray dogs ran out, but Wren simply stood there as if she had forgotten how to cook, how to clean up and how to serve customers. She simply stood, breathing fast. Then she thought of Wyatt.

Having no idea whether Wyatt had even known Jessy's family, she thought of his temper and his cruelty. This was a rough area with thieves and fools, men who beat their wives, and those too poor to feed themselves. With a gang forming every week, needing to build their reputation, there could be the terror of brutality even without motive.

Reverting slowly to habit, Wren scrubbed, collected the live eels from the tank amongst the buckets, prepared pastry, dough and bread crumble, then built up the oven, slammed the iron door against the building heat, and finally sank down on the one small stool.

She was again thinking of Wyatt. She hoped the sheriff would turn up later, and talk to her. Jessy's hanging corpse remained in her eyes. Then the oven was burning, time for cooking, a stream of customers, and Wren had no more moments for thought.

Having been late to open the shop and late with the cooking, Wren muttered apologies to Pansy when she strode through the back door, eyebrows raised.

Pansy demanded, "It all looks excellent, as usual, Wren. What's the apology for?"

"Because I was late. And I have to tell you about it." Simply telling the story made Wren sick again. She leaned back against the wall, hardly able to explain and hoping desperately that Pansy would not ask endless questions. Pansy simply stared, not wanting to believe it.

"Did the sheriff call you?"

"No, I called on him." Now Wren was crying once more. "But I have to go and see him again and find out what – you know."

Pansy took the solitary stool. "Wren, you're being stupid. It's impossible. With one rotten bastard tying up the first poor bugger, the other three would knife him."

Wren sighed. "Perhaps it was a gang. There is one starting here now. I don't suppose you know. A giant of a lout started it just days past. This must have been him. I sort of know him and he's certainly cruel."

"Gangs make too much noise. They'd be shouting and your friends would be screaming, people would have heard. You can't do that sort of sick stuff quietly."

"I don't know. I don't want to know." Now Wren was making the noise that the murder of her friends had not. "Yes, I do want to know. But really I just want it all to go away."

"I'll take over," Pansy said with unexpected sympathy. "Go see Sheriff Wilson. And don't tell this awful story to anyone else. We'll get no one in the shop."

Wren again grabbed to creased bundle of her cape and ran out into the wind. She stood, catching her breath and rubbing at her nose and face. She managed to stop crying but the wind stung her eyes and they watered. It was a cold day, autumn's entrance. From a distance, already she could see the crush at Jessy's door. Bodies were being carried from the house to St. Mildred's church. Wren knew she could not afford the funerals. The church itself would have to do it for free. The sheriff's four assistants also crowded the door, alongside a tall man far too well dressed to live locally. She assumed he was a doctor, a solicitor or some other official determined to solve a vile crime. Buffeted by wind, Wren walked towards the crowd.

Having to push between the audience of twenty or more who had stopped to watch with curiosity, or because they knew the family, Wren said nothing and bent her head. Two women were sobbing.

"Keep those dogs away," shouted one man. "Dirty buggers are smelling death. Kick them off."

Wren had no dogs, but looked behind. The two starving mutts from the night before stalked her, a short haired creature with huge brown eyes, long ears flicking up as soon as Wren turned. The other, even thinner, was black furred and wisps of long hair curled over its skeletal neck, brown eyes gazing in hope. It stopped as Wren looked, one paw raised, waiting.

"I'm so very sorry." Wren was sobbing again. "That's my fault. It was for the dogs. Stray dogs they are, not mine. But they're starving."

With a blink of contempt, the sheriff pushed past. Wren caught the sheriff's arm.

"Can you tell me anything?"

"Ah," mumbled the sheriff. "It's you. I'll be wanting to talk to you at some length, Mistress Bennet. Go and wait at my office if you want. My men'll serve you ale and you can keep warm."

Wren turned and slowly walked in that direction. Both dogs, dribbling apple juice, followed her. As she sat, so they sat close. They waited as she folded her arms on the sheriff's empty table, and bent, cradling her head on her wrists.

First to enter was not the sheriff, but the well-dressed gentleman she had seen outside, and two liveried guards flanked him. He nodded to Wren, polite and careful. "Madam, these wretched murdered souls are from your family?" She shook her head having no desire to speak with strangers. "My apologies," the gentleman continued, "I am Morgan, Earl of Thamesdon, and I may be able to help. You are grieving for the family you knew?"

She gulped. "They were friends. Jessy and Randle and their little boys. They were lovely people. Poor and so kind. This is – it's a nightmare."

The earl was unusual, sweet faced and bright eyed, clearly concerned and spoke kindly. "I've no wish to trouble you, mistress, but I believe their surname was Ford. Am I correct? And there seems to be little or nothing within the house apart from those poor souls. So they were a penniless family? Or has their property been stolen?"

Although wishing he would leave her alone since he would not be the one who investigated and found the killer, she answered quickly. "Yes, my lord, the Ford family. And they never owned anything, poor people. Half the time they were hungry. I tried to help but I didn't do enough."

"And I presume you have no idea who might have committed this horror, nor why?"

She told him no and turned away, but he thanked her before leaving. He wore scarlet velvet with golden trimming and Wren hated that, seeing him as a fire intruding on the vile black death which surrounded them.

The sheriff, once returned, ignored the tail wagging dogs and their ragged protruding bones.

"So you knew the family? Tell me all about them, anything you think of, tell it all. Not relevant? Tell it anyway."

It surprised her to admit how little she knew. Jessy had never been a friend for talking together, shopping together or even relaxing together during summer evenings. Wren had admired Randle's stoicism, she admired the boy Martin who worked harder than she did and she enjoyed small Peter's childishness. Most of all she had cared for Jessy and pitied her poverty.

"Such nice people. Innocent people. Half-starved and yet coped with it. None ever stole a thing." Well – not from her.

Then she retold what had happened the day before, that took a great deal longer.

"And the gang you mentioned, Mistress Wren. Who is this Wyatt?"

Another story to tell. However, during the explanation Wren did not mention the deaths or Landry who had been both saviour and the killer.

It was nearly supper time when Wren left, promising to return to the sheriff should she remember more. She walked home without looking up, she watched only her shoes, hearing the rhythm of patter, then the echoed patter of the dogs keeping pace behind.

Pansy said, "You were a long time, Wren. I had to cook more." She wore a flushed frown. "Late this morning. Late now. Wren, you've had a hard day, but so have I with all this extra work. Now you'd better start cleaning. And get rid of those filthy dogs."

Wren breathed deeply, gulping on a sob, and said, "I'm sorry but I think I have to leave."

"Leave what?"

She thought she'd stopped crying but now felt the tears tickling her cheeks. "Leave here. Leave everything."

Pansy said, "Running from that Wyatt person, I suppose."

And Wren nodded. "I'm so terribly sorry after you gave me such a lovely room and taught me about eels. Two years now isn't it?"

"Two years and two months," Pansy told her. "But the first month doesn't count because you were still learning."

"I think you're fed up with me anyhow." Wren was only thinking of the past and not the future.

"Everyone leaves sooner or later," Pansy said without expression. "No loyalty of course. But you've been good enough. Your cooking's good. But you bring in those mucky old dogs and that dirty pig from next door and now armed gangs and sheriffs. I don't mind if you go, but you have to finish the week off first. I can't find a replacement that quickly."

"You'll make more money on your own."

"Too much hard work," Pansy smiled faintly. Half a smile. "I'll find another helper, and pay less. Young boys looking for work without an apprenticeship are common enough."

"I'll finish the week then," muttered Wren. "Tomorrow's Friday. I'll do Saturday too and leave on Sunday."

While she worked, she watched the door. While she cooked, she watched the door. She was very careful locking the doors she'd been watching, front and back, each evening.

While Wren worked, the dogs sat permanently on the floor, ate up dropped eel tails, heads and entrails and licked the scattered flour, pastry scraps and drips of onion and herbs. Wren visited the first butcher in Pudding Lane and bustled home with every scrap of meat she could talk them into giving free. A wedge of pork was thick with gristle. There was lamb with the first touch of mould, and a huge bone with only scraps and shaving left.

So the dogs ate well for three days, drank river water without having to wade down the banks, and slept on Wren's bed without Pansy knowing. First time up the steps on fleshless legs had been difficult for both animals but the restful warmth soon beckoned and was worth the struggle.

Wren continued to feed them often and generously with the food she'd begged from the butcher. At least their bones were just a touch less visible, and their energy was certainly increasing. Slipping her fingers over their ribs and backbones showed the flesh growing across their skinny bodies. Their fleas were probably enjoying themselves too.

Without the effort of imagination, Wren called the hounds Red and Shadow.

It was Sunday and she avoided church deciding instead, to pack her small heap of belongings in the little hessian bag she owned, knelt to pray for Jessy, Randle, Martin and Peter, then remembered to pray for herself too.

"Dear Lord, I don't know where I'm going. Please could you lead me somewhere that isn't terrifying or dangerous or painful. I don't mind if you kill me but please make it quick."

Someone was knocking on the door downstairs. Red barked. Shadow whimpered and began to slide down the steps on his rear, front paws grabbing at the wood where it had splintered. Wren followed him. The shop was shut, forbidden to open on a Sunday and Pansy was no doubt in church.

This was probably some hungry soul who had come begging. Unless it was Wyatt or one of his men. Perhaps just the sheriff asking questions. "If you open the door," she told herself, "you might find out."

She pressed her ear to the wood. Red was still barking. "Hush, darling," Wren begged. Red sank silently to the floorboards.

The soft voice from the other side of the door answered her.

"Hush," said the voice, "without the additional *darling*, is invariably considered sufficient."

So Wren knew who it was immediately, and yet was surprised when she opened the door.

"Landry," she said.

She had heard him more than seen him, and the one occasion she had seen him, he had seemed little more than a shadow amongst the fury of Wyatt's gang. Now the man was younger than she had expected and beneath a low brimmed black hat, his hair was longer than fashion, thick silky brown and brushing over his shoulders. Although his hair was dark, his eyes were light grey, almost hidden beneath heavy lids and lashes darker than the eyes themselves. His nose, a little long, was very straight and his mouth was wide but thin.

Not a thin man except for his mouth, Landry was tall and even beneath his cloak, again longer than the fashion, the muscled outlines were clear. Beyond the plain black hat, a sheen of drizzle lit the dull clouds.

Wren said, "You're not the way I thought you'd be. But that's not the point. I don't know why you're here, what do you want?"

Landry said as softly as always. "I am here to discover whether you know more of Wyatt Mason. My own actions will likely change according to what you know."

Her voice sinking to whisper, Wren asked, "You want to join his gang?"

"Answering questions with questions rarely brings the information either questioner hopes for." Landry's expression did not change as he added, "That is certainly not my intention nor ever will be. Now, do you personally know any more about him and his followers?"

It was Wren's attraction towards her unexpected visitor that brought fleeting irritation. "I don't know anything, and I don't want to either. He's vile. We both knew that from Newgate and the other evening here." Her voice sank. "You might have even saved my life."

"There's no need to thank me," he continued. "I simply wished to warn Wyatt of my intentions and my opinion of him."

"Oh." That stung, almost felt like a slap. "It doesn't matter. You helped me but unfortunately I can't help you." Then she changed her mind. "There's one thing though, four days ago a whole family was killed in such a horrible way. It could have been Wyatt. I can't know for sure, but I believe it very possible."

Landry lifted one straight dark eyebrow. "For what reason would he have killed them? And for what reason do you believe it was him?"

It seemed to dilute her conviction. "Just – thoughts. It would have taken more than one man and that family didn't have enemies. Poor as a spider without a web. There's only Wyatt around here who could have done it as far as I know."

"There are others," Landry murmured, "whether you know of them or not." He nodded, taking two steps back. "My own apologies for disturbing you without result. I shall leave you in peace."

But Wren was staring back over her shoulder, then started to run. Both dogs raced ahead, barking in panic. The door was left wide open. Then Landry also smelled the strong scent of burning.

CHAPTER SIX

WREN

I knew something was burning so I ran. It had to be the oven, though surely, I hadn't been stupid enough to leave that door open. I'd been startled by Landry. He now suddenly seemed fascinating. But whatever burned was all that mattered now.

The oven stood stout and black in iron, huddled in the corner. The door was firmly shut and even when I opened it, it was obvious that the fire was little more than ashes. Of course, the heat still rushed out until I slammed that shut again. I looked desperately around.

Shadow and Red both quivered, tails between their legs, whimpering now instead of barking. I looked where they looked.

Shit, beyond the serving area were three deep shelves of utensils and a pantry of sorts where I kept the ingredients needed for cooking. In front in a row along the top shelf were tall jars of flour, milk, herbs, onions, and tiny amounts of other stuff. All these shelves lined the far wall, just past the shop's back door which opened onto Pot Lane. Immediately I saw the scarlet glow and then the shooting flames from behind the jars.

I shoved every jar aside and at once saw where the flames had started and were growing. There was a box of herbs in flour, a large box which had been sitting there for weeks so the flour would absorb the sweet herbal perfumes, and the fresh juice from their stems.

Risking my own hands, my fingers had been burned before and would survive, I dragged the box from the shelf and dropped it to the tiled floor. One of the tiles cracked but that didn't matter. I snatched up the large wet towel I used often for so much and slammed it over the flames. It sizzled. I heard the flames spark and surrender with a puff of smoke.

The other items, boxes and small sacks which had stood beside the one burning, were glowing with the first threat of heat. I grabbed and sat them on the wet towel on the ground, adding to the fizzle.

Then the towel itself glowed, embers building along the drying edges. I stamped them out, bent over, peering for every tiny spark.

A jug of water splashed abruptly over the floor, swamping the boxes and packets, leaving no possibility of new flames. It splashed me too and that was more relief than surprise. Landry stood beside me, the bucket he carried now empty.

I sighed with that same heartfelt relief. "Did you collect that from the rainwater barrel outside?" Almost falling backwards now, I gasped my words. "Thank you," I repeated. "You've saved me again."

"Few fires are untouchable until they reach the thatch," Landry murmured. "But this was no accident."

He was right of course. At the back of a high shelf, a large dry box catches fire? Impossible, surely. It had been there for weeks. And this was early October, the weather was cold, and it was drizzling. There was no possible trigger in sight. I said, "Oh Lord, what now?"

"I saw a man, older than myself," Landry said. "I was outside collecting water from the barrel and saw him run."

My already muddled brain had some trouble with that. "A stranger lit the fire? Or did he just smell it and run from the danger?"

"It was too soon and there was no visible danger outside,"

Landry answered. "The man's arm had come from that scrap of a window by your back door. His fingers were poking into your shelves from behind. I shouted and he ran. Having no time, the window did not catch the flame, but the evidence was there."

I was shaking with shock. "He must've been one of Wyatt's gang, then."

Landry shook his head. "Doubtful," he said as softly as always. Had he really shouted at the man running away? His voice rarely rose above a whisper. "You appear to believe Wyatt is the only criminal in the area. I assure you that's hardly true."

"Why doubtful? Would you recognise them all?"

"One or two. But this fool was elderly. Perhaps in his forties. Men of that age don't join street ruffians often. And this one ran, immediately on seeing me. He was small, no hat, with white curls, grey streaked, and tufts of grey beard."

"Then I don't know him," I insisted. "Why would a stranger do such a thing?"

Landry almost smiled, then instead raised one eyebrow. "He might once have thought himself cheated here. Possibly he dislikes the shop owner. Or he finds fire exciting and plays his own games."

I had heard of people who liked to start fires. But I had another problem. My entire life from childhood had seemed a trap of fear and nonsense until I worked hard to change the pattern. I'd succeeded but after years of monotony, this strange return of violence seemed more than absurd. My father had been chucked into Newgate accused of murder, and I'd been obliged to visit him several times in that terrible place. Putting up with him staying in my bedchamber had seemed almost as bad. Wyatt was the most brutal creature I'd met and suddenly he was free and wanting me murdered. The worst, of course, had been Jessy's death. So, I'd gathered the courage to leave that horrid little eel shop and on my last day, I was attacked by fire and a stranger's anger.

I leaned heavily against the wall and breathed hard, avoiding the clump of dripping rubbish on the ground, and stared instead at

Landry. His grey eyes suddenly glittered as though they'd caught the flames.

"None of it is fair," I mumbled.

"I have noticed no element of fairness ever occurring in my life nor in anyone's I've shared. We imagine that fairness is expected in life. It is not."

I almost smiled at him. "I need to clean this up," I said. "Then I'm leaving. I don't work here anymore. Pansy owns this place and she'll be at church for hours. She's a bossy woman and I don't want her coming back thinking I've tried to burn the place down." On my knees now, I bundled the towel around the remaining sticks and ashes and carried them out to the street gutter. Releasing the muck, I dropped the wet black lumps, taking the towel back to hang over the one stool, hoping it would dry and hide those singed edges. I should have swept them further off, but my hands were still badly singed and damned sore.

I noticed Landry kicking the rubbish down the gutter, and then disappear. When he returned, he said, "The lock on your back door is broken."

"I can't mend that now."

"I've closed the door," Landry said. "But it'll be noticed."

Shaking my head, I was back on the floor wiping the last ashes and puddles away. Landry remained, watching. "I've already given my notice," I explained. "I packed my bag before you knocked on the door." I paused but Landry didn't say anything, so I pulled the front door shut and locked it, hopefully no one would think to use the back door, then shoved the key under the gap beneath. "So thank you again and goodbye," I finished.

He wasn't moving, and asked, "Where are you going?"

I did actually manage to smile this time. "I don't know. I just want to get away."

After a short pause, he surprised me again. With two fingers in his mouth, he whistled. Then he turned, looking down the street. It was the loudest, most vibrantly piercing whistle I'd ever heard. And then we both heard the horse's hooves on the cobbles. It appeared from one of the small streets leading to the river, shook both mane and tail, came directly to Landry, bent its nose to him, and waited. Landry kissed the soft brown forehead and scratched it beneath its chin.

Both of them looked up. "Come," said Landry.

I remember obeying like a lamb to the shepherd without thinking. I had no idea what this man wanted to do with me, but I walked towards him anyway. Then so quickly, I was in the air, wind beneath my skirts and my hair over my face, no hat and no qualms.

Then, gasping for breath, I was sitting astride the horse, with my feet dangling. The drizzle was in my eyes, but not tears thank the heavens. One hiccup later, Landry sat behind me, his left arm so tight around my waist, it took my breath away.

Never having ridden a horse in my life, I was amazed at the horse, amazed at Landry and amazed at myself for not falling off. With the hem of my shabby gown stretched across the saddle, my ankles were more visible than decency permitted. I had nothing to clutch at except the rich mane, which gave me a moment of panic until I realised that the insane closeness of the man holding me from behind, was the cause of a rich tingle running through me.

Not only had I never before ridden a horse, but more importantly, I'd never ever been held so tight by any man. It was deliciously and worryingly strange.

"I don't think," I stuttered, when he interrupted me.

"You need not worry," he said, his soft voice now tickling my ear, and the tingle inside my stomach increased. "I am simply removing you from whoever seems intent on attacking you."

He'd slung my little collection of baggage over my shoulder, and I could hear the desperate panting of Red and Shad running behind. I suppose they feared the regular food disappearing.

I said, "Could you ride just a little bit slower?"

"You worry about yourself or the dogs?" he asked without expression.

"All of us," I said.

"Once through the gate," he told me, "and past the slums, you can relax. We need to leave London first."

It was damned Newgate again. Those high dirty stone walls loomed over us, the guards sat on the steps playing cards and took no notice as we passed, and I saw no grimy hands waving from the low windows at road level. The drizzle was in my face, and spangled the horse's neck, but in one breathless moment, we were through. Almost immediately Landry slowed. Now the pace was significantly less, and I looked down, checking the dogs had caught up. I had no scrap of food to give them anymore and had expected to leave them in Black Spoon Row. That, however, was now a mile away.

Heading west, I knew only that we'd cross The Fleet by the bridge. Nearer the banks of the Thames would be my father. Much further on would be Westminster with all the palaces and cathedrals. I'd never seen any of them, and I had no idea what lay further on.

"Where are you taking me?" I mumbled, still utterly confused.

"The docks," he said. "To see Haldon Bennet."

"My father." A rather pointless thing to say but I was surprised and even more puzzled. "He'll be shocked, but I think he'll be pleased." I paused, "when you escaped from Newgate, even my father was impressed. But why leave London through Newgate instead of Ludgate? Surely that was a risk?"

"Just common sense," Landry informed me, "Leaving the city through any gate is a risk as every guard will have been warned, and on watch. Newgate, however, does not expect an escaped convict to pass so close, and rarely watches."

I could see the point, though it still seemed too much risk. To ride close to the very people you had to avoid. "Clever, I think," I said. Then I realised something which seemed genuinely clever. "But how do you know where my father lives?"

"I appreciate your cautious comments," he chuckled into my hair. "However, it's misplaced. This ploy has been proven many times. And as for your father's new home, I've seen him working at the docks. So naturally, I know."

"Oh." I couldn't think of anything else to say.

"And this," Landry told me while pulling on the reins, "is where your father lives. While that," and he pointed towards the cranes and warehouse by the river, "is where he works."

The docks banked the Thames and were virtually banking the Fleet, but the small house where he had stopped the horse and dismounted from behind me, "Your father rents two rooms on the upper floor.

Suddenly I missed his warmth at my back and the security of those capable arms at my side. I felt quite stupidly alone. With the gentle pace of the horse, Landry had not only been deliciously close, but beautifully relaxing with the horses swaying and Landry's warmth.

Yet as he held out his arms, I had no alternative but to slip down to the ground. Another glimmer of heat, but he released me too quickly though I managed to smile.

"You really have been kind. Will you come in. You seem to know my father well enough."

"Only from the exceedingly temporary acquaintanceship of those incarcerated." He turned from me, speaking softly to his horse. He slipped the reins into a loop on the saddle, made no effort to tether the animal, and wished it a good evening. With a whisk of a thick tail, it bounded off into the distance.

"You don't feed it or tie it?" I asked with a slight glower.

He was striding to my father's front door. "If he's hungry," Landry said without turning around, "he'll find his own out in the fields, go back to his stables or he'll return to me with a belligerent expression. Your dogs do the same?"

"No," I said at once. "They were starving. I feed them when I can. You can still almost see all their bones. All that running behind your horse has probably made them starved again. And anyway, they're not mine."

"Indeed a trial," Landry said without noticeable sympathy for the dogs or me. "Now I suggest you call on your father."

I wanted to say, *Well of course I damn well do, do you think me an idiot?* But, busily being a polite female with gratitude and most certainly not a female of sarcastic arrogance, I remained polite. I smiled, knocked briefly on the door, pushed it open, and called my father.

"I'm here, Dad. And so is Landry." When there was no answer, I added, "he's probably still at work."

"They bring in the eel boats and empty the crates early. Your father works one of the cranes. Look to the docks and you'll see those cranes no longer moving. Therefore, your father is either here, or out."

So that made sense.

I stumbled up the stairs. Somewhat wobbly after a long time in the saddle on an animal I found somewhat daunting, while held tight in an embrace I found glorious but refused to admit, my legs were still unbalanced. However, I reached the top of the steps and knocked on the smaller door, pushed at it, found it locked, and called again for my father.

"What now?" demanded the bleary voice from inside. The door squeaked open. Dad's less than attractive head poked out. His expression changed which was quite a relief. "My lovely little birdie," he croaked, "come on in." And he opened the door wider.

Landry didn't wait to be invited. He walked in beside me.

My father's house was not delightful, but it was larger than mine had been. There was a pallet bed in one room along with a row of pegs for hanging clothes, a somewhat smelly pissing pot and a stool beside the bed. The other room, where we now all sat, had four small wooden stools, no fireplace and no place for cooking, but contained a little rickety table and a shelf holding a jug beside an assortment of cups and platters.

I presumed he didn't cook his own meals, but bought all his dinners elsewhere. Perhaps another eel shop since this was the docks for the eel wherries, but there were also plenty of pie shops around.

"It's wonderful to see you again," I told him, an exaggeration, but he seemed happy.

"She needs a place to sleep," Landry interrupted.

It was true enough, but I would have told it differently. As it was my father just nodded, sighed, and pointed to the jug and cups. "I've no wine to offer," he said. "Nor ale."

From the whimpers and little whines from outside, I assumed Red and Shad were waiting on the landing there. "I don't need anything, Dad. But I suppose you haven't got anything hidden away for the dogs?"

This made no sense to him. "You want dog scraps? You says don't need anything, lass?"

"No," I giggled, which wasn't really fair. "My dogs are waiting outside and they're starving. Even though they aren't mine."

"Well, I ain't got nothing for you nor me, let alone fer dogs. But there's a shop at the docks. Eels, but other fish, maybe a few bones."

"I'll walk over there," I said. "Aren't you working today?"

"I start work at bloody four of the morning clock," he scowled. "Till the afternoon starts and then I comes back to sleep. You woke me up."

"My apologies." Another exaggeration. I just wanted the walk. The piss pot was in the bedchamber, but this room still smelled of it.

Landry stood, scraping back the stool's three misshapen legs. "I shall find your hopefully open shop," he said. "I will buy food for myself, for you, and even for your dogs."

So I wasn't getting fresh air and an escape after all. I didn't insist on going with him, still being uncomfortably polite. I'd soon learn different.

CHAPTER SEVEN

NARRATIVE

The young stallion trotted back to his whistle and caress, disliked the insistent stink of eels both raw and cooked, and so backed away before depositing his rider at the docks. There he waited as Landry wandered to the small open shop. He bought whatever appeared sufficiently interesting and piled the packages into the stained sack attached to the saddle.

The horse sniffed and then snorted. The smells had not appealed. No food for him then. Landry leaned over the broad brown neck before him and waved a fat carrot at his mount's snout. "Feeling ignored, Arthur? Do I ever forget your appetite? Take this and apologise."

Arthur grabbed the carrot with eager teeth, trotting cheerfully back beyond the docks.

Landry returned to Haldon's rooms and deposited the food on the floor. "Help yourselves. The dogs which aren't yours," he grinned, "are still outside praying frantically not to be forgotten."

A large fish that had been long dead and squashed. Another smelled just a touch unclean. Wren took both outside and fed Red and Shadow on the landing. She left them to eat every scrap and probably lick the floorboards as she returned to her own meal, hopefully more appetising.

Hot fish pies were now numerous on the table. "Two each," Landry told her, "and one remaining."

Wren tasted crab, took the two which smelled the best, and watched her father take the last one.

Wren sighed. "Strange how eating can be so exhausting. It's like a dream in a blanket that wraps you up all warm and cosy."

"Then I suggest you discover the obliging blanket," Landry said, "While I speak with your father."

She had no wish to leave, wondered if she had been somehow dismissed, and turned to her father. "May I?"

"Tis the next room," Haldon waved a pie crusted hand, "with only my bed. Use it now, cause you'll be sleeping on the floor tonight."

She heard nothing of Landry's discussion with her father, and when she woke, she was surprised to see the sky black, knowing she had slept for far longer than she could have expected. Shaking down her clothes, Wren hurried back into the other room. It was empty. Another surprise.

Having no idea where her father had gone, out with Landry perhaps or back to work, Wren cleaned the mess the food had left, managed to put together a make-shift bed for herself, then sat on the vacated stool and stared peacefully into space. The space was neither attractive nor interesting and she quickly decided that work, however boring and however exhausting, was preferable to doing nothing at all. The nothing at all which now clouded around her head, was growing steadily more unattractive.

The clank of the door opening and closing sounded suddenly sweet. But it wasn't Landry. Only her father.

He grunted, "That's a fine fellow, that man. I never thought it when we were both in gaol, and he called me guilty, saying I murdered my own daughter. This time he was proper nice. But I doubt we'll see him again. Says he's heading southwest away from Newgate. But I made a couple o' pennies doing what he asked."

Wren muttered, "Stealing isn't going to help keep you out of gaol."

"I didn't say naught of stuff stolen, brat. He gived me the coins hisself, saying as how I should use my work here to get me back on the treading caracks." Haldon frowned. "But there's no place on no trading vessel for you, so what d'you think on doing, then? Walking the street to pick up a few desperate buggers? I don't want a daughter o' mine doing the whore's run."

Annoyed, Wren grimaced, "I've no intention of that. And never have. Never would. I'll move on tomorrow. I just wanted to see you and have a rest without eels."

"No chance of that here," Haldon sniggered. "'Tis only eels and more eels. But we ate well. Sleep again if you wants, but I'm off to bed now. I start work mighty early."

"You told me. And you're right, we all ate well. Sounds as though you've been drinking well too."

"Fish and ale paid by Landry. I'll never say no to that."

"He's a thief, isn't he?"

Haldon was halfway to his bed when he turned, one eyebrow raised, "What else, girl? Food costs coin. Some folks have plenty of coin and others don't. I work at the docks and Landry does what he wants."

He was asleep in a blink. Wren lay awake for half the night, wondering what she should do, where to go, and why. She wondered if she'd been a fool to leave the eel shop, wondered why Pansy hadn't even tried to keep her with an offer of more pay or a better bed. Clearly, she'd not been worth keeping. Then she wondered about the four dead bodies hanging from the ceiling and felt sick. A shadow of misery sent her to sleep, dreamless, without waking as her father left the house, heading for work.

It was later when Wren awoke and combed her hair, pinned it beneath the small cap, and scuttled downstairs carrying the little she owned in the bag over her shoulder. Using the wrap from yesterday's pies, she left a message for her father. *'Off to find work south.'*

She was immediately followed. The two dogs on the landing were awake instantly, jumping from dreams to staircase and keeping as close to Wren as she permitted. They had been well fed the day before. An etching of flesh across the scrawny skin and bones was now quite visible. This was a promise of being fed and they wouldn't risk being left behind.

Not my dogs, she reminded herself. But perhaps they thought she was theirs. No breakfast for either them or herself, but yesterday had been a day of feasting for all three and would suffice sufficiently to cover a day bereft.

The warmth of sleep under cover had helped, though now it was colder but dry. Not even an October drizzle spoiled their run. The autumn sun rose late, so the sky was still dark with a last hint of moon sinking behind the clustered rooves. Having no idea where to head and knowing only that she had to cross the river if she intended going south, she reminded herself that she had missed the only bridge more than a mile back by the Tower. She could not afford a wherry, but had little choice. Starting her escape by walking more than a mile would mean immediate exhaustion. She might as well swim the Thames. Laughing, she called the wherry and hoped it wouldn't be Bryce, the Newgate inmate who had once been a wherryman but would probably now be swinging on the scaffold. That brought thoughts of Jessy again, and Wren bit her lip, forcing herself to think of sunnier things.

No sunshine came. The small boats had unloaded their catches overnight, now the cranes were clanking and wheels squealing, the men shouting to each other, and Wren did not look for her father, who would hardly help. But one of the little eel boats, stinking of eels although now empty, was heading out from the docks when it hit the bank, then stopped to turn and right itself. Wren hurried over.

"I'm Haldon's daughter." She pointed vaguely towards two of the cranes. "I have to cross over to Southwark. Could you drop me on the southern bank?"

The elderly man hanging onto the low gunwales turned and smiled. "Reckon I can if you don't want no specific dock."

"No, anywhere is fine. Though I'd sooner not get wet on the banks. I mean, not have to wade ashore, I can't swim."

"Climb in quick, then we're off."

Both dogs, however, proved they didn't like boats, shivering the whole crossing and climbed ashore before the boat hit dry land, they were in such a hurry.

Wren had never crossed the Thames in her entire life. "I have," she told herself when standing on dry cobbles and watching the first pink glaze of the dawn, "been a woman of monotony. I've been nowhere. I've done nothing. No friends and no family left. Except for Dad. He's not much of a friend though."

She hoped her southern choice would prove warmer. Folk had told her this on the rare occasion such a thing had been discussed. Yet Wren had not the faintest idea what lay south, whether there was an ocean, fields, cities, towns or villages. *Ignorance again,* she whispered to herself. Nor had she ever had a reason for leaving London. Walking for days without food had never seemed sensible. It wasn't really sensible now, but perhaps she'd find something better.

And so she walked on, following the road that called her.

Life, after all, had never really brought comfort. She had never known her mother and had no idea of her own age when the mother died. Once Haldon had informed her that her mother had died giving birth. However, she found it exceedingly unlikely that her father could have brought her up from birth. Her father had presumably taken over her care once she could walk, talk, and do as she was told. She vaguely remembered being fed twice a day, but usually with the meagre rations of boiled oats and stale bread. Whether it had been a mother or a father supplying this, she could not remember. Yet she could remember loving apples, and was sometimes given half when her father had finished his own helping.

A neighbour had taught her to read and write which she had adored learning. But without anything else to learn on offer, she had taught herself addition and the value of the pennies her father brought home. She also learned to cook, teaching herself with the help of the neighbour. If a meal was vile, Haldon told her loudly and slapped her, although usually ate it anyway. Too badly cooked, he would throw it back at her. She learned to clean, learned from those times. Her father often beat her although she rarely understood why, and he dismissed any questions that might answer. "All good fathers beat their brats. Tis the right way to raise a child."

At around the age of nine, she had left home and worked in a tailors, sitting on the floor to sew, to sharpen needles, to measure customers, and to sit very quietly when there was nothing else to do. The floor grew familiar since that was also where she slept.

Two years at the eel shop had at least given her a room with a bed and a place to light a fire, and that had been a luxury. The benefits overwhelmed the disadvantage of the smell that disgusted her, a boss she disliked and work which lasted for long hours for only pennies in return.

Those were not her reasons for leaving. She had no eloquent motive. But leaving felt like a relief, a pleasure, as far as she understood what pleasure might be.

Riding with Landry's arms around her had also been pleasure, and a good deal faster than walking, and eating two hot crab pies had also been a pleasure never experienced before. Now she could explore the added pleasure of freedom.

The dogs, shaking their coats dry, trotted behind as though glued to her heels. Wren was becoming hungry again, and she guessed the same would be true of the dogs.

Gulls watched from the riverbanks. Flying upstream from the estuary where autumn rains flooded the lowland, they found food where people dropped crumbs and fish lounged in fresh water. Flying low over her head, two gulls brushed her hair with their wide white wings, and both dogs barked. The gulls squawked back, swirling ready to swoop for fish near the river's surface.

The wind also blew upstream as though chasing the birds, and Wren quickly walked from the Thames into the broken streets of the Bishop of Winchester's Southwark. Men lounged outside the ale houses, and it was ale houses, inns and taverns which filled almost every street. The gulls gathered. Bird shit covered roof tops, and sometimes the shoulders of the women who walked, watched, waited and smiled at the men outside the taverns.

Wren had heard of the whores of Southwark, known as The Winchester Geese, but would not have recognised a whore from a respectable matron herself. Instead, she heard the shouting of a rabid crowd and knew that a cock fight was finishing outside the old castle ruins, someone killing the wretched loser, kissing the winner, and counting the results of the wager.

One man had chewed the meat from a pork chop, leaving the bone on the street. Wren bent to rescue it, snapped it in half, and gave the pieces to each of the dogs. She was hungry but not enough for scraps from the street.

Beyond the tenements and collapsing dregs of old houses, the fresh air from the distant farms called, and Wren walked on, slowly enough not to tire herself too quickly, but fast enough to reach somewhere offering shelter by nightfall.

Southwark, they said, was the way that penitents trudged barefoot towards Canterbury Cathedral, and the forgiveness they hoped to find there. Wren wanted blessings but decided she had few sins to confess and aimed instead where the wooden stiles led to soft green grass and the last of the daisies.

A field, thick hedged, was boarded by another, another and another, each ploughed down to the dry earth and neat beneath the glowering clouds. A pretty dawn had slunk into the promise of later rain. The clouds remained watchful.

Wren led the dogs to the stile and climbed, crossing the first field by the roots of the hedge, Red and Shadow following although nervous at their first sight of open land and a sky not peeping between buildings. Eventually the farmer's cottage sat snug in a hollow, planted with vegetables and herbs. But no one seemed to notice Wren and she continued walking until the storm hit.

It was just the lightning at first, a great fork of light ripping through the clouds over and over again, then a rolling, incessant roar of thunder, before the rain too heavy, split the clouds open and the dark rivers of water tumbled in curtains and covered the land around her.

She ran. There was a long shed at the end of the next field. The lightning struck again and again, and the thunder growled far louder. The frightened dogs, soaked, stumbled, heads down, backs low with fear and tails between their legs.

Without a tail to hide, Wren raced to the next stile, almost fell over it, and finally reached the shed. The door was shut, and she feared it might be locked, but the dogs hurtled forwards, heads to the slatted wood, and pushed it open. They fled into shelter and Wren collapsed behind them.

Puddles of water trailed from each of them, but Wren tugged the door closed behind them and stumbled to the heaps of dried straw and hay, now blown loose from their stacks. Both dogs spread themselves beside her, their heads to her lap. She lay breathless and listened to the explosion of thunder outside her new haven. At least, she thought vaguely, while the rain poured, there would be no farmer crossing to throw strangers from his shed. She curled, stroking ears, snouts and foreheads. The dogs licked her fingers.

There was a dead sparrow beneath the hay, and Red ripped and ate it, spitting feathers. Shadow watched, trembling. He sniffed at the straw but found only rest there, not food. Winter gloom was already falling, and the light came from neither sun nor moon, and only from the jagged flashes splitting the sky.

No window brought light to the shed and Wren saw nothing. She only heard the thunder and the pounding of the rain against the thin wooden walls. Tired, but only from walking, Wren thought it too early for sleep, but closed her eyes.

She was asleep in minutes and lay curled between the dogs, now both snoring a little as all three slowly dried, snuggled into the wealth of dry hay, and feeling the comfort of warmth without the threat of fire.

The storm thinned by midnight, shrugging off the torrents as it drifted into a damp chill. But the hay stayed warm, and the winds drowned in the puddles outside where the horse-ploughed earth lay its stripes, now muddy bog and stagnant streams. An owl called, then its flight was silent as it hunted. Yet Wren heard nothing and already flew that same darkening sky within her dreams.

CHAPTER EIGHT

WREN

When I woke I could hear both dogs snuffling in their sleep, there was no rain, no thunder and no gales. I had no idea whether I snored as well, with no one to tell me, and I doubted the dogs would care. I stayed warmly snuggled and tried to make plans without success.

To be excited by finding myself on a farm for the very first and perhaps only time, was proof of what a dullard I'd been. I needed life, I told myself, and not just existence. So a muddy farm and a prickly bed in a shed could not be an adventure, but at the very least I faced change.

At least we'd dried off overnight and although there was still a large puddle just inside the door, presumably where the storm had leaked in, our hay beds were still warm and dry. If it hadn't been for hunger, I would have stayed another day, perhaps a week.

We left around midday, which was far too late, but I kept putting it off. Even the hungry dogs were keen to stay lounging in the warm. But there was only cloud when we left and sheltering beneath it was no shelter at all. It was freezing and even colder than the storm.

The dogs and I hurried across the fields, both to keep warmer and to get away before the farmer saw us. Beyond the last field was a lane, thick glutinous mud after last night's rain, but banked by grass and beyond that trickled a small stream. It was enjoying the breezes, overflowing its banks and sloshing fast, supplying a good morning drink for all of us. My shoes were ruined anyway, so we kept walking in the same direction, telling myself I was simply floating downstream.

Having no idea what day this might be, I decided it must be approaching November. After that the Christmas season would arrive. Surely, we'd passed St. Andrew. I was hoping for St. Nicholas. I laughed and tried to skip a little. I only managed to dislodge a little of the mud from my shoes, and gained more immediately as we wandered on.

The first village we reached was pretty. The cottages crowded together. Thatch to thatch, wattle to wattle and daub to daub. I found the tiny square and three market stalls crouched beneath their striped awnings. Delighted to see that two of the stalls sold food, whereas the third was a knife sharpener flashing his metal, I hurried to the butcher.

"I'm going to be walking for some days," I explained, "I have two starving dogs that follow me. So something I can eat myself, and any old bones or scraps you can't sell, please?"

He peered at me over the spread of his wares, little bloody lumps of dead creatures I couldn't recognise. "I ain't got no meat what won't sell," he complained. "I got prime meat cause I's a prime butcher what sells the best. Now – what you want?"

I shook my head and stared down at the two dogs sitting dutifully at my feet while gazing up with frantically hopeful eyes. But nothing cooked was on offer. "Bones, then, and any fat and gristle you've trimmed off."

He reached down beneath his trays and hauled up an armful of bones, then shook his head. "You'd best gnaw them bones yerself," he muttered, "or go to the tavern up that lane over there."

He'd pointed and I nodded, grasped the sticky collection of raw bones, walked off to the lane, and dumped the pile down on the grass. The dogs swooped, tails so active they nearly fell off. Red grabbed the larger bone, but Shadow chewed the smaller bone which still held more meat. Fatty skin with a heap of gristle was spread beneath the dogs' noses. There was a lot for them to eat and certainly more than the day before, so I left them to it and approached the tavern. I could smell the cooking and it made me suddenly ravenous. My appetite swelled.

But my money hadn't swelled so I asked for a pie and held out sixpence. I got the pie and one penny change, sat on the corner stool and ate the pie in less than a blink.

But once I'd finished it, I was still hungry, sat over a small cup of ale, and closed my eyes. The dogs would still be eating and so I relaxed from the strains of the journey, my thoughts drifting.

The voice that interrupted my sweet doze was more dream than the dream I'd been dreaming.

"A strange coincidence, little bird."

I opened my eyes, and sat up straighter and stared. I knew Landry had told my father he'd be travelling southwest but surely there was a lot of possibility there. I had no idea where I was although south somewhere. But meeting up again with Landry seemed suspicious. What was fate trying to do? That wheel of fortune was whirling fast and had some sneaky plan in mind.

It was still the same Landry but somehow away from my father, this man looked more relaxed. He wore a highly unfashionable hat stuck with feathers and an enormous black cape which I remembered from before. He hadn't shaved that morning, but the stubble was little more than a shadow, and his pale grey eyes were almost invisible beneath lowered lids.

"It's you." my thoughts hadn't caught up.

"Yes indeed, it is me," he said in that soft voice, "Were you expecting someone more interesting?"

Since I'd never met anyone more interesting, I just nodded with a faint smile. "I wasn't expecting anyone."

"I confess," he continued, "I had no intention of entering here, but I saw your dogs outside. They can hardly be missed."

So, he was simply passing and then came in on purpose to see me. I loved the thought of that.

"Arthur," Landry suddenly smiled at me, "is waiting for us both." The smile stretched between those two deep tucks at the corners of his mouth and the narrow lips seemed softer. "Depending, naturally, on where you hope to go."

That was an offer from heaven. "Anywhere," I said at once. "I don't know anyone, and I don't really know where I am now. I just wanted out of London. Where are you going?"

"I go where the road takes me." He was still smiling.

A little surprised that he had no objective, just like me, I gulped the last dribble of ale and stood, ready to follow. "Well," I said with my own smile, "it just so happens that's exactly where I'm heading too."

His invitation had not been put in those words, but I was more than ready, both for the idea of having somewhere to go, and for the sheer pleasure of his strong arms around me once again. I quickly followed him outside.

The stallion was regarding the dogs with obvious contempt, but was eating as well. A clump of hay was disappearing fast. Red and Shadow were busy licking around the grass trying to find any forgotten morsels. They weren't bulging yet, but they were on their way.

I was tentative while stroking Arthur. Sitting astride had seemed perilous at first but when Landry held me, I felt reassuringly safe. I believed I owed Arthur a thank you, so stroked his beautiful brown neck. I suddenly found myself mounted without any effort on my part, Landry simply hoisted me up, and there I was with my skirt improperly hitched, and my body waiting for his embrace.

We had not been riding long when we heard noises, they were audible from some distance, but there was no suspicion they were aiming for us, at least not until they surrounded us. Five mounted men, tall and liveried in scarlet, two held pikes, the others unsheathed and pointed their swords at Landry.

They shouted, "You are under arrest, Landry Crawford, for escaping imprisonment while awaiting trial for the crimes of theft and aggressive robbery. And you -," his sword swerved in my direction, "are now under arrest for aiding and abetting a criminal."

I hadn't, but it seemed pointless arguing now, though with swords, pikes, and all those horses, I admit I was nervous. I tried to catch my breath and appear courageous.

Landry just looked bored. "Again?" he demanded, shrugging.

"You're damned right, again," the guard insisted, and flashed the sword blade closer. "Get up behind that female. You'll ride back to Newgate with us. Forget any attempt to escape or this sword will end up through your eye." I shivered. Landry just shrugged and settled in the saddle, put both arms forward and held me tight and close. My fear began to fade. But Arthur's reins were held by one of the guards, while the others surrounded us even closer. Another pointed his sword directly at Landry's side and kept it hovering there as we rode.

The butcher looked up as we passed, saw the dogs running hard behind, and shook his head.

With barely time to think, my thoughts were in a knot of confusion. The wheel of fate was probably pissed. I had relished freedom, discovered the beauty of the countryside for the first time, and although had no idea where I was going. I had strangely been discovered by Landry, a coincidence I could barely believe. And then? Arrest. Landry had found me. The Newgate guards had found him.

When Landry began to sing softly into my ear, I was delighted and amused. The fear ebbed again. But then I realised what he was humming.

"Little bird, little bird, this is all so absurd. There's no need for sorrow. I'll be out by tomorrow, and you'll come with me." I leaned my head back against his shoulder and it felt so sweetly warm. "Back to the city, with one so pretty, so see what we shall find." His mouth nuzzled my hair, and the suddenly invented tune tickled. Although little more than a whisper, his singing was sweet. "I look for a fat man who works on a farm. A dangerous fellow, but no cause for alarm. David's his name and has a brother the same. Both fat as a cart horse, but I cannot think of a rhyme that might fit with the wretched horse. At Newgate I'll meet those to ask, with no need to stay more than a day."

Although I was laughing at the game, I guessed he was telling me his intentions. Why he'd search for two fat brothers, I wasn't going to ask. It didn't matter to me, and I certainly knew by now that he could look after himself. In the meantime, I probably couldn't and knew I'd have to fight if anyone tried to chuck me into Newgate too.

This meant at least one night sleeping in those filthy cells, trying to prove my innocence to those who rarely listened. I'd left the city because of that hideous day seeing Jessy and her family dead, with Wyatt striding the streets ready to attack. I certainly didn't have enough money to bribe the guards, and whether or not Landry was a thief, I doubted he was rich enough either.

And a thief. A robber! Did I really have such a fascination for an unrepentant felon who lived on what he could steal? Now I was feeling sick and could hear my heartbeat pounding as loudly as yesterday's storm.

"What day is it?" I whispered back.

"I seem to remember Saint Simon." He laughed at me. "Is it so vital to remember which day you've been arrested?"

"No. Yes. Not for the first time in my life, it's absolutely unfair," I said, my voice topsy turvy as Arthur trotted and my head kept bumping against Landry's chin.

It seemed like a long ride back to Southwark and then over the Bridge. It had been mid-morning when the guards had turned up. Now it was dark, no stars, or moon, just blackness all around until we saw candles flickering in windows of the houses across the Bridge, and then down Thames Street towards Ludgate.

Twisting up past St. Paul's Cathedral, I saw the huge towers of

Newgate looming over us and suddenly wanted to cry. It was Landry's hands that stopped me. He held me so sweetly and one hand caressed my hair as he caught my hat. It had blown off in the wind.

No rain, but blistering gales slammed into our faces, blasting down from the north. Almost too quick, we were within the shelter of those great stone walls, and I would have so much preferred to freeze outside.

It was a tiny office, with a haughty seeming guard watching us over his table.

"Welcome back, Master Crawford." he said, glaring even though his words seemed humorous. "What a pleasure to see you again. And it seems you've brought us another friend. Who is this? Your sister? Your wife? Your whore?"

I just stood there like an idiot while Landry smiled. "None of those, John. This is simply a friend, and an innocent one who your men grabbed by mistake. You'd best release her at once, or risk looking a dolt. She's a respectable female who works in the eel shop down Black Spoon Row. I know her only slightly."

"Humph," said the guard without any sign of believing him. I tried to smile but it probably looked like a snarl, twisted into a threat.

The guards who had brought us were crowded behind, the leader who had arrested us now stepped forwards and haggled very quietly with the one sitting. They mumbled. I understood very little, which I suppose was intentional.

"If you work in Black Spoon Row," demanded the sitting guard, "what were you doing all the way south in Humble Village?"

"It was my day off." Feeble, but it was the only thing I could think of. I was also wondering where the dogs were, hoping perhaps they'd wandered into the countryside. "But I swear I haven't stolen a thing, I never have."

After a few moments of more muttering, the seated guard scowled up at me. "I've no warrant for your arrest and I'm told you've not been seen doing aught wicked. So, I reckon you can go. But not you, my man. You'll be shackled in the dungeons."

It was a massive relief, but I felt both sorry for Landry and for myself. I'd spent all that time and energy walking south, escaping that horrible storm, not to mention telling Pansy I didn't want to work there anymore. And now I was back again so soon.

Two guards took Landry's arms, opened the side door and marched him along to the horrid stone steps going down into hell. Landry shook off the arms and walked ahead. Well, he certainly knew the way, but he didn't even turn to say goodbye.

After a moment standing like an idiot, I returned to the freezing wind outside. The dogs were sitting, waiting, patiently after their long run. Still weak and skinny, I bent, scratching behind their ears and telling them both how wonderful they were. I certainly wasn't going to say I'd wished they'd stayed in the country, although it would have been the truth.

I pulled my hat and cloak tighter, with the bag of my bits and pieces over my shoulder. Then I walked through the gate over The Fleet, and off to the eel docks and my father's house again. I was crying. Just a few silly tears trickling. I was sad, confused and definitely frustrated. I was also angry although I didn't know who with. The ridiculous wheel of fate perhaps.

Damn, life was tiring even though momentarily interesting, for Landry had brought some brief excitement. And yet here I was again, exactly where I didn't want to be.

CHAPTER NINE

NARRATIVE

"Oh, you. Well, come on in. Bloody woken me in the middle of the night again." Haldon opened the door to his daughter, him in a wrapped blanket, and Wren in an increasingly shabby cloak over even more shabby mud caked boots. Haldon pointed with dislike. "You can leave them muddy things outside." Then he blinked, seeing something else. "And you can leave them muddy hounds outside and all."

Bending to remove her shoes and whisper to Red and Shad, Wren mumbled, "I won't be staying long." She didn't want to stay at all but knew this would not be the best greeting for a father already reluctant.

"That's what you said before. Come on, brat. Tis cold."

Wren scrambled inside and snuggled on a stool, no fire and no blanket for her, but cosier than outside. "Thanks, Dad. It's been a sad day."

"You look plenty alive to me, girl. But you ain't going to sleep on a stool, is you, daft brat! Your bed's still on the floor by mine, more or less. A touch messy but t'will do. Move it. I'm bloody tired."

In front of her father, she swallowed back tears and made no complaints. The snuffle of the dogs settling outside helped, with the knowledge that they had followed all that way, and still wanted her close. But there was no food to give them except two small crusts of stale bread. She peeped outside, gave each a hard crust and watched them devour the bread with eager appetite.

Morning for Haldon came quickly, and Wren woke as he rolled from his bed, his bitterly cold and unwashed feet to her face. Unable to sleep again after he had left, she redressed herself with the cape pulled tight and walked back to Newgate. As always, the dogs followed but there was nothing to give them except the morning scratch beneath the ears. She stood sheltering under the archway as the church bell rang for opening, the gate unlocked, slammed back against the stone, and Wren walked again into London.

Both Red and Shadow smelled the butchers close past the gate, the reek of blood and fresh meat hung to dry. The crowd of aproned housewives and young pages, kitchen staff and children sent by working parents clustered at shop doorways, already too crowded for joining any queue and instead Wren ignored the dogs and walked on.

Drifting aimlessly towards the river, she sat for some time on the banks, watching the wherries, the Thames as busy as any market. The dogs returned, bloody hair and offal around their snouts, but still searched in the gutters for more food scraps. A wind whistled up from the estuary, so she turned, the wind at her back, and the gusts pushed her once more towards Newgate.

The smell of dying cattle and the fresh cut meat was immediately overpowered by the stench of the prison, from above and below, wrapping every corner in gloom.

"I'm visiting," Wren told the guard on duty.

"That Haldon fellow ain't here no more. Got released," the guard told her.

"I know. I've come to see Landry Crawford. But I'm surprised you recognise me."

"Not many pretty young girls come here," he grumbled. "And now I'll be remembering you the more. But them dogs best stay outside, and don't you go helping that fellow Landry to escape again."

"I won't. I wouldn't know how."

The great swarm welcomed her back. Her eyes adjusted very slowly as she looked for Landry and was first surprised to see Wyatt.

"Tis the slimy little eel wench," Wyatt waved as though his words had been complimentary. "Seems we all comes back sooner or later."

"I'm just visiting," she told him. "And not you." She doubted he'd care, but she added, "But I'm glad to see you here, and not raising violent mobs in London."

Wyatt snorted. "You want the bugger wot knifed my friends?"

Faces peered at her, a couple familiar, but most were strangers. Wren avoided the stares. She was adjusting to the reek and swamp of aimless bodies. Landry seemed nowhere amongst them, either invisible, or already escaping. Still standing in Wyatt's shadow, she felt disappointment and was annoyed.

"They fought and would have killed me. And don't accuse others of murder when the guards might hear."

"I does as I wants," Wyatt grumbled. "You and him, the bastard, over there in the corner, you killed my mates. And you just wait fer I's gonna get my own back."

She looked in the direction which Wyatt had indicated. Then the soft voice reached out, seemingly a gentle drift of smoke.

"Your kindness, little bird, will surely be repaid. Though first I need access to the well, the pump and the day's light."

Feeling the direction, Wren groped through the shivering darkness. "Landry, are you close?"

The hand startled her. "Close enough, I believe." His breath tickled her ear, she let him pull her back into the deeper shadows away from the row of high windows and sat with him on the bench. Someone she didn't know was sprawled on the filthy stone at their feet, sleeping it seemed, or half dead. No one else was near enough to hear what was said.

"I'm so sorry." Wren meant it. "It seemed so horrid – just as we set off. And royal guards. Why? You haven't killed the king?"

Landry's expression was still indiscernible. "If so, I'm unaware of it," the soft voice drifted. "I've neither fought for him nor against. Edward is a sovereign of great skill in battle, but little else." He had avoided explaining the royal liveried guards who had arrested him.

"They say he spends like a rich man, but most is borrowed and never paid back." She was smiling and hoped that he was too.

"I doubt anyone would expect repayment when lending on request of a king."

Wren's response was interrupted. The heavy door was once again unlocked, and the skirmish interested every man's boredom. They heard the sweep of skirts, though this was not who they expected.

"Our Lord God," bellowed the masculine entrance, "will forgive even wickedness, but only when the sinner repents."

Some inmates sat up, most sighed and rolled over.

"Father Jacob," announced the guard who now retreated, "I'll leave you to your good works. Just thump on the door when you wants out."

The priest nodded but stood still, facing the filth and the bodies before him. Landry leaned back. Wren sat forwards. The priest spoke as though at the pulpit.

He was thin, although almost as tall as Landry, and his mouth seemed etched in permanent sympathy. His voice, sadly sepulchral, echoed. "No confessional exists for me to offer the proper privacy between any sinner and our Holy Lord, but any man wishing for salvation may kneel here, ask forgiveness for his sins and swear that he will never sin again."

Two of the men hurried forwards and both knelt at the priest's feet. Both muttered their repentance, one after the other. Wren recognised Bryce and was surprised.

"I'm glad to say it, sir, and mean every word." Bryce lowered his head to one knee. "I'm mighty sorry for what I've done and swear never to sin again." In the darkness and his head bent low, whatever honesty Bryce felt was not visible. Wren had disliked him previously although he had complimented her father. A man covering all possibilities, she decided.

Then she was astonished when Landry stood slowly, and then walked to the priest's side. He did not kneel, did not kiss Father Jacob's hand, and spoke more quietly than most. The words sank into a murmur of unrecognisable noise as the priest nodded and Landry returned to his seat on the bench. Wren looked at him with curiosity. He did not return her gaze and said nothing until the priest had left.

First was the bustle of a sermon, a little strident although the routine lessons dragged on without originality.

Impossible to leave, impossible to speak, Wren found she was dozing. Having been awake since well before dawn, she forgave herself. But it was as the priest banged on the door and called the guard that he also turned and nodded to Landry.

Wren blinked. Landry also nodded, and the priest left. "You know him?" Wren asked.

Landry gazed back at her, one eyebrow raised. "My answer is that it involves motive more than holy religion." His hand on her shoulder was light, but she was again startled.

"Sorry. I know it is not my business."

"Do you have any business?" he asked her.

She shook her head. "No. But almost everything you do seems so unexpected."

"Probably since we have a diversity of interests," he told her, which made her smile once more. "But listen little bird. Rather than crouching in the discomfort of your father's slum, I have another place to recommend."

Wren accepted the tease. "Any slum will do. I had decided to go back to Black Spoon Row and that's a slum."

"Indeed," he said. "However, I have a more interesting habitat to suggest. Between Bread and Fish Streets runs an inlet to a Mews of stables owned by a gentleman I doubt you know. On the more dismal side of the lane to the side and above a stable, steps lead to a two-storey building. It's pleasantly grim outside. Somewhat less grim inside. I offer it to you for living without payment, neither of coin nor service required. There are two bedchambers but since I shall return soon, I may choose to keep the larger, as no doubt it smells of me. The smaller room contains a bed of some comfort, and your canine companions are free to share your room, or move into the stable with Arthur. I admit I am generally away."

Wren simply stared, realised her mouth hung open, and snapped it shut. She stuttered, "No rent at all?"

He shook his head. "The key, your own for a month at least, should be found with the older stable boy, Prad, who lives in the straw over the stable next door. Go to him, get the key, and arrange your own comforts."

"Landry, I can't – I mean, I can, I'd love to. But you hardly know me. It's too kind. Much too kind. I'll get a job, so I can pay you."

"I have no need of money." His eyes glinted in spite of the shadow. "But no doubt helping at the stables will pass your time."

"I don't know anything about horses."

"Learn," he advised. "You'll find Arthur there. He returns there to Prad when I have little need of him."

It was unwise, and had she considered it first she would not have done it, but without thinking at all, she leaned over and kissed his cheek. "I won't refuse, it's a wonderful offer. No doubt I'll see you again soon."

"A day or two," he nodded. "No longer."

"Oi." The last word from Wyatt was unexpected. "If you sees any o'my gang left alive, you tell 'em, that I's gonna stay here this time. Tis as good a roof as any and fair grub when I threaten them guards. I ain't got a roof nowhere else."

Bryce called. "I shall fit you into my prayers, Wyatt."

"Don't you go telling no gods about me," Wyatt exploded. "I don't want none o' them knowing wot I done."

"You think He doesn't know who you are by now?"

"I bloody hopes not."

"And you talk of gods?" Bryce pretended to tremble. "How many do you reckon we have?"

"I thought as how there be three, ain't there?" Wyatt looked confused. "There be the father and that son, and then there be a ghost or sommit."

"Holy Mother Mary." Someone else shouted, shocked. "You say that again next time the priest comes, and I reckon he'll accuse you o' heresy. You know the punishment for that?"

Wyatt picked his nose.

"It would seem," Landry murmured, "that I may choose to leave here sooner than originally planned."

He lounged back against the damp stone, seemingly at home. Wren stood, avoiding Wyatt, "I'll find the Mews and the man Prad. I hope you come back soon. Are you sure I can keep the dogs? They're waiting for me outside."

"Keep whatever you wish," he murmured. "Dogs, horses, bears or camels. It may even make life more interesting."

CHAPTER TEN

NARRATIVE

Both sides of the lane were crammed with stable blocks, stalls facing each other and others single, set back, but larger. Every space appeared occupied. Wren was not accustomed to the smells of horses but did not find it as unpleasant as she had expected. Better, she grinned at herself, than the stink of Newgate, and even better than boiling eels.

Arthur watched her from the stall attached to the narrow climbing steps, tossed his head and whinnied. Wren scratched between his ears and smiled at the young man who had been brushing the stallion's rump, and now leaned against it, regarding the woman.

"Are you Prad? I'm Wren," she told him. "Landry said I could stay upstairs. He said you have a spare key."

"Yes, I got it," he admitted. "But how do I know he sent you?"

"Because obviously Arthur knows me, and I know this address," she said. "I know your name because Landry told me."

"Fair enough," said Prad and turned, taking a large hanging object from the back wall. He handed Wren the key. "Those scrawny hounds going in with you? The master says that's allowed? Do you know when the master's coming back, then?"

"He said a day or two." Wren removed the small dirty stubs of straw stuck to the key and carried it to the steps next door. She did not mention where Landry was nor that his arrival home would mean escaping from gaol. The steps were steep, dark and hardly welcoming, but she pushed the key in the door at their peak, turned it, and walked into Landry's property. It was as unexpected as every other aspect the man had ever shown.

She closed the door behind her, both dogs inching in at her side, but large windows remained unshuttered, and she could see clearly. Wren adored what she could see already.

An unexpectedly spacious room with unexpected comfort stared back at her. Shad and Red had shuffled in and were standing directly behind her, nervous but with tails so active, desperate to express their delight.

Two long wooden settles were heaped with pillows, a large fireplace was outlined with sturdy dark logs, but the huge logs holding the ceiling firm, had been painted with small scuttling animals of the woodland, deer of several kinds, beavers and badgers, little red squirrels, weasels and mice, rats and foxes, and every bird Wren was able to identify. There were even bats, fish and frogs, brightly coloured and dancing.

A table sat central, holding a variety of candles, two roughly bound books, a tinder box and a huge pot of oak resin with several quill pens. Around it stood stools of different sizes, both three and four legged, and also brightly painted. A large woven scarlet rug lay beneath.

The hearth held no wood for the fire, but there were three large trivets and a hook for a pan to hang over once the flames were lit. The pans themselves in various sizes, both copper and iron, were stacked beside. On either side of the chimney breast were shelves with platters, spoons, knives and a variety of cups, jugs and a roasting spit, ready set with its handle responding to the slightest appetite. Windows, their shutters somewhat broken, gazed both front and back, and the back window watched the grooming and exercising of the horses.

The window seemed to belong to a house even grander, for without an outer frame of heavy wood were a dozen metal framed panes of real glass, thick with central swirls making them harder to break than the shutters lifted against them.

Wren dared climb up the narrow wooden steps and found both bedchambers. The smaller, was the home of a bed of luxurious comfort, she had never slept in the like before.

A four poster with bedraggled red curtains gazed back at her, a table holding a candle next to one side, and even more, a tiny garderobe lined with pegs, a table with an empty washing bowl and jug. Her own garderobe was a luxury she had never experienced and thought a true marvel. An even greater luxury was the small inlet she had passed, wedged between both bedchambers, for this was a privy. Such a commodity existed only in castles, manor houses and palaces. "This is," she thought aloud, "a home as unexpected as its owner."

She did not dare peep again into Landry's larger bedchamber but could imagine nothing better than her own. She collapsed on the bed, discovering a deep feather mattress and a linen sheet topped by a feather quilt. Now beneath her head was a feather stuffed bolster and it cradled her.

Red and Shad, energised with food and hope, leapt on the bed beside Wren, all three fell asleep even though it was only dusk with the flash of the first rising stars. Almost November. As always, the sun fled by four of the afternoon's clock, but bliss, always brings sweet dreams.

It was a short sleep, however, all three feeling the discomfort of hunger. Reluctantly Wren rolled from the mattress and staggered, thoroughly creased, back downstairs. Then, making sure the dogs remained shut inside, she clutched the key and hurried to Black Spoon Row where the eel house still flickered its candle and clearly remained open.

Pansy was serving but appeared exhausted. She looked up with a tired smile then saw Wren and beckoned her quickly inside.

"That sheriff was here looking for you two days back," she said under her breath. "He's still trying to sort out that nightmare with Jessy's family. He wasn't pleased to find you'd gone but I said wicked murder sends us all running. Besides, it happened weeks past."

"Yes. One of the reasons I left," Wren said, half sigh. "It was so ghoulish. There was that horrid gang gathering around here too. I'd wager it was Wyatt who did all of it. But anyway, and thank the good Lord, now he's back at Newgate."

But Pansy had no idea who Wyatt might be. "I reckon you should visit the sheriff tomorrow. Do you want your job back? I've not found anyone else to help."

"Sorry, I don't think so. For now, I just want food. I've still got a few pennies left from my last pay."

Pansy scowled which quickly changed to a smile. "I get so tired, sometimes I shut early. Today was busy, but folks asked for pies, and I can't cook pies like you did. I need your skills back, my dear. And your bed's still waiting upstairs."

It was pleasant to feel appreciated, but Wren easily recognised the meaning in her words of bribery. Having often discovered Landry's odd behaviour suspicious without being able to trace the cheat behind the actions, at least Wren found Pansy's frauds transparent. She shook her head. "Sorry, I've got a new home. You'll find someone soon, there's plenty out there desperate for paid work. Giving a bed too, that's a big bonus. But all I need is food. And I can pay. Well, not much but enough if you've got a dumpling or two. And perhaps some leftovers for the dogs if you have any, maybe from yesterday?"

She passed over the small jingle of coins. Having hoped Pansy might be generous, she was instead disappointed when the woman grabbed every penny. "What's left of what I paid you? Well, here's everything I have left of the food. And all the rubbish for those skinny dogs of yours."

"The dogs aren't mine." Wren sniffed as she saw her very last ha'penny disappear into Pansy's apron pocket.

Wren marched back to her new home cheerfully though, with a large sack of food between her arms. Oil, slime and pale blood seeped into the hessian and leaked down the front of her already ruined skirts and onto her even more ruined boots, but once she unlocked Landry's door, the dogs leaped, smelling whatever seemed edible.

There were two somewhat congealed eel dumplings for herself, and a variety of mush beneath. Red and Shad buried their noses and Wren hurried back into the shelter but had no logs nor even twigs for a small fire. Instead, she cuddled on one of the settles and stuffed lumps of eel dumpling down her throat. Hating eels did not stop her eating them when hunger rose.

She knew she must visit the sheriff early the next morning. That did not trouble her, but she did not want to remember all she had seen when visiting Jessy's home that day, had desperately tried to block the memory in fact. Landry's appearance and his offer to stay in his more than glorious home had swept her into far happier thoughts. But now thinking of the sheriff, Jessy's death surged back into her mind.

Once again opening the door, Wren checked that all scraps and grease had been licked away from the landing, and called the dogs back into the warmth. It was still not late, but she staggered upstairs to her new bedroom and accepted the comfort of the two large furry bodies against her as she curled onto the soft billow of feathered down. Both dogs snored a little, which was strangely reassuring. Wren closed her eyes and breathed deep.

But sleeping brought dreams.

The dream was blurred, yet she recognised the front of Jessy's family home and walked unwillingly to the door, pushing it open.

Four long shadows swayed towards her, doom ridden and threatening. The shadows became the bodies she remembered in brutal detail. Hanging from the ceiling beams, first were the two small children, so pitiful, bare footed, clothed in rags, fingers hanging loose, eyes closed over the repeated loops of dirty string pulled so tight it dug into the flesh, and thin lines of bloody strangulation like necklaces of evil had wrenched them into death.

Their father hung behind them, boots almost reaching the ground, the vomit still smelling rank down his shirt, the last drip frozen to his lips. There was heavy rope fastening him to the ceiling beam, cutting into skin, flesh and bone. His head hung, lolling as though ready to fall.

Jessy swung like a fragile bundle of twigs, the noose around her neck blood stained. Her tongue hung from her open mouth, and her eyes were open and glazed as if covered in whitewash, one hand loose fingered, the other gripping a tiny knife, also bloodstained, and blood smeared the flesh around her nostrils.

When first seen, there had been no wind and the room was entirely enclosed. Yet now as Wren dreamt, the bodies began to swing, sighing, their eyes popping and their dead pale faces glaring. They hurtled towards her, spraying blood and whispering of devils and monsters. Immediately Wren awoke crying. The bolster beneath her face was cold and wet. She turned over and tried to blind herself to the nightmare. The dogs seemed undisturbed. She wished she could remain the same, closed her eyes and forced her thoughts into sweet warm gardens, and into the embrace of a man on a horse. It was the image of Landry's lips brushing against her own that helped her sleep.

The following morning, she dragged herself to the sheriff's office. Her only clothes were now ruined, and she thought the sheriff might think her a beggar, but knocked on the door, telling the dogs to wait outside.

"Mistress Wren isn't it. You're the female that took me to that house of horrors with the family hanging?" he asked her. "Of course, I remember you looking a good deal different, when you worked the eel shop. Looks as if you've been in more trouble."

"I've had a few unfortunate days since then," she shook her head, "and don't have anything to change into. But nothing's as bad as finding Jessy like that."

"They've been buried in consecrated ground with a priest doing his business," the sheriff nodded. "All done right and proper, though we found no relatives. And I've found no suspects. I wanted to ask you some questions."

"I'd love to help," Wren said, "but I really don't know anything."

"I was told you knew about that gang up from Newgate. It has to be them. Those brutes to hold the others while each one was killed. It would have taken a pack. But I know none of the names, though three of them were found dead later, floating in the river. Bodies got stuck under the Bridge." He shook his head, sighing. "Those louts fight amongst themselves, and the dead always end under water. Nibbled by fish. A nasty business. The church buried the dead gang members too, and got no payment, so the priest wasn't happy. But Father Luke always has a moan whether paid or not. According to him it's either nothing or too little. No one went to that funeral except me, so I donated, but I wasn't going to pay for three scum pigs when I didn't even know their names. So, tell me what you know."

She was sitting, the stool facing the sheriff's paper strewn scrivener, trying to look honest. No one trusted sheriffs not to grab the first opportunity, and arrest anyone so to boost his own reputation.

"I met the gang. They came pushing into the shop where I worked, wanting to steal what they could. I knew one of the ruffians. Wyatt Mason, but he's back in Newgate now. And I don't work at the eel shop anymore. I don't know if the rest of the mob are still around."

"They certainly keep out of my sight," the sheriff grumbled. "I've not seen or heard a hint of any gang trouble lately. But I reckon your friend Wyatt must be the killer."

Wren glared. "He's not my friend. I met him, but I hate him."

"No matter," the sheriff stared down at his quill. "I can't arrest the bugger if he's back in Newgate anyway."

"Can you prove he did it?"

The sheriff looked back up, staring at her. "Of course not. How do I prove a damned thing? You think the killers will leave a note confessing? What I need is a motive."

Wren had no idea of motive and accused Wyatt only because she knew of nobody else. "Jessy never said anything about enemies. They were poor, but the husband worked in the lime pits."

"Then I'll ask there."

"And the oldest son worked at the bakers. Sullivans up the road. That's all I know."

"And what of the female, Jessy?" the sheriff asked. "She knew you. Who else?"

"Yes me, and Pansy who owns the eel shop, and I think even my father who stayed with me and helped in the shop for a few days. And her neighbours on both sides, though one side is the Duff family and I doubt those were friends. Milly Sullivan of course, who owns the Bakery. And Jessy would have known the local priest. She was quite religious. But Black Spoon isn't a friendly street, there's the old couple at the end who spits at everyone out of the window. But Jessy was so kind and sweet, and I think all that family were good people. That's all I know."

"I reckon I can rule out the priest," sighed the sheriff. "No one loves the Duffs nor Lea and Oddy Fratten down the other end. But there's no one you're telling me who sounds guilty, except this Wyatt mob."

"Which is why I thought he did it too. But that's not proof, is it?"

"And no footprints on the floor, nor good stuff as could have been stolen. The family being as poor as the robbers. Who has enemies when they're like sheep just up from the gutters?" The sheriff was talking to himself but looked up abruptly. "It's definite then and I'll need just a wink of proof, no more. So where did that Wyatt fellow live?"

"I think he did really sleep in the gutter. Now he sleeps in Newgate and wants to stay there for winter, a shelter in a cell is better than none at all I suppose." Wren was becoming uncomfortable and could hear the dogs whimpering outside.

"It's raining," nodded the sheriff. "Even that unravelling cape won't keep you dry. Best wait here till it stops."

"It'll probably rain all day," Wren said into her ragged lap. "I'd sooner hurry home. It's not too far." In her mind she could hear the sweet call of the house she was now claiming as home, and might even manage to light a small fire, perhaps even cook some supper. No fire ever blazed in the sheriff's office.

"Give me your address then, mistress, lest I want to ask something more." She explained where she now lived, and the sheriff stared, suspicious while trying to remember. "You share with the horses? I think a strange fellow lived there once, and there was another who spent a good deal of time at Newgate. But that whole Mews is owned by the gentry."

"Very possibly," Wren stood and turned to leave, "but I live there now." She offered no further explanations and marched out into the rain, the dogs scurrying behind. The walk was only minutes, and the rain washed her boots. Once back between the stables, she waved at Prad. He was dry and smiling. She and both dogs were dripping but not yet soaked.

"Leave them hounds here," Prad waved. "Plenty o' dry straw for rolling, and I might have a little food."

Wren thanked him and wished she might share the food as well but didn't ask, the dogs thanked him with their tails, and Arthur snorted cheerfully. Alone now, she ran up the first wooden steps. Then unlocking the door to the house, Wren threw her wet cloak to the boards, kicked off the boots complete with the remains of sodden mud and ran directly up the second staircase to the bedchamber she already loved.

There she collapsed on the welcoming blankets. Outside, although the small window was shut tight, she could hear birdsong and their cheerful twitter, their feathers dust free while bathing, sparrows delighted with the rain. She knew her hair was soaked and tried to keep her head from soaking the pillow. A damp dusk drifted beyond the window but it could not be late and Wren knew it. She'd slept through the night but now she simply wanted to sleep in the warmth again.

This time, however, she hoped not to dream.

Then a voice spoke very softly over her and a cup of hot spiced wine was pressed into her open palm. Steam rose in a tiny circle and the heat of wine and cup was warmer than gloves around her fingers.

"Now drink your wine and tell me whether you like your new home."

CHAPTER ELEVEN

WREN

This man was one continuous surprise. Could he ever be predictable?

"It only seems like minutes past when you were in Newgate, you're quicker – much quicker than I expected."

"Expectations," said that soft drifting voice, "interrupt reality. So naturally reality interrupts expectations."

This was a man who had told me there was no reality. "But," I said, refusing to fall into confusion, "how on earth do you escape that vile place so quickly and easily?"

"Too easy would be far too dull," he said, "but quickly is certainly an advantage."

I nearly begged him to start talking sense, but I kept my mouth politely shut. I knew he did it on purpose. Perhaps he just liked to be difficult, but now I had an idea his main reason was to avoid real explanations. He wanted – perhaps needed – his life to stay in the shadows. As a brat of a child, being polite, with my father as my closest example, had never been known. But working for my betters and then serving customers in the shop, manners became my protective overcoat. Now it was genuine gratitude that kept me polite, with Landry.

So, I changed the subject. "I adore your house," I said with what I hoped was obvious enthusiasm. "I never expected anything this comfy and grand. This bedroom is such luxury. The dogs love it too." I was still clutching the cup of spiced wine, but already I'd gulped half of it, loving its unusual taste, the steam in my mouth and its warmth down my throat.

I was still fully dressed even though I'd hoped to sleep, so I staggered up as he strode back down the stairs, expecting me to follow. I wanted to ask him how he'd escaped gaol yet again but knew he wouldn't tell me. Instead, I sank into the cushioned settle, sipping the wine before it cooled too much.

"Warmth is the one necessity missing," he said, still standing over me. Then he opened the door again and called Prad. "We are in desperate need of fire and food, my friend," he called down, and I heard Prad answering, then his footsteps galloping fast as the horses. "It won't take long," Landry assured me.

And it really wasn't long. Prad came back with piles of twigs, logs and bags of food. I sat and watched and didn't say anything while Landry knelt and built up the wood on the hearth, finally setting light to a huge blazing golden fire. Not warmth but real heat, and so welcome. Then he cooked. I most certainly hadn't expected that.

He settled the trivet high and placed both slabs of meat with a little lard on the flat pan now balanced on top. He chopped onions on the tiled hearth, scattered them onto the meat, then turned and turned all the contents, using a large wooden spoon. Everything sizzled.

Without a word, Landry passed me a metal cask of wine from behind him, his arm silently outstretched. I took it and poured some into my empty cup, the rest into his own cup on the table beside me. This wine was not spiced nor heated, but a great Burgundy, though it was the food that lured me the most. The smells of fried onions and steak made my hunger double. No – quadruple.

I had already heard the dogs calling me from outside the door, little squeaks and yaps, and was once again surprised when Landry marched to the door and threw each of them a very large bone covered in gristle. Their immediate silence told me exactly how happy they were.

Our meal, a slightly late dinner, soon appeared on platters on the table and I rushed to the stool opposite my new landlord. I thanked him so much, he actually frowned. He certainly didn't owe me such extravagance.

It was more than delicious; it was lifesaving.

I was stuffing the food into my mouth like a starving brat from the gutter, which is actually how I'd been feeling a couple of days ago and was ready to start expressing a flood of thanks all over again, when he looked up, rested his knife on the platter and gazed at me with his usual lack of expression.

Landry's voice was deep and soft as always, but his eyes were cold. "I shall be here rarely. Consider yourself free to live at these premises as you wish. When I return, I shall be interested to hear of developments involving that family you knew and their horrific murder." He paused, watching me, then continued. "Prad will supply food when you ask, bring wood and any other necessities. I have ordered him to look after you in my absence."

Good news and bad news all together. I was mumbling on the last scrape of onion when I managed to say, "It's so wonderfully kind and thank you so very much. But I have no money left to pay Prad. I'll find a job soon. Perhaps the eel shop again."

"Prad has all the money he needs," came that amazing voice again. "He'll supply whatever you wish."

I stared, mouth open, then snapped it shut. Was I supposed to be his mistress? I didn't want to accept actual coin without giving anything in return, but I had no intention of sharing beds. He'd made a point that no service was required, and he'd be away most of the time. "At least let me look after this beautiful house."

"That will be appreciated." The tucks at the corners of his cheeks flickered into half a smile.

"It was Wyatt and his gang," I floundered on, breathless, "who murdered my friend and her family. Now even Sheriff Wilson thinks it was Wyatt. It had to be. But he's back in Newgate anyway."

"It was not Wyatt," Landry said, pushing back his platter and standing, still looking down at me.

"How can you know that?" I was genuinely interested. I'd thought about it so often, and Wyatt had seemed the only possibility.

"I spoke with him while we shared the dungeons," he said in the usual silky soft murmur. Even discussing murder didn't seem to change his voice. Then he piled our empty platters and spoons and tipped them into a large bucket of water at the other end of the room. He spoke on, but no longer bothered to look at me. "Wyatt has no capacity for planning such a strange business, would be incapable of it on several different points, had a small crowd of idiotic imbeciles who followed him for a day or two, no more, since he brought them no benefit, and they would not have helped with such a venture. This killing was carefully planned by more than one person and carefully undertaken with intentional cruelty. It appeared well practised and yet no similar murder has been reported, even at a distance. Finally, the motive is unknown but must certainly have been the cause. Wyatt had neither motive nor capability." Having also rinsed his hands in the water bucket, he shook off the drips and walked back to me. "While in Newgate I also inquired about two other men I have never met but have heard of offering to kill for payment. I received no answer."

Interest switched to fascination. "You really are trying to help, aren't you! But you didn't even knew Jessy or her family."

"Some situations need understanding. Perhaps I could admit they attract me."

I was shocked. "Killing attracts you?"

With a twitch of smile, he told me, "Not death and certainly not killing. But the mind of a man without sympathy or love, who is prepared to kill."

With a probable glare, I said, "I hope you don't mean yourself?"

The little itchy grin travelled to his eyes. The first time I'd ever seen his eyes change from ice cold to flickering warmth. "Luckily not myself, or I should know the answer and have no interest in solving it further."

"You said something about some fat men." Now I was not just interested, I was completely absorbed.

"Brothers of peculiar appearance," he actually yawned. "But I have no knowledge of their names nor home. My reason for travelling south carried its own motive, and my return was equally motivated. Unfortunately, I had no questions answered within Newgate's walls. I assume you know no one of such description?"

By now Landry was halfway up the stairs and I just watched him disappear as I called back. He knew it already. "No idea. I've never seen anyone like that."

He'd certainly thought about this. Previously when I'd mentioned it, I'd thought him barely listening. Now I realised that he'd been very interested indeed. I stood to open the door for the dogs who came leaping indoors to jump up and lick me. Uch, now I would need to wash again.

I set out cleaning the platters, spoons and knives, placed everything to dry by the fire, and then flopped back onto the settle, trying to think. My clothes were ruined, and I no longer had the serving gown and starched apron which Pansy had first given me and then taken back. Looking like a gutter whelp felt embarrassing, I'd need to trudge off to the wash house. But again and again, it was Jessy's death that coloured every thought.

If it hadn't been Wyatt, then I just didn't know a single other possibility. It wasn't as though I'd ever known Jessy or her family that closely. And it just seemed weird that Landry clearly had thought a good deal about it, even though he didn't know the family at all.

The knock on the door broke into my shallow swirling thoughts and I assumed it was Prad, but the visitor pushed the door open himself and strode in, looking around. Startled of course, I blubbered something about Landry being upstairs.

"I'll wait for him," muttered the visitor.

Then I looked at him again, and when he pulled his hood off, I saw his ecclesiastical haircut, shaved and bald in the middle. So, life had no intention of stopping the surprises.

"You're Father Jacob," I said in amazement. Then I apologised in a panic. "You came to Newgate. I mean, sorry, I'm just a little confused."

No one seemed interested in my confusion. I'd assumed Landry had gone to bed, but now he appeared back from the shadows above the steps and walked over to the priest now sitting comfortably on the other settle.

"You're here, Jacob," he said. He was now wearing full riding gear beneath a fur lined hooded cape. "Good. Then we had better go."

The priest rose again, although was not wearing ecclesiastical robes, then said, "Prad has my horse. No doubt it'll rain."

"Of no consequence," Landry shook his head, and both men marched to the door. Landry turned briefly to me. "I may be back tonight. I may not. It might be several days. Stay comfortable." And the door slammed shut behind him. Even the dogs looked startled.

"I'm living in Bedlam," I told myself. "But I couldn't care less since it was also paradise."

I just sat staring at the closed door for some time, while trying to make sense of Landry, the odd priest, me, and everything else. It didn't help. Shad had landed on my lap, while Red cheerfully sat on my feet. Having kicked off my ruined boots already, my stockinged feet were now tingling with the dog's heartbeat and very warm fur.

So other than the dogs, I was alone again. I needed a job of some kind, but now with no worry of starvation, it would simply be a help. I had the house of a king – perhaps not quite – but in comparison to my entire life so far – I would eat at least once a day and it wouldn't be eels. I had the company of two loving dogs, I paid no rent except to clean up after myself, I could even pay the wash house and have baths and be clean too, and I might stay sheltered indoors on a cushioned settle in front of a blazing fire. It had happened without warning and without any sense needed.

I'd turned into a withering child after that gruesome sight of

Jessy and then spending the night with her. Now I decided I'd never, ever, feel that way again. I felt like a queen and might even sometimes have a horse to ride. And not lonely since I had two dogs who I could sort of have conversations with, and a sort-of friend in the shop down the road.

Then I quickly realised that I had one problem still. Boredom. It would help if Landry came home more often, though he'd probably ignore me when he did.

I was fairly sure I had a brain. I'd have to start using it.

CHAPTER TWELVE

NARRATIVE

"Yes, I saw them," said Haldon. "Talked with the fellow once. Can't remember the silly sod's name, but he wasn't too bad. We chatted. I liked them for the few moments I met them."

"You didn't seem much concerned when I told you about the murder," Wren mumbled.

"Cos they weren't of interest," her father insisted. "I can't even remember their names."

"Jessy and Randle and their sons Martin and little Peter," Wren said, feeling that they should be remembered.

Without wishing to become a regular visitor, Wren saw her father twice when sufficiently bored to wander far enough. Reluctant, Wren called it duty yet never felt more enthusiasm from Haldon than she felt herself. She wandered the markets, walked up the Fleet and encouraged the dogs to run, even ran across the grass herself sometimes, skirts lifted to save the last ragged twists of hem, worked one day a week at the eel shop principally to make pies as Pansy had asked her so many times, and also sometimes helped Prad with the horses.

Having earned a few coins at the shop and collecting the penny tips given by the owners of the horses, Wren saved with avid determination until she had enough money for some new shoes and a new gown with double sleeves and a higher neckline than most. This, however, was kept for best and she continued to wear the rags most days.

Haldon said, "You look a right mess, girl. This Landry fellow be so generous, then get new clothes."

"Have you got any money spare?"

"Don't be daft, girl."

"Well nor have I," she said. "I eat well. I keep warm. I love my life – or most of it anyway. But I don't have money."

"So, think yourself lucky."

"I do," said Wren. "Very lucky."

It had been a disappointment when Landry still hadn't returned. He had said a day or a few, yet it was considerably more. In some ways this was an advantage. She could eat what she chose, as little or as much. She could sleep when she chose, and undress entirely so her rag-taggle clothes remained a little less creased. Her attempts to help Prad and her conversations with him helped relieve the solitude, and her safety now seemed pleasantly secure. Yet Landry's strange pale grey eyes often sneaked into her dreams, the hot strength of his arms around her as she sat astride on Arthur, skirts almost up to her knees, and the thrill of knowing that Landry's gaze sat firmly on her legs until he sat behind her and adjusted the stirrups.

Without Landry, the house was hers. Her home. The deep warm sense of being in her own home was blissfully attractive. And, she supposed, with Landry so long away, he was making good money. Stealing was a vulgar business, but she managed to ignore her disapproval while curling on the cushioned settle watching as Prad built up the fire.

The stables were busy, and the horses talked far more often and far more loudly than she had previously supposed.

Dally, a small black mare, neighed repeatedly every morning until fed, and snorted violently once she was hungry again. A larger mare, Winnie, was a variety of colours quite oddly mixed, with a copper tail, a black mane, huge brown eyes, and a coat patterned in black, white, light brown, dark brown, and a few beige spots. She snuffled a good deal and stamped if ignored.

Wren admired the tall stallion, Remy, elegant and gleaming, who kicked up a frenzy when he wanted exercise, whatever the weather. He seemed rather fond of a light rain but complained regarding the wind.

She was combing Remy's high soft back one bitter morning, when she was interrupted. The horsed squealed in delight, and kicked up his front hooves, which knocked Wren backwards. She banged her head on the stable door. A tall arrival faced her as she scrambled up, yet at first seemed far more interested in the horse, removed his gloves and caressed Remy with obvious affection. Then he turned to Wren.

His voice was autocratic, his accent imperious, but his smile was pleasant beneath round blue eyes.

"What a pleasant surprise," he said, regarding her. "We meet again. A delightful change from the usual groom."

Prad was grinning over the top of the stable door, and nodded, half bowing. "My lord. Tis a great to have the new lass help. Wren, her name is."

The tall man snickered. "Then I shall take unfair advantage and address you as Wren. I, am Morgan, Earl of Thamesdon. I assumed I introduced myself before, but no matter. And don't bother trying to curtsey, I don't require such nonsense and you would surely fall over the hay bucket." His laugh was warm and just as delicious. "Perhaps you remember me."

It seemed rude to chuckle but on the other hand it seemed rude not to. "That's kind, my lord, I'm proud to remember having met you before at the sheriff's office. You have the most beautiful horse."

"I do, mistress, certainly I do," and his lordship returned to caressing his stallion's ears. "And now I need my beautiful Remy, so have him saddled, if you will, as quickly as possible."

Prad, knowing perfectly well that Wren had not the slightest idea how to saddle a horse, let alone to the Lord Thamesdon's preferences, and pushed in. "This will be done within a moment or two," he said, "if your lordship will wait."

The earl stepped out onto the cobbles, Wren extricated herself entirely and drifted towards the next stable. Once she saw the earl ride off, she asked Prad, "So he's the one who owns the Mews. Does Landry have to pay a high price to stay here?"

"Not exactly," Prad grinned. "He's a bloody nice gentleman, he is, never acts the *'kiss me feet'* stuff. Comes, pays, goes, and sure is the only lord I'll ever get to call friend."

"Does he always wear such grand clothes? All that fur and velvet." But this was not the question in her head.

Prad nodded. "He's an earl, so I suppose he has to dress pretty. Besides, tis cold today." He nodded at her. "I'd wager a new born donkey you're half frozen."

Wren agreed, shivered, and asked the question repeating itself in her mind. "Does he know he's renting one of his smart stables and the lovely house above it, to a thief who spends half his life in gaol?"

Prad frowned, then changed his mind and smiled. "Reckon he does. Landry and him are good friends."

Now it was Wren frowning. She couldn't see how a thief and an earl could be even acquaintances, let alone friends. Yet she also admitted, although only to herself, that she was delighted to call Landry her friend too.

She missed his company, but time passed, and he still did not reappear. It had been getting colder day by day and it was now creeping into November, Wren needed more wool, hemp and fur but could not afford the latter. Woollen gloves were her best hope. She had visited the nearest glover on three occasions, had offered her small hand for measurement, but had only paid a deposit. A muff would be easier made and so cheaper, but no one could work with both hands stuffed into a muff.

More consistent were Wren's unwanted thoughts of Landry, and what he was doing with a priest and even an earl. The church enjoyed donations and payment for many things – demanded it in fact, but few priests changed into normal old clothes and marched the countryside on horseback, stealing from both rich and poor. Wren's curiosity crept back immediately she stopped thinking deeply of anything else. And so, she was annoyed with herself all over again.

The sky turned to a permanent dark grey, the sun had left for some warmer country, and when it rained the rain turned to ice on the cobbles so that folk slipped and slid, and children seemed to be laughing constantly. The dogs had evidently decided they needed no exercise and lived either lying on the small red rug by the fire, or on the warm straw as Prad fed and tickled them. Other dogs howled, but Wren shut her ears. Adopting more than two would be impossible. Instead, she watched the children kick the round stones they found, chase each other, hop and laugh, and play with the occasional wandering goat or pig. Rappo the pig was certainly still around, always eager to play as long as there was an edible reward.

Finally, Landry returned as November danced into its first week. "I have," said the voice drifting in from the doorway while Wren had been dozing, the dogs snoring in front of the fire, "returned. Sleep, little bird, but do not be startled when you finally wake to the perfumes of braised kidneys. Wake and eat your share or stay sleeping and dream of greater feasts."

She sat so suddenly, she felt quite dizzy. Although certainly not starving, the attraction of food and Landry's return was quite enough to banish the boredom which had led to sleep.

Wren said, "It's nice to see you again. It's been – what? Weeks? Or more?"

"I cannot count anything except coin," Landry murmured absently, "so do not know. More than one day and less than one year."

She watched him throw his cape to the rounded end of the banister, kick off the wet boots, and sling the large hessian bag he had carried to the table beside the fire. Both dogs were sniffing and watching with huge hopeful eyes. Although now constantly well fed, more food was still their dream. Landry pushed his fingers into the bag, grasped a couple of large kidneys and threw one to each of the hounds. They leapt, excited, and Wren smiled. She continued to watch as Landry poured wine, pushed one cup towards her, and started cooking the remaining contents of the bag,

Shadow and Red had eaten their treats in two bites, and now sat, tails wagging. Landry ignored them and continued cooking.

It was when she sat at the table opposite him, her platter now full and her cup now empty, that Wren said, "This is such kindness. I've never met anyone like you before."

His brows were lowered as he ate. He did not look up, but the glint of shining grey appeared beneath the brows. "That is perhaps just as well."

Now eating quickly, the food as appetising as it's perfume, Wren had a mouth full when she asked, "Where's the priest?"

Having emptied his platter, now Landry had returned to the fire, adding a large log and balancing it across the smouldering twigs. The flames jumped. Again, Landry did not bother to turn back, only his gaze shifted sideways, the eyes reflecting the light of the fire.

"Jacob left some days back. Why? Did you wish to ask for a blessing?"

"Not really." She raised an eyebrow. "But I'd love some more wine. If I may? I just thought it odd that the priest wore ordinary clothes and seemed to be your friend."

"Help yourself to the wine," Landry still bent beside the fire and did not look around. "Jacob has long been a friend. Should a priest not befriend a thief?"

"No. Yes. Maybe for confessions. But I don't believe in blessings."

"Nor do I believe in confessions." Landry stood. He had not refilled his own cup. He sat once more on the stool, pushed away both platter and cup, and rested his elbows on the tabletop. He spoke softly, "I wish to ask you some questions. You don't need to answer any of them, but I'd prefer it if you did."

"Of course I'll answer," she sat up straight, cup in hand, "as long as I know what the answer is."

"Then tell me about your father," he said softly, "and then as much as you know of your murdered friend Jessy."

"You sound like the sheriff." Wren stared, surprised. "It's hard to judge my own father, especially when I've never had a mother. We were never close. But I can tell you unimportant things about poor Jessy."

"Simply tell me what you can," Landry now looked directly into her own eyes. "I am neither sheriff nor priest, but some matters interest me. And also, if you feel obliging, tell me what you know of your mother."

CHAPTER THIRTEEN

WREN

I'm not sure which feeling was uppermost. I felt surprised and completely puzzled. I was also slightly annoyed.

But I was living in his house, warmed by his fires, and eating his food. Even drinking his wine. So, I stopped myself telling him to mind his own business, or ask why the devil he wanted to know such intimate things. I decided that murder interested him for different reasons, and he'd possibly done his own share of killing over the years. He didn't seem brutal, but I always found it hard to judge. Of course, what he'd asked wasn't his business, but why he asked these things wasn't my business. So, I gulped some more wine and nodded.

I told him. "My father never told me anything helpful about my mother. I used to keep asking and he just slapped me or sent me to bed. He said she died in childbirth – but then he said it was a couple of years after my birth and she'd looked after me till I was 3 years, so I don't actually know anything except her name was Gilith. I look a bit like her evidently."

Landry sat somewhat sprawled on the other settle, not drinking, and looked tired. Sometimes he shut his eyes. They were closed now, but he blinked them open, which startled me, they were so bright and seemed more silver than grey. "Very well," he murmured. "Now tell me of your father, including his last arrest for the murder of his second wife."

I blanched. "It wasn't really murder and," I said somewhat louder, "he was found innocent. It was an accident."

"You were watching? I understand that you acted as witness during his trial?"

So, I said, "Yes, I did and no, I didn't. But I did because he didn't. Am I making sense? He's not a really bad man I suppose. He isn't the father I'd want or anything. I've never liked him much at all. He hit me a lot and shouted when I was younger. Twice he made me eat charcoal, but that was when he was drunk. But the worst was when I was about seven and eight, he tried to touch me and to make me touch him. After getting away, I hit him and ran. Everyone I've talked to, not so much the boys, but they say the same stuff. Especially the whippings and beatings – that's just what fathers do. But he stopped after that. Sometimes I didn't eat for days but it wasn't all Dad's fault. We were poor. He didn't always find work. But then he worked on the carracks, and you know he's working now."

For a moment I wondered if I was boring him, he'd fallen asleep. But when he opened his eyes, he sat forwards, eyes quite silver again. "Now tell me what you saw when you discovered your friend killed."

"Jessy was sweet," I said quickly, I'd rather not think of it again. "I liked her so much. She had a sense of humour, even when she was sad and hungry, and she loved making me laugh. I tried to do the same back, but I got funny ideas muddled up, which in the end just made her laugh at me anyway."

"And her age? Even a guess?"

"I can't remember asking but it might have come up while chatting, since I know she was thirty-one. Her husband was nice as well, but he worked long hours in the pits, so I only met him a few times. The oldest boy was only nine and worked all day at the bakers. The small boy was just four so didn't work, and of course they were always starving. I used to give her free meals when I could."

"She had enemies?"

"No. Well, actually I haven't the faintest idea. But she couldn't have enemies, that wouldn't make any sense. She didn't like the Duff family next door, but then nobody does,"

"But you knew her. You walked in and found her dead."

"It was so horrible." And I began to describe all over again the scene I just wanted to forget. It was one of the main reasons why I left Pansy and the eel shop. And yet of course, here I was living fairly close, and working Saturdays back in the shop.

Then Landry wanted to know what sort of string was used – the children hung on string and the others on rope – must I talk about this? I kept on answering his questions, getting more and more reluctant, but I did as asked. Of course, that whole scene floated back in detail, I could even remember how the rope was knotted and all sorts of nasty points which I hadn't ever wanted to remember again.

"What was the time when you saw them?"

"Late. Dark." But I never really knew what the time was. On summer days it's easier to nip out and look at the sun but I know the sun had set. "Maybe around twilight."

"Did you touch? Were they warm?"

Now I shivered. "Cold and stiff. But the room was freezing anyway. It was an icy day, and they didn't have any fire on the slab."

It went on and on, and I was relieved when Landry, abrupt as always, said, "You have a good memory, little bird. And you have been a great help. I daresay you are wondering why I wished to know so much concerning matters gone, but now I intend going to bed. Leave the fire, it's low enough to stay as warm ashes. So, thank you, and good night."

He stood immediately and climbed the stairs without looking back. I poured myself another cup of wine and finished the jug. I'd never afforded wine in the past but now it was free, and I had learned to like it very much indeed. It also helped me into oblivion.

Once I clambered up those creaking steps, I cheerfully trotted into my bedroom, but first, without conscience or shame, listened outside Landry's door. Silence. No sound. For one moment I thought I heard the rustling of papers, but that stopped instantly.

Is voice carried through the door. "Unless you are summoning courage in the hope that I invite you into my bed, I cannot see what else you expect to hear." Shit, he'd heard me. Did I breathe so loudly? I was trying to think of something to say, making the decision whether to be polite or outright rude, when he added, "And since I am both tired and busy, I have no desire tonight. I therefore wish you a deep sleep without sinister dreams."

I was furious, how dare he think I would do that, I wanted to kick the door. I didn't of course. The damned man must have fantastic hearing. Instead, I shuffled off to my own bed and pondered the ups and downs of being the guest of someone you wanted to shout at. Had it been anyone else I most certainly would have shouted. But this wretched creature was my very generous landlord, and I was immensely grateful.

I did indeed have a beautiful sleep in that beautiful bed and did not experience, as far as I could remember anyway, any sinister dreams.

Waking to snow was exciting. I forgot my complaints concerning Landry and almost flew down the stairs. The fire had been built up, hot water sat beside the grate, simmering in a metal bucket, both dogs had raced down the stairs before me and were now sniffing at another saucepan, and I could smell something sweet. But Landry was not there. Ridiculous perhaps, but I felt that sudden jolt of disappointment.

He had been up earlier and left. Although he'd clearly built up the fire – boiled water – and left me a delicious swirl of porridge in the small pan, a crust of honey decorating the delight of breakfast.

Such kindness. I sat at the table, ate my porridge straight from the pan so I wouldn't have another platter to wash, and dropped a couple of small blobs of porridge for the dogs on a platter and left it on the floor. Once I'd finished, I looked out of the front door. There on the stone landing outside was a breakfast of meat and bone lying for both Red and Shadow. They leapt at it, so I shut the door on them. They could go running afterwards if they wanted to brave the snow.

Days without Landry flitted past again. I enjoyed cooking for myself and usually sent some down to Prad. I helped clean and clear downstairs, and of course cleaned upstairs. I played with the dogs, cleaned and brushed them. I was able to do the same with myself.

Yet the routine began to feel as dull as my past. Late one morning, sitting on one of the little stools, I just stared from the back window. The white softness of the snow was so gorgeous. As the wind strengthened, the flakes began to twist and increase, pelting against the outside of the window in a wild fury. Yet even the gale was snowed into silence and the hush swallowed back the wind's song. It must have snowed heavily in the night since the ground was thickly enclosed, and a frosted white carpet covered the already rimed cobbles, the gutters and whatever was in them, the trees and bushes nearby, the stable roofs and even the doorways, half open with snuffling horses staring out, one with a cold white tipped nose.

Remy was opposite, kicking at his door, and the snow fell from the edge. Yet now it fell so thickly, I could barely see the horses or the grooms.

Snow perhaps meant that it was getting deeper into November, and winters promised arrival.

I sat there without moving, elbows to the window ledge and chin in my hands. I had nothing else to do, and I wanted to stay and stare. But my wishes were spoiled as the icy carpet began to close in the window. Building like little piles of uneven white sparkle, and then painted even the glass.

And it was real glass. I had thought that a marvellous luxury when I first moved in, attached to this wonderful house in a back alley of stables. But I knew they called this the Thamesdon Mews, and of course a rich earl would want proper glass windows, even for those renting it would have been his treat.

Once having opened the door to see if the dogs had yet returned, I heard the loud footsteps, and peered down. Hoping it was Prad come to tell me something, but it wasn't. The dogs both rushed into the warm, wagging their tails so that white crystals flew in circles, and directly behind them with snow on his hat and shoulders, was Landry.

I couldn't remember where I was up to with him – anger or pleasure – so I smiled and sat back on the stool, though now facing the room instead of the window.

"I'm pleased to see you back again. Thank you so much for the porridge," I said, the smile carefully wide. "And food you left for the dogs. Prad has been supplying everything ever since and says it's on your orders. You are incredibly kind."

"Indeed, I am both kind and incredible," Landry murmured as he sank back on the settle, his feet up on one of the other stools, his ankles crossed. "But I have no intention of staying here for long. One day perhaps, or I may leave again this evening."

"I suppose you have to keep running, or they'll arrest you," I nodded. "Do the guards know about this house?"

"No." He almost smiled and then thought better of it. At least he didn't mention bedding. "The property does not belong to me."

Of course, he rented it. No surprise there. "And are you still interested in who murdered Jessy and her family?"

He looked up at me then, those eyes turning silver, almost like snow eyes. "I continue to be interested," he said in that usual deep softness. I began to smile at myself. "There appears no one else except yourself and the sheriff you called, who saw the initial scene. The bodies were then quickly removed. I know less than I might consider useful."

Now I was staring too. "Useful? Why?" I demanded.

And there was the smile, just the tiny tucks at the corners of his mouth. "There are reasons for my interest, and as yet there are no suspects which arouses my curiosity further." He replied.

"What about the one who tried to set fire to the eel shop while I was talking to you at the back door? Are you curious about him too?

You saw him briefly, you said. All sorts of crimes seem to attract you. Perhaps you should be a sheriff."

Now his smile widened. "I have not yet met a sheriff I admire," he said through that smile.

"Well," I smiled back, "they all want to arrest you. That probably spoils any admiration." I was using his own sort of sarcasm so now he was almost grinning.

"You appear to be a clever little bird," he said, his words almost as soft as the snow. "Can you use that intelligence to tell me more of the deaths you saw. Your friend's ceiling was higher than many, six foot to the ceiling plaster directly above the beams. The beams were thick, so brought the space lower. Can you remember how much space remained beneath the feet of all four bodies?"

He was weird and I was uncomfortable again. "So, you actually went there and measured the room after the sheriff finished? That's horrid."

"I accept your opinions," he said, no frown and no smile anymore. Just blank ice again. "I am evidently kind, incredible, and also horrid. Your answer will have relevance, since when hanging a body, the drop tells – just answer my question."

So, I just mumbled into my lap, not wanting to look at him. "All the rope nooses were very short and all about the same size. Randell's feet almost touched the floor, but the boys' feet hung up in the air. Now, please, I really don't want to talk about it anymore."

CHAPTER FOURTEEN

LANDRY

Although I thought her intelligent, I was pleased that she hadn't yet discovered the truth. That made life easier. I may often speak to the contrary, but when the dig is easy, I am pleased.

Lies are not a problem. They are necessities. What folk then think of me is not of interest to me, nor to Thamesdon.

The girl Wren had been useful and would continue to be so as far as it was possible to foresee. I intended to keep her at the house, and return there occasionally, watching and continuing to ask questions should any arise. I'd rarely used a girl but this one would stay until the final solution. I was beginning to like her yet liking could bring bias and was therefore a disadvantage. Bedding, as I had warned, would not be part of our friendship. Yet now that possibility crept towards me, and more than once

She was naturally one of the suspects as I was myself, however both of which could be ignored. Her father remained. Wyatt, however, was now cancelled. I was not so secure concerning Pansy, the woman who owned the eel shop. There was no written list, but one that sat in my mind as the creation of a tree. Certain names would constitute the trunk, sturdy and unbending. But there were branches, stronger and higher, others slim and near to the ground.

The roots had not yet been resolved. They would bear the names of those I considered more significant and any who appeared to be the power behind the assassin.

As yet Wren, Wyatt and myself hung, fingers slipping, to the lowest branches. Wren's father and Pansy sat higher, but not yet attached to the trunk. I needed more suspects. Adding myself was no serious consideration, but one I knew Jacob would offer if not already attached.

It was a slower and longer job than usual. Both irritating and welcome, since the difficulty made the situation more interesting. As did Wren.

The short trip south of the city brought disappointment since those unnamed twins, recognisable as vastly overweight and identical, did not work on the Kentish farm I had been told. It had then been simple to return, discover Wren as Prad had spied, and informed me, and arrange for the next Newgate visit. I therefore was able to arrange for Wren to become my lodger, but Newgate had brought no further clues.

I entertained Wren for some days. It amused me to play the Moorish guitar, the only instrument I now owned, which meant I also entertained myself. I doubt I'm yet beyond discovery. Nor do I consider disguise a necessity although I prefer to remain unknown.

Wren is perhaps twenty. She could be a year more – or less. That doesn't matter – but those additional years sometimes bring additional wisdom.

My suspicions regarding Pansy, the owner of the eel shop, were based on her denial of ever having met a member of the family now dead. She worked several hours each day in the shop and must have known all her regular customers, encouraging their custom. She also must have known that Wren gave free food to her friend Jessy, who lived only ten doors along from the shop. These are areas where folk know their neighbours, useful, even essential for many reasons. I doubt Pansy was fool enough to know nothing of this. She was middling in age although dressed as a young girl and had never been married. This did not add to my suspicions but nor did it weaken them.

Avoiding Wren, I had returned twice to the empty house of the erstwhile Ford family. Never having met any of them and having been able to witness the murder scene only as it was being dismantled, I was aware of missing clues. Returning the second time, I was greeted by an elderly woman who lived next door.

She was screaming at me, so I stopped to listen. "Wot you think you're doing? Ain't it enough they's all bloody dead??"

"I am here to discover," I said. I invented a smile. "I am Landry Crawford and I live close by. And you are?"

"None o' your bloody business," the woman told me. True enough. "But I's Doria Duff and I'll be calling for the sheriff if you don't bugger off."

Since this could mean that she was either protective or violent, I immediately took an interest, and told her that I respected her desire to protect the property of those killed so brutally. "I am – let us say – investigating," I continued. "You, Madam, would be my perfect guide. I have many questions. You would naturally be free to answer or not as you wish."

Whether to be rude or polite is a simple choice.

Naturally I had made the correct choice, as I usually do. She invited me into her home which was identical in size and shape to that of the murdered family next door. I wandered her home, asked some questions of importance and others of no importance whatsoever.

"I presume," I said as I finally left, "you have no key for the empty house?" I knew the answer, but I had continued with the irritating choice of being polite.

"Tis open, young man, now it's empty," Doria began. "No key needed."

Another woman suddenly burst into the room, shaking snow from her cape. Clearly younger than the wrinkled Doria, though this new female was equally small, plump and unattractive.

"Tis bloody snowing," she said, then raised her voice to a screech. "Who the bloody hell are you, then? Wot you doing ere?"

"I am your mother's visitor," I said, looking at her with considerable dislike. The relationship between them was now obvious.

"But I don't know you," the girl still shrieked. Turning to her mother with a whine that caused pain in my ear. "What's Dad gonna say?"

"No doubt he can speak for himself," I told her. "But it's unlikely that he'll see me, since I intend leaving."

"Scared you off, has I?"

She was so absurd that I laughed. This seemed to upset her further, and now her mother was also screeching. "Shut up, stupid brat," she told her daughter. "I can see who I wants to see, it ain't up to you."

"Mum, he could be the bugger what killed Jessy."

"So, says you, Lyanna, but I knows better."

"You never knows nuffing, Ma."

The nauseating conversation remained so high pitch, it was giving me a headache. I had no further use of the mother Doria and doubted I would ever have a use for the daughter. I therefore left their hovel and walked next door.

However, with a continuance of the day's irritation, as I left one house and entered the other, the girl Wren was passing, head low as she avoided the snow. Perhaps my delightful shoes attracted her since she looked up, forehead furrowed. "It's you! How can it be you?"

This sort of remark did not improve my level of concentration. "It is indeed myself."

"But the screaming I heard," she mumbled at me, "what was that about? You're going back into that wretched house. You didn't - ?" and she halted, staring.

Her eyes, such a bright blue, enlarged as she stared at me. I thought that she looked like a frightened kitten with those stunning black pupils in her enormous sky-blue eyes. Not that the sky was blue at the moment. It was white, and both Wren and I were soon gilded with snow.

Although I avoided any liking I already had for this girl, I answered with more of a smile than usual. "I am looking for something that has no name," I told her, and of course, she did not seem to have the slightest idea of what I meant.

"What –," trembling, "have you done to the people next door?"

"I should have murdered them," I told her, "but did not. Knock and ask them whether or not they are dead."

Her voice shrank to a whisper. "Please don't do anything dreadful. Though you don't seem cruel, are you?"

I sighed. Did the wretched girl suspect me as the local murderer? After a moment considering the options, I was quite sure that as a Luna-type killer, I would probably not politely admit it now. "I can promise you," I said, kicking open the door where I stood unsheltered and increasingly covered in snow, "that I have killed no one during the past two months." And I went into the house and let the door slam behind me. I heard Wren's footsteps retreating. She had no doubt stood gazing before finally trotting off to wherever she had originally intended going.

Amused, and wondering just how much she was learning to dislike me, I closed my eyes and chuckled, leaning against the wall beside the staircase, while realising that I was more attracted than I had thought. Indeed. She held a spark that she didn't show often, but when she did, my smothered desire to bed the girl increased dramatically. Yet not something I imagined would ever occur.

The days were crammed not with pleasure but with duty. Yet it is not usually the brain which first ignites attraction, and the same is true regarding Wren. However, after more time spent in her company, I discovered that my brain had involved itself. Now the girl I admitted to wanting, was wondering if I was the murderer. Since she could have no proof, my crimes were not about to see me hanging from the noose, just as those four had done in this very room. My own hanging was likely to be far more public.

This anchored another thought in the stormy tidal waves of my mind. It seemed that not one of those wretched corpses had kicked during such a slow death. I have witnessed the brutality of the scaffold and during the long misery of waiting to die, all criminals had fought, kicked and struggled for sometimes as much as an hour.

Yet even the two children had evidently hung placidly as though welcoming escape. I asked myself the question and immediately knew the answer.

Once again, I studied the beams. The scrapes of the rope indicated which beams had been used as supports. Even the youngest boy left behind a faint stripe of the string's threads. However, not one beam was cracked or bent, no splinter had been pulled open and there was no other violent sign of such a murder. Had the victims kicked and fought, especially the heavier body of the father, the beams would surely have shown the stress.

Nor were there indications of fights before when the killer arrived. Nothing was broken. I had entered this room moments after the removal of the bodies and would have seen any signs of destruction. It is true that this family owned very little, but the window remained peacefully covered in parchment, no platter was out of place, and no cup broken.

Over the following days I had visited Jacob and then Morgan, discussing the situation once again. Often tedious but necessary and had been entertained by a significant amount of wine on each visit. Since the journey south had served only to discover Wren, I travelled north, then to less intimate friends such as Swinda, a whore who avoided danger, and Trig, the wherryman whose memory was remarkable. Those days, sadly, had also brought me no useful information.

I returned home. The snow had stopped but it lay thick on the ground, on rooftops, and on trees. Footsteps, including those of birds and horses, were distinctly visible. Wren was already in the house, a little earlier than probable had she been at work.

Sitting on the settle closest to the fire, which I presume Prad had kept blazing, the girl was gazing at the flames dancing in the grate. She clearly heard my entrance since the dogs had jumped up to wag their rear ends at my arrival. She did not, however, greet me nor turn her head.

"Presumably you are still considering the possibility of my having eagerly and without other motive, slaughtered your friends. Do you seriously believe this?" I asked.

She turned her head and bit her lip, whatever that was supposed to mean. So I poured myself a cup of wine, and with the jug still in my hand, looked at her, waiting.

Finally, she mumbled a 'Yes, please' barely audible. I poured her a cup and handed it to her. I sat on the other settle, stretched myself comfortably, and drank my wine. Since I had been asking questions in the nearby tavern for more than two hours, I was already somewhat cup-shot, I closed my eyes and leaned back.

Wren spoke into my vague scatter of thoughts.

"Please, tell me it wasn't you."

"No," I replied. No doubt it was the wine which spoke rather than myself. "Make up your own mind. Decide according to my personality, or what little you know of it, and the accumulation of facts so far uncovered." I re-shut my eyes. I would have been perfectly content to doze and snore.

"Do you talk to Father Jacob for moral advice?"

"I have no morals and I rarely if ever, ask for advice," I said, now half asleep. Almost immediately I heard her footsteps trudging up the stairs, and I called more loudly. "Your own bedchamber, not mine."

I then heard her slam the door.

Whether she had eaten, I had no idea. I had not eaten since breakfast, but the hours spent drinking had blocked all appetite and I waited only moments before I wandered up to bed myself.

CHAPTER FIFTEEN

NARRATIVE

Still the snow hurtled, windblown at an angle that slanted past buildings, pathways, trees and any crack it found. Through the dark of the night, it billowed like falling silver stars, an attack of white softness against the dark. It hushed the scramble of the tiny bats and the great owl's hunt.

Sitting at the window of her own bedchamber, Wren slept little. She watched the snow as though mesmerised, but her thoughts were just as wild, although never landing, never settling, and never making sense.

The sun did not rise at dawn and the snow continued, building thick crusted blockages outside doors, blinding windows, heaping over roofs, thatch and slate, then froze the horse's breakfast into brittle and frosted ice as it blasted down chimneys, turning fires to icicles.

Wren was later waking than usual, having slept so badly, therefore she discovered breakfast already on the table when she staggered downstairs. Having expected that Landry would have left as usual, she was both pleased and a little disturbed at his casual appearance, sitting at the table with her empty platter waiting opposite.

He did not look up, but his eyes followed her appearance, and remained in her direction as she sat.

"Naturally I expect you to help yourself," he said, hardly more than a murmur.

She was helping herself to the crusty bread rolls, the small wedge of butter and the bowl of thick honey, when she responded, "You seem to take a few other things for granted, Landry. You assume, quite mistakenly, that I am longing to leap into your bed. So, I can tell you now, not only don't I want to, but the idea is actually quite disgusting."

He paused, looking at her for one tiny moment, then he flung down his napkin and burst out laughing. Wren hadn't wanted to catch his eyes, but now she couldn't help looking, bread roll halfway to her mouth. She had been annoyed before. But now she was furious.

Her voice echoed her anger. "And how dare you laugh at me? I might be a penniless idiot, but at least I don't kill people."

Still grinning, Landry put both elbows to the table and nodded. "I am appallingly rude and reprehensible. I apologise."

Her bread was dripping honey. "Then why do it? Just to upset me?" Wren wiped the honey from the table and licked her fingers. The table smears remained.

"My motives?" He laughed again. "Are not to insult you, little bird. That would serve neither of us, although I admit when cup-shot, I judge by different standards. I can only admit that I would adore to take you into my bed. My denials are directed at myself, as I imagine you deliciously naked, then smiling while climbing cheerfully beneath my sheet."

Wren gasped before her voice had shrunk. "I don't want you to think of me like that."

"Unfortunately," he told her, "such thoughts are difficult to discipline." He took her empty cup and filled it with ale from the jug. "Drink this and forget about me, my dear."

"I can't," she said, gulping ale. "I've been having thoughts all night, and I can't get rid of them either. I mean – did you?"

"Dream of bedding you?"

"No." She blushed. "Murder those poor people? Did you set fire to the shop before pretending it was someone else?"

The grin remained. "Do you believe that?"

Wren simply stared. "I don't believe it. But then sometimes I do."

He refilled his cup, then drained it, pushing the jug and its last drips of ale across the table to Wren. His grin had drained as much as the ale had. "You saw me kill Wyatt's men when they attacked your shop and yourself. I am capable of violence, little bird, but only when I consider it essential. I protected you and myself with those deaths and as such they do not count as murder. I kill but I do not murder. I am amused and also disturbed to find you believe me capable of that. No, little bird, I did not murder that wretched family, though I've been trying to discover who did. Nor did I set fire to the shop, which would have been ludicrous. I saw the man who did it but have no way of identifying him."

Landry had spoken softly, his voice deep, gentle, and with his eyes central to her gaze. Then she nodded carefully and looked away. "I know you didn't. I just couldn't be sure yesterday. But that was silly of me. You've been kind." She looked up again. "Perhaps kind people get angry – well, we all do don't we. But you're hard to understand. You're a thief and keep getting arrested. But you are kind and generous and you've helped me so much." Having finished her ale, she began to twist the cup on the table, fidgeting and still looking down at her hands. "And you hardly ever move your head, even when someone speaks or calls you. You just move your eyes, and they go all silver, like ice."

"Not a habit I'm aware of."

"You do it all the time." She poured herself the last dribbles of ale from the jug and drank. "But I'm sorry about thinking you could have – that was fear of the moment. You have a friendly priest even though you spend ages in Newgate. You're even friends with an earl. But why on earth are you trying to find who committed the murders? Why does it matter to you? You didn't even know Jessy.

And you don't talk to the sheriff. He might already know who did it, and they're probably in Newgate now, waiting to be hanged."

"Your sheriff," Landry said, "hasn't the faintest idea and no one has been properly suspected, let alone arrested. My own interest is another matter. Perhaps excessive cruelty interests me."

"Then you must be sick too."

"Then, little one, you have a sick landlord. Which will hopefully keep you away from my bed." Wren opened her mouth to shout at him, but Landry laughed and raised one hand. "It seems my sense of humour is also diseased, and so I should start each day with an apology for what is bound to come later." He eyed the empty jug and sighed. "But if you are also interested in discovering who has the capacity to kill in such a manner, then you may either permit me to explore in peace, or you will help me. I offer both just as I offer this home and its comforts. As always, you are free to choose."

"Then I'll choose to help." Wren leaned forwards and clasped her hands on the table beside her empty cup. "Because I liked Jessy and felt awful for her family."

"And because a killer capable of such infamy, should not be left free to commit such horrors again. Or worse."

"There isn't any worse." Wren heard herself stutter.

"Believe me," Landry murmured. "There is."

With a deep exhale, Wren nodded. "Then I'll make a list. Wyatt. Your strange priest. The noisy family next door with four or five children, and all horrible. Any of Wyatt's gang. Whoever it was who tried to set fire to the shop. And you."

"The neighbours," Landry said, "are on my list, although I've not yet met them all. However, that's unlikely for several obvious reasons. Wyatt and his gang lack the mentality necessary for such a crime. Jacob, now evidently known as my personal priest, helps me with solving such situations but he does not create them. My own mentality is certainly sufficiently twisted, but I had neither motive nor acquaintanceship." He smiled. "You, my dear, might be added to the list."

"Yes, alright, I'm getting used to your twisted idea of humour."

"You might be interested to know that a friend of mine who helps with this type of puzzle, has you high on his list."

This time, believing it, Wren was horrified. "The priest? Or someone else. Do you have a gang of your own?"

"The one who suspects you, my dear, would be highly indignant at being called a member of my gang."

Collecting the platters, cups, cutlery and jug, Wren didn't answer, bent to the water bucket and piled everything in. The small remainder of food was replaced onto the shelves. Then she looked back. Landry was shrugging into his cape, hat, scarf and gloves. The cape was black and thick, the fur lining even thicker, the unadorned hat was also black. But the scarf was scarlet, and the gloves were knitted green. Beneath he wore the same clothes, once smart but no longer.

She regarded him. "You're leaving again? Is there anything you want me to do while you're away? Will you be gone for hours, days or years?"

"Neither the first nor the last," he said, not bothering to turn. "Arthur comes with me. I expect to be away for several days, but expectations should always be avoided. As for what you should do – think. Simply think, remember any details. That would be an advantage."

She answered in a hurry. "I want to help so I'll think. I know it wasn't you. Of course I know it wasn't me. I suppose I know it wasn't your priest, and now I accept it couldn't have been Wyatt. Nor the Duffs next door, they couldn't organise a Yule feast, let alone a cold vicious killing. So that leaves nobody."

The door clicked softly closed behind him, and she heard Arthur's cheerful greeting. Wren immediately sat on the settle by the fire, which blazed high, and closed her eyes while thinking. Everything idea to be a no. She accepted that Wyatt was too much of a fool and a man who acted on impulse, yet he planned other matters for himself, such as staying in gaol. And all the others now seemed doubtful. But that left the unknown bastard who had attempted setting fire to the eel shop. There seemed no motive for that either. Nor had it been a crime efficiently concluded.

Murder surely, was committed by mad men. A mad man might secretly plan and plot, ponder his intentions and devise an idea based on his madness. Wren often decided that she barely understood her own mind, let alone that of anyone else, Landry especially. Yet now she refused to think him capable of any deviousness.

She had heard men smirk over mumbles of self-pleasure. She had no idea what that might mean to most and would surely conjure different pictures for different men. Her own idea of self-pleasure had been little more than rest, warmth and food. Now, however, it included discovering the warped monster who had murdered and could do so again.

This was not the first time she had wondered how it would feel, hung up, roped and death without knowing why.

Wren decided to visit Pansy, not to work, but to talk.

CHAPTER SIXTEEN

NARRATIVE

"Yes, of course I know all about it," Pansy said, scowling as she rolled out the batter. "But whoever that Jessy person was, I didn't know her. She was just another customer without money or charm. As for trying to burn me down, someone hated you, Wren, not me. I don't have those sorts of friends."

"I doubt he'd have been a friend."

"Well, I don't have enemies." She banged down the rolling pin. "You really should know by now, Wren, I'm better than that."

"And I'm not?" But Pansy turned away and refused to answer.

The shop was open, but the hour was too early for most customers. The oven supplied the heat and the light which the sun now failed to do. The smell of eels, raw and cooked, filled the shop with a suffocation of the senses. It would attract the beggars who couldn't afford it. The poor were always nearby.

Pansy thumped the oven, crackling the flames inside. "Perhaps it was one of those bloody beggars who tried to burn my shop, just to get in and steel the food. Or that bastard Wyatt and his nasty followers."

"No, it wasn't Wyatt. Perhaps he was already back in Newgate."

Wren sighed, and started to make pastry, boiling eels and onion for the filling. "I'll help while you think of anyone who might have wanted to hurt you."

"I told you." Pansy piled the eel dumplings into the huge pot that topped the oven and began the second round. "No one hates me nor has reason to." She smiled suddenly. "But I've got a new friend. He's nice. A bit old, lonely maybe, but we're good friends."

"But he doesn't help in the shop?"

"No, dear." Pansy sniffed. "He's an important man. Very clever. His name's Bryce." She paused, watching Wren. "You're only making ten pies. But you know I can sell a lot more than that."

"But it would take all day to make them, and I can't stay." Wren stared back at Pansy. "I used to know someone called Bryce."

"Well, it won't be the same man." Pansy returned to her dumplings. "My friend is far too superior for you to know. He's a lawyer."

Wren was curious. Pansy never left the house, and certainly never had need of a lawyer. "How did you meet him?"

"A customer, of course."

It was customers who entered now, running in from the blistering cold, hands on hats, fingers clutching at collars. Wren served them, made another ten pies which would have to wait to be cooked anyway, and scurried from the shop. She had forgotten how irritating Pansy could be. Now Wren intended visiting someone even more irritating.

It was Sheriff John Wilson she faced over the table at his office, placed both hands on the tabletop as she sat, then realised her hands were still thick with flour.

Wren apologised and used her thin old glove to wipe the flour to the floor. "Sheriff Wilson, I just came to ask about the Ford family. I wondered – I hoped –have you arrested the killer yet?"

"It's not so easy," the sheriff eyed the last smears of sticky flour. "These terrible crimes aren't the ones we solve quickly, I'm afraid. The killer must be a close acquaintance of the family, with a strong motive for the murder, you know, miss. And that's not something I'm going to discuss with you."

"Surely you remember me?"

He nodded while frowning. "You're no suspect, Mistress Bennet, but why should I take the eel shop girl into my confidence?"

"You mean you don't have the faintest idea who did it." Wren frowned back, stood, and marched out. The sheriff did not call after her.

Another freezing walk to the Mews. The cobbles were thick with ice and where the snow had partially melted, there was sludge. Wren almost slid her way back home and bumped into the gentleman standing at the doorway. The two dogs were sitting at his feet, gazing up, impressed. Wren expected a stumble but instead the visitor caught her, straightened her, and wished her a good afternoon.

"I have come to visit Master Landry," he said. "But it seems he is not at home."

Although his face was heavily shadowed by the brim of his hat with four heaving feathers blowing in the wind, Wren recognised the grandeur immediately. "My lord, you're the Lord of Thamesdon?" She bowed but didn't risk a curtsy as she knew she'd surely fall once more.

Having thought Landry was smartly dressed, Wren now smiled at herself. In comparison to the gentleman now smiling at her, both she and Landry were practically wearing rags. The earl looked even more glorious than the previous time she'd seen him.

Lord Morgan of Thamesdon was now a wide splash of crimson velvet and blue satin. "Yes indeed, my dear," he was saying without arrogance, "that's me. And have you any idea where your landlord might be?"

Having no idea, Wren shook her head and explained. She remained puzzled that such a gentleman was frequently visiting the frequently arrested thief. She had decided that he might not know who Landry truly was. Alternatively, perhaps the earl had come to claim unpaid rent.

"I don't know when he'll be back," she concluded. "Can I do anything to help? Perhaps with the horses? Does your stallion need grooming?"

"No, mistress," the earl found this amusing. "Remy is very warmly tucked up. Master Landry is my friend and expert. I doubt you know much of his private work."

True. Having thought his skills covered such matters as theft, escapes from gaol and general misdemeanours, she was puzzled, even alarmed, that an earl of the land would involve himself and consider it acceptable. As for proper work – no – she did not know that Landry worked at all, what that work might be. She opened her mouth and started to speak, changed her mind twice, then sank into the obsequious manners of a slum girl to a titled gentleman.

"Whenever he comes back, I'll tell him you need him, my lord."

Listening to the tremor in her own voice, she disliked its timidity and tones of servitude. While wondering what she might say to change pathetic uselessness to signs of determination, she was interrupted.

"My apologies, mistress," said the earl with smiling eyes, "but since speaking with my friend late yesterday evening, I am expecting his return very soon. Would you mind if I enter here to wait for him? I am a shocking coward in the snow and ice. I shall most certainly not get in your way."

"Really?" She was surprised and knew she had no choice. "Of course, come in, my lord. This is Landry's home and I'm sure you are more than welcome."

Wren offered wine, which was refused. She then curtsied and began to climb the stairs, content to stay in her bedchamber until called. But the call was sooner than expected. Someone else was rapping on the outside door. Turning, she ran down to answer it, hoping it was Landry who had perhaps lost his key.

Five men glared. They wore the dark livery Wren remembered from Newgate, the somewhat dusty and ill-fitting uniform of the prison guards. Now each held swords unsheathed, their dark caps over their eyes while staring beneath the tiny worn brims. The taller man stepped forward, his sword pointing high, the other hand thrusting the door further open.

Tiny white flakes drifted like soft butterflies coating heads, hats and shoulders.

"In the name of his highness, King Edward, Mighty Crown of England, Wales, Ireland and Norman France, we come to arrest the felon Landry Crawford, and take him into custody."

The snow tipped his nose in a tiny soft peak. Wren stared back, cleared her throat and mumbled, "He's not here. He went away three days ago."

"Stand aside," the guard ordered as the other four pushed from behind. "I have the authority to search the premises."

"You do not," said the voice over her head. The earl glared at the glare of the guards but did not unsheathe his sword.

"Then you must be hedge-born Landry Crawford," accused the guard. "Now I arrest you –,"

"I shall introduce myself," the earl announced, moving in front of Wren as she shuffled back. "I am the Earl of Thamesdon, Morgan Harris, close friend to his majesty the king, and owner of this property and the entire mews. I warn you that if you attempt to arrest me, you will end on the gallows yourselves."

The guard looked from him to Wren, and nodded, slightly flushed. His eyebrows were encrusted with snow. They began to drip.

"It ain't him," the guard turned to his companions with a sniff. "I reckon this be the earl as he says he is."

"Bloody hell," murmured another, stepping quickly backwards.

The first guard, abruptly sheathing his sword and indicating for his men to do the same, bowed hurriedly to the earl and began his apologies. He had said nothing relevant however, when he discovered the edge of a metal blade pushing up beneath his chin, his mouth jammed shut and his hands shaking. The next voice came loud, imperious, from behind.

"You are under arrest, for threatening his lordship, Earl of

Thamesdon. And I hereby inform you, fool, that no one calls for the arrest of Master Landry Crawford unless permission is first granted by his royal highness, the king. Landry Crawford is under his majesty's protection until further notice."

Six guards in the gold and scarlet livery of the royal palace had surrounded the guards of Newgate, and Wren gasped as the earl smiled. Words whirled around her unbrushed hair and mixed with the snowflakes.

"We got good reason to arrest a thief what got away," complained one guard.

"And I have good reason to bounce you on your head all the way down the Cheaps," roared one man beneath his shining scarlet cap, the badge now snow-crusted too.

One of the voices crept in behind the dithering crowd. "They say that a horse likes to jump in snow drifts, but Betsy hates it."

Several other men turned their heads, confused.

"What the devil you moaning about," bellowed a Newgate guard.

Prad was grinning inside his high turned-up collar. His interruption had calmed the opposing guards and brought the realisation of absurdity.

The earl raised both arms and clapped his hands. The colourful velvets brought him to notice, but his height had been insufficient to rise visible amongst the liveried throng.

"You will all calm yourselves," he ordered. "As the Earl of Thamesdon, I have the ability to demand the arrest of every man present."

"Perhaps," Wren called in a wild moment of amusement, "you should all come indoors and wait for Landry, since his lordship tells us Landry is on his way."

An unappreciative shove first blocked the doorway, then dispersed, allowing the thunder of footsteps up the creaking stairs, the earl now leading the way. It had originally seemed a large room with its large hearth, two settles both cushioned in embroidered pikes and swords surrounded by flowers, the hefty wooden table and stools, and the cupboards of books and kitchen clatter, platters clinking as anyone bumped past. The bumping now filled the room. Lord Morgan stretched himself on one settle and nobody dared sit next to him. He regained a modest height while sitting and became centre of attention.

Clustered beside the large glass window, every leaden frame now thick white in a hundred tiny peaks, were the royal guards, glaring at the Newgate guards who sat on the lower stairs, blocking the way to the bedchambers, looking rightfully worried. The royal guards held unarguable precedence, but the head guard of Newgate had given orders that every one of his men feared to disobey.

Meanwhile Wren and Prad had claimed the second settle, so Prad risked building up the fire behind the grate. The flames hurtled abruptly, tossing their peaks up the uneven brick chimney while at the same time, the dark smoke puffed back into the faces of all present.

The earl coughed. "Thank you, Prad, but I think that will do."

It was while she was trying to appear relaxed, that Wren heard another knock on the door downstairs, and sighed. There were already fourteen folk, mostly large in height as well as width, plus two large and sprawling hounds, all squashed into a room that had once seemed spacious and now seemed minute. But since no one was talking to her, nor indeed taking any notice of her whatsoever, Wren stepped out and down the steps, determined to scowl at any more visitor unless it was the king himself.

It was the sheriff.

"Sheriff Wilson, how unexpected."

Stamping the snow from his boots, the sheriff asked what trouble had been aroused here, and who had caused the disgraceful noise which had so annoyed the neighbours, their back yards attached to the rear of the Mews. "Three complaints I've had to deal with," the man announced through a clenched jaw. "I had to swear I'd see to it. Now, what's been going on?"

"Just the Earl of Thamesdon and six royal guards," Wren smiled through her teeth. "All upstairs."

"Mistress Wren, what rubbish," concluded the sheriff. "I demand to see what's going on upstairs."

"Oh, please yourself," sighed Wren. "Come in."

CHAPTER SEVENTEEN

WREN

I didn't laugh but I wanted to. Sheriff Wilson's face flushed into rusty copper.

"My lord," although speaking to the earl, he was gazing at the fire-reflecting sheen of the uniforms by the window, "my apologies, I had no idea."

"Teach you to believe me in future," I said, with the courage inspired by the earl smiling at me and the sheriff twitching into a tremble. He bowed, managed a double turn almost as though dancing and didn't trip over, though I wished he had.

Actually, when I was young, I'd liked the man and just accepted that he did a good job. Of course, I now knew he was not the best at his job, and I was frazzled at everyone scowling at everyone else when the Landlord wasn't even at home. I once again offered wine to the earl and made it obvious that I wasn't offering a thing to anyone else.

The words which still hung, repeating themselves, at the back of my mind, were those claiming that Landry Crawford was under his majesty's protection. Landry – who rode the back streets and stole whatever he could? I'd heard folk say the biggest thief in the land was indeed the king, but that was a very different matter, and not something to say in public. You'd be quickly arrested. I sat quietly contemplating.

Prad smiled at the sheriff and with polite deference and began to explain. "Since you know me," he nodded, "you might prefer my explanations, and not in this crowded room where everyone will listen even if they pretend not to. The stable directly downstairs is warm but empty, until Master Crawford returns with Arthur."

The sheriff nodded. "Arthur?"

"His stallion," Prad grinned.

Prad led the way back down the stairs and the sheriff shook his head but followed. I peered over the banister to make sure the door was safely closed behind them, when there was a clatter and push on the lower steps, and someone was forcing his way in before the others could force their way out.

"Clergy – make way," thrusting his way up the stairs, Father Jacob waved both arms and appeared beside me with a grin that didn't fit his ecclesiastical gown.

I gazed at his face splitting smile, the priest's hair cut with the top of his head shining as though polished silver, leather sandals toes covered in snow peeping from beneath his long black linen robe, and the sleeveless top from neck to waist in vibrant scarlet with all its full swinging edges embroidered with crosses and bells.

It wouldn't have been sensible to demand what church he belonged to, but I had a sneaky idea that there was no church who would want him. Naturally I smiled back, welcomed him into the warmth of the room, and informed him that Landry had not yet reappeared.

"But he's coming," said the priest, then saw Lord Morgan and marched over to the settle. The earl moved sideways, and the priest sat next to him. "Landry should be here soon," he nodded, "unless he's been arrested on the way." This began an irritating squabble with the guards all over again.

The large room had not only shrunk, but the comfort and placid decorations were. Once the smells were of the crackling fire and rich burning bark, the perfumed glimmer of dry hay, from the encrusted mud imported into the room.

It was different now of course. Sweat was predominant. Unwashed armpits and feet. The earl smelled of sweet but artificial rose petals, and the priest brought with him a waft of incense.

I think I smelled of badly rinsed soap suds.

Though now it wasn't smells that mattered as the squabbles turned to fights. One of the royal guards punched one of Newgate's guards to the floor, where the fallen guard rolled over and tugged a short sword from his leather belt. The royal guard's boot shot out and kicked the sword. It clattered to the wall, almost at my feet. Although probably not sensible, I picked it up anyway.

"Stop fighting," I yelled, swinging the blade, careful to keep it at a distance. "This is a private home. Not a palace and not a gaol, and if you start punching, then someone's bound to fall in the fire."

The swish of legs and livery was already shooting the flames higher as though I'd used the bellows. I hadn't since we didn't have any. I dodged the sparks and raced to the other settle where I'd sat before. But the fire smelled more strongly than anything else, right until one of the Newgate guards lifted both arms in front of me and swore loudly.

The Newgate gaoler said. "I got orders. You lot of hedge-shitters can arrest me, but I's gonna arrest Landry Crawford first."

The royal guard, I guessed their chief, flashed his livery. "Our authority, fool, is greater than yours, and you know it. You arrest Landry Crawford, and you will be immediately taken into custody in the king's name."

It was the perfect moment for Landry to walk in. He pushed the door wide, strode into the middle of his own bulging room, and frowned.

"It seems I am entertaining guests."

As always, his voice was low, little more than a murmur, yet somehow coldly threatening.

He was his usual self, tall, dark hair wind and snow encrusted, boots so thick with snow the mud beneath didn't show through, with no weapons to see. He wore a thick black doublet beneath a long fur lined cape, and his long muscled legs were prominent in their crimson knitted hose. Red legged but black shadowed elsewhere. His grey eyes had narrowed beneath those prominent brows, appearing as thin streaks of ice.

Yet Landry's expression drifted from threatening to sweet appreciation when he turned to the earl and the priest next to him.

"My lords," he half bowed, and half nodded to both. "We meet as arranged. Yet to the best of my memory, we had not expected the London guards, high and low."

The earl chuckled. "This type of chaos rarely happens in my home, Landry. We should have arranged to meet there."

"I never feel comfortable swearing in your halls, Morgan," Landry said. "Oddly, I tend to feel more at home here usually."

Still smiling, the earl pointed to me. "Your friend has coped remarkably well," he said. "But I think you should take over now, Landry."

The Newgate guard with his horribly sweaty armpits had walked forwards and even though Landry's back was turned, the guard declared, "As the appointed administrator of his majesty's Newgate gaol, I hereby arrest the felon Landry Crawford for the offences of theft, injury and the unlawful desertion of his incarceration."

"Beautifully put," said Landry, turning towards the guard, smile in place. "However, I believe the royal guard has precedence and will hopefully over-ride your intentions."

The taller of the royal guards, his crimson and gold as vibrant as the fire, pushed past the Newgate guard and made his own announcement, his voice louder as he thumped the base of his lance against the floorboards.

"I hereby announce that his majesty, crowned monarch of this land, has overruled all other authorities including this attempt at the arrest of Landry Crawford which is hereby denounced as unlawful. Landry Crawford is under the temporary protection of his royal highness King Edward, and therefore remains a free citizen until such time as his royal highness cancels the warrant of protection."

Landry looked from one guard to the other. "Difficult, isn't it. I sympathise."

The Earl of Thamesdon stood. "Right," he announced cheerfully. "Off you go, the whole damn lot of you. Take your arguments outside. The snow will make a perfect witness. Come on – off with you – now."

The five prison guards grumbled reluctantly, stared down at their boots, and began to shuffle down the stairs, each step grinding beneath the weight. The outer door was pushed open, perhaps kicked, and I could immediately hear the horses snorting and neighing, smashing at their stable doors and complaining loudly.

The members of the royal guard, thanked briefly by both Landry and the earl, stomped downstairs directly behind the others, and eventually I could hear the door shut. Hopefully Prad had also got rid of the sheriff, and even the horses calmed as the guards marched out from the Mews and headed west.

It was the priest who nodded at me. "Well now, do we include your lady friend?"

Since it was damned obvious that I was no lady, I probably blushed. "I'm Mistress Wren Bennet," I said, half mumbled, "and if you'll excuse me, I'll retire to my bedchamber."

No one seemed ready to object. Landry said nothing. I would have loved to stay. The talk about Landry's royal protection was fascinating. I wanted explanations but wasn't going to be able to eavesdrop on the conversation to come. With a hopeful glance at the collection of wine jugs, I was going to offer refreshment, but Landry got in first, pouring for the earl, the priest and himself. So off I shuffled and flopped down on my unmade bed, closed my eyes, and cursed.

A faint murmur of distant speech tried very hard to tunnel into my ears, but even standing inside the closed door with that eager ear against the wood, I couldn't make out more than a couple of words. Naturally they were words that didn't help. *'no result.' 'I have* no need of Newgate now.' 'What?' 'How?' 'The quarry, perhaps,' and 'Tomorrow.'"

None of it explained anything, even the remark about Newgate. And there was certainly no mention of *Mistress Wren has the intelligence to help if we explain first*!

Wishing produced no result as usual, so I crept back to bed.

CHAPTER EIGHTEEN

NARRATIVE

W ren did not sleep although her own banishment from the downstairs warmth continued for several hours. Her bed was a tangle of linen and blanket when finally she heard the door downstairs close, and the click of the lock within told her that Landry had remained.

Delighted, she straightened her hair and clothes, and hurried downstairs.

The fire still blazed, and new logs had been stacked. The dogs had also remained, stretched without shame across a Turkey rug. Landry sat, stretched in exhaustion like the dogs although not on the rug, and his eyes were closed.

Although he must have heard her arrival, he did not open his eyes. But he spoke softly, "You must have questions. But they can wait. First we eat, and this time, you will need to do the cooking my dear. Whatever you find, whatever you prepare, will be for both of us. The choice is yours."

Landry continued to doze until sometime later Wren whispered. "Dinner is ready, if you want it."

"I want it," he said, opening his eyes into the fire glow.

It was across platters of pork chops and spinach with split figs that Wren accepted the cup of wine poured for her, and said, "I wonder if it's time for questions?"

"But whether it is time for answers," Landry murmured, "I'm not so sure. First, I compliment you, little bird, on a supper better than those I sometimes produce myself."

"I like cooking, except for eels," she told him, mouth full.

"Then you deserve at least one answer," he smiled back, raising his cup. His cape now lay tumbled on the floor, and one of the dogs had chosen it as a pillow. Landry's hat and gloves had also been tossed to the rug. Although the rug was an item of expense and unusual luxury, offering greater comfort and insulation than the strewn rushes many poor households used against drafts and spillage, Landry treated it with little respect.

While finishing her own meal and draining her cup, Wren, bright eyed, watched Landry's tired expression over the brim of his own cup. Finally she said, "So, I'm allowed one question. In which case, who are you really?"

He smiled. "A gentle beginning," he acknowledged. "Landry Crawford would be the obvious answer. Yet if I answer kindness with kindness, I might say a good deal more."

"So do you feel kind?" She reached for the wine jug and refilled his cup before her own. "I can see you're exhausted. I leave the choice to you."

These were words he often spoke himself. Landry sighed. "Then I make an easy choice. I am not hedge-born, but nor do I have title nor position of importance. But I am not the thief I seem. I work for the Earl of Thamesdon." Then, abruptly smiling wide, his eyes directly grinning into hers, he added, "That I'm afraid is all I can answer."

Wren sat with her mouth open, her now full cup halfway. "You won't tell me what on earth you do for an earl who calls you a friend? So, it's not just scrubbing the floor or looking after his horse."

"Prad does that. Although he's a friend too." Landry's grin remained.

"You know you have to tell me now." She promptly drank, gulping as though half dead of thirst.

Landry threw the bones from his platter to the dogs. Both Red and Shadow were now buxom hounds layered in muscle and flesh, passionately in love with Wren, Prad and Landry himself. Four chops meant two bones each, although with little meat left attached.

Cup in hand, now Landry stood, wandered to the nearest settle and Wren, leaving the cleaning up until later, sat herself on the other settle, watching and waiting for the explanation she needed.

"No doubt you've guessed by now," Landry leaned back, adjusting the cushions, legs stretched past the slobbering dogs by the hearth. "Thamesdon is a gentleman of considerable intelligence, and overflows with the virtue of kindness we often mention. Some years back, his friend's young sister was killed. I knew the earl already for other reasons, and he asked me to discover the nature of this girl's death, and who, if anyone, was responsible. The investigation was comparatively easy. The earl switched his anger to moral virtue. I am paid, and have been for many years, to discover justice and find those who kill and torment. Not always so easy, but permanently profitable and of great fascination to me. You may think it hard to believe, but I am frequently successful."

Landry's pale silk eyes remained warm, his hair ruffled, no longer snow splattered but glowing with reflections of flame and candlelight.

Wren said, "I'd guessed it might be something of that nature. But I'd never imagined it all. It's unexpected. I thought – but I shouldn't have."

"That I'd murdered your neighbours?" His voice continued low and soft. The ice had gone. "I pass many days in Newgate gaol. Yet the crimes for which I'm arrested do not exist. Both my detention and my escapes are conjured by Jacob and the earl both. Unfair, of course, for the guards who feel obliged to chase a disappearing criminal."

"You've never robbed anyone?"

"Not since I was twelve years of age. Before then I had no interest in morals or church. Hunger was my only preoccupation."

Wren was surprised. "You're poor – no parents?"

"Another story, but without relevance."

She breathed out, smiling, relieved but hoping for further details. "You go to gaol yet you're under his majesty's protection. That's amazing. It sounds so exciting." But her smile dropped. "And now you're looking for the killer – the one who murdered my friend Jessy and her family. I hope – oh, how much I hope, you know who it is."

"I don't." His answer was abrupt, and Wren sighed. "There's no secrecy now since that is precisely why I invited you to live here."

"Me? You thought it was me?"

But Landry shook his head again. "No, little bird. My assumptions are not so blind. But I needed to know your connection, and who you knew that also knew them. I needed the information I believed only you might have. And I believed you'd wish to help."

"I do," she told him at once. "You know that. I could help with anything you want. I live here free, I eat free, it's warm and beautiful and I love it here. But I'd love even more to find that monsterous killer."

Landry reached his arm back to the table, grasped the wine jug and saw it empty. He stretched as he stood, murmuring, "All day, for many days, in the saddle can crack a man's back." He collected more wine from the shelf and shared it between them. "My weeks of investigation have uncovered no more than suggestions. Overweight brothers with names unknown. One brute, too difficult to blame since he wears a title. Wyatt, of course, a favourite for any accusation. One or two others, but all so unlikely." He sat again on the opposite settle. "But I managed a pebble of insight, and I discovered the fool who set fire to the shop before you left it."

Excitement again. "Who?"

"His name," Landry nodded, "is Cadby Bracks. You know him I believe, or at least you know of him."

The excitement was extinguished by amazement and shock. "He was Magg's father. Dad's wife Maggs." She blushed. "The one he killed."

"The slaughter you exonerated when you stood witness in court for your father?"

Wren was still blushing. "Surely I wasn't wrong? My father could be nasty and violent. But he isn't a murderer."

"The dead woman's father believes he is," Landry said without sign of judgement. "This was the crime I investigated before the death of your friend. I understand a daughter's impulse to protect her father, just as I understand a father's impulse to avenge his daughter's death."

"But if she –," Wren paused. "You think Dad was guilty?"

"Naturally," Landry said.

Wren stared, shocked, and almost burst into tears. "I believed, I really believed him. But Dad has always been a mean bastard, so why did I believe him? How stupid. But Maggs – she did leave the babe. Didn't she?"

Wren curled away, Landry was sitting next to her. The soft murmur of his voice was now directly in her ear. "You did not hear the full story and of course your father lied. Why would he admit a crime that would send him to the gallows? Your own blame is simply that of duty to your father. But his young wife, hearing that her mother was dying in pain, rushed to her side. Without the ability to travel apart from her own two feet, she could not carry an infant, and left it in the care of the midwife, Sara Peck, who she expected to nurse the child until Maggs returned. Unfortunately, your father returned from the carvel days earlier than he later admitted and told Sara Peck he would take over the care of his child. Meanwhile your well fed and healthy half-sister lay alone in her cradle, waiting for the love, care and sustenance all infants expect."

Wren had wiped her eyes, determined not to cry. But, with a stuttered gulp, she wiped the tears from her eyes.

"Are you sure about this?" She expected no explanation and sank back against the cushions. "A tiny baby, starving, for six days," she mumbled, her tears louder. "Perhaps Dad didn't know how to warm milk for feeding. Although I know there was a linen infant's bottle there held in wood, expensive too, because I gave it to Maggs myself, but Sara should have shown him how to use it."

Landry insisted that Wren drink. "Such misery and desperation is common enough in our miserable world," Landry said as Wren took the cup. "Your stepmother returned after six days, weeping for the loss of her mother but delighted to be reunited with her child. She was, perhaps, equally delighted to see that her husband had returned from his work on the oceans. I doubt her pleasure lasted long."

"Dad killed her in fury then?"

"His temper seems violent," Landry nodded. "But he knew she was not responsible for the death of his daughter, yet clearly offered her no explanation. Indeed, seeing her infant, your stepmother may not have resisted. Her own father, Cadby, however, quite correctly believed that your father had killed both her and the child. At the time your dutiful attempt to exonerate him seemed to me both naive and understandable, which is why I made no outcry. Cadby, however, attempting revenge for your words at court, saving Haldon from the gallows he deserved, seems also excusable. Who would you blame? Everyone involved? Or no one? Including yourself?"

For a moment, Wren felt Landry's arm around her shoulders. She was still sobbing. But his arm was removed, and Landry crossed back to the other settle, leaving Wren sniffing into her cup. She wept quietly into the last of the wine.

She looked up, trying to wipe the streaming tears from her face. "I never cry. I got hit and beaten and I only cried when I was very little. But first my sister and then Jessy, I cry all the time. I can't help it. I try to stop, it's pathetic."

"And naturally you believed what your father told you."

"Now I know." She stuttered, sobbing again. "I trusted Dad. But I trust what you're telling me. Perhaps I'm just too trusting."

"Your father carries full blame. But," Landry said, watching her, "the one who killed the Ford family carries the heart of a demon, and I will not stop investigating until I find who it was."

Once again Wren saw the vision of the four hanging bodies and choked on more tears. She saw the bodies roped to the ceiling beams, and the shadows stretched across the floorboards. Now Wren thought if she failed to control the nightmare visions, she might never stop crying.

Once again, she felt Landry's arm around her shoulders, holding her warm and close. She felt his hot breath on her cheek, and the grasp of his long fingers pressing her against him.

She did not make any move away, nor disentangled herself, but cuddled to the comfort she needed. "I should never have believed him. I know he lies."

"And perhaps I should not have told you the truth of it, since nothing can be done now." His whisper tickled, and she loved the warm breath and the smell of the wine. "But facing the truth is essential in this job. And from now on," he continued, "the only lies you can believe, are my own."

CHAPTER NINETEEN

NARRATIVE

"If you investigate a crime," Landry's voice murmured against her ear, "you cannot allow misery in and lose your own judgement. Weeping for the victim colours your thoughts too much. Even hating the killer can spoil your understanding. Now listen, and let my words take precedence. The creature who slaughtered your neighbours had a motive. This was no act of sudden temper. It was carefully planned. There were either four killers, or the family was dead, probably poisoned, before being hung. There is therefore a specific motive for what was done, not simply murder, but also a motive for hanging the bodies in plain view."

The words finally sank through the tears and Wren gulped. "It was planned?"

"You had thought that fury and hatred are sudden brutal emotions?"

Wren thought of the ice in Landry's eyes and voice when his own anger flared. He seemed static and cold. "I know," she said into his shoulder.

"Now," he asked her, "when you can describe this crime using careful evaluation dismissing all emotion." He allowed the long pause, then nodded. "Then you are ready to tell me the pertinent details."

His arm still held her close to him, her head still resting on his shoulder. It brought her confidence. "I think I can do that." She straightened, lifted her head and gazed at him, yet not dislodging from his partial embrace. "The family already knew the killer or killers. Someone – male or female – came to their house and was invited in. The family trusted the visitor and accepted a drink that they brought. They had no idea this drink was drugged or poisoned. They all died of the poison or fell deeply asleep from the drug. Then the killer or killers hung up each body from the beams with the ropes they had intentionally brought for that purpose."

"Because there are no signs of struggle?" Landry nodded. "But there were some signs, though limited. Do you know what they were?"

"I suppose Jessy's husband woke up or wasn't completely dead." Wren frowned. "There was blood on him and on the floor where he hung. They all had blood on their necks, but Randell most of all. Perhaps none of them were totally dead, but the poison would have made them weak, useless. Unable to resist."

"Excellent," Landry said, quietly impressed. "There is one small point which corroborates your words. Once dead, a corpse does not freely bleed, yet the husband did so. I saw the blood on the floor myself, even though the bodies had been removed. There were also puddles of piss. As any man or woman dies, they piss out whatever remains in the body. So, they were drugged or poisoned then died on the rope. So why does a killer wish to exhibit his crime, instead of hiding his guilt?"

"Because he's evil," Wren said at once, "and wants to show off."

"That's possible," Landry nodded, "although there is no other evidence of such a nature. Instead, the crime was careful, cold, and unusual."

"So, he was sending a message," Wren said. "Hanging out a sign for someone to see. But what message was it?" Climbing into the crime in such a manner now fascinated her.

"There are two possibilities," Landry said. "Either he was shouting the proof of his own power. Or he was showing what would happen to those who crossed him, denied him, or cheated him. Both are possible, as are both together."

"So, the killer was someone with a particular motive. And he or she is experienced." Wren no longer wanted to cry. "I suppose even monsters do things for a reason, I suppose."

"Indeed. Entirely true. Well done." Landry eased her head back to his shoulder and his voice softened even further. "Can you imagine what your friend's husband might have done to inspire this cruelty against his family?"

"If it was him – no. I hardly knew him," Wren mumbled, now trying to think past the warm comfort of the man who held her. "And I'm sorry, but I'm so easily distracted. I feel – well, warm."

With no intention of confessing the extent to which she enjoyed his embrace, she had found the courage to say a little. She had disliked Landry at the beginning. She had suspected him of violence, and certainly believed him a thief. But she had found him attractive, though that alone had not made her like him. Now Wren relished his touch. She hoped he wouldn't move.

Yet as she wished it, he did. Abruptly he stood, moving back to his own settle. Wren felt the lack of his arm like a sudden chill and the loss of protection.

With his voice cold, Landry spoke again, "A man, almost certainly, proved by the strength used lifting the bodies, unless there was more than one. A man who had reason, however vindictive and however mistaken, to hate one of the family sufficient to murder them all. Murdering a small child in that manner, certainly an innocent child, is surely the act of a creature without proper feelings. Think, little bird. Have you ever met anyone capable?"

"I hope not." She stared across at him, annoyed to discover herself feeling lonely again. "I think not. He'd be cold without feelings. He'd be cruel." For a moment she thought, "I don't know anyone important enough. I don't think I know anyone cruel except Wyatt. He's hot tempered, but I don't think he is calculating."

Landry smiled. "Let us leave Wyatt from the discussion. Wyatt is cruel dependent on hunger. The brutality in his nature requires action and no one has ever taught him differently. So, Wyatt now ceases to exist within our discussions."

"I don't know many other people, at least, not well."

"We search for a man more organised, yet without pity." Landry chuckled. "More alike to my own character, perhaps. Though I dislike cruelty and loathe the thought of a mind so devious. I can kill. I have killed. But for reasons of the danger my victims represent, or the brutality they've committed. If I kill, then I kill someone dangerous who is no victim. My job is to find the killer. He is a dangerous and twisted man."

"It's interesting, you're telling me more about yourself." Wren said, "I'm not sure why, unless you want my trust. Or perhaps distrust."

He laughed, leaning forwards. "Trust would be helpful. But it's a level of understanding I need from you if we're to work together." The iced eyes had opened into tunnels. "To admit I have killed and will kill with little compunction, but this doesn't mean I enjoy it, nor wish to hurt others."

"Randell Ford worked in the old quarry north of Cripplegate," Wren remembered. "It must be someone he knew there. We couldn't know who. I certainly never went there and hardly knew Randell."

"I agree, and have been exploring the quarry, with a pretence of working as an inspector." Landry once again refilled his cup but when he offered the jug to Wren, she shook her head.

"I'm half asleep already."

"Then go to your bedchamber, little bird."

"But I'm interested," she said. "Too much to sleep. I want to understand it all. I wish I could think better. Now I'm feeling the way I know you do. And I really want to work more closely with you."

"Most folk would loathe such an idea," Landry smiled. "These situations are rarely a pleasure."

"I don't mean that way," Wren sat forwards, her elbows to her knees. "This whole situation is unbelievably horrible, and I want it to go away. I can help make it go if we solve it. And helping by putting the bad people in Newgate would be – well, worth it. I'd know I'd done something important instead of washing cups and platters and staring at windows all my life. I try and help with the horses, but I doubt they appreciate it. I don't understand much about them except for perhaps, Arthur."

"Arthur will appreciate that when I tell him."

Wren managed to laugh. "So, I can help with whatever you do?"

"Whatever I do might cover a little too much, little bird. But I shall inform the earl that now you work with me. Jacob will be delighted."

She wasn't so sure about that and nearly asked what on earth he was – priest or disguised sheriff – and whether he only went to pray at Newgate in order to help Landry escape. Instead, she looked at the neatly clasped hands in her lap and mumbled, "You've met a lot of criminals in Newgate. Why do you do that? Do you suspect some of them?"

"Invariably. I've investigated many crimes over the years. I don't object to a few nights in gaol. Though neither comfortable nor pleasant, invariably useful." Landry seemed placid now, his eyes blinked out the cold and he appeared content to answer her questions. He stretched back against the settle's wooden panels, a deep green cushion behind him, his ankles crossed before him.

The only candle was guttering, and the shadows lengthened, but they were split by the consistent spark of flame from the hearth. The room fizzled, the fire sank, then rose. Gold and scarlet lights splashed against the walls and shook the shadows.

Above them the dark wooden beams striped the plastered ceiling. They had been treated, and that had darkened their colour. Having seen bodies hanging from other beams, she now avoided staring up at ceilings, but here they enclosed her in safety and the beauty of their scuttling pictures. But when Wren saw Landry stoking the fire again and a new rush of heat flushed against her.

For distraction, she changed the subject, "so Magg's father wanted revenge, knowing about his daughter's death. His granddaughters too. He must have thought I knew the truth but twisted it to save my own family. I feel sorry for him but wanting to burn down the shop with me in it wasn't – well, was it? Almost as disgusting as what he thought my father had done."

"Several weeks back I found Cadby Bracks and spoke with him." Landry drained his fifth cup of wine. "The man is an idiot, but first his wife died in his arms and then he heard of the rest of his family murdered. A simple fool, he was too distraught to act any other way than to respond in kind. He still harbours fury. But he knew nothing of the Ford family and their wretched end."

"So, we can leave him out of it then. I can't even remember what he looks like. I only met him once for a moment or two." Wren drained her own cup, just the last trickle of wine she no longer wanted. "I feel a little sick," she said under her breath. "Too much wine. Too much thinking about murders. Remembering that baby, knowing the truth about Maggs and imagining my father slaughtering her. Then of course the hanging – I don't want any more of that tonight." She looked up quickly. "But I still want to help you, honestly I do. I suppose interesting is a fair word. But justice is even more important."

"No nightmares permitted tonight," Landry told her. His smile was almost lazy. "The wine should help with that."

Wren stood, shaking a little, and pushed herself towards the stairs, grabbing the banister for support. "I'll try," she said, still mumbling. "I don't want any dreams at all. But I need to sleep."

"Then I wish you a night of deep rest," Landry told her, although not moving. "And tonight I change my usual advice. If you prefer my own bedchamber to yours, then you are free to enjoy my bed. No doubt you'd be asleep by the time I join you."

Not sure whether he meant it or was laughing at her, she neither knew nor admitted caring. "It's my own bed I want," she hiccupped. "And I'll stay there with the door shut."

This time she could hear the gentle laughter, but as she climbed the stairs, almost tripping, she wondered if she was making more mistakes than she knew.

CHAPTER TWENTY

NARRATIVE

A slim girl, her black hair long and loose at her back, waited quietly in the shadows.

His royal highness, King Edward, gazed frequently, smiling, into those shadows. He seemed considerably more interested in the young woman than he was in the liveried sergeant at arms who now addressed him.

"Your highness, I beg you to inform me as to your ruling on his lordship the Earl of Thamesdon, who awaits your highness in the great Hall."

An impressively tall man, Edward IV, turned reluctantly, and looked from shadow to light at the kneeling figure of his Master Guard. "Usher him in, man. Bring him in." The king's smile was engaging, it lit his face, and his blue eyes shone with sapphire. His once golden hair was now thickly streaked in grey, but this added wisdom to his face. He was once considered handsome, quite beautiful indeed, and his depth of voice had proclaimed him a man to admire. Since then, his highness had not realised that girth had begun to spoil the image, but the width of his waist and the rolls of fat above and below, were mostly hidden beneath the grandeur of his clothes.

The guard backed almost to the doorway, then turned and strode to where the earl waited. "My lord, his highness wishes to speak with you. Follow me, my lord."

Morgan also knelt and bowed his head before his king.

"Get up, Morgan," ordered his monarch, dismissing the girl behind him with his fingertips, his appreciative smile still in place. He spoke softly to the retiring guard. "Bring that female to me after supper." Then turned back to the earl. Thamesdon stood now, waiting patiently. "Sit here," Edward ordered, tapping the stool beside his cushioned chair. "Tell me, whatever it is."

"Sire, our monthly meeting has been delayed this time, and the fault is mine. The crime I had hoped to solve before now, remains a mystery. The number of those willing and able to work for me within these circumstances, as your highness so graciously knows and kindly finances, has increased, yet no new suspect has been traced."

His majesty, still graciously wrapped in smiles, nodded. "Morgan, I know you well and you know my beliefs. I promised this country justice when I first took the throne, but I'm well aware of the corruption which leaks into every layer and class. You're one of the few amongst my court who wishes to work against it, in spite of the peril that involves. Now, enough of apologies. What do you need?"

"Permission, your highness." The earl uncomfortable on his stool, gazed up meekly at his king. "Your permission to investigate, and possibly speak against another of the royal court, sire. The young man who works for me as I work for your highness, has uncovered not simply possibilities but also probabilities."

King Edward IV chuckled. "I distrust half my court. But not you, Thamesdon. You have my permission, and are free to investigate whatever and whoever you wish. You remain under my royal protection, as does your assistant Crawford and his friends."

❧

It was the following morning when the earl returned to the Mews, dismounted and ordered his groom to call Landry. Within a few moments he was sitting on one of the long settles, and Landry was offering wine or ale.

"Ale," Morgan said. "So, tell me about your new recruit. I've met her of course, but I know little of her. You've never asked me to include a female before. I'll always accept your recommendations, Landry, but this one needs more explanation."

"You've reported to the king?"

"He made neither objection nor seemed much interested. Not unusual. He has an entirely different view of women, and only one use. But now I await your report, Landry."

"Wren Bennet seems to breed insight, intelligence, and prompt understanding, although sometimes muffled by youth. She loathes boredom instead of cherishing it, and searches for purpose."

"You like her," Morgan decided. "You're attracted, just as the damned king delights in passing time in that manner."

"Yes, I like her," Landry snorted. "But I've no intention of bringing a bed mate into this business simply because of my affections."

Wren had heard nothing of what was said.

She was drifting in the butcher's market within the Shambles. Not yet Friday, she had no desire to cook fish, since the salt smell reminded her of eels. Instead, on this chilly Thursday, with the snow having stopped overnight and melted into a dirty sludge, she planned on a generous dinner to share with Landry, hoping he had not yet disappeared, as he usually did, without a word.

His long discussion two days previously had delighted her. It had also disappointed her, although she was ashamed of that particular reaction. Landry's offer of his own home free of any charge, including the supply of daily food, she suspected, had been made solely on the need for the examination of someone who knew more of the Ford family's murder than he did. Did that mean that any attraction had been non-existent, and no part of Landry's motive? Yet if had he actively disliked her, surely the offer of sharing his own home would have been too repugnant to press.

Instead, he wanted her to share her knowledge, and even help him with the investigation. That was both welcome, and flattering. It could be the promise of a future, but maybe a delightful one. Now there was a growing hope, even conviction, that she could help solve the crime that haunted her.

The smells of the butchers' displays heightened those memories. She remembered the blood on Randell's smock. It had dried almost black, but the stink of it had hung like the noose.

It was early. Some of the shops were only just opening, having first spent those necessary hours slaughtering the animals brought by farmers, or bought at the farmers' markets. The farmers led cattle, sheep, goats and geese to the open fields, and those from the Shambles would either choose, and order their choice killed, or would do the butchering themselves. Consideration for the animals was limited. There were those who watched, and the law supplied the Watchers.

Brutality while killing any creature for food was illegal, and yet some man, or several, seemed capable of hideous brutality against not just the innocence of a goat or cow, but against a woman, a man, and their children.

Carcasses were hung for some days before cutting, the blood falling to the cobbles. The entrails and hooves, discarded, ended in the gutters. Blood and the stench of killing sank into the woodwork, the stone, the beams, and the roads. Stockyards set up along the old wall helped with the killing, the distribution and the sales.

The Shambles close to Newgate was not Wren's favourite destination, no more than the eel shop. She told herself, however, to hold her thoughts, and accept the uglier aspects of life. Hanging carcasses were seen here every day, except Friday when only fish shops opened. The butchers attending market on Fridays, discouraged visitors. The masters sent to oversee the killing were the only men welcome. Wren had never been, she would rather avoid watching the death of a frightened animal.

Yet if she was to work as an investigator of crime, her sickening at the sight of bloody slaughter would need to be controlled or hidden. Wren wondered if the final result would make her stronger, or simply more of a fool.

The heavy wooden shutters were being lifted down from the shop windows, the bottom ledge lowered to serve as the counter, the doors unlocked, and the carcasses hung from the large hooks along the top of the open window spaces. This time no dogs accompanied her. They stayed, dozing and well fed, with Prad. Death and blood seemed starker than previously, and those wafting smells the dogs adored, were what she was now learning to hate.

Ready for business, Wren stopped at the Bailey's Butchers where she had often shopped before. Avoiding the swing of the meat above, Wren pointed at the small sheep hanging further back into the shadows. "A shoulder is all I want," she said. "That one," and she pointed, "perhaps. How long has it hung?"

"Just two days," the butcher, round faced, pursed his lips.

"Then I'll take that shoulder. It's smaller than the others so it's just right for me."

Wren didn't watch as the entire weight of the body was slammed onto the stone topped table inside the shop, and the butcher, his round face now crimson with exertion, raised his cleaver. The smooth cut fell clean, and the meat seemed fine, without the suspicious stink of decay, or the crawl of flies sheltering from the cold.

She stood longer than was comfortable, clutching the bag she had brought to hold whatever she acquired, but it was Newgate she was watching now, the huge threat of the gaol standing at the end of the street. She prayed silently that her new work would not mean her arrest and imprisonment there, as it often had for Landry.

Wren found Landry at home for a change, he was outside talking to Prad, Arthur nuzzling his neck. He unlocked the door for her and followed her up the steps to his living-room.

"I'm going to cook dinner," she said, unpacking her bag on the table. She bent to fix the trivet over the fire, and reassemble the spit, sliding its point through the shoulder of lamb. Then she crouched on the floor, slowly turning the handle.

"Prad could do that," Landry told her. "I'd offer myself if I was less of an expert at avoiding boredom."

"I've done it before, but I'll rest when my hand burns." she said, "I've already cut figs and shelled the winter beans. They're in the pan, and I'll put them on the trivet once the meat's almost cooked."

"You've planned a feast." He grinned at her.

"Because it's Saint Nicholas' Day. The Christmas season has begun. Haven't you counted the days, soon it'll be mid-December."

"Then we need Prad," Landry repeated. "Otherwise, he'll sit down there on the hay all day. I'll call him. He can turn the spit handle for you."

Wren was grateful. She had no desire to acquire more burns, already her fingers felt scalded. "While at the Shambles, I was thinking. There wasn't any slaughtering going on, but I've seen it other times. It's sickening. I never go there on a Friday." Landry raised an eyebrow. "Shoppers go to the fishmongers so butchers can do their butchering in peace, but it's not peaceful or quiet for the animals. What I mean is," Wren said in a rush, "This murderer we're looking for, he didn't like blood, did he. He was no butcher. Poisoning before the hanging. I'd guess he found bloody hacking as revolting as I do. He's cold hearted and disgusting and evil, but he's not a person wallowing in the slaughter."

"Correct, little partner. Unlike most killers. Yet, since there was likely more than one killer, their characters could be varied." Although his words were serious, he was smiling, even his eyes seemed warm. "Now, before the meat burns, I suggest you call Prad."

The chance of a sweet evening with only Landry for company

was disappearing. She marched downstairs. "Prad, sorry to interrupt, are you busy? If not, then Landry's hoping you'll come up. Do you know it's Christmas?"

"Umm," said Prad, sitting up. He had been sprawled on the dry straw beside Arthur. "You sure?"

Immediately doubting herself, Wren once again changed the subject. "Well, I'm cooking dinner anyway and you're invited, and Landry asks that you to turn the spit."

"He would." Prad staggered upwards. "I had a good drink last night. My head aches, but no matter, I'm coming." Having padded upstairs behind Wren, Prad saw the meat speared on the spit over the crackling flames across the grate, and his eyes glinted. "I will certainly join you to eat, just as long as you don't have me burn these fingers so bad I can't touch my dinner."

"Get working," Landry grinned. "This is Wren's grand Christmas feast, so it's her you have to thank for the food, and me to thank for the burned fingers."

⭙

Once it was cooked, the lamb fell from its bone in a gentle layer of fat and burnished skin both sizzled, and the roasted meat perfumes were bewitching. They seeped into the woodwork, the cushions and the stone hearth, creeping up the old brick chimney like moths in the night. The meat, now on the huge platter, oozed its own juices as Landry began to cut the thick slices, sharing onto three smaller platters where the roast figs, onion and winter beans had already been divided.

Prad, enthusiastic, was open mouthed. Wren said, "Looks good, smells even better."

Landry continued to carve the joint. "I have neither the space nor the patience to lay out platters for you to help yourselves."

"Whichever platter you think is mine," said Wren, "has too much on it already."

"Nonsense," Landry told her. "Food is good for you, and having bought it, you deserve a generous portion. Here. Now eat."

She was still eating, and Landry was pouring ale from the barrel tucked beneath the stairs, when Prad stretched and rubbed is stomach, "Well that was flaming wonderful, but now I suppose we got to talk about that fellow Cadby?"

Landry passed the full cup. "Naturally."

Wren gulped her last mouthful. She had not planned the feast as a meeting to discuss work. "You mean Cadby who tried to burn the eel shop?"

"A man you're shortly about to know better," Landry told her. "He's due here soon, if he turns up as agreed. Having had a good deal of time to think over everything I told him, I'm assuming he has a great deal to say. If not, then I shall – let us say – encourage him to do so."

"Threatening him with gaol for burning down shops," mumbled Prad.

"I feel sorry for him." Wren seemed uncomfortable. "Losing your wife, your daughter and your granddaughter in one week, is tragic."

"Yet revenge on someone who committed none of those deaths, is an act of absurd spite."

"But I told lies to the court, and got my father free."

"As most daughters would," Landry nodded. "And most of what you said, was what you believed true at the time. Nor was the shop your property. The attempt at revenge was stupid, but in a few hours, unless he changes his mind and runs, he will be here to explain, and hear the truth. It should be interesting, and he is still one of our suspects in the killing of your friends, although he is at the bottom of my list."

"He's at the top of mine," Prad said, scowling,

"And the earl agrees. Even your strange priest?"

Landry drank his ale and smiled. "Morgan's input in this business is one of generosity and encouragement. I rarely listen to his opinions. Jacob, on the other hand, has not yet decided, but will be here within the hour, and will take an equal interest in what Cadby Bracks has to say."

Sipping at her ale, Wren was digesting the best food she'd eaten in a year or more, and enjoying the comfort as she sat on the second settle, with the blue downy cushion at the back of her neck. The smell of roast lamb remained, although Landry had removed what small part was left, into a cupboard, door shut.

She said, "What a long strange Saint Nicholas' Day this will be. I suppose I'm pleased."

"More so when I uncork the wine barrel," Landry smiled. The wooden tub balanced above the ale barrel, both were oak and mightily heavy, while full beyond the bilges. Both were kept in the shadow under the stairs.

Bending to remove the spit, Prad put it onto another empty platter, and pulled off the scraps of meat. "For the dogs," he nodded, "though they don't care what day it is."

The heat of the fire still sizzled when Jacob arrived in a swoop of snow spattered cloak and mud encrusted boots. He brought the wind in with him, and marched at once to the fire, held out his trembling fingers to the flames, and drank in the blazing reflections. The flying snowflakes shot from his clothes to the ceiling beams, chimney, red rug and table.

"A day of reverence and celebration, of holy prayer and joy," Jacob said, both cape and boots now kicked to a corner beneath the shuttered window. "The start of the Christmas season, thanks to the blessed Saint Nicholas, and good luck to all those priests on their knees in the snow and ice, setting up their scenes of the nativity." The priest crossed himself. "Blessings on the birth of Christianity, good wine and the discovery of a criminal, even our Lord Jesus Christ would have loathed."

"I thought our Lord loved and forgave everyone?"

"My dear Miss," Jacob smiled at Wren, "murder is one of the deadly sins, and this sinner has certainly not yet been forgiven."

"Nor by myself, though it would help if we knew who he was."

Landry pointed to the wine jug. "And stop swirling around, man. You're covered in snow and it's damaging my Turkey Rugs."

"Most nativity scenes include the snow beneath the manger," Jacob objected.

"I thought Jerusalem was a hot country," Wren bounced up to pour the wine, including replenishing Landry's cup.

"Frankly, I have no idea," said the priest, claiming the second settle. "Never been there. Never will. But the sixth day of December is a day to be celebrated across the country."

"Yet my tree of suspects," Landry smiled, tapping one finger against his own head, "although a few shadows now cling to the roots, recognises Cadby only as a chestnut at the end of a small branch, and about to fall."

"I've come to meet our dabbler in fire, Cadby Bracks," Jacob said, happily accepting the over-flowing cup. "but depending on what he says and does, I might consider killing the swine myself."

Not having expected such a remark from a priest, Wren hovered, then sat next to him with a wide smile of surprise, crossed her arms, sank back and awaited the wine-induced pleasure she knew would follow.

CHAPTER TWENTY ONE

WREN

Landry's coldness was slowly melting.

He spoke with humour, he smiled, he even laughed. He had enjoyed the dinner I'd cooked, and he had explained so much.

Then he had invited me to join him in the work I'd never known he was doing. And brought with it an excitement whizzing around in my head, in a way I had never felt before.

I'd thought only children experienced excitement, though I didn't even remember knowing it when I was young myself. I'd accepted life as a monotony of duty and necessity, but this was so different. I also have a buzz inside, which is more fear than excitement, and that tells me that Landry would kill me if I ever proved untrustworthy.

I was gradually discovering more about myself, and that made me think of all the things I'd never even glimpsed before. I don't remember having a mother, but despite Dad's confusions about her death, I'm damned sure she must have been around at some point. Then it was just him, and of course he was never warm and comforting. He poked, punched, pinched and made me work, washing and cooking when I hardly knew the words. So – simple soul that I am – the slightest comforting touch was wonderful to me, and so far, Landry was the only one who'd ever done it.

Cadby definitely wasn't going to bring excitement, trepidation though was definitely present

It was so long since I'd seen Magg's father, and I really hadn't wanted to see him now. Feeling wretchedly sorry for the man, didn't mean I wanted to spend the evening with him.

He trudged slowly up the stairs as though his back was broken, and just stood silent in the upper doorway, while Prad tried to push in past him. Evidently it had started to snow again and Cadby's shoulders were dappled with it, and over the top of his small black hat. His boots were covered in slush. Short, skinny, hook nosed and black eyed, he appeared half starved.

I whispered to Landry, "Give him the left-overs." I knew not much remained, but they would be appreciated by someone half starved.

Landry nodded to Prad to unearth the food, and then nodded to the man himself. "Come in Cadby. Join us."

I think Cadby had half expected a knife in the back, so sitting down to a hearty dinner, even if cold, seemed a glorious surprise. The little man was awfully polite about it, and expressed his gratitude so often, it got a little annoying.

As usual I didn't know what to say, and it was Landry who interrupted his repast.

"You are welcome, Master Bracks, for reasons I shall explain while you continue to eat and drink. Naturally you don't know me, and I doubt you know Father Jacob here. However, you may know Mistress Wren Bennet. We are all deeply sorry for the recent loss of your wife, your daughter, and also sadly your granddaughter. That is partially the reason for this invitation."

Cadby looked up, a half-eaten fig between his fingers. "You mean for pity?"

"Not exactly," continued Landry. "Sympathy, certainly. However, there is another reason, and the presence of Wren Bennet may indicate part of it."

Refusing to answer, Cadby kept his eyes on the platter and cup before him, eating and drinking fast. He clearly expected trouble and possibly intended starting some himself, but food came first. He was a fair way from home, and obviously hungry, while too poor to eat at any of the taverns or pie shops. I sympathised.

The food finished, the poor man scraped his spoon around and around, trying to capture any final drip of pleasure stuck to the earthenware.

Seeing all our eyes stuck to his every move, he coughed and mumbled. "This ain't been a good year for me." He sniffed, gathered himself and stuck his nose into the wine cup. "I had time to stop and admire every nativity scene before every church, and there was a play with music set up in the courtyard by St. Pauls."

It was Father Jacob who picked up on this thread. "Indeed," he said politely, "all members of the clergy will have their Christmas presentations ready for St. Nicholas's Day. Now may I introduce myself in a little more detail? As Father, I administer to the inmates of Newgate Gaol, such a sad and needy extension of my parish. I work principally at the church of Saint Nicholas nearby. I therefore hold no bias, no anger and no desire for vengeance. I have no intention of involving sheriffs nor guards. The conversation will be between ourselves alone."

Swallowing loudly, Cadby looked up. "I'll talk to you, Father, but I'll not speak with that female present."

"You don't need to answer me or speak with me," I said at once. "but, I want to say something important, so please listen. Firstly, I want to apologise for not knowing the facts when I stood witness for my father at his trial. None of us knew, and at the time, I presume you didn't know either. Back then I said what I truly believed. In court I said what I'd heard and I'm still not absolutely sure of the truth, but now I know I was at least a little bit mistaken. Perhaps more. If I was really wrong, then I'm sorry. So very sorry."

Cadby gazed down at the table, gripped his cup between both hands, and stayed adamantly silent.

For the few moments the only sound was the spit of the fire, to which Prad had added two more small logs. They sent glorious beams of scarlet light darting across the room, chasing the shadows.

At least Cadby was surely now warm and less hungry. He'd not left a single fig seed. The two dogs lay stretched as usual beside the hearth, but I knew they'd leap up if Cadby started fighting. Surely, he wasn't stupid enough to attack while so outnumbered.

It was Landry who spoke next. He stood and wandered over to the unshuttered window.

"It's still snowing," he said in that soft icy voice, "but our fire burns well. You have eaten, and both wine and ale are offered when you wish. You are welcome. None of us plot or plan, and none of us wish to harm you in any manner. The home is mine, but you may talk with whoever you prefer. We have only simple questions."

"I'll speak to the priest," Cadby muttered.

"Very well." Landry nodded. "First, I wish you to know that I did not agree with Mistress Bennet when she declared her father innocent at trial. However, daughters tend to support their parents, and she did not know the true story. Are you sure you know them, Master Bracks?"

Those silken iced eyes always demanded obedience. So now although he'd said he'd only talk to Jacob, he answered Landry.

Cadby was blinking a tear-filled gaze. "I knew. You think me a fool? The midwife was my dearest Magg's friend of many years, and she'd nursed her before and after the birth. When Maggs came to say farewell to her dear mother, she told us that Sara had taken the baby for safekeeping. Maggs only stayed two days. My sweet Effie died at dawn on the second day. I wanted my daughter to stay for the funeral, but she said she had to rush back for the baby. Then that foul husband of hers, sailed home and killed them both."

I interrupted, which didn't help. "I knew nothing about the midwife. I knew Maggs had gone away for six days and left the baby to starve. When Dad saw his baby daughter lying dead, just bones, he thought Maggs – well – it was his reaction – temper. He told me it was all an accident."

"An accident? First half strangled. Then your vile father's knife through my daughter's neck. No accident, just murder."

I hung my head. I thought she'd fallen downstairs as Dad told me, and he had seemed genuinely upset. Now it sounded so awful. At least he could have talked to her first. Dad wasn't a monster, just a useless pig and I didn't think Landry had any way of knowing the truth, any more than I had. Neither of us had been there watching.

It could have been murder. It could have been an accident. I'd thought about it so often over the past week, and since every detail I'd been told immediately contradicted the details anyone else had told me, I was left thinking the actual truth was probably different again. I had even gone looking for the midwife. I knew her, so it should have been easy enough – but no – why should anything be easy these days? One muddle after another. The midwife had gone off somewhere. One disappearance after another.

"Poor wretched little Hannah, six days alone. Six days starved, and she wasn't even a week old. She must have screamed and screamed. Why didn't the neighbours hear the baby screaming and look to help?"

"Because," and Cadby looked at me with eyes so nasty, I felt sick again. Landry's eyes were ice, but Cadby's were black fire, "everyone hated your bloody father."

Now it was Landry who interrupted. "Another question it seems, little bird, and one I shall follow up. But these tragic deaths are the sad background to my questions." He turned to Cadby again. "This tragic story alters a little each time, depending on who tells it, but whatever the details, I understand your fury, but cannot altogether sympathise. Why did you come to the eel shop and set the fire to kill? Why race for revenge instead of praying and mourning the loss of your family?"

Cadby's silence dragged on. He was staring down at his twitching fingers resting on the table. Finally, he spoke but his mumble was hard to hear. "Rage. Misery. I didn't know where to find Haldon Bennet, but Maggs had told me where Wren worked. I wanted to kill the world."

"A girl no older than your daughter?"

"Who lied in court and swore her father hadn't done what I knew he had."

I was feeling so damned guilty and so horribly sad, I could do nothing but watch Cadby looking haunted.

Again, Landry barely raised his voice. "Rage at the horror of a man slaughtering the innocent. Yet that was exactly what you also set out to do."

Finally, Father Jacob spoke, "In the Lord's name, I can forgive those we speak of. Such a terrible tragedy brings a sadness, impossible to digest. Trying to blank out that misery, we turn to anger. But acts of cruelty must stop here." He was looking only at Cadby. "Another appalling act of sin occurred nearby just before your attempt to start the fire. A family of four were murdered in their home. I would not accuse, nor imagine that you would commit such an act on strangers, but I need to know what, if anything, you saw. You were in the right area for several days, plotting your vengeance. Your own actions are forgiven, but what did you see of others?"

Of course, it hadn't been him and he hadn't seen anything either. He'd just been one of the possibilities, which needed clearing up too.

Cadby was looking horrified all over again. "Four folk killed? A whole family?" He was crying again, a silent weeping he seemed unable to control.

"Mother, father, their son of nine years and another son of only four or five years." Father Jacob was almost whispering. "I have announced the Last Rights for Maggs Bracks, Hannah Bennet, and for each member of the Ford family. Blessed each one with the necessary rites and penitence on their behalf."

I'd never heard of this being done by any other priest, but I certainly didn't know everything about the church doctrines. I just hoped it would help both the dead and the living.

I watched the snow falling outside the window through the cracks in the shutters. Prad had closed them, and it brought an even greater cosiness. Prad had also lit three beeswax candles and the tiny flames threw their reflections against the larger ones covering walls and ceiling, but I was staring through those shutter cracks. The swirling snow was thicker now, a white curtain closed off the world outside.

Cadby just sat like a vacant sculpture, like the saints in churches, though not as pretty. Then I realised he was still crying. "Death," he said, "it rules the world. We all die. It would be better if we weren't ever born."

"The deaths we speak of," Landry leaned forwards, "were not simply dying, but evil killings. That is very different, and that is why I am here, to find true justice."

So Cadby sobbed like I had, too often for me, but he had every reason. Stupid or not, I nearly joined him. I just couldn't think of a baby starving to death. I started hating all the neighbours, the midwife too. So unfair, but anger writhed inside me. Then I realised I was doing what Cadby had done, without even being sure of the truth.

It was the world perhaps, that I hated. Though it had never been kind to me, it had been far worse to others. I wished I could lie down and sleep and pretend it had never happened.

Landry woke me from my meanderings. Then he stared at Cadby again. "Before setting fire to the eel shop, where did you sleep?"

Sniffing, "Against the door several houses up the road. There was a concrete ledge over the door. The only one with a spit of shelter. Not real shelter, but a little."

"That was next door to the Fords," I said at once. "On the other side to the Duffs."

Now we all paid attention. Landry spoke even softer. "And who did you see? Who entered the house next to you?"

I suppose he felt under scrutiny, as if we suspected him. "We know it wasn't you," I said quickly, "but did anyone go in next door, and if so, who was it?"

I looked hopefully at Cadby who frowned back.

And that was when all hell's demons let loose outside, screaming, shouting, banging. Cadby rushed back into a dark corner against the wall, while Landry and Prad went racing down the stairs. I sat frozen on the settle, and Father Jacob turned white as the snow.

None of us had the faintest idea of who was pounding on the door and shouting up at the windows, but it sounded like a vicious mob. The horses, who had been standing quietly in a chilly doze, now woke, kicked, snorted and neighed in fear. I was suddenly afraid. It didn't help when both dogs leapt up and barked even louder than the chaos downstairs.

CHAPTER TWENTY TWO

NARRATIVE

Wrenching open the door, Landry glared at the group standing in the falling snow.

Prad rushed past him to get to the horses, calming them. One kicked him and Landry, furious, heard the yelp.

"What in the name of Mercy are you wanting here?" Landry demanded.

The Watch had been called. They held flaming torches high, and behind them reappeared the Newgate guards. No sign of the placid sheriff who was presumably asleep in a warm bed. The torches, held high, were spitting, the flames first cowered into thin windy stripes and then doused in a waxy puddle.

Three men walked the Watch each night, but had never before needed to tramp through these mews. "We've had complaints," the first man said, large eyes beneath the brim of his snow-covered hood.

Landry stared. "The absurd rampage of some hours past," Landry said through his teeth, "was the work of those guards behind you. Unwanted, and un-needed. This house and the entire Mews has been sitting in sweet silence for the last several hours."

"I beg your pardon," said the leader of the Watch, now relighting his torch from one of the others. It sizzled and flared. "but when there's news of a fight or possible danger, I'll always be wanting to find the truth."

"We need no help," Landry said, "and the existing danger left when those fools behind you left. Yet the fools are back again. Take them with you as you leave. They're unwanted here."

"Ahha," roared the leader of the Newgate Guard, pushing forwards between the men of the Watch until his nose almost touched Landry's. "You may not want us, my man, but it seems we want you. The escaped criminal, Landry Crawford, you'll come with us now."

Sighing, Landry shook his head, the glare remaining. "You know well that the royal guard explained my royal dispensation. You may feel thwarted, fool, but the king's protection overrides everything else. So, you'll get away from my doorstep now, or I'll have my groom ride directly to the palace."

The leader of the Watch wavered, stepping back. The Newgate guard's leader pushed forward, full of rage and determination, considering himself the master now. He looked up and snarled, showing crooked teeth and the gap in the centre thickly cabbage decorated. "I know that woman sitting up on them steps. I reckon she's forged that Royal Pardon."

Both dogs, having first leapt up from their comfy sleeping, now sat obediently beside Wren, and continued their persistent barking, both angry and frightened.

Wren had attempted to calm them and was sitting on the top stair, each arm wrapped around a dog's furry neck. Now she stood, glaring down. "Yes, I've met you, how dare you accuse me of such rubbish. You don't know a damn thing about me." Now she shouted in such a rush, no one properly understood her. "I'm Wren Bennet. How dare you suggest I forged anything. Besides, it was royal dispensation, not a pardon. Nothing was done that needed pardoning."

The three men of the Watch kept back, ready to see what might happen next. The Newgate guard had taken over and the leader's shout was louder than the dogs. Arthur was kicking at his stable door and Prad, hurrying from a different stable further along the Mews, again ran back to calm him.

The Newgate leader stamped as loudly as the horses and the slush of snow splattered into his furious face. "I'm telling you now, whatever you think you are, tis my warrant I'm serving. I got authority from the baron hisself, arrest Landry Crawford, as that protection rubbish is a fraud."

"What baron? There is no baron renting any property here." Father Jacob marched towards the confused mass, and held up the cross he had been using before. "I personally witnessed the Royal Seal of Protection, and its presentation at Westminster Palace."

"I'll not argue with a man of the Holy Cloth," the leader of the guards hurried back, crossing himself, "but the baron can't be wrong."

"Then tis time for that arrest." Another of the guards pushed inside the open door and waved his fist. "And I reckon that female too." He glared up at Wren. "Gave false witness, you did, and there's no king's dispensation for you, miss."

"Not unless you have a warrant," Landry said, pulling him once again outside and into the snow. "You'll not barge into a private home to arrest a law-abiding woman without reason or without a legal warrant."

The horses were in uproar. The guardsmen were shouting, one waving a knife over the other heads.

The Watch stamped, raising the torches and shouting for quiet. "We're leaving," called the leader. "I've no rule over the Prison Guard." He once again disappeared into the shadow of his hood, but the voice echoed beyond the dark. "But I'll pass information, if you ask for it, Master Crawford."

"Yes indeed." Speaking deliberately slowly, virtually imperious, Landry wore no hood, but his eyes were as dark, hooded by his brows. "You'll inform the Mayor of these unlawful demands and outright injustice, and get a ruling for these buffoons to run back to their gaol."

The leader of the Watch touched his hood, nodding, and thrust his path beyond the stamping mass, his two companions close behind, and their torches held almost into the faces of the guard.

Remy, one of the earl's horses on the opposite side of the Mews, a destrier once trained for the battlefield, was screaming in fear, kicking out and rearing. As Prad rushed over to the vibrating stable, the stallion then calmed, snorted a roar before Prad blew into the stallion's nostrils, calming him further, and stroking the snow flecked mane.

Prad was exhausted, rushing from one stable to another, each horse he calmed then rearing once more as he hurriedly left. Beneath the riot of horses and dogs, little else could be easily heard, with each man shouting louder than his companions. The snow continued to fall yet brought no sweet hush. Crowds out to watch the mummings, plays and join the singing beside each holy nativity, had now deserted their late evening celebrations and stood staring, pushing into the Mews, curious to see what caused all the noise.

"You want the Earl o' Thamesdon to go marching to the palace again?" Prad called, a roar as loud as the horse in anger. "I'll ride there now, if you try and touch that innocent young woman."

Landry barred his own doorstep. "You'll leave now," he said, voice hard, eyes colder, "unless you want to risk your jobs, perhaps your lives."

"We're leaving," the chief guard shouted. "But I warn you all, if I get a warrant, I'll be marching back for both of you. Two warrants, and at least one for the hangman's noose."

They pushed at each other, turning to leave, while cursing over their shoulders. Wren had released both dogs. They now jumped the stairs and rushed to the doorstep, barking and snarling. The departing guards quickened, but the leader yelled, "And I'll report you for them dogs too."

"They're not my dogs," Wren yelled back, and Landry laughed, shepherding her back up the stairs, dogs at his heels. The outer door slammed.

Landry had snow in his hair and the dogs were white coated.

Prad was now also covered in the freezing snow, and it fell from him like a soft cloak of downy feathers. He leaned back against the door as the others returned to the room above. Quivering and wet, Red and Shadow settled again, stretching before the fire. Their breathing calmed, eyes closed, while the snow melted onto the rug in small puddles. "It's crazy," Wren muttered as she shook the snow from her hair. "How many times do they want to make this ridiculous attempt" They're turning up almost daily to arrest you."

She couldn't tell whether Landry was angry, or simply amused. "Clearly the guards have been punished, their pay docked or some such, for their incompetence at letting a vile criminal escape without ever bringing him back for trial."

"Perhaps they think you're going to pay them off."

"They'll have to pay off the royal guard themselves if they keep this up," Prad muttered, now slouching in the doorway.

Cadby had remained in the corner until Landry's reappearance. He crept from the shadows and stood facing the confusion, waiting to see what would happen. Landry grinned at him. "You, Master Bracks, have been thrust into some highly unfortunate situations. Now, will you answer my last question? Since you have no proper home in the city and it's now too late to walk the miles back to your own bed, I suggest you sleep here. It will only be a cushioned floor, or, if you prefer, the straw above the stables where Prad and two other grooms sleep, but it's warm and safe. I'll happily offer a blanket or two."

"The stable straw," Cadby muttered, now staring down at his boots, "that's a mighty good offer, and a blanket. I thank you most sincerely."

"But first," Landry repeated with a yawn, "an answer to my question. Did you see, and if so, can you describe those entering the home of the Ford family, just two doors from where you stayed."

The small man was hesitant. "It's hard to remember, you see. Not knowing, back then, it being important, which it wasn't to me. Yes, very difficult. I think I did. I'd say a man and a woman, but this was days before – well, you know what before. Naught to do with what happened later."

"Describe the man and the woman, as best you can."

Cadby shook his head and rubbed his eyes. He still stared at nothing above the level of his boots. "A big man. I remember big shoulders, but it's hard, you see, and the woman, I remember very little. A dark gown under a short dark cape. I don't even know what day it was, and maybe they just walked past. Tis impossible to be sure."

He fell silent and then clutching the blanket Prad brought him, was led away to a bed over Arthur's, dry hay for both, the smell of horse droppings hopefully mellowed by the smell of straw. The mumbled thankyous disappeared into their echoes.

Father Jacob appeared to have enjoyed the puppet show played out before him. "Amusing, but badly scripted." He grinned, shaking his head.

"Not that you achieved any improvements," Landry pointed out.

"Since I never know your intentions, your plans or prepared untruths," smiled Father Jacob, "I prefer to let you master your own battles."

"It was fairly clear," Landry said, "that the arrival of the Watch and those damned idiots, was no plan of mine. Simply an added irritation. I'd hoped for more from the other fool, but the visit of the man and woman, if he remembered correctly, was possibly of some interest."

"Cadby," said Father Jacob, "described what might have been true. Where he was staying might have been confused, and even his misery and anger at the death of his daughter could have been false. That is a man who lacks the confidence to speak at all. He'll hide and start a vengeful fire, but he'll never face the one he truly hates, nor risk the truth which might bring trouble from some other path."

Wren had begun to remove the platters and cups in need of washing, and mopping the puddles brought in by each of them, including the dogs. "He hates me," she said briefly, "but doesn't say it. Yet he had the courage to speak against my father, though not to his face. He's going to be so damned lonely from now on."

"I shall try to discover more, regarding visitors to the Ford household, including this possible man and woman." Landry lounged back on the settle, as Wren clanked terracotta within the cold-water bucket. "I might even permit a return to Newgate after all. A wretched place but holds fascinating gossip."

"Do it," Father Jacob nodded. "And I shall take confessions."

"You expect someone to confess to murders when already in gaol, with everyone listening?" Wren said, placing the crockery on the shelf to dry from the warmth of the fire."

Prad, now back on the landing, was waiting for the moment to interrupt. Landry raised one eyebrow. Prad said, "If you don't need more, then I'll follow the fool, say goodnight to Arthur, and talk about the Fords and their visitors. Easy enough while he's tired."

"By all means." Watching Prad leave, Landry pushed his head back to the settle's final balanced cushion. "I also have a few ideas, but I must admit, that none of these are hopeful of finding the solution."

Wren leaned against the wall behind the buckets, breathed deeply and swallowed on a gulp. "I could go back to Newgate myself. If I surrender to that idiot guard, without him having a warrant, he can't keep me in. I'd be safe, but I can put up with a night and a day. They can't keep me any longer, can they!"

The slant of surprise was briefly visible. "An unnecessary risk," Landry said, immediately returning to his usual expressionless diffidence. "And women are now separated from the men, once incarcerated, you'd be talking with whores and cut-purses, a heap of wretched women accused of beating their husbands even while defending themselves, and others stealing to feed their children. Nothing of that is likely to help."

"I was quite friendly with a young woman who sometimes walked the streets for money," Wren said through a distinct glare. "She worked at the licenced house on the Bridge, because her husband was crippled. I liked her."

Landry answered her. "Like any group, little bird, there are always the good, and the bad."

Wren stared back, unsure whether he was thinking her incapable.

"I could do it, and see if any of the women know anything useful. I'm not a coward."

Abruptly, Wren stopped speaking, looking at the fire spread over the hearth, and then at the door to the stairs. Finally, she ran to the window. Landry and Jacob looked confused, but after a pause, she spoke in a rush, loud and sharp. "I can smell burning from downstairs. There's a fire."

CHAPTER TWENTY THREE

NARRATIVE

Landry jumped the back of the settle and flung open the door leading to the stairs. The dogs were barking again, then howling. Father Jacob was trying to open the shutters at the window, and Wren ran behind Landry, the dogs close at her side.

She yelled, "Cadby is mad, he hates me, but why kill the innocent?"

The priest left the window, dropped the shutters, and pulled open the door. "I'm worried for Prad."

"And us?"

Landry was already down the stairs and opening the outer door. The stench of burning rose in the smoke. Outside the chaos swirled as horses broke free of loose wooden enclosures, others kicking in terror, rearing and trying to burst free.

From the night's shadows and the sudden streak of scarlet flame, Prad ran to Landry. "I let Arthur run," he shouted over the pounding and spitting. "He knows where to go. Reckon I should let them all free?

"Do it," Landry yelled, his voice no longer soft ice, but as wild as the flames themselves. "At worst they'll escape fire and death, and there's ten will know to gallop back to the manor. Others – well - lost but living at least." He ran to the far shadows of the Mews where the flames hadn't yet reached, pulling open the stables where screaming horses shivered in fear. Every animal galloped west, giddy and frantic.

Landry's home was now alight. Wren grabbed the water bucket, sluicing down the steps leading up to what she now thought of as her home too, dousing the crackled and creeping sizzle, then on to the empty stables and the flare of hay and straw. She'd not had the time to tie up her hair, and singe threatened, as her loose curls sweeping around her face as she ran.

The snow still dithered from sky to ground yet across the growing heat of the cobbles, it melted. Over the stone it was a slide of broken ice and the slush and slip of wet dirt. At the closed end of the Mews where the last stable was wide, that normally held horses left by customers to the taverns and markets. The flames were now strong and flared high, eating into hanging bridles and the thick laid straw, but this was not the weather for market or tavern, and there had been no more horses.

It was Saint Nicholas's Day and across the city the church bells were ringing for midnight. One minute past, and St. Nicholas's Day crept out but no stars were visible above the rising scarlet of the flames.

The dogs had almost tripped Wren, keeping close and barking frantically into the uproar. There was shouting, horses escaping, men racing about, as the flames swirled upwards against the night, leaping from stable to stable. The burning straw floated upwards, ash and cinders were caught in the wind, carrying fire from one point to the next. Horse owners from the local tavern burst up the Mews, doors burned, men slipped and fell, their hats burned, their hair burned, friends dragged them clear, screaming to help them.

Two young grooms woke and slithered from ladder to blaze. Landry grabbed one. "Run to the next street and bring the rain tubs from outside the houses."

Wren felt the scorch across her shoulders, and twisted, falling abruptly into the snow puddled below, then darting away from the mill of flame and windblown ash.

The blazing heat at the Mews' closure, was now leaping into the homes that backed the walls there. One dog cowered, its tongue hanging, its throat too sore for barking, but the other had fled. Wren screamed, "Red, here," but no dog returned. Scrambling up, her hair and the back of her clothes now soaked, Wren saw Prad tipping water over new flames in the waning shadows. Wren grabbed his shoulder. "Cadby did this, didn't he?"

Prad stared, confused. "Poor little bugger was asleep. I pulled him safe. Reckon he'll run. Too much of a coward to help."

One great black stallion, lost and bewildered, had galloped his way back to what he knew as home, turning, dizzy, kicking up dirty water. From the other end of the cobbles, a groom just returned from church saw the stallion and rushed to grab him, one arm to his tail, calling and pulling. "Neddy, I'll get you safe, calm now," and threw himself onto the horse's bare back, using his mane as a bridle, and leaning forward to whisper in the flattened back ears. Within moments, they had gone.

The buckets had held water for the horses, other tubs caught rainwater, but now all were empty. Yet still the fire grew.

A hand gripped Wren's arm, pulling her backwards. She wrestled away but the grip was the stronger and Landry shouted into her hair. "Get out while you can. This is beyond us. Rain would help but snow doesn't. Get out before it's too late."

"You too?" Wren shouted back.

"I have a place to go," he told her. "I can't take you. I'll find you in a day or two. Just get yourself somewhere safe."

"And you find Cadby and kill him." Wren was crying now, one hand to the dog's neck, the other wiping her eyes.

"He's dead already."

The small body lay cradled by flame. As the fire surged, the back of Arthur's stable which had supported Landry's house, had been destroyed. Lower down, where water bubbled in the heat, the blackened wood and planks were now little more than splinters.

The collapse of the higher ledges, used by grooms for shelter and sleep, had built a pitch of soot and ashes, a mess of destruction, still hot with flying cinders. And there, beneath the piled horror, lay the one poor soul eaten by the blaze.

One of the horses sniffed at the cinder covered corpse, then turned and galloped away. Wren reached out one finger to Cadby's scorched face. "Justice, then. Killed by his own fire. And saved from loneliness, and possibly gaol."

The ruin gradually mounted as the fire surrendered to the hurtling water, the cold, and the battle from the newly returned grooms and others, who, hearing the onslaught, had rushed out to help and to save their own homes in the streets behind and beyond.

Finally, after nearly four hours, only the stink remained, along with the wretched, fleshless remains, of a man who had never even lived there.

Clutching to the sides of the remaining dog, both shivering with fatigue and fear, Wren stared down at Cadby. The body was cooked, the smell increasing. The body's remaining clothes were ragged and partially burned. The hair was now only ashes, the midriff showing its bones, the hips jutting upwards in pale nudity, as the water below had kept some of the flesh intact. The grimace of pain and fear also remained.

Renewed courage had kept her fighting and her ragged skirts were now singed at the hems, her hair still gathered sparks, and in utter exhaustion Wren stood limp, half bent, half crying, half furious. "He deserves it," Wren muttered, trying to burn away her own disgust and pity.

Prad called from a distance. "Mistress, tis not safe yet. Get to a friend if there's one near." And finally, with his face and hands scorched and smeared with soot, Prad ran.

It was not so far to the eel shop, and Wren stumbled from the horror, into the main street, then slanting off and finally facing Pansy's shop which had once been home. Here, the night sky held echoes. No stars powered through the pink haze above, and a faint reminder of the stench of burning, oozed into the cracks in the windows and through the draughts beneath the doors. But the fire hadn't reached here, and the shop stood sedate, dark, closed, and whole.

Sinking down to the front doorstep, Wren leaned her head against the wooden solidity of the entrance, closed her eyes, and tried to throw off the panic and the thump of her heartbeat. Now long past midnight, and thinking morning must be close, she thought she would never sleep again, but within moments she slept, her skirts dragging into the snow clad cobbles.

The shop opened early, Wren awoke without knowing how long she might have dreamed of disaster, and thumped on the door. Pansy peeped out, startled, and quickly helped Wren into the warmth.

"Where in mercy's name have you come from?" Pansy squeaked, kneeling, her hands already white with flour.

"It wasn't that far." Wren tried to stand, hoisting herself with both hands to the counter frame. "There was a fire. Everything burned. And me almost with it. It was horrible."

"That explains your hair."

Wren gulped. "I haven't anywhere to go. Can I – just for a night or two – stay here? I'll work."

"You want a bed for just two nights?" Pansy sniffed. "Bit of a cheek, isn't it? Are you hurt? Well, you walked out on me and left me with no help at all, and now you think I should help you?"

Wren also sniffed, but her reason was quite different. "I gave you notice. You said you'd find someone better. Then I came back and helped with making pies."

"I suppose you did." Pansy half smiled. "Well, you can stay two nights and make pies. No pay. Is that a deal?"

Staring, Wren said, "You've enough flour and onions for that much?"

"I reckon so."

Customers had evidently increased. "I'll do it, but I can't make many pies if I have to serve people as well."

"No, Bryce'll do that." Now Pansy was grinning. "Didn't you

know? We're a real pair. He loves me, well, I love him too – but he's a fair bit more smitten than I am. He's helpful and such a nice gentleman."

Wren realised her mouth was hanging open, and snapped it shut. She simply nodded. There was no possibility of identifying Bryce until she met him. Then she would know if he was the Newgate inmate she had met, or a different man altogether, the unlikely lawyer who had seemingly given up his work, to help a woman serve cooked eels.

"So, I work two days and sleep in my old bed?"

"That's what I said."

"And I can sleep now? An hour, perhaps, or more if you let me." Her hair was singed, her face was as white as the snow, in spite of the sooty smudges, and she appeared both frozen and exhausted. "Please, just let me sleep two hours and then I'll start work. I'll work faster and I'll make fifty pies even if I have to work after you shut the shop." She looked and sounded desperate. A woman with that appearance would be a bad advertisement in a busy shop, and Bryce might complain. Pansy knew which problem was best avoided.

"Yeah, that's fine. Go up now. I'll carry on making the dumplings. In two hours, I'll call you."

Silently thanking the Lord God, rather than Pansy, Wren crept up to the bed she knew so well. It was unmade, but topped with folded blankets, so Wren flung all of them around her, and curled on the linen sac of straw, adoring the warmth. She doubted she could face the oven flames yet, but escape from the freeze was as important, so once again, Wren slept.

It was neither Pansy nor Bryce who woke her. The face staring down at her as she awoke, was the one she now knew better than any other.

"I came to find you." Landry neither smiled nor frowned. "Your bed offers little comfort, it seems. You are simply a bundle of rags."

She felt exactly as he described. "I don't know – I mean, I had no choice. I don't know anyone else. Just my father and he's too far away, actually, he could be anywhere. Then there used to be Jessy, but –. Only here – once Pansy opened. I had to wait on the doorstep."

"I have a somewhat more attractive alternative to offer." He stood, unmoving, his hands clasped behind his back as he looked down at her.

Wren gazed up, watching the inexpressive pale grey eyes, like tightly closed doors, their meaning withheld. Like some magical music she was not permitted to hear. "You actually found a better place for me? And thought of me?"

Shadow was up, reaching to lick Landry's hands, eyes huge and hopeful. Landry remained unmoved. "My memory is not so poor. Yes, I managed to think of a woman I call friend, and this is not a place of sanctuary. Your own memory, I presume, is sufficient to know who it is who works downstairs."

The guess was easy enough. "So, it's the same Bryce."

"Indeed." Landry leaned back, shoulder to the wall and his voice soft silk once more. Wren was unwrapping herself. "Bryce was held in Newgate for the rape of women and the theft of their belongings."

"Shit." She managed to stand. "Although he was the only one in the prison who tried to be nice."

"The well clothed frontage can hide the ragged back."

"I almost liked him, but what you say means he's disgusting. And she thinks he's a lawyer. She's so daft and he's a rotten rapist." There was no time to wonder how she could have liked someone without seeing what he truly was underneath the smiles. Wren shivered. "I should warn Pansy."

"You should, though I doubt she'll believe you. You'll lose one friend and gain another enemy. The right choice is not always the best one."

It didn't sound right, but Wren accepted what Landry had said. There was no time to think anyway. "I'm ready," she told him, running her fingers through the knots of her hair. "I'll follow you."

Landry, then Wren, and Shadow, each hurried into the shop.

Pansy was rolling the dumplings, poking onion and wet squares of skinned eel flesh into each centre. She looked up.

Bryce closed the oven doors, stepping back and around.

"Landry, my dear friend." He grinned, delighted. "Never thought to see you here."

Landry replied. "You being here, is a greater surprise, you're free, and working. You also have found a partner."

Pansy interrupted. "My beautiful Bryce, yes. He's my dearly beloved. Really a lawyer, weren't you, my darling," She shook the flour from her hands and turned to hug him. "but took a holiday just to help me. Such a wonderful gentleman."

Only Bryce and Pansy smiled.

"I'm leaving," Wren said in a hurry. "I'm sorry – there's no time to do the pies, but I only slept an hour, so I'm not cheating."

"No pies?" Pansy scowled. "You promised -,"

Wren shook her head. "And I've folded up the blankets again. It's all tidy."

Pansy started to speak, saw Landry's face freeze, and stopped. "Yes, of course, I suppose that's fair. I wish you well."

Bryce nodded. His smile was as bright as the flames behind the oven doors. "Good luck to both of you."

"We have no need of luck," Landry said softly, and turned, striding immediately from the shop. Wren followed close, Shadow at her heels.

Outside, sugared in snow, Red, the missing hound, was waiting, wagged his tail in delight, and joined the procession. Shadow jumped, licked his friend's nose and Wren bent, hugging Red's neck. "I missed you and I was worried. I hope you aren't hurt." Clearly, he was too active for much injury, now jumping to lick her fingers.

Arthur was also waiting. Landry threw Wren up to the horse's back, and mounted behind her. It was not a long ride, although Wren wished it was longer. She adored the closeness of Landry's arms around her. After a disturbed sleep, Wren would have chosen to sleep again, if she could, curled against the warmth of Landry's caped body.

CHAPTER TWENTY FOUR

NARRATIVE

The Thamesdon earl's home backed onto the London Wall, directly north of the Mews, where now only destruction lay in a blackened turmoil. The sky no longer echoed the rich blush of flames, and offered neither sunshine, nor the colours of a winter dawn. Even the stench of ruin had blown away as the ice returned, but it would be long months before repair would overtake the wreckage.

This was no palace, but the house was large, many windowed, and fronted by a parade of bushes and vines, grown tall, hiding the two lower floors of the three-storey manor. The many tiny panes of window glass in its façade, reflected only wind - blown shade.

Landry entered through the high iron gates, laying already open. The short distance from gate to house, sided with bushes and leafless trees, led them to the front of the great doors, carved wooden lintels and a huge brass cat's head as a knocker. Dismounting, Landry held out his arms to Wren, who dropped cheerfully into the embrace.

Wren was surprised to see Prad waiting. He grinned at her, not the normal behaviour of a simple groom. He took the reins and led the horse around to the back of the house.

Landry strode the four wide stone steps and knocked. The brass cat's head boomed. A liveried figure, seemingly important, in black and gold, opened the door wide, stepped aside, and said, "His lordship waits in the main hall, sir."

It was Father Jacob who greeted her, and not the earl. His robes still bore the damage from the fire, yet he appeared, as usual, delighted with everything that happened around him.

"I doubt we can expect his lordship to keep us all warm and well fed forever," he chuckled. "but for a week or two, it seems he will. Spends more time in his manor in Kent, but always comes to London for Christmas at court. But, he's here now, though he doesn't roll from his eiderdowns until approaching midday, but you'll meet him soon enough. In the meantime, come and warm up by the fire. Yes, yes, dogs allowed too, the earl has a pack of them himself. They live by the stables, but he lets them wander free."

All Wren managed was a whispered thanks. She was now in awe, and still stood staring around her.

"You appear somewhat subdued, little bird," said the soft voice behind her. "Does wealth silence you? Your dogs are inspired it seems, and already exploring."

"They're not my dogs – and I'm – sort of – shocked." Wren was staring upwards at the vaulted roof and the beauty of its vast elaboration.

Landry told her. "Pleasure tends to be short, make the most of it, though I am, as usual, off again with little prospect of pleasure. I shall return tomorrow."

She was sorry. "Definitely tomorrow?"

The small crease beside his mouth deepened with the shadows of a smile. "Definitely tomorrow. Today you have only pleasure to discover."

Landry left her standing awkwardly in the centre of the grand but empty hall, unsure of what to think or what to do next. Eventually she sat on a high-backed chair, set before the enormous hearth, where a fire of huge logs was burning, flames like wings of scarlet eagles. Warmer than warm, she sat and dozed, cooked in considerable comfort. The other fire which had destroyed so much, was pushed from her thoughts, and she basked, eyes closed.

Nearly two hours later, the earl coughed, surprising her awake. It became a day of surprises.

"I'm delighted to meet you again, Mistress Bennet."

The earl looked down on her as he stood before the fire, hands cossetted in the huge decorate cuffs on each arm. Sitting up in a hurry, and trying to stop being embarrassingly slouched, Wren managed only a gulp. "I'm – I mean – it's so generous of you. I'm so very grateful."

"No need for gratitude," the earl assured her. "Indeed, you may not realise, but I have been employing you for some time, ensuring your health through young Prad. Food, firewood, and so forth. Now I can continue in the same manner, as well as enjoy your charming smiles at the same time."

She felt like kissing his feet. "That was you? I mean, your lordship? I thought it was Landry."

The earl sniggered slightly. "Same thing, mistress. I pay him whatever he needs. He passes on the necessities – and some of the luxuries – to those who accompany him."

Wren had realised none of this and could not think of herself as having accompanied Landry in any valid use.

"My lord, I'm Wren. Your servant." She heard herself stutter.

"In which case, Wren, I beg to be just an advisor and friend, and you may call me Morgan. Being known only as a title seems appallingly conceited, I certainly would prefer you call me Morgan. I may be an earl, and I certainly enjoy the benefits, but I inherited the position and have never earned it myself."

"I think you have, Sir Morgan. I'm learning something of what you do."

"My father knew the Mayor of London," the earl continued to smile, "Dick Whittington, a man of amazing altruism, my dear Wren. He put huge sums of money into helping and improving others."

She knew. Newgate, after all, was one place she had visited more than once, and had heard many times of Dick Whittington's attempt to improve the gaol. But despite how much had been donated, Newgate remained a place of nightmares. "What you do, sir, seems even more important."

Morgan sat, after pulling up a similar chair to Wren's, while stretching his legs to the fire. Considerably longer than her own, his legs were slim and well-shaped in their tight silken hose. He was, Wren thought, the prettiest man she had ever seen in spite of being shorter than Landry. His eyes sparkled blue, and his short blonde hair was cut in the height of fashion. She judged him to be a little older than Landry, so perhaps in his mid-thirties.

"And now," Morgan interrupted his own thoughts, "you gaze at me in curiosity. I wonder what you think. Or do you puzzle over my family? Or perhaps my age?"

Embarrassed again, Wren flushed. "Very perceptive, sir."

"So perhaps I should introduce myself with a little more detail, my dear. I am forty-two years of age, and it is nine years that your friend Landry has been working with me. Indeed longer, although previously in another less interesting capacity. I claim no wife, and no children, I am not what you might call the marrying type." He laughed. "The death of my friend's sister when I was younger, terrified and puzzled me. It inspired me to work as I do, but I can be as lazy and self-obsessed, as can we all from time to time, so I employ others to be far cleverer than myself. That includes you, Mistress Wren.

She had never thought of herself as intelligent or clever at anything, except cleaning a kitchen, and fostering the patience to deal with her father. "I've led a very plain life, sir. I've never achieved anything clever. I've regretted things – but that's not important, and I'll work hard. This will be far more important than anything else I've ever done, since being born."

"We only ever appreciate the wisdom of others," he smiled. "and Landry has described how efficient and courageous you were during the inferno yesterday."

"I just did – well – no one is just going to stand there and burn."

She thought a moment, frowning. "Although it seems that's what Cadby did." She looked up. "Apologies, sir, I doubt you know anything of the man Cadby setting fires."

"I may not be an intellectual, Wren, but I'm no blank simpleton. Yes, Landry told me the details. Cadby was your step-mother's father, and he was once seen setting a fire at the shop where you worked, but I can assure you he did not start yesterdays' destruction."

"He must have." She flushed again. "Apologies, sir, but -,"

"I call you Wren and you must call me Morgan," he interrupted. "and I have Prad's word that the man Cadby set no fire within the Mews. Prad was with him, climbing the ladder to the area above the stable, where both men intended to sleep. Prad tells me that from the moment of leaving Landry, they were never separated. The fire could even be an accident, sparks, perhaps, from a tinderbox or torch, but whatever it was, it was not started by the man you so distrust."

Wren stared. "I didn't know. I assumed – assumptions are stupid, aren't they, but the fire was too wild to be some little accident with a candle flame. If it wasn't Cadby, who was it."

The earl chuckled softly. "That's the eternal question in this house, Wren. *Who was it* echoes endlessly."

She nodded vigorously, trying to think. "And if Cadby slept, perhaps he started it before – no – impossible. He was in the mews house with us for hours." The nod turned to shake. "Have you seen what's left at the mews, sir? I mean Morgan."

The earl did not complain. "I've not yet visited what I know will make me quite sick, but it seems I may know more about some folk than you do, my dear."

"Do you mean Landry? I wouldn't want to ask, but if you're happy to say – something."

"Gossip is always better than supper." He smiled, just one side of those rich thick lips lifting, the opposite eyebrow tilting as if to question his own words. "How would you like a bedtime story?"

Was it really that late? The sun still slipped its pale shimmer through the window. Midday, perhaps. "Must I wait until then?"

The earl chuckled. "A good story can be relished night or day, I believe. Landry almost grew up at my side. I know him well. Nor do I feel any compunction telling another man's secrets. But maybe it should wait. Perhaps you should return to the mews and examine the damage and loss first. I have no loss that matters since I own the land and will order the necessary rebuilding. No one was killed."

It was true, although she hated the inevitable misery when she saw the ruin, and knew her own few possessions gone.

⋇◇⋇

The road from the Wall east of Cripplegate, served as the high back of the Earl of Thamesmead's large London property. From his iron gate, leading into the city towards the mighty Guildhall, Lawrence Lane led down to the Cheaps, and then the Poultry. St. Swithin's Lane turned towards Candlewick, then slipped southwards to the jumble of narrow laneways, their gutters ever more heaped with the refuse of wet feathers, chicken feet and faeces. Here Black Spoon Row whispered of misery and poverty.

Yet, with a mist of light snow falling, the children played, some still bare foot, skipping, hopping and chasing across the crisp topped cobbles, calling to each other and laughing, running after the cockerels as they called territory at the dawn, then searched the gutters for breakfast. Stray dogs joined the games. Mothers called from their doorways. "*It's too cold. Don't slip on the ice.*"

Yet only the wealthy owned the grounds attached to their mansions, and if children played in the tiny rooms their parents owned, they'd cause as much chaos as could leave barely the space for a beating. It was the cobbles and gutters outside that welcomed children, stray dogs and cats, hungry pigs, goats, poultry and scavenging birds.

Outside the Wall, the slums further east towards the Tanneries, sat in part ruin and the twisting paths were uncobbled. Here only beaten earth served as a walkway, little more than a swamp when the rain battered, and the Tannery surrendered. That was a place of stench worse than Newgate, where even the stray dogs found nothing to eat amongst the waste. Folk living there had little enough food themselves, but now mid-December and already well within the Christmas season, the churches were full, and the people sang. The mid-winter feast was planned. Whether it would be roast goose, fig puddings, roast apples sprigged with holly, baked parsnips, jelly, cream and platters of curds, whey and kidney pie, spread across the wealthy families' white linen tablecloths, or the more common celebration of minced goat rolled in parsley stuffing, and buttered bread rolls beside cups of strong beer, for the poor.

The mid-winter feast, celebrated on the twenty fifth of December, a holy day, started late, since midnight mass had been attended the night before. It called excitement to everyone, young or old, wealthy or dismally poor, religiously fervent or morally uncaring.

Those with homes beyond the London Wall knew themselves as gutter born, so those within the city's cobbled lanes, whether they had food or none, were neither trash nor beggars. The great city's inhabitants were therefore respectable, adults wore shoes, folk sheltered beneath hoods, and their capes were lined. Every flake of snow whispered of the celebration to come, and many of the poor ate with the wealthy, for although the bitter misery of the old French and Norman feudal system had long died in England and Wales, many of the lords included their staff at the feast of Christmas Day, and invited the folk living nearby as well. There were songs, dancing, games and enough food to fill some stomachs for weeks.

Now approaching, but not yet the day, here on the alley's wide corner, the Eel Shop boasted of a shuttered window, turning to an open counter, once the shutters were removed, a door to the shop with a wide painted lintel, and a back door onto the tiny path with no name. Pot Lane, they called it, because broken pots littered the gutters.

Within the freeze of snow and the sharp stab of the wind, Wren gazed at the welter of poverty, having just come from a welter of bliss and luxury. She stood where once there had been the entrance to the Thamesdon mews, but where now lay a blackened tumble of shrivelled and splintered wood, fallen beams, and the remains of leather reins, metal stirrups, even some scattered straw now all stinking with the hovering smell of destruction and burnt cinders. It was a stench which hung like a mist, although the smoke had been carried away by wind and water.

Daring to walk into the mess, it took time even to realise which pile of wreckage had been Landry's home. Some steps led up, yet led to nothing. The floors had cascaded and the beauty of those painted beams showing the wildlife of the English countryside were now simply ashes.

It had been some time since Wren had cried, though not long enough. She didn't want to cry again. 'Only babes cry,' her father had once shouted at her when she had been little more than a baby.

Yet now she felt the tickle of tears on her cheeks and her sight was blurred with loss. Fear, almost the disappearance of one of the dogs which weren't even hers, and now not knowing who had created such destruction. She adored her new amazing bedchamber, but she had loved the one in Landry's mews house as much, and it had seemed like her own.

After a meal celebrating the Christmas season, her stomach still feeling the comfort of a well-cooked feast, the misery of sudden horror had swamped her again. Now she felt, smelled and saw only the nightmare.

Something else was also obvious. Cadby's vile death had not been justice. It had been cruel. He had carried no blame and was innocent of the fire's terrible malignancy. And along with virtually everything else in her life, she had no idea who had caused it.

Standing very still, the stench made her bilious, but it was her thoughts which were strangling her. Turning quickly, she ran through ice, snow and the uneven cobbles which made her slip. As she ran, she also realised that she was once again sobbing.

CHAPTER TWENTY FIVE

LANDRY

The Earl of Thamesdon gazed at him like a rabbit faced by the flames from a torch. "I feel a terrifying burden of blame. Your enemies come from the work you do for me, we both know that."

I was the proof of my enemies. Clothes, face and hands covered in soot. Drifting black ash and doused embers flew as the white drifted as thickly outside. "It has not been a day of reassurance," I told him. "More searching, yet still no answers."

Morgan had collapsed into one of his elaborately comfortable chairs. "You have never agreed with my ideas. But this wretched family was desperately poverty-stricken and afforded nothing beyond your friend's eel pies. That would be close to starvation. Therefore, they possibly killed themselves."

I shook my head again, sending the last black and white specks of embarrassment flying. "Hands tied and necks noosed. An unusual method of suicide. I also believe they were church goers who respected the laws of their religion."

"Anyone desperate with hunger might overlook that which is regarded as sin." Morgan had convinced himself.

"And is it so easy to tie the noose around your neck, and then tie your own wrists? Indeed, the father might have sedated his obedient family and then, sobbing, have managed the rest. But himself?"

"He had the noose fixed already, climbed on a stool, popped his head into the noose and tightened it, then kicked the stool away, and while hanging, waiting to die, slipped his wrists into a ready prepared loop. It's far-fetched I know, but it seems to me that anyone else would also be unbelievable."

"Is it acceptable," I smiled down at him, "to inform a kind and titled gentleman of the elite royal court, that he is an absolute idiot?"

"For you, yes. You frequently do." Morgan had a pretty grin, when it was genuine. "No one else would dare. Except Tim naturally."

Although I doubted that Tim had ever insulted Morgan that way, I was too tired to prolong the discussion. "They were definitely murdered, and I intend discovering and naming their killers. I believe at least three killers, but I have as yet, no conceivable notion of motive. A declaration of some kind. The 'why' remains." Then I'd thought of something else, although less important. "In your various visits to the palace," I asked him, "have you known a cold, unfriendly and unresponsive baron?"

Morgan paused, stared, and promptly laughed. "No, my friend. Lord Hastings perhaps? But I avoid the unresponsive and mostly, I avoid the court."

It was an answer I had expected. Exhaustion carried its own trickle of irritation, and I had rarely been so inept. Past investigations had been – if not perhaps, exactly easy, – easier than this. A life dedicated to only one aim, needed that solitary aim realised.

My childhood had passed in a miserable manner and family poverty was taken for granted. Until I turned twelve years, I remember the ugly twists and topples, with the painful side accepted as normal, by a child who knew nothing else.

I was twelve when I killed my mother. I then spent a few pointless years parading the streets, stealing food for my father and myself, practising strength, then showing it off, and sleeping where and when I could.

The earl already knew me, and thought me, accurately, a criminally inclined fool. My father was one of his grooms, but died of dysentery when I was sixteen. I took over his position, slept in the hay above the stables, missed my father and sobbed into the night. In time, when Morgan understood me better, he employed me properly, and slowly, he organised my future. A far more interesting future than I had ever imagined, and a damned fascinating apprenticeship as well. Morgan was not my teacher, but he had provided hope, bed, and coin. It was the outlaws, the fools and the criminals who were my teachers.

Genuine friendship between the earl and myself took some years to solidify, but now it's a bond beyond measure.

Investigating the death of Haldon's new wife and recently born infant, I began to know Wren, long before she met me. An advantage of some depth, yet she seemed a pleasant young woman, as much as any other, and more attractive than most, although less than others. It has been living with her that has deepened my interest and respect. I have even enjoyed imagining her naked as she clambers into my bed, but I do not expect it to happen. Her appearance entices me, yet it is her character than I admire.

And it is the murder of the Ford family which engrosses me, and which is the only real matter of importance, presently, in my life.

Except, of course, the destruction of my home and the entire Mews beside it.

It is not the stench of Newgate Gaol, the dark seeping stink of damp walls, nor even the shit filled gutter clogged through the centre, without any genuine privy as an alternative, that makes me hate it. Newgate makes me puke because of what it is. It mixes the weak with the strong, the innocence with the brutal guilt, and yet, simply because of this personality, many times the dungeon and the inmates have brought me knowledge, and answers to my questions.

I use it, as I use Morgan, Prad, Jacob and now Wren. A larger workforce would be useful, but more difficult to control. Wren is a useful addition, although she tempts me with attraction, even sympathy. I have made the choice to try to avoid both.

The earl's home is excessively beneficial on many levels, not simply the comfort. A huge wealth of staff means I do not cook, make up the fires, or clean. Not that I ever bothered with much of that, making beds, supplying stables with horse food, or delicious food for us. Instead, I enjoy a place of ease, for discussion, as well as silent thought and contemplation.

Having lived here since I was young, although first within the stables, it keeps that sense of home. It welcomes me and even my brain functions better within these undemanding boarders.

The Ford boy worked at a bakery nearby, and I have been there, studied the possibilities, however unlikely, and decided it has no place for further investigation. The eel shop brought me Wren, but little else. The female Pansy is a creature without brain, though she fosters ambition, yet what she covets is money, not blood. Now, on learning that Bryce is involved with her, I shall investigate further, but not on behalf of the Fords. He was in Newgate when that was done.

My tree of suspicion grows in my head, its branches increase, and then diminish. The roots, however, are failing to attach, and without them, the tree will fall. I have seen the glint of opportunity when as yet unknown possibilities fly over my treetop. A baron of unpleasant disposition. Too vague perhaps, but a murder scene so meticulously planned, needs a leader of resource and ugly determination. The two large brothers remain undiscovered, yet I am losing faith in any of these hinted branches. My tree will soon fall.

I have been to the quarry beyond Moorgate, where Randell Ford had worked for most of his life. Mining had been failing for long years, due to famine, disease and war. However, overlapping the marshes, close to the city, and therefore comfortable both for hiring workers, and for trading and selling the product, was the limestone pit which was considered an example of particular success. That ruined stretch of landscape shouted wealth. There had once been deeper mining and metallurgy, yet now the quarrying for stone was its principal work.

The pits had once been separate, but had now been dug together, sloping in a huge devastation of chopping, carting, and digging, to create great ugliness. Wooden huts had been roughly built along one edge where the limestone still upheld some solidity. Softer than some other forms of limestone, this was said to be easier to quarry, yet both more hardwearing and more supportive than other types, once dried.

A multitude of workers, appearing as little more than slaves as they sweated into the pits, dared not stop their work to answer my questions. However, many had known Randell, liked him, then named him as too quiet and too moral. No one offered any hint of understanding his death.

Those in charge seemed rarely present, and the one I eventually discovered, remained mute, refusing to acknowledge my presence.

I need reminding that Wren, now wears rags, and lost other items in the fire, though I doubt she had many. It will be necessary to buy replacements, or she will eventually end half naked in stained, torn and unravelling linen. Although I might welcome aspects of that possibility, it is clothes she needs, and I will have no problem in supplying them. The small difficulty is simply in remembering to, since my thoughts are concentrated purely on discovering those who are brutal, and fixated on bloody murder.

The original capture of Wren when she ran south, had been Prad's plan. Jacob had disapproved, but I, on the other hand, thought it both sensible and entertaining. Prad ideas are often uniquely helpful.

The women in my life, apart from the strange madness of my mother, have been useful in the usual manner. I grew almost fond of one once, though she became popular with so many other men, I eventually let her go. Wren does not enter that category, yet my fondness for her grows, so needs curbing, or that may threaten my focus.

My mother was a whore, a career my father strangely accepted, even when her customers were taken to their bed. However, perhaps only to keep me from prying, at such times I was locked in a small wooden shed, barely room to move, with two breathing holes in the roof. When eventually I outgrew its dimensions, I was chained outside, where a tiny yard was used to stack wood and coke for the fire. My chains, and the yard itself, became an almost permanent home, whatever the weather brought, and I adapted quickly to the cold and the pain.

I was aware of affection since my father came at least once each day to feed and embrace me, whispering of his feelings and admiring my skills, although I do not believe any existed at that time. My mother ruled him so entirely, he remained, whenever possible, at the Thamesdon stables, and as such I suffered regular periods without any food or warmth. However, when my father returned, which was often, he brought me blankets, food and love. All would be quickly removed when my mother came out to collect wood for the fire, but I learned to be patient for my father's return.

I also delighted in the affection of our hound. He was my father's long-lived companion, and stayed close when permitted, bringing more warmth and comfort than any blanket. I also shared my food with him while he licked my face. He died when my father died, both above the Thamesdon stables. By then I was long free of my mother. But she had taught me a great deal that has later been of benefit, her methods and need for control, for instance. Principally she taught me the machinations of a mind capable only of cruelty, and what such a soulless soul sees as pleasure. The hunger for control by bringing great pain to others, is a strange business, but one I now at least partially understand. For someone who investigates the worst of crimes, this understanding is extraordinarily helpful.

Wren has no experience of love whatsoever. Her mother died

before she can remember, and her father has only ever offered rejection and the unscrupulous demands of his own needs. He does not resemble my mother in any manner, but I dislike him just as much.

She is not alone in her lack of experience of love, but I consider my childhood superior by comparison.

The quarry was owned by a baron with vague reputation. During my last short stay in Newgate, I was told of a fat man with a brother, the elder being capable of harrowing crimes. Since most of the existing inmates are thieves and killers, what they consider harrowing, must indicate a creature of real horror. I have never met this villain, and originally followed the word of an inmate who swore the man worked on a Kentish farm. I searched and found no such man there. Now I hear there exists a leader of gross appearance at the quarry. I have not seen anyone of that description during my visits past Moorgate, but I force myself to keep the possibility in mind.

The woman Jessy, worked at home caring for the younger son, while earning a pittance as a seamstress. Her employer is an unlikeable woman, but there would be no possibility of her having ordered these killings. Neither the neighbours, all unpleasant, or some keeper at the quarry, are my last suspects, who seem able to twine themselves in my tree of suspicion, but instead of sitting loose and undeveloped on the branches, they tunnel and reach for the roots.

Drinking, invariably too much, is another benefit of the Thamesdon mansion. The earl's cellars need occasionally reducing, or he will have no space for more stacked barrels. I find that an excess of wine blows away the absurd and extraneous detail of my life, and banishes unimportant memory. A simple and delightful remedy, it also ensures sleep, which would otherwise be rare.

So my work rolls on, with disappointment, and frequent anger, within its tailored seams. However, optimism pillows me, as do the earl's velvet cushions, and the vile situations I examine daily, will one day surrender their solution.

CHAPTER TWENTY SIX

NARRATIVE

Being Sunday, the shop was closed and locked tight. Upstairs two cramped bedchambers sat behind the long narrow salon. Pansy sat on the smaller stool, her back against the wall. She was mending a pair of brown woollen hose, the threaded needle between her lips as she adjusted the two sides of the small unravelling split.

She smiled as Bryce strode from their bedchamber.

Bryce did not smile in return. "I gave you two pence. I told you to get new hose. You do as I say or you get no more."

No longer surprised at these daily squabbles, she told him, with her voice carefully humble, "But the two pence will buy bread and ale, my dearest. New hose cost five pence or more, and I can mend these so the holes won't even show."

He glared. "You do as I say, slut, not as you think, and don't twist my words to sound righteous. The shop's profits pay for bread and more."

Laying the repairs on her lap, Pansy smiled. "My darling, yesterday's profits you took, except for the two pence."

He stood over her, glaring down. "Are you arguing? Do you dare tell me different?"

"Never." And never would. "Tomorrow I shall hurry out and buy the beautiful new hose you want, my dear, and if I mend these, then you'll have two pairs, as you so deserve."

Now Bryce smiled. "You decide nothing, bitch. If I want ten pairs of hose, then that's what I get. If I want bread and ale, I get it. Do you hear?"

"Oh, yes, my dearest. Always, I swear."

She cowered back against the wall. Bryce moved faster, although having expected the punch, Pansy expected to fall no further than the wall behind her. But he grabbed her hand. Her fingers were clean. *"Sunday morning purity,"* And he grabbed her index finger in his mouth and bit hard. Pansy started to cry but Bryce did not release her, and she screamed as he bit down again. Giggling slightly, Bryce dropped her hand. One finger hung limp. He had cracked the bone. Now he licked his lips. "What a good breakfast, my dear, better than bread, so tasty, your sweet little fingers."

Still sobbing, she pulled away but Bryce already held her hand, this time her middle finger between his teeth. Now Pansy did not dare struggle. Pulling her hand away would increase the pain, but this time, when he broke the larger finger, she lost consciousness and tumbled from the stool.

The needle she still clasped in the other hand, pierced his wrist. Bryce swore, punching at her face. She sank deeper into the faint. Bryce kicked her. She did not wake. He marched away.

Pansy woke alone, and prayed that Bryce had left the building, even that he might never return. When she tried to stand, she realised that one of her own stockings had been wrenched from her leg and was now tied and knotted around her neck, the needle, still threaded with fine black wool, piercing her ear.

She screamed, and fell back, sprawled on the floorboards. The pain of her two broken fingers was less than the choking and strangling. Desperately quick, with her uninjured hand, Pansy attempted to untie the restraints that strangled her. First, she pulled out the needle from her ear. Blood poured, but the pain lessened. Finally, she loosened and then removed the stocking from her neck, but she had no means of healing her two broken fingers.

The room contained a small settle, now used exclusively by Bryce and she sank there, lay back her head, closed her eyes and wished she could faint again. Her leg, now bare without its stocking, felt pinched and sore, but she had no energy, and did not examine it. When she opened her eyes, Bryce was standing over her again.

"Well, ugly little whore of mine, what sweet pleasure that was. Perhaps I'll do something a little more tomorrow."

Without daring to reply, Pansy scrambled from the settle and returned to the stool.

"I'll cook dinner, beloved." Her voice was a small croak, her throat too painful for speech. "We have some chicken left from yesterday. Not much, but I don't need to eat." She didn't think herself capable of eating, nor indeed, of cooking. Trying hard to smile, she cradled the hand with broken fingers, hoping she might find something to use as a bandage.

Remaining quiet, she used a strip of linen to bind together the two limp fingers, enabling the cooking of the chicken leg in a soft sauce. Bryce sat at the table where Pansy spread the linen cloth and served his platter with a small cup of ale to the side. Then she crept from the room, down the stairs, and out of the back door into the winter freeze.

The ice-streaked air woke her and refreshed her determination. So, very slowly, Pansy limped to the sheriff's small back street office. Sunday closure blocked her, and Sheriff Wilson refused to open the door to her call. Crumbling onto the doorstep, she closed her eyes and stayed, half unconscious, for some hours. When John Wilson eventually realised that the bundle outside his locked door was not simply rubbish, he clattered downstairs and unlocked his office door. She was skinny enough, in spite of his own size, for him to carry a few steps, sufficient to bring her indoors. The sheriff quickly realised that she was frozen and might well have died.

He wrapped her in blankets, laid her on the ground, a cushion beneath her head. Her hair was brittle icicles, and crackled as she was lifted. Wilson hurried to the tiny hearth and lit a fire. He had a stronger fire already blazing upstairs, but he knew himself incapable of carrying the woman all that way. He might risk dropping her down the stairs and killing her entirely.

As the little flames sizzled higher, Pansy blinked, almost opened her eyes, and then closed them again. Wilson was watching closely. However, apart from thawing the woman, he had no idea how to treat her, whether or not she returned to life. The thick scarlet bruising around her neck and the beads of dried blood beneath her ear, were obvious; That two of her fingers were badly bandaged together was equally clear. The dribble of blood, still gleaming on her ankle, was something he tried not to see. A young woman's ankle, even one wounded, was not the proper part for gazing, especially for a man of law-abiding respectability.

She woke so slowly, neither she nor the sheriff were confident of reality. Then, finally, Pansy whispered, "You brought me in."

"Indeed, mistress," he told her. "being Sunday, I don't answer calls, I'm afraid. I ignored your visit for far too long. I apologise, mistress. The fault is all mine."

"The fault," Pansy tried to raise her voice, "is his. Him. Not you."

"Him?" Carefully slow, soft and simple, the sheriff sat firmly on the floor beside his unexpected visitor.

After weeks of increasing abuse, she was no longer herself. Yet this, she realised, was the time to remember previous claims of courage. "Bryce," Pansy muttered. "Bryce Judd."

John Wilson brought her water, then wine, and finally a small platter of slightly stale bread, with very ripe cheese. The medicine worked. He was able to help her up to his own rooms, bundle her onto the settle by the fire, adding a pillow from his own bed, and began to hope for greater signs of life.

When she started to tell her story, he was appalled.

"By biting?"

Pansy shivered, then spoke fast and clear. "Two fingers broken between his nasty, dirty, rotten teeth. It hurts so much. I wasn't able to bandage anything properly with just one hand."

He carefully untied her bandage, and was horrified as the broken fingers appeared, purple, and limp, with large bleeding spots where the teeth had dug through. As a sheriff, Wilson had bandages, creams, salves, tonics, willow bark and other medicinal objects on a shelf, and was able to use them with reasonable and practised dexterity. As he worked with salves and bandages, he asked her, "Now Mistress Pansy, tell me the rest about this violent husband of yours."

Pansy leaned back, breathed in the considerable warmth, watched as her skirts visibly dried, tried to flex her fingers, stopped quickly and bit back the tears while attempting to explain. "No husband of mine, thank the Lord above for it. I thought I loved him, and I thought he loved me. He was helpful and sympathetic and kind. He smiled from morning till night. I was so stupid, and when he wanted to move in, to look after me and help with the shop, I was delighted. For the first days, a little more than a week, he was – adorable. I hate to say the word, but he was."

"There are folk who act the saint until they feel secure," said the sheriff, who had met some similar himself, including Bryce Judd, already knowing him as the convict released from Newgate. "Then they turn into the devil. An innocent lass like yourself, mistress, is never to blame. I'll wager you didn't know of that man's criminal past."

"He told me he was a lawyer, but we never married, he never asked me," Pansy admitted, staring at her now well bandaged fingers. "I was dreaming of marriage. If he'd asked me, I'd have said yes. I never had such a hope before. I'm thankful at least I realised the truth before any wedding. It started one night, when he crawled into bed, stuck a pillow over my head, tied my hands together and – well, I can't say what he did then. It was horrible, and day after day it got worse."

Wilson nodded gently, immediately emotional and on the verge of crying himself. "I trust you don't intend to return, Mistress Carlton."

"Call me Pansy, please."

"I only know you from the eel shop, mistress."

"But you're so kind." And she called him John. It was a long day and their conversation developed.

The following morning once his three assistants arrived at the office, the sheriff explained his intentions. "Mistress Carlton stays here to recuperate," he announced, a little gruff. Emotion and shock had not yet abandoned him. "We head to the Eel shop, make sure nothing lies damaged, arrest Bryce Judd, march him to Newgate and lock the shop behind us."

A busy morning was always preferable to sitting bored in the cold, and without delay they set off to arrest Bryce Judd. However, he was not at the eel shop, which sat dark, closed, and the shop front still locked. The back door was open, but no one remained within. They searched the two local taverns where men, some with children on their laps, huddled by the fires, their noses in their cups.

"I ain't seen that bugger," the sheriff was told. "but the bastard considers hisself bloody rich now, wiv a shop's profits at his dirty fingertips, and the lass willing in bed."

The church bells rang from north and west, chiming eight of the clock. The winter sky had only just lightened, and the city gates were unlocking. The first rush of those pushing their carts to market rumbled through, heads down. Several taverns had not yet opened but still Bryce was nowhere to be found. Next, they tried the nearby shops, the beer brewers, even the haberdashery, with its swathes of silk, linen and gossamer. Bryce Judd, the sheriff told Pansy on his return to the office, had entirely disappeared.

"Does he have relatives in London?"

"Not that I know of."

Wilson patted her hand. "I have already called the local medic, Mistress Pansy. I trust we'll arrest that dreadful man within a day or two at the most. Meanwhile, if all be well, you shall look forward to a Christmas celebration as happy as you wish."

It was difficult, and the sheriff knew that Pansy could not stay within his home, or further trouble was bound to mark the remainder of the season. A respectable sheriff hoping to keep his reputation intact, would not survive the scandal of living with a young female, already known as a bit of a feather-tipped doxy herself. Yet until Bryce was safely incarcerated, John Wilson believed forcing her back home would mean further horrors. Possibly even a death sentence.

"Mistress, until that wretch is safe back in Newgate, I can't permit you to return to that shop."

"But it's my living. There's nothing else I can live on."

"For a short and most temporary period," the sheriff emphasised the words short and temporary, "you may stay here. In the sola, naturally, and I shall make up a *makeshift* bed on the floor by the fire. If it takes too long to arrest Master Judd, then I shall have to find you a place in a convent or even an inn."

"I can't afford an inn," and Pansy once again croaked into tears.

Sheriff Wilson sighed.

CHAPTER TWENTY SEVEN

WREN

Pansy and I had always pretended to be friends of a sort. Of course, I worked for her, which made real friendship difficult anyway. The woman was no lady, but she thought I should treat her as one, being my employer. I hadn't ever really liked her.

I'd wanted more friends when I worked in the shop, and had got to know Jessy. I liked her enormously. I tried with Pansy, because working with someone you like, must surely be better, but she was always superior and a bit rude.

Two days since I had visited that sad remnant of the mews, I met the sheriff and his three assistants buzzing around the corner of Black Spoon Row, and I was extremely interested in what he told me.

He asked me if I knew Bryce well?

"No," I said at first. "I met him a couple of times and he seemed almost nice, but there was always something brutal peeping out right at the back of his eyes. Of course, I knew he was a criminal too, capable of some nasty stuff. He told Pansy he was a lawyer, though I never believed it. He used to be a Wherryman, but he only rented the wherry."

Sheriff Wilson looked woebegone. "He's known to the lawmakers as a wicked man."

"How he got let out, I've no idea. He's a bad man, but a good liar, so perhaps the court believed him. Either that or he paid the judge."

"But now he's gone and we don't know where to find him?"

I had no idea, none at all. After what Landry had told me, I realised Bryce was one of those who knows how to seem saintly, and then once they've got your love and your money, they turn sinister and cruel. That made me think of Jessy, who was much sweeter than Pansy, and had suffered worse. But although I knew why Pansy had fallen for Bryce, I had only met him once other than as a prisoner and I had no idea if he had his own home, or family, or even friends. Then the sheriff told me what he'd done to Pansy. It made me feel sick.

So, I visited the poor woman, and thanked John Wilson for taking her in. "But it's a difficult situation," he told me, loud enough for Pansy to hear. "Very bad for my reputation, and for hers. I must find her somewhere else to sleep." He looked at me hopefully, but I stayed firmly silent.

It was as she sat and described the awful behaviour of Bryce, who she had thought she loved, and was positive that he loved her, when I discovered that she was crying for her dreadful pain, for the loss of a man she had thought an intelligent saint, and now also because the sheriff didn't want her permanently in his bed.

Pansy had her clothes and probably a little money too, back in the rooms over the eel shop, so I went back there with her, offering to help. The sheriff came too, in case Bryce turned up, and called one of his assistants for protection.

I should have expected it, but none of us had. The rooms were ransacked, everything torn, broken, tossed around, and the clothes left there were either purposefully ripped, or chucked in a heap on the floor, with a bucket of eels emptied out on top. Some of those eels were still alive, and trying to catch them was hard work. Disgusting work actually. Clearly Bryce had been furious, and hoped to find money as well.

Any money from the box in the shop had been taken, and the

box tossed, empty, on the floor. Yet, knowing Pansy had left on a Sunday when all shops were shut, I doubted whether more than a penny had been in it at all.

In her own room, Pansy pulled on a little gap between the wall's wooden planks, and with a creak and a snap, the opening grew. A small linen sack sat in the dark. It was quite full of money. It looked as though she'd saved a fortune, a good deal more than a few pounds anyway. So, at least Bryce hadn't found that.

We were collecting up any clothes worth saving, and a few items Pansy loved, when the back door was slammed open downstairs and the heavy climbing footsteps had to be Bryce's. No one else would have barged in that way. So, we kept quiet until he marched into the room, when the sheriff and his guard quickly walked to bar the doorway behind him. Bryce turned in shock, seeing us all, and swore loudly.

Pansy screeched loud as a trumpet and flew at him. Bryce slammed out, his fist missing her, as I grabbed and pulled her away. That wasn't going to help, even though I'd have liked to punch him too. Wilson marched forwards and his assistant lunged at Bryce's back. The stupid man was trapped between the two of them and he knew he couldn't get away. Bryce wasn't going anywhere. Naturally he had his own ideas and immediate surrender wasn't one of them. He whirled and kicked out.

His wooden toed boot cracked directly into Wilson's codpiece. Wilson howled. He sounded like one of the dogs. Tumbling backwards, he left the door free, and Bryce raced towards it. The assistant was as fast, grabbed out at one fleeing ankle and Bryce tripped at once, hurtling down beside the sheriff.

I watched as they pounded each other, blows to noses, eyes and chins. They both yelled and swore, Bryce considerably more blasphemous, but his nose was the first to break, spitting blood as it poured from his nostrils to his mouth. Hammering back, Bryce did not pause and now Wilson's nose broke and was instantly blubbering scarlet, as voraciously as his assailant's.

Pansy was trying to hide in the corner. I grabbed up a couple of squirming eels from the bucket where the assistant had previously rescued them from the floorboards, and threw two of them at Bryce's furiously stamping feet.

Bryce slipped on one of the eels, falling beside it, face down. I actually heard the snap as his nose broke again. He was lying in a pool of blood but only for an instant. He grabbed the wriggling eel, stumbled upwards and swung it outwards.

This slapped into Pansy's face and then Wilson's. Wilson staggered back against the closed doorway, and Pansy yelled, dropping her sack of money. Untied, it rattled, clanked, and burst open. Coins spread across every the floor, rolled, spun, and disappeared beneath the settle, some beneath the gap below the door, and more under the eels, which were once again slithering in confused desperation.

Immediately Wilson grabbed both Bryce's arms, and the assistant chained those slimy wrists. "I arrest you, Bryce Judd, for the brutal assault on Pansy Carlton. I shall take you directly to Newgate where you'll stay until trial."

Pansy, of course, was on her knees, attempting to collect every ha'penny, and every farthing, peering desperately into shadows for where the coins had rolled, squeaking as she fumbled for them.

I doubt he had ever been captured this easily and Bryce didn't seem to believe it either, trying to free himself, wrestling his hands and kicking out. Actually, I decided that the pig couldn't fight. He knew how to beat women but was useless against practised men of justice.

Wilson dragged him towards the door. Some of those swear words were actually quite new to me. The nose bled from both sides and Bryce was definitely furious. "I've done nothing wrong," he yelled. Pansy cowered back. "Tis said a man can beat his wife is she deserves it, and this slut deserved it, and more." I wished I had the strength to smash his teeth out.

"I'm not your wife," Pansy squealed from the back of the room.

"You damn well are," Bryce roared twice as loudly. "A proper handfasting, it was. We're wed, and you stole my money."

Aghast, Pansy shook her head.

"Call your witness," Wilson demanded.

"My friend Col," Bryce shouted back.

"Impossible," smiled the sheriff. "Col Flanders has been in Newgate all this month and more. Try again."

"A different Col," insisted Bryce. "and anyway, I don't need no witness."

"For proof, you do, since this female doesn't admit marriage," the sheriff said, "and wed or no, your assault was brutal, and I saw the result if not the attack. You're a wicked and brutal pox-ridden nonce, and you'll hang when I tell the court what you did."

I kicked the bastard as he passed. He kicked back but I was quicker and I dodged. "And Pansy never stole your money, since you never had any," I shouted in his face. "You tried to steal hers. We've seen what a mess you made here, ripping her clothes and smashing platters all over the place. And telling her you're a lawyer, oh, I'm sure you'd make such a good lawyer with all you must know about the law by now."

I think his glare was quite a bit uglier than mine. I wished Landry was with me.

"Common-Law wife. Lived together. Done plenty and helped run the shop. That's marriage, that is."

"It isn't," Wilson said, and between them, the sheriff and his assistant pulled Bryce down the stairs, into the icy wind and the new curtain of sleet. The snow had drifted off, and a torrent of pounding sleet and rain had replaced it, one freeze turning to another.

Pansy clung to me as we watched them march off into the growing storm. She heaved a great sigh of relief. I suppose she was reluctant to go back to a bed on the floor where she knew she wasn't wanted. Besides, I held half the pile of her belongings, so I felt obliged to help her clean up the shop.

With Bryce safely locked up, she could stay in the shop. Because of her injuries, Pansy wouldn't do much of the cleaning. So, guess who would! Unpaid, since I was now supposed to be a friend.

But she surprised me and pleased me too.

"No, I never want to go into that shop again," she said with an enormous intake of breath. "It's made money, but it's always been such a trial. Now, with the recent memories, I hate the thought of getting into that bed where that monster hit me and cursed me. I'm going to sell it."

"The bed?"

"Everything, some of the eels and onions will still be fresh enough too, if someone would buy quick."

I shook my head. "Not me," I told her. "I couldn't afford it anyway, it'll be expensive, won't it. A popular shop with the oven, and everything ready for cooking, in a good position too. A nice place upstairs as well, three rooms with furniture. The sheriff's bound to know who might be interested. Probably you should rent it out and get money back every month."

I added that now she had rescued all that saved coin, she could rent her own new home.

"No thanks, Wren. I shall move back with the kind sheriff until I can afford a lovely home, once I sell the shop. He won't mind."

"Pansy, at least you should ask first.:

"No, dear." She grinned. "I'll give him no opportunity. And he'll enjoy what I have in mind." I followed her to the sheriff's empty office, and watched as Pansy started putting away the stuff she had collected from above the shop. She certainly had a lot more clothes than I did, and three pairs of shoes, which I considered wildly extravagant but was secretly envious. Her grin expanded. "John knows me now," she continued cheerfully, "he'll be glad to have me."

Sadly, we stayed longer at the shop than I'd intended. At the earl's wonderful manor, I did no housework at all, now I was sweeping, wiping, washing and tidying.

Finally, she sat upstairs on the bed, and I sat on a stool, and we stared at each other. "Thanks for your help," she said, polite at last and sinking back against the pillows. "Now I'm going back to Sheriff Wilson's place, and hopefully, John's going to be home soon to tell me all about the arrest and what's going to happen next." She smiled and tried to look appreciative. "But," she continued with a humph, "honestly, I'd like to be there alone when he comes. I mean, thanks for everything and I could never have done it myself, but I'm rather keen to hear what John has to say. I'm sure you understand."

I certainly did, I wasn't that stupid, nor did I have the slightest desire to stay close to her in the shop, or house. "You need a doctor now," I told her. "Not a sheriff."

"John will take me to the right place," she assured me. "or perhaps call the doctor there. I just need some time with John alone."

"Well don't eat him up," I said, knowing I was being bossy. "He's an odd man, never married, and totally lazy. Not the best sheriff in London, but alright, and he's kind."

"He's – *wonderful.*"

"You only got rid of Bryce two days gone," I said, but I just mumbled and pulled on my cloak, ready to brave the freeze outside.

She stopped me. "You will come back and visit, won't you? I shall need friends."

So, of course I smiled, and said yes, but John Wilson, sheriff though he was, had never found any clues as to Jessy and her family's terrible deaths, and he behaved rather like a shut shop himself. However, I wished Pansy well. She wasn't about to be my friend for life, but I supposed I could visit her now and again.

For me, home. Home was now a mansion, with velvets and paintings and a real outside, with trees and hedges, stables and a laundry. Real privies inside. Water brought in by the staff. I almost felt like a countess myself. Except that I owned just one pair of shoes and no Sunday best clothes.

Actually, in my wonderful big bedchamber I had a beautifully polished clothes chest. It sat – entirely empty – at the end of the huge carved bed. Landry didn't seem to care that my only gown was burned around the hem, stained with eel slime and smells, raw and cooked, with sweaty underarms as well. I couldn't even clean the damned gown, since I'd then have to walk naked until it dried in the sun. Which was even more of a problem, since I didn't expect to see the sun for at least three months.

In the meantime, it snowed, rained, made thick frost, rime between the cobbles, and any day now was bound to greet us with lightening, thunder and a deluge to follow.

Naturally I didn't know the date, but I damn well knew it was winter, and close to the end of December. It might even be Christmas Day.

✳◈✳

When I got back to the house, Landry had returned. He was sitting by the fire, and I trotted in after the steward had taken my cloak. I sat close by, and the fire was a paradise.

It simply seemed miraculous that this house of glory was my home, even if just temporary, and here sat the most fascinating man I'd ever met. I still wasn't sure I how I felt about him, but fascinating was a definite yes.

"I met up with Bryce again." I told Landry as he looked up, no welcomes, no hugs, not even a smile. "He attacked Pansy. The sheriff arrested him, and he's back in gaol, but what do you think about him killing Jessy and her family? He's a nasty cruel man. He could have done it."

He didn't really look up, but his eyes lifted and focused. "Time," Landry murmured, hardly bothering to open those lips, "is invariably difficult to measure, unless you live beneath a church bell, and do nothing else to distract the moments passing. However, little bird, even you may be capable of an occasional memory, and the memory would inform you that Bryce was most certainly locked in Newgate Gaol when that murder was, sadly, committed."

Sadly. I'd been poorly treated by my father when growing up. But no man had ever treated me as Bryce had treated Pansy. She might not be the sweetest or most intelligent woman in the city, but she hadn't deserved theft and torture. If Bryce tried to bribe the judge at his next trial, I decided I'd march in and accuse corruption.

CHAPTER TWENTY EIGHT

WREN

I t was after a light supper when we sat together before the crackling fire.

"Bryce," Landry told me, ice-eyed, "creates pain and terror for those he attacks. He once raped a child, then tossed her into the Thames and watched her drown in the freezing water. That is not the way that your friend died. Bryce revels in first earning trust, and then gleefully watches, as he cruelly destroys that trust. Jessy Ford and her family were left hanging as a warning, but murdered by poison. Those deaths were careful and that is not the work of a monster like Bryce. Therefore, even had you not known that the vile creature was already incarcerated at the time, you should not have suspected him."

I was disappointed. I knew the truth of what Landry told me, but had hoped I'd miraculously solved the crime.

"So, we still haven't got a single clue?"

Landry's feet were almost in the fire. He'd kicked off his shoes, which lay, one beside him, and the other over by the table. He wore only black hose, and they looked quite wet, in spite of the fire. I guessed he hadn't been in for long.

Now he raised one eyebrow at me. "No. Sad, yet invariably true."

I was surprised that his toes hadn't caught fire. "However," he continued, "I have discovered who set the flames that destroyed the Mews, our home, and much else."

"Who? How do you know?"

"I claim no credit. Yesterday I questioned Prad and the other grooms present at the time. Prad saw a shadow running, almost dancing, a flaming torch in hand. He described the shadow, which was helpful, and two other grooms heard a cackling laugh. Naturally they had recognised no one and so assumed what they'd seen would be no help. However, the arsonist had to have a reason, and delight in creating fear and destruction. Bryce is the answer to all such."

"You can be positive?"

"Once I've questioned him in Newgate, yes, I shall be sure."

It almost all made sense. "So, you'll threaten him to get the truth? But you said he had a reason, he never hated you."

"He will, once I've questioned him," Landry smiled faintly. "But it was you he followed to my house."

"Why would he hate me? He might now of course, but that's different."

Landry, as usual, looked glazed. "Because you might expose him to Pansy, and of his jealousy when you went to the shop, because of the compliments Pansy made regarding your skills. I spoke to her some days gone. She admitted as much. Yet she still believed in the lawyer, and as he thought you her friend, you were the one who could ruin his dreams."

I suppose I understood. What a vile beast. "And he nearly killed Pansy too. Thank the Heavens he's back in gaol."

Landry said. "I have heard considerably more from the sheriff."

How did he know everything, and squeeze into the tiniest corners of whatever was happening? "I'm surprised." I admitted, but it all made sense.

My mind, and the endless pictures at the back of it, were dancing as usual. Instead of the endless swinging bodies, now I saw those painted animals on the beams where we'd lived until the fire. I saw squirrels running from badgers, tiny deer running after their mothers, beaver jumping from rivers and staring at foxes, birds nesting, a dozen eggs nestled in the treetop, fish leaping and hawks flying down to catch them. I even envisaged a hedgehog jumping on the back of a weasel, while a frog watched, laughing.

Now all gone and burned to cinders.

Then I asked, "You've been somewhere with puddles. You've got wet feet." I smiled. "Anything I can know about?"

"You hope to hear of fights and prisons, or brothels and bordellos?"

That would have annoyed me once. Now I just smiled. "Naturally."

But what he said next really did surprise me. "I went to visit your father," he told me without expression, as if this was utterly without interest.

"Without telling me? Without asking if I wanted to come? I've been meaning to visit him for ages."

"I would not have stopped you."

"I should hope not," I glared and raised my voice. The temptation was to shout, but I wanted this wretched man as a partner not an enemy. "So, tell me what he said, and what you asked? Or was it just for a cup of ale?"

"None of those," he nodded, "since I did not find him. He has left the work at the docks, and he has left his rooms behind the quay. No person there had any idea why he had left, nor where he had gone."

I muttered. "I'd wager he was sacked."

"And if so," he looked at me again – or perhaps he was looking through me, "where might he go?"

My father was no genius, and I thought his first move would be to expect sharing with me again, and so would come to the shop. But either he saw Bryce, and backed off, or maybe the whole place was already locked up, with that ghastly mess that Bryce left inside. "No idea," I said. "but he made friends in Newgate, and I suppose some of them have homes somewhere, even wives. So, he'd have a list of places to go. Why do you want to see him?"

Landry smiled, but somehow it wasn't a nice one. "For you, naturally."

Leaning back and feeling myself a bit scorched. I asked, "you were gone sometime, and you got very wet. You didn't fall in the river I hope?"

Now he laughed, and this time it was warm and sweet. "Not a habit of mine, and no. Neither drowning, nor swimming, nor booted from the docks. I galloped on an unwise visit to the fens in Kent. But this had nothing to do with your devoted father."

Devoted. I wish! "What for? And all that way?"

His smile slipped sideways. "For excellent reasons."

"Private – then?"

"For crime." He half smiled, the top lip twitching. "But not my own criminal acts this time. I wished to explore, without being seen, the home of an unappetising baron."

So, I gave up asking. I sank back into the warmth again and just enjoyed having Landry to myself. Wine was brought, and a platter of warm apple dumplings, which I ate immediately, so couldn't speak. I just sat there with my mouth full. "Ummph."

"I am sure you're correct," said Landry, with that twitch at the corner of his mouth. "However, there is another subject I consider relevant, and you may have more success with the necessary investigation." I nodded and tried to swallow. I choked instead. He continued. "There's a good deal of gossip surrounding the death of your friend and her family. A considerable amount is unpleasant. Gossip is the popular diversion of many, but in such a situation, it may be more. I am surprised you've not followed the more spiteful of these stories already."

I'd finished my first dumpling, although a fair amount of hot batter still clung to my teeth.

"Gossip?" I asked. "I haven't heard a word. What's being said?"

"That the Fords were killed for revenge since they had murdered others, that they were a family of spies for the Lancastrians. That they were killed on the orders of the king, and that they had stolen from the Mint at the Tower. The most interesting claims are that you killed them, my dear, since you had been adulterously involved with the husband, and the wife had therefore threatened you. It seems you killed them all to quieten such possible scandal. How you managed all four at once has not been explained. Quite dexterous, I imagine.

I gaped at him, and dripped a piece of stewed apple. "Someone actually said that? Or did you make it up?"

"My imagination," Landry said, one hand to his forehead, "is not sufficiently remarkable for that, but it is why I suggest you make the investigation yourself."

"Bother." Not relevant of course, but I couldn't think what else to say.

"I have heard a fair number of bright conversations along these lines," Landry said, and the twitch of a smile was back. "It seems likely that the Ford's neighbours have birthed most of them, needing to enjoy the public interest in the vile crime, so close. There is also a faint possibility that they saw something that might be more interesting than the gossip. I spoke with them once. It left an unpleasant taste, but I should have returned."

"I've met some of them. It's a big family," I told Landry. "They're all equally horrible. I'll go tomorrow."

That cramped family, living on the house on the other side of the Fords, had never been my friends, and Jessy had always said she didn't like them. I thought them far too muddled and gossipy, to be guilty of a carefully planned murder, but living next door could mean they'd seen or heard something, yet been too stupid to realise the importance.

"An excellent idea." Landry's eyes were half closed again. "I shall almost certainly remain here to speak with Morgan on a number of matters. Come back for me if you need me, and take Arthur by all means."

"Not without you holding the reins," I said. I wasn't an experienced rider even though Arthur was quite a friend by now.

"I'm used to walking. It doesn't bother me, and nearly all the snow has gone."

"You consider rain, sleet and hail more comfortable?"

No, I didn't, but I was fairly used to it anyway. My boots were strong, and I had a thick cloak with a hood. I explained all of that, as Landry patiently smiled at me. At least, I think it was a smile.

"And if my feet get wet, I'll come back and stick my toes close to the fire, just the way you are."

"Wet feet," Landry was still wriggling his black woolly toes at the rising flames, "are a common problem, even when riding a horse. That reminds me, you need a few clothes for visiting. Are you content to arrange that on your own?"

I think I blushed. "Yes, it's true but I don't exactly have much money." I didn't have a penny.

"On the contrary," Landry answered. "You are wealthy beyond measure, little bird. Simply ask, and should you dislike the thought of asking, then I'll arrange for chests of silver to be delivered to your bedchamber."

I sort of giggled. "I wouldn't say no." True enough.

"It will be arranged," he said. "I presume you lost clothes and more in the fire?"

Not that I've ever had a closet full, but my second shift, gown for working in the shop and the apron too, and my only gloves, had all gone. I had a wonderful vision of buying a hoard of bright new clothes. "Yes, I lost everything. New clothes would be a luxury," I admitted. If I spend some hours tomorrow with those vile Duffs, then perhaps I could go to the haberdasher and the tailor the next day, even if it rains, pours, snows, sleets and thunders all day."

I was standing now, denying myself the temptation to sit and talk with Landry all night. I probably needed a good night's sleep more than a cosy evening.

Landry nodded. "Excellent organising skills," he said, although I suspected more sarcasm than appreciation. "I wish you a good night, little bird and if you find your own bedchamber too cold, then you're welcome to join me in mine." Now I was sure it was sarcasm. I just sniffed, and hurried off so I wouldn't have to answer.

My bed was not cold since one of the maids had heated a brick and pushed it between the sheets. Once cuddled, snuggled indeed, in the beautifully heated bed, it was not the Duffs I dreamed of that night. Lying warm, but unable to sleep for long hours.

CHAPTER TWENTY NINE

NARRATIVE

Although invariably open, this day, the Duff's door was closed. No doubt due to the thunder, and wind driven rain, Yet it was not locked. The family did not appear to fear the arrival of murderers, such as had killed the family next door.

Wren stood, soaked and shivering, knocked on the door as loudly as she thought might drown out the thunder, then pushed the wet wood open, walked in, and pulled the door closed behind her. She called, "Mistress Duff, are you in?"

Indeed, she was already visible at the end of the long-shadowed space, trying to light a small fire beneath the trivet. Candles, being too expensive, had not been lit, and the room was darker than the storm outside.

Doria Duff abandoned the home-made fire lighter and scurried over. "My dear Wren, what a pleasure. The all the girls are upstairs. Mistress Uptort gave them the day off because of the weather. She said it would just bring in more mud."

Having deciphered this message, Wren sat on the nearest stool, without being invited, and interrupted. "It's you I'd like to talk to, Doria, but first, I'd like to know who's been making up these nasty stories about me killing your neighbours."

The blush was not visible in the density of shadow, but Doria's voice echoed it. "I have no idea, Wren, honestly, I was shocked to hear that and of course it was no one in my family spreading lies. As if we would! I have not a single notion, but of course I've told everyone it isn't the truth. I've known you as poor Jessy's best friend."

"Forgive me for saying it, Doria, but your daughter Lyana always did like making up stories." Wren half expected to be slapped off the stool. Instead, Doria apologised profusely. "It's true, sadly, I know that's the truth, but never about you, Wren dear. She never would."

"I'd appreciate it," Wren leaned forwards, "if you could tell everyone they're wrong about these stories. You know all that nasty gossip might make it harder to find the real villain." Wren managed half a smile. "Now, as the neighbours, folk will think you're the ones to know best. So, start telling it would never be me, and that it's an impossible and ridiculous idea. Then make sure they know Jessy's family were honest folk, not spies, not wicked in any way, they worked hard with very little thanks. Like your children, I'm sure. They deserved happiness, not such an evil end." Her false smile peaked. "And naturally, everyone will believe you."

"Oh, indeed, Wren. They all know us as helpful folk who always tell the honest truth." She clasped her hands with a virtuous gaze to the heavens. "As were the Fords. The Padre at Saint Muriel's knew us well. He's quite a friend, and my dearest husband knows the sheriff. We're good friends with all and sundry. The most honest folk you could imagine."

"So, you're the perfect people to stop the horrid lies and gossip," Wren nodded. "I shall listen out for the locals changing their silly stories."

"I shall do my best," Doria assured her. "But I feel I should put you right on one thing, Wren dear, since you seem to hope someone might guess who the killer was. After all this time, there's no hope, dear. You haven't any experience of course, but I feel I should put you right."

"That's kind," Wren suppressed the desire to kick the woman.

"but I helped my father a few times you know, in Newgate and in court. I do know a bit. For instance, I know the family was probably poisoned first before they were hung."

Doria Duff clamped her hand over her mouth and croaked. "How horrible. How can you know that? Is that just a guess?"

The thunderous gallop down the stairs was louder than the thunder outside. Lyana's voice was louder than her mother's. "Who you talking to?"

"Me." Wren glared. She distrusted the eldest daughter more even than Doria herself.

Missing the annoyance in Wren's voice, Lyana supplied a good deal more. "You ain't no real friend of my mum's, and you know it. You just like to make trouble. I wouldn't be proper surprised if I found - ,"

"If you say anything about me killing Jessy next door, then I'll drag you off to the sheriff," Wren stood, facing the girl. "So don't you dare. And, I know damn well what you've been saying to others."

"I never. Well, I wouldn't," Lyana flopped onto a third stool and glared.

"I want to ask something extremely important," Wren glared back. "It's hard after all this time, but the sheriff must have asked this when it all happened, and Landry Crawford asked you too. It really is important. Did you see anyone go into the Ford's home on that day, or the day before, or even the day before that?"

"You think folk tell us, *I's gonner kill them Duffs. Watch me?*"

"Don't be ridiculous," now shouting, Wren's glare turned to fury. "This is too important for silly stories. Your door's always wide open unless it's raining, and I know it wasn't raining on that day. You all like seeing what goes on in the whole street, so you could have seen someone, or heard them knock on the door, or anything like that."

"Tis too long ago," Lyana stared at her toes. It was her mother's glare, not Wren's, which quietened her.

Doria nodded, "Quite right, Wren dear, and if what you say is right, then we'd best be bloody careful. The bastard might come again."

Wren sighed, "do you remember anything at all?"

"Well, I do, as it happens," Doria leaned forwards, enjoying the attention. "and so does Belinda. She's only little but she ain't stupid." She turned to Lyana. "Go get Belinda, and be quick about it." Then back to Wren, "Trouble is, I can't rightly remember what day it all was. I never knew what terrible stuff went on till a bit later, when the sheriff turned up, but a couple of days before, I seen shadows go in, and some fellow shouted."

A very small voice broke through the rumble of thunder outside and the rumble of Doria's voice inside. It seemed to squeak from the top of the stairs. "Ain't no person gotta come and get me," it insisted. "I done heard all you been saying and I saw folks too."

Wearing one of her sister's shifts, so long that she needed to hold it up to her knees, the child, Belinda, shuffled downstairs, beaming brightly. Being wanted for anything except housework or a telling-off, was exciting to a nine-year-old.

She stood cheerfully in front of Wren, who was sitting again. Wren explained. "It's very important, Belinda dear. Can you remember what day it was? All the details would be so very, very helpful."

Belinda hopped to one foot, back to the other, grinned, and settled. "I did, honest I did. Three big men, there was. In a mighty big hurry too. And one says, *You sure?* And the biggest says, *Tis done.'* I was sitting on me doorstep playing wiv pebbles wiv meself, so I saw clearly and I heard it like I says. The biggest man were all fancy dressed, but them other two was just normal. Then they all hurried off, almost running they was."

Doria smiled warmly. "Clever girl."

Wren was staring in astonishment. "That's wonderful. Incredible. Did you tell this to the sheriff?"

The child shook her head. "He never asked. He never wanted to talk with me. Me mum didn't know neither. Well, no one tells me nuffing. I didn't know about them nasty killings, so I just thought them big fellows was friends on a visit. How could I know t'was important? Wasn't till loads and loads later, when me Mum says as how Jessy's gone to Purgatory, I tells her about what I saw."

"And you didn't go to the sheriff even then?"

"Well, it was a bit late by then, so we didn't bother," Doria interrupted.

Bending forwards, Wren took both Belinda's wrists and smiled. "Would you come with me to meet someone else and tell your story? There's some people who want to find out what happened to poor Jessy. I'm sure you'll get a lovely dinner."

"I'll come too," said Lyana immediately.

"No, no, I shall bring my little girl wherever you want," Doria interrupted.

"It's the big house up by the Wall," Wren smiled while also shaking her head. "The Earl of Thamesdon. I'm afraid I couldn't take anyone else. Just Belinda."

Belinda gazed, stunned as though the thunder outside had burst through the wall and exploded around her. "The earl?"

"He's a very nice man," Wren said, "but it's awfully cold and wet outside. Have you any cloaks or warm clothes?"

"I got a proper gown for church," Belinda nodded with enthusiasm. "Reckon I'll put it on. It ain't Sunday, but earls is earls."

By now the third daughter had stumbled from the stairs into the firelight. Mary Duff interrupted her little sister. "What's up? Is something wrong?"

"No, tis proper right," squeaked Belinda.

"Naught to do with you," Lyana yelled. "No one wants us. Just that little brat."

Doria stood and clapped her hands. "Quiet, all of you. I need to think. Belinda, get back upstairs and change into your best clothes. Mary, you go and help her. Comb her hair, make sure she looks clean and tidy, and get your father's cape. Tis the shortest and might fit the child down to her toes."

"Can't. He's wearing it," said Mary.

"Oh yes, of course. Bother," Doria sniffed. "Lyanna, how long is yours. Would it fit Belinda?"

"No, and she ain't having it anyways," Lyanna screeched. "Let the stupid brat get wet." She stamped both feet one after the other and the fire puffed and went out.

"Stupid girl," Doria yelled back. "Go get it and I'll see," meanwhile trying to relight the small cooking fire with a lacklustre tinderbox.

With her own tinderbox in better condition, Wren went to Doria's side, pulled it from her purse, and lit the pile of twigs. "I'll look after Belinda, I promise," she said. "This is important. If she hasn't got a cloak, I can pull her inside mine beside me. She's little enough."

With the vibration of three pairs of feet on the stairs, now louder than the fading thunder, Lyanna, Mary, and the fully dressed Belinda, reappeared. The smallest child appeared neat, sensibly dressed, and wore a smile of pure excitement. Wren smiled back, only too aware that her own clothes were little more than rags, and her appearance was far worse than the child's.

Lyanna tossed a bundle of dark blue at her mother. "If that goes with Belinda, you'd best make bloody sure she doesn't go dribbling nor sneezing on it. She comes back with stains, I'll thrash the brat over the stool."

Belinda shouted as Doria grabbed the cloak, and puffed it out, testing the size. Made to fit a girl considerably shorter than Lyanna, it seemed perfect for covering Belinda. Clearly Lyanna had owned it for years, having no means for a replacement. Doria spread it over her youngest daughter's shoulders. It was unlined but made of blue wool, thick and hooded, a little voluminous for the skinny Belinda, but ideal to keep her dry for the first few streets, if they hurried. Covering down to her ankles, it would certainly be in risk of splashed puddles and mud, yet was unlikely to face ruin.

"It'll do," decided Doria. "and don't you say a single word, Lyanna. I won't have my little treasure going to meet an earl all soaked to the skin and covered in ice. Besides, you never paid for that cloak yourself. Your Papa got it for you."

"My Dad got it off a friend and I looked after it ever since. I'll wager that little brat drops it in a puddle."

Wren took Belinda's hand and marched quickly to the door before a worse squabble overtook them. "I'll look after both child and cloak," she said, "and I'll be back before dark or soon after. Don't you worry."

Doria opened the door for them and peered out. "Looks as if that rain's fading a bit," she said, and then to Belinda, "Now, don't you go showing off, nor behaving badly, nor crying and snivelling like you always do to get attention. You be a good girl and just tell the truth. No fibs. No making out you know more than you do."

Wet but delighted, Belinda skipped through the rain, happy both to be considered special, and to be the guest at a house of luxury belonging to one of the titled elites. She was also thrilled with what she saw as freedom, away from the boring arguments of mother and sisters.

Skipping and dancing involved kicking up water, but Wren smiled quietly and objected to nothing. Some of the puddles had begun to freeze, and the risk was of sliding and slipping, but Belinda's delight continued.

The earl's house against the northern wall, stood proud beneath the thunder, and as she pushed open the iron gates, Wren looked down at Belinda's expression of astonished wonder.

"One room," Belinda whispered, "is bigger than all my house."

"True," Wren nodded, "but let's hurry into one of those rooms before we're utterly soaked." Already the power of the rain was forcing a path through half their clothes, hoods, cloaks and boots.

Wren knocked and the steward answered, bowing and pulling the front door open wide, welcoming the face he already recognised. Belinda's awe increased as she shivered, trotting meekly behind, and into the huge candle lit hall. Landry stood by the fire, elbow to the mantle. He walked forwards as Wren entered, smiling at her and then down at Belinda as Wren introduced her.

"As our possible great saviour," Landry told the child, "take off your wet cloak and shoes, which the kind gentleman here will clean and, dry for you. Meanwhile, sit by the fire and tell me in detail what you saw concerning the house next door." He took her hand and sat her on the comfortable fireside chair, then added, "Sometimes our memories invite us to elaborate beyond the truth. In this instance, the truth is far too important to alter in any way, however tiny, but first I imagine a hot drink and some food would help all of us."

Wren sat on the second chair, while the steward, clutching a pile of the clothes virtually ruined in the prolonged storm, nodded and bowed to Landry, then disappeared. Within short moments he returned with a well piled tray. He stood this on the table and began to serve mulled wine to Landry and Wren, and a hot mixture of milk and other spices for Belinda.

There were three empty platters, and two others with oat biscuits, warm fig pies, and finally, a variety of minced meat mixtures wrapped in pastry,

It was some time before Belinda could tell her story, for she was far too busy eating, drinking, licking her fingers, and drying off her toes at the fire.

CHAPTER THIRTY

NARRATIVE

Belinda sat straight, wiped her hair down with both hands, hoping that might help her look more respectable, then cupped her hands in her lap and beamed. She was the centre of attention and felt as though the sun shone only on her for the first, and probably last, time in her life.

"One of them was ever so fat. He wore a big black hat, I never saw his face, but he sort of limped on one leg, or was that the other more skinny one. Not sure. Sort of wobbling, being so bulging round middle bits and legs. Fat curly arms too."

Landry was bright eyed. "I have been told of brothers like that," he said, smiling. "I believe, Mistress Belinda, you are telling me something of extreme importance."

Doubting if she had ever been addressed as mistress before in her life, Belinda sat up even straighter and beamed like the sun, which had not appeared outside. "He wore dark brown everything, except for the hat. I remembers him the most 'cos he was funny. Wobbly fat legs under the cape, and I know I giggled. The other looked ordinary like everyone else. Ordinary clothes too, and a little hat. Stomped and stamped, and I saw his face, but it was ordinary with big ears and a pudgy nose. It weren't raining or nothing then, but I ain't sure what day it was. I reckon it was the day before the sheriff came, or two days, I dunno what, but it were afore they died, cos I could still play sometimes, in the street with Peter nextdoor."

"So probably the same day I found them in the evening, or even the day before that. It was the next day when I went to tell the sheriff in the morning." Wren was forced to recollect the details she'd seen, and felt sick again. Her hands were so tightly clasped and rigid in her lap, the knuckles were turning white. "Two days is quite likely. I already smelled death."

The rain battering against the windows had ceased, and the hush, when they paused, was broken only by the spit and crackle of the fire, its flames brighter than the candles. The word death echoed. The great hall was dazzled in warmth, but Wren shivered. Landry frowned. The colours of the fire reflected across Wren's face, and a gleam of forehead sweat, shone scarlet. Clearly Wren was not cold, and her shivers were memories of those nightmares.

"The death of others," he murmured, looking from Belinda to Wren, "has discoloured much of your life, little bird."

Wren didn't answer, and instead looked only at Belinda. The child was eager. "Getting dead don't worry me much. Folks die all the time, but I hope my Dad never does. Me Mum lost a baby when I were five. I saw it on the bed. All red wiv blood too. Poor thing were just bald head and teeny legs all curled up."

Looking quickly away, Wren spoke to her lap. "I think I may have killed my mother. Not really, I mean just being born. I hate thinking about it." Feeling the chill of misery, she sniffed and stared again at the fire.

Belinda tapped tunes with her stockinged feet on the rug. "I can't think of no more about them men," she said, "but I don't want to go home yet. I doesn't have to, does I?"

"Not until after dinner, which is coming very soon," Landry informed her. Her grin widened. "and I haven't yet finished with questions. For instance, did any of these men carry any large objects or bags?"

"And I have an idea," Wren abruptly sat forwards, "You've mixed up the one who limped and the one with the squashed nose. Who had which? You told me it was the other way around."

Belinda stuck her grubby thumb in her mouth and sucked hard in concentration. "I doesn't reckon I remember rightly. There were one wiv this and one wiv that. I saw all three, one in front, them other two was behind. So the fancy dressed one was a bit tall, wore a hat wiv a feather, and a cape wiv fur under, and fluffed up around the neck." She smiled in all directions. "Got it? Fancy fellow first. Wish I had a cape like that."

Landry and Wren nodded. Landry said, "If these recollections help us find these vile killers, I may celebrate by buying you one. For now, start with the fat one again, please."

"Right. He come next. Fat curly legs in brown hose, wiv a hole at back of the fat bit. Had a mighty big hat. Couldn't see his face. Brown everything 'cept a black hat, what made shadows. Then we comes to number three. Last fellow was just plain ordinary, but wiv a squashed nose and flappy ears, limped a bit, he did. Then the fancy one done talked, and talked real fancy too."

"Can you remember anything he said?"

"It weren't nothing interesting," Belinda said, temporally removing her thumb from her mouth. "Stuff like 'Quiet' and 'Quick.' He talked more when they come out. That were ages and ages later, and I were back indoors fer me supper. We had grit and veggie stew stuff wiv bits o' bread. I remembers that 'cos the fancy gent's voice were louder outside. Our door were open 'cos it was nice and warm."

Landry again asked, "Weapons? Any packages?"

"The fancy one had a sword on a big red belt thing, over his shoulder. Them others had naught, but flappy ears carried a sack, not that big, but not teeny neither." Belinda again tapped her feet, lurching to the tune she heard in her head. She was enjoying every moment. "Yep. A big dirty sack wot he dragged, so I reckon it were heavy."

Sitting at the grand table, with a sparkling white linen tablecloth, was Belinda's first experience of opulence, never having seen a table so large, nor one neat under linen. Wren had sat here for several dinners and various suppers already, but the experience had been new to her too, and had verged on intimidating.

As the earl now appeared and took his place at the head of the table, Belinda gazed open mouthed and silent.

"A fruitful meeting, no doubt?" he asked, looking at Wren's expression and the child's incredulity.

"Highly useful, although with limits," Landry answered. "and I'm hoping you'll stretch those limits, Morgan. Leading the group into the killing, this delightful young lady has told us there were three men who arrived at the house, and the leader was dressed and spoke as a titled gentleman. Immediately I am reminded of a baron having been mentioned. Someone you might know, if luck's on our wheel."

Leaning back and scratching his chin, the earl lapsed, forgot his meal and didn't speak for some time. Wren said quickly, "It's always possible he wasn't titled at all. Simply a thief and murderer, who stole sufficient to make him rich enough to buy the clothes he shouldn't be wearing."

Very softly, Landry agreed. "That is certainly possible," he murmured. "but I have an idea who that might be."

"You might. As I might," The earl wore gold rings, some studded, on every finger. Absently he turned them, twisting them in sequence as though this aided his concentration. His eyes half closed. "I've met the younger brother, a cousin of sorts. We are not friends, but I remain polite when we're forced to meet." He smiled at Belinda. "See if my description fits. This cousin is almost as tall as Landry here, though a little less I believe. He holds no position and no land, but enjoys expensive clothes, bright colours, and peacock feathers in his hats. As the second son, strangely, he was never introduced to either the church or the political houses, and no doubt is the type to have fought against such prospects. Yet he seems particularly wealthy, more so than most second sons, considering that the family was never a rich one. He is largely disliked, but I don't know him well enough to judge his friends. His face is almost chinless, but his other features are average. His hair is pale brown, almost fair, but lifeless, and he wears it long and straight. Does this sound like your wicked killer?"

"Proper close," Belinda told him at once. "I doesn't know all them words yer lordship done used, but he done had fancy rings like you m'lord, but not so many. And had shiny teeth. I looked cos grand people don't never come down my street. Dunno bout the chin cos he wore a big collar, all fur, what near nigh come to his eyes."

"Interesting." Landry took up his cup of wine. "I speak of the same man. I don't know him, but I know of him. Paul Waddington, younger brother of Baron Lyle. Indeed, many have said that he seems unusually wealthy for a younger brother without position, and has more money than morals."

"He's a cockroach," the earl agreed, "I shall see if I can discover where he lives. Not an easy task since I don't really know the man, he may be a cousin, a fourth cousin actually, but never a friend. As for Baron Lyle, he makes no friends. I doubt he'd allow his steward to admit me to the house."

"If you find either of them, take at least four of your guards with you," Landry advised. "If we're right, then both could be dangerous."

"Always 'if. Will we ever know anything for sure?" Cautiously, Wren added, "But wouldn't a man like that wear a disguise, or at least something less noticeable, when intending to slaughter, especially a murder so outrageous?"

"Not if he is an arrogant idiot," Morgan said, the food on his platter ignored and now cold. "Indeed, he might purposefully have wished to be seen, making his threat to others."

"And invariably wears a crimson leather baldric, whether or not the holster holds his sword," Landry spoke to himself, adjusting his memories.

"But my lord, how could you have a cousin capable of such things?" Wren stared at the earl.

"I don't choose my relatives unfortunately ," Morgan smiled, remembering his platter, and spoke after he swallowed. "He is clearly corrupt, I disliked him as a child. I've avoided him ever since, and now know very little of him. I doubt his brother is a pious creature. I was once sure he indulged in piracy. I rarely see either of them. Perhaps now I'll pretend to friendship, but both will immediately distrust my intentions."

"Not relations to welcome or trust sudden attempts at friendship, I would think" Landry smiled.

The earl pushed away the platter of cold food. "Only fourth cousins, no closer, thank the good Lord. Somewhere in the north, my father informed me I have sixteenth cousins who own a small farm and help shear the sheep. Odd, yet better than these foul criminals. Never met them either."

"If you arrange to visit this baron, call me if you want me," Landry said. "or send me instead. You'll more easily gain admittance, but I shall more easily be seen as someone wishing to trade wickedness."

"This is going to mean a highly interesting discussion after supper," the earl grinned. "but I accept you are the better actor."

Dusk was heavy in the narrow lanes as Wren guided Belinda home. The rain had stopped but the wind had increased, whistling through alleys, chimneys and poorly shuttered windows. Huddled within her sister's now newly cleaned cloak, one hand keeping the hood tight, Belinda clumped over the cobbles in her boots, now shining brown after the first clean of their existence.

"One hop, two hop, five hop six," and Berlinda hopped.

"There's three and four before five and six," Wren told her. "You may need to count your fingers again."

"But you ain't hopping," objected Belinda.

Wren did not feel at all like hopping. She was deep in thought. It mattered little concerning the two assistants when their leader might already be known to Landry. Too soon, perhaps, for the sheriff, but Landry might identify the killers within the week. Success sped closer. She avoided the questions she knew would fly if she was forced to face Doria, so pushed Belinda through her unlocked door, and quickly retraced her footsteps.

Even a few steps distant, she could hear Belinda's voice squeaking, high pitched. "They got a tablecloth wiv lacey stuff on the corners, and them cups is all silver and is matching too, wiv silver spoons what dazzle in the firelight. Candles too, loads of them, smelling proper lovely, not like our one."

Smiling silently, Wren hurried back to her glorious but temporary home, while reminding herself of the cape to buy for Belinda, knowing she desperately needed a new one as well.

⋈

Landry and the earl sat facing each other beside the fire, and Wren knew herself unneeded. She hurried upstairs to her bedchamber, discovered the flicker of fire warming the room, shutters already raised, and a cup of spiced wine, still steaming on the stool beside the bed. The dreams that followed were sweet.

⋈

Waking to a soft white flurry outside the window, Wren rediscovered her sense of excitement. The beauty of the snow, as delicate as icing on a cake, seemed to promise something special. She ran downstairs, not even bothering to remake her bed. This time, just for once, she would leave it for one of the maids.

The breakfast table, however, was entirely empty. A kitchen boy heard her arrival and apologised, promising to serve the reheated food. "T'was Master Crawford being so early as sent us out o' time," he attempted to explain. "Got up so early, he did, and went out soon after."

Earnestly assuring the boy that his confusion was understandable, and she wouldn't dream of complaint, but Wren was disappointed. She'd not see Landry for some hours now.

She also expected the earl to have accompanied Landry, but as she finished her breakfast and pushed back her chair, throwing the linen napkin to the empty platter, she heard the earl entering behind her. She turned at once.

"No problem, Wren," he called, "I'll not bother with food this morning. Ale is the only necessity."

Wren smiled. "You're busy, I presume, my lord."

"Not in the least," he told her, accepting the brimming cup brought by the steward. "Simply tired, and eager to know the latest news once Landry reappears."

"Speaking of Landry," her excitement was bubbling more than the ale, "Morgan, my lord, you once promised me a bedtime story."

The earl had clearly forgotten. "My dear," he frowned, "I'm just out of bed. Not time to go back to it quite yet."

She renewed the smile. "Landry's not likely to be here for some hours. It was all about him you said."

Chuckling, the earl sipped his wine and beckoned. "Then we will sit by the fire, and I shall enjoy the company. It might be a long day, thick snow outside and boredom within. So a pleasant and secretive gossip is a damned good idea."

Having followed her host from the small breakfast chamber and into the vast hall, Wren saw the fire leap high into the chimney, the heat of its light illuminating past the still shuttered windows.

"I'll be – fascinated – whatever you choose to tell me," and she leaned forwards to take the cup the steward now brought her, avoiding the embarrassment she was sure would once again turn her pink. She then slipped back into the comfortable depths of the chair. Previously she had hoped to pass the day speaking with Landry. Now she decided this might be more informative.

Morgan also leaned back, his huge blue eyes static, and his hands spread together beneath his chin as though supporting it. "Well now, let us see if I can re-exercise my ancient memory. Landry was one of the grooms' sons, born just as I became independent, and considered myself adult. But a soft skinned bundle of beauty made me want to keep him nearby and I saw him many times until he grew out of his nether-cloths. The groom was no friend of mine, but when he died, I found the son in need of a home. And buffoon though I was, I couldn't help realising that I had a half empty house to share, and a desire for companionship. By that time, Landry was becoming an adult. Highly different, I remember, from his infant state."

Wren had permitted an eager move forward, and now she sat on the edge of the chair. "Because of being an orphan yourself?"

"Perhaps." Although speaking of sadness, Morgan's voice remained eager, soft, and pretty. "I never met his mother, but I soon heard of the cruel misery she'd caused when Landry was young. He was sixteen when I got him. Yes, he'd changed. Polite, quiet and dutiful, but also angry and ready to steal, cause damage, and be rude if crossed. Eventually that also changed, and we grew closer."

Wren sat silent before gulping a request for the earl to continue. "I can't think of him as small and rude. Please tell me more."

"My dutiful titled father saw little of me, and I spent my early childhood with my nurse. I cared for the woman, but she was more of an organised soldier than a substitute for my mother. How delightful all parents can be. If I complained, my father thrashed me as fathers seem to do."

"My father," Wren smiled, "had the same idea. Discipline is such a bore."

"As a young man I saw little of Landry's father, but I did notice that he avoided going home, so attended the local tavern and then went home only when piss-trodden." He sniggered, remembering. "So, when he died, puking over the stable where he slept, I was happy to call Landry back. Unrecognisable of course. Just pale sulky eyes."

Wren nodded. "And his mother?"

"I know nothing of her except that she was already dead," Morgan nodded. "There was some mumble of Landry disliking her, even being afraid of her, but I never heard proof."

"But Landry is never afraid."

The earl rang a tiny bell sitting beside the hearth, a page came running, and this time he ordered wine. While waiting, he reached forwards and patted Wren's hand, now gripping the wooden seat beneath her. "Landry is unusual," he said softly. "My best friend, perhaps. I have never aspired to be his equal, as my courage is kept locked in a tiny brass box in the back of my mind."

She laughed, waiting for the wine to be poured. She was surprised to be handed a handsome pewter cup, almost full to the brim. She drank. The wine tasted like nectar itself.

Morgan grinned, finishing his own wine and pouring himself another from the jug. "Now we are friends," he said, laughing through wine-stained lips. "I do my duty to my king, and I remember my parents as dutiful souls, but my joy is with Landry, and of course at my country home with my partner Timothy. I chose a partner instead of a wife, a rarity perhaps, but not unknown, and so I am happy. A rich and happy man can afford to help others."

Her nod was vigorous enough to spill her wine as she wobbled, eager. "I don't think I could call myself happy, but thanks to you – Morgan – now I can help people too. Maybe it's a strange sort of help to find killers and send them to gaol, but it is helping in a way, isn't it. It would help people who wouldn't be the next victims after all, and it will maybe make me happy too, especially staying here. Your house is a palace."

"Not quite, but whatever you wish to call it, you are welcome to it." Sighing, Wren leaned back, eyes closed in contentment, but she did not mention her own growing feelings for Landry. "I doubt," Morgan refilled her cup, "whether seeking murderers is a pleasant pastime, but surely satisfying. When I'm here I try to help, but Landry invariably ignores my suggestions. I'm no sheriff."

"Nor are most of the sheriffs."

"It seems that Landry enjoys finding out who did all these foul deeds, and tossing the culprits into gaol. So, going back to the story, eventually he needed his own space, and the rooms above the stables already existed and sat empty. That suited him perfectly. But now we're back together again and I've no complaints." The earl was now beaming. "Sometimes Timothy accompanies me to London, but usually I join him in the country. He is certainly the one I love, but Landry's a friend I trust and value. He asks for five pounds, I give him ten, and he kills a few more bullies, saves a dozen folk or more, and puts a great number into Newgate. He's the hero no one knows about. Except myself, Timothy and Jacob. The priest is a nice fellow who never criticises me, Landry does, but that's what true friendship allows. We all do what Landry tells us, even my steward." He smiled at the thought.

Peering into her grand pewter cup, Wren realised she'd drunk the lot and was frightened she'd end up as ossified as Landry's father. Morgan might pride himself that he was never intoxicated, but she smiled as she heard his slurred words and watched him stumble. It was only midday, the earl wasn't long out of his bedchamber, but he'd already drunk enough for the day.

"Thank you so much for telling me," she said, wondering if she ought to help him upright, "and I'm so proud to be part of such a wonderful group. Does anyone else work alongside you all?"

Half standing, Morgan frowned. "Can't remember," he said. "Couple of dogs. Couple of horses. Oh yes, and Prad of course, and now you."

"I'm thrilled to be included," she said, and although she was silently laughing, what she said was true.

The earl tottered back to the grand staircase, and Wren stayed curled beside the fire. Wide awake but still dreaming, she waited through the long hours. But Landry did not reappear.

The next morning dawned without the light of even a reluctant sun. It was the twenty fourth of December, the eve of Christmas Day itself, and the city was roused for more celebration.

Rising late to a cloudy sky and a thick layer of frost outside, Wren expected another day of lonely disappointment, both the earl and Landry to have left the house, eager with investigations surely already started. Because of bored inactivity the day before, she had gone early to bed, yet had risen late, imagining more of the same. The bed had been so warm, and the dreams so encouraging, she'd taken advantage of what she had supposed would be an empty house.

Yet Landry greeted her as she slipped into the small breakfast room in the hope of bread, sausages and ale. He regarded her over the rim of his cup.

"The rags you wear will be ideal for today's business," he told her, unsmiling. "Later, should there be time, and both still live, I intend to enlarge your clothing collection somewhat." He did not mention that this had been promised before, but no clothes, not even a shift, had yet appeared. He smiled. "But for now, your appearance seems ideal for the part I wish you to play. So don't bother combing your hair."

"I've combed it already." Wren was confused.

"Then perhaps a new comb can also come later," Landry continued. "For the moment, I believe we match well enough."

Wren remained puzzled.

"You may not have noticed," Landry added, "but I am clothed rather differently to my usual appearance."

He put down both cup and bread, and Wren saw his drab belted tunic, unbleached linen, no collar and no cuffs. As he stood, crossing to the chair by the fire, she also saw that beneath the unturned hem of the tunic, he wore roughly knitted brown hose, which did not cling, and folded unattractively around the knee. As yet, he wore no shoes, and the hose flopped, longer than his feet, wrinkled around each ankle. She had certainly never seen him like this before.

Wren nodded, smiling delightedly. "You actually want me to come with you?"

"My unappreciated wife," he told her, "needs to be less talkative, but extremely useful. I am John Spelding and you, my dear, are Lizzie Spelding, a housewife without food to cook."

Guessing what delighted her, she said, "We're poor then, and you don't work."

"Luckily," he regarded her gravely from beneath his heavy

eyelids, "I worked long hours yesterday and finally discovered a good amount of what I have passed frustrated months wanting to know. We are finally closing in and nearer the discovery than any time before. So, my beloved but poverty stricken wife, drink your wine. We have a long way to go."

CHAPTER THIRTY ONE

WREN

The house was long and low, the upper storey rising only centrally, and sufficient for just one room. Inelegant, it was more of a large shed, roofed in a thin thatch, which hung loose, carrying more mould than tight reeds. It slumped close to farmland, and the calls of the cattle floated through the trees' bare branches, as the cows were released from their winter shed, for an hour's exercise in the cold. I had never worked on a farm, but I'd visited a few, when searching for work years back.

Some miles north of the old postern of Moorgate, having waded through the start of the moors and their filthy mush, we avoided the worst by heading west.

This was not far, Landry pointed out, from the quarry. A quick trot on horseback I expected, but an uncomfortable walk. I immediately thought of poor Randell Ford working in the quarry. I expect he had the sense to keep away from these marshes.

Landry and I looked like the beggars I thought sadly I was not far from it. Landry limped slightly. I didn't know if that was an act, or whether it was caused by those horrible flat wooden shoes he now wore, and so we hobbled to the front doorway of this ugly old building, and Landry knocked.

A small fat man answered. I wondered if this was the obese killer that Belinda had described.

"I ain't worked afore, but I needs it some now," Landry said in a voice I certainly didn't recognise. "The lord met me long ago, so he knows me trusting. We're mighty hungry, so any food if there ain't no work, but both if he can."

I stood obediently silent. I couldn't have thought of anything to say under the circumstances. The fat man thought aloud. "Dunno, would he? Don't usually. Might though, if he remembers you. You wait here whilst I finds out."

We waited patiently as the door was closed in our faces. Landry didn't even look at me.

After more waiting than I'd expected, and at the point of patience disappearing, the door opened again. "There ain't no work," said the fat man having finally reappeared. "but there be bread and honey."

I thought it quite a nice offer under the circumstances. However, as we were led into the kitchen quarters, separated from the main house by a half door, and told to sit on the three legged and lopsided stools, I understood the reason. His lordship, though I wasn't sure he counted as a lord indeed, strode in behind us to stare at Landry, checking whether he had ever met him. The idea worked well. Something about Landry obviously seemed familiar, but no memory of who he really was could creep in. Landry looked even more like a mouse-brained beggar than I did.

"Umm," said the gruff voice behind us. "maybe I know you, or maybe I don't."

Landry turned, and looked obsequious. Even beggarly. "My lord, tis an honour to see you again. I knowed you long ago. T'was your brother the baron I worked for."

"In what capacity, man?"

"Whatever his lordship done told me," Landry said, and I felt like laughing. "Scrubbing and other kitchen stuff, grooming his lordship's horse. Fanny she were, but I reckon t'will be another by now. An I done plenty more, getting the whores in, and then chucking them out, a bit o' fishing sometimes, but mostly thumping folks what owed him coin and didn't pay up."

"I remember the mare Fanny," the tall man said without giving his own name. "I remember you from somewhere, no doubt that's the one, and perhaps you could be useful."

I was acting the dutiful and thoroughly bullied wife as Landry had ordered, keeping my head down. It helped when I wanted to laugh, but had to stay silent. It had been Morgan who had evidently given us the name. He'd even told us about Fanny the mare, but this was no baron living in luxury, it was his brother, Paul Waddington.

The fat man had dumped a platter before us, a small terracotta pot of rich dark honey, and a pile of dark bread. I wasn't hungry but I had to pretend I was, which wasn't so hard when I smelled the honey. So, I sat, nibbled, and hopefully seemed sullen, starving, and stupid.

Ignoring me, Landry and Paul Waddington spoke for some time. Landry kept up his East London twitter, and lied for a good half an hour. In case I had to know the same stories, none of which were true of course, I tried to listen. Not difficult, since no one bothered speaking to me.

I could hear the rain starting again outside, thumping against the old shed walls, but also heard the interest growing in the man's replies. Everything was going well.

Then he said, "Yes, you'll be mighty useful, so I'll give you the small shed at the end of the fence out there. It's small, but a damn site better than sleeping under a bridge. You'll get blankets and free food. Once I've tested you out, both of you that is, then I'll discuss the possibility of wages. Your wife can start in the kitchen, but she'll be more useful later. Do you object to sharing her? Not for myself, naturally, but there are other men working here from time to time."

"Reckon I'd object," Landry said with an apologetic smile. "She ain't the type, nor me to let her."

I was utterly amazed and even more horrified, but since Landry had already discussed how little time he expected us to stay here, I managed not to react except for concentrating on the last piece of bread and honey.

Waddington seemed disinterested, and half nodded. "Of no importance. There's matters of far more interest."

Halfway through his answer, I heard the door behind us open again, and the pounding of footsteps followed. I didn't want to show curiosity, but Waddington looked up, "Looks like we got new workers. Come in." But whoever it was rushed out again, and the door slammed behind him. Presumably, new companions were of little curiosity, but I thought the fat man looked surprised, and he immediately crossed the little room, following the unseen newcomer outside. Landry and Waddington simply went on talking.

After what seemed an endless conversation without any useful information, our disgusting host said, "Follow me. I'll show you your sleeping quarters and send Hamward to get you blankets. Stay there until I send for you."

We dutifully followed him, looking grateful. I just kept my head down. It rained on us, and the wind was icy, but it was only a few steps away. Once left alone, we stood in the centre of the tiny mess and stared at each other.

Landry put a finger against his lips. "Whisper, or nothing," he told me in his own whisper, and I was so pleased to hear his normal voice again. "You act your part well. One day only, and we'll be gone."

"And one night?"

"Unfortunately, yes." Of course, Landry had slept in worse. Newgate for example. Here it was tiny, dark and stank of mould and worse. The walls were thin wood panels, the roof was poorly thatched, and the ground was a mess of broken stools, untreated leather, and a large tin pot, probably once used for bleaching, although now empty, since it still stank of urine. Landry pointed at the bed. "One night only, and you wake on Christmas Day. Morgan will no doubt have a celebration waiting for us."

The blankets were brought. There were four of them, all amply decorated with unravelling holes and a variety of stains. I made a sort of bed, moving away the rubbish beneath, and promptly flopped down on it myself. Landry sat beside me but facing away. His whisper eventually broke through my boredom.

"Doubtless this day and night will be unutterably dull, but that is better than having to start scrubbing ovens and killing neighbours. I simply need to know whatever I can discover as soon as I can. For instance, the man he calls Hamward is a total stranger to me. If I meet any of the others working here, hopefully they'll not know me, or at least not recognise me dressed in this manner."

Agreeing, since I considered him entirely unrecognisable, I muttered a few pointless additions and closed my eyes. I thought I could even smell the marshes. They stretched for miles, and this was about as close to them that anyone would agree to live. So, the quarries weren't far. I didn't know which one was where Jessy's husband had worked, but none were too distant.

I'd only tumbled out of bed three or four hours previously, but I was almost asleep again when everything started to turn against us.

First, there was shouting from the house. We weren't far off, but even so, I wouldn't have heard a thing if it had been normal speech.

Then Hamward waddled over. Our tiny shed had no lock and even the door didn't fit well, so the outside was a slushy half puddle. When he pushed the door open, the fat man stood in this muck but seemed unbothered.

"Master wants you," he said, and pointed at me. "gotter hurry. So come on."

Why me and not Landry? With a reminder of what Waddington had seemed to think my more obvious use was, I didn't stand up. Staying exactly where I was, I said, "Sorry. I'm so very tired."

But Hamward shook his fat arms, which wobbled. "Master says come, you gotter do it." He reached out a large fat fingered hand and tried to grab me.

Pulling my arm away, I glared at him. "What's he want me for?"

"Dunno," he glared back. "It don't matter. You come, or I drags you by yer hair."

Landry looked up as though barely interested, and I thought he might be more annoyed with me for arguing, but he said, "You ain't doing no such thing, this being me wife. Ask nice, and tell her what for."

"Dunno what for. Washing platters. Washing floors. Washing summit no doubt."

Having heard the shouting, I didn't believe him. "The master sounds angry. Why?"

"Dunno, but you come and you comes quick."

Very softly and under his breath, Landry told me, "Go, but be careful. Call out for me if you need. Remember, just yell for me if there's the slightest hint of danger." Loudly, and to the fat man, he said, "No fellow gonna hurt my wife. You hear me? Best look after her, or I'll look after you."

So, I took my time standing, nodded without diminishing my glare, and followed Hamward. He grabbed my shoulder and pushed me, I managed to shake him off, but only for a moment.

The house door was open, but no one stood there, so we walked into silence. Then almost immediately the door closed behind me, and I turned.

"It seems," sneered Paul Waddington, "that you and your husband are better frauds than I gave you credit for, but I am relieved to have discovered the truth so quickly."

I felt sick. I also had an idea of what might have happened. The other person who had walked in and slammed the kitchen door while we were there, had recognised Landry? They had known who Landry was – and who he wasn't? That was why the visitor had left and not faced us. Landry would know so many of the Newgate inmates, and others too of course. It had always been a risky idea, even though his disguise had seemed so good.

Evidently not so perfect and now I expected – well – some form of retaliation. I was ready to scream for Landry, but I wasn't convinced of anything yet.

"Take her away," said the pig. "You know where, and tie her hands at her back."

Hamward did as he was asked, and so tightly, it damn well hurt. That was all I needed, and opened my mouth ready to shout. But as my mouth opened, the fat man stretched it open even further, forcing in a dirty smelling rag that filled my throat. I shook my head wildly, trying to spit it out, but it was too large, and I had no hands to use. Fear coursed through me as I thought I'd choke.

The stringy rope bit into my wrists, and the beast clamped his massive hand on my upper arm and thrust me forward. Outside the back door and directly at our feet, was a steel lidded hole in the ground. A rusty and broken pump stood at the edge. I assumed it was a well. Already afraid and expecting a beating or worse, I couldn't think. Then he kicked off the lid and shoved me forwards.

The force of his cold hand pounded against the small of my back and I fell. All weight, all sight, and all understanding was gone in that instant. I was overwhelmingly dizzy, terrified and in pain.

I whirled, and slammed against rock. The faint turned to agony. My hair tumbling below me, feet struggling to find purchase, skirts blinding me. But there was no doubt I was tumbling down the well. Suddenly I was upright again, shoulder against rock, bouncing back, knee on rock, such pain. My foot almost in my mouth.

With my vomit flew the rag. And desperately I tried to scream.

I had no time to imagine what death would be like. I simply knew it was close. My ragged skirts were streaked with vomit, and vomit in my face. Terror was all I could feel.

I just hoped Landry would hear me and be warned, so escape his own murder. Blackness overtook everything else.

CHAPTER THIRTY TWO

NARRATIVE

Kicking open the locked door, Landry strode in. Inside Paul Waddington looked up, surprised at such an almighty disturbance. He toppled as Landry suddenly wedged his arm and inner elbow around the man's neck from behind, his other hand pulling his head back buy the hair.

Tightening his neck lock, the grip on his hair now wedged hard to his skull, Landry was within one squeeze of strangling the man. Waddington's feet slid, his knees buckled, and he was held upright only by the arm beneath his chin.

The attack had been instantaneous. Panicked, Waddington struggled, wheezed, trying desperately to grab Landry's face, scratching and punching, his hands twisting, unable to find purchase, only air, reaching nothing, then hanging limp as the breath was forced from him.

Landry's voice was his own, very soft, it slid like silk into Waddington's ear. "You will tell me where she is, or I will kill you now."

The struggle, determined and frenzied, did not remove Waddington from Landry's grasp. With his captor behind him and his legs sliding from beneath him, he had neither means nor hope of defence. Although choking, he was able to croak once, calling for Hamward.

The fat man heard the noise, and surprised, looked into the room.

"What?" Though he could see what.

"If you attempt to fight me," Landry spat, "I will kill him within a heartbeat, then you."

Waddington's struggle surged, lapsed, then surged again, proved useless, but he continued. He had long known himself as a fighter of undisputed success. His failure and his own impending death now clamped black and heavy within his belly.

Landry tightened the arm around Waddington's neck, forcing his chin up beyond its normal rise, while skin of his face turned white. He then released the man's hair, grabbed a long-bladed knife from within his belted tunic, and thrust this to the scrawny neck beneath the squeeze of his arm. The shallow skin cut began to bleed.

Hamward stared, then shouted. "Pays well, he do. Let him go. And he'll pay you too."

Landry raised an eyebrow. "Once he is dead, which will be after you answer my question, you can search this house for every hidden coin. I imagine there will be plenty once you start looking, but first, where is the woman who came here in my company."

"My mate said as how you wasn't wed," the fat man insisted.

"Where is she? Quickly, or I'll kill this fool and you both. But tell me now and as long as I find my friend at once, I shall leave you to search for whatever you want."

Hamward rubbed his nose. "Won't be proper easy. The wench is down the well."

Landry's eyes narrowed to fire blown fury, and he slid the edge of the knife deep into the neck below it. Waddington's eyes opened wide, as the blood poured from the cut, he slumped without noise, falling to the ground in the deep red puddle. His cut neck open to bone and divided artery pouring blood from the wound. His head tumbled back, almost severed.

For one fleeting moment both legs twitched as though pedalling for life. Then the lump lay face up in his own oozing puddle and was motionless.

Hamward pulled himself together. "That were bloody quick. I reckon he hardly knew he were alive afore he were dead. Right, I reckon I goes fer the coin then."

"First you can help me rescue the woman," Landry held up one blood-stained hand. The thought of a narrow stone well, and the woman falling, blasted through his mind like the knife he'd just used. Wren's death was already likely. He swallowed back the thought, he needed to find her and he refused to think beyond that.

"Not much point," Hamward said, "Reckon she's gone. Tis a mighty deep well and no water. Smash the head I reckon, but at least she won't drown. You come along, you never knows yer luck."

The whistle of the wind seemed to come from her own body. The fall held such horror, battering her head and body against rock as she tumbled, unconscious when she hit the base. Laying crooked, bloody and comatose, unaware of what time passed, she escaped the pain and the darkness that enclosed her.

Wren regained consciousness not long after and awoke dazed and dizzy, the pain made her sick, and she vomited over her clothes again, she knew only that her head screamed. One arm and one leg were bent beneath her when she had landed, and surely were broken. Wren lay on wet earth. The well, long abandoned, was an oozing swamp, littered with dead birds and mice half stuck in mud.

The stone walls, rising high above her, would be, she knew, impossible to climb. Too smooth, slippery with rain, and so high she could barely see the mouth above.

For long dark minutes, Wren stayed very still, feeling the pain strike every part of her. Yet needing to test what was really broken, she inched her arms to the right, then left. Both arms raged. One leg more painful than the other she struggled first to her knees, then lurched, sobbing, and fell back to sit against the unforgiving rock face. Her head still a thunder of explosions with no method of calming it, so finally, she rose again to her knees. Although painful both legs still worked.

Wren's hands, no longer tied, lay in her lap. The twists of her fall had loosened the rope, it had also wrenched her shoulder. Having regained the use of her arms despite cursing the pain, she stretched herself back into mobility. Then wondered what god or fate had kept her alive, when she knew she should have died.

Unable to see in such absolute darkness, it was her hand that discovered the passageway leading off to her right.

Yet discovering a path to escape would surely be unlikely, however, the tunnel was waiting. It was too low for her to walk upright, nor did she believe herself capable of standing. With excruciating pain, she crawled.

The minute prick of light from the well's mouth, far above, blinked out as she moved into the passage, crawling into an even denser darkness.

She only knew she was crying when she felt the cold tears falling on her hands. Wren forced the tears back, feeling out for sudden drops, she crawled on.

Sloping always up, sometimes steep, it promised a return to reality, yet her greatest worry was the man who wanted her dead might see her, and try to kill her again. Crawling upwards exhausted her, the palms of her hands on the jagged rock base were cut into a thousand bleeding holes and scratches. Pausing, crawling, gasping for breath, then pausing again, was her only way to push onwards.

Wren paused, hearing a voice that told her she was lucky and should welcome the life that was now being restored to her. She only realised it was her own voice when she collapsed, lying in her own bloody stains, she closed her eyes, sobbing once more.

Unmoving for what seemed eternity, she prayed, for safety, for strength, even for sleep. Only sleep – or death.

"I hear something," Landry said. Hamward stooped beside him. Get me rope, netting or anything that might help me down."

Hamward grunted with complaint.

"There's rope here," Landry growled. "Get it. Every length you find."

"Bloody hell," sniffed the fat man, toddling back into the house.

Landry sat on the well's rim and continued to call. He heard the echoes of his own voice repeating downwards into the gloom, yet there was no further sound from way below.

He needed rope but there was another risk, in that he might reach the bottom, and even discover Wren alive, but once he was down there, Hamward would surely leave. Landry might be capable of climbing back up, if the man had not dislodged the rope, but even his highest hopes did not include Wren being able to climb. She would at best, be severely injured. He did not think climbing such a distance on cheap rope, would enable him to carry Wren too.

Loathing indecision, he was unused to fear.

Interrupting Hamward said from behind, "I got bits of rope. More n' I thought, but it ain't enough."

Landry controlled his fury, fearing Wren must indeed be dead and broken, whilst knowing that he still had to reach her. "Tie the rope around your waist, if you have one. Then wind it three times around the trunk of that tree. Stand behind the tree, and hold on to it with both arms. I shall then stretch the rope down into the well and climb it as far as it will take me."

"Umm," mumbled the fat man. Landry turned. Hamward held up a length which might wind twice around the tree trunk but little more.

Landry paused. "Then I shall need blankets and sheets to shred for additional length. Is there wire in your sheds? What else might lower me to the well's end?"

Hamward shook his head. "It'll be mighty easier if you goes t'other way."

Staring, "What other way? Quick. She's down there dying."

"I tells you," Hamward pointed left. "The lass surely be already dead, but you trot along with me, mate, and I takes you a better way."

The lassitude of the grey rain had blown into Landry's head. He believed nothing, but stood, and quickly followed the fat man around the back of the house, and then a short march amongst the trees.

There was, he saw at once, another well. He sighed, "Not much of an improvement, but can I hope this is not as deep, and connects with the other?"

"Oh yeah, joins together they does, but this ain't no well, it be just a muddy slope. Long past when that well were a well, this helped all the rain fill it up. Reckon you can walk down it. I ain't done it for years, but I done it twice before, and I seen others do it, and come back an' all."

This was a blessed improvement. Kneeling, Landry stroked one hand into the hole's edge. Immediately he felt the soft earthen slope. Reaching into his tunic's belt where the bloody knife blade now protruded, he pulled out a tinder box, and lit a clump of dry twigs from amongst the undergrowth. Now he saw the slope more clearly, and the proof of its continuance.

"You'll come with me," Landry told Hamward, "and walk first."

"Bloody hell," mumbled the fat man. "I knowed you was gonna say that." But without further complaint, he sat, pushed out his legs and slid onto the top of the slope. Then he managed to stand, bending only his head and knees, called back for Landry to keep the tiny torch blazing, and continued to walk, half slipping, part bent, but able to move forwards.

Landry followed. He gripped the rope, which he thought might still be of help, held up the light, and did not slip. His feet were covered only in the loose hose, as he had left the wooden clogs at the top. His toes gripped and although he was bent almost double, he had no intention of stopping.

The low roofed, tunnel, continued downwards. Landry refused to think, refused to entertain any doubts. The pitch dragged, seemingly endless, and the torch Landry had made spat and started to burn his fingers. The scramble down was steep, yet not steep enough to fall.

Landry heard a sudden scuffle ahead, too muffled and too far ahead to be Hamward. He paused, and then called, dropping the ashes of the torch and holding both palms around his lips to increase the sound.

The call of her name floated, repeating, doubling, each call amplified until abruptly the voice changed. Then, so much fainter and so much more desperate, it was no longer the word 'Wren' which dominated the tunnel. A new call echoed although faint and tentative. "Is it you? Is it you Landry?"

At once Landry ran.

CHAPTER THIRTY THREE

WREN

When I heard his voice, I knew I must be dreaming. I knew my own mind was marking me for death.

But then I didn't just hear him, I saw him.

Although the roof above me was higher, I was still on my knees. I'd tried to stand, but one leg bent pitifully, just as one wrist had done, ever since I woke from the hopelessness.

I couldn't run into his arms, but he almost ran into mine, and I found myself lifted. Immediately I knew safety, and I closed my eyes in utter relief.

Landry lay me down and sat beside me on the muddy slope. The feet of someone else, leading to extremely fat ankles in brown woolly hose, flanked me, but I wasn't interested in anything but Landry. I think I muttered something, but I doubt it made sense.

He whispered back, "Bless you for living. I feared you gone. The creature who meant your death is now dead himself."

"You killed him?"

"Naturally."

"And how long have I been down here?" I asked. It really didn't matter, so an absurd question, but I felt I'd been half dying and crawling around for a week.

"A little less than a day," Landry told me in that soft voice. "and now I take you back so you can sleep, and find the cure for your injuries."

He must have carried a torch, as a tiny bundle of twigs was almost under our feet, spitting and guttering, but still offering a meagre light. I could stare up at the roof by that scattered flicker, seeing shadows dancing above me. Landry's profile glowed, then spun, long and dark, that strong and unusually straight nose, the straight line of a square chin then rising up into thick dark hair, the low brows and the eyes flashing bright with flame.

Beside us, another long shadow lay,

"What's that?" I whispered, pointing to the rocks sloping ahead.

It was, whatever else it was, lying almost beside us. At first, he saw nothing. "Fallen rock or piled mud probably. But now I'll carry you back to the world above."

His arms around me were magical. I tingled with the warmth. As he turned, his feet kicked against the unmoving bundle. "Hamward," he called, "what's that? Do you see?"

I had no idea who Hamward was, but heard his voice. "Dunno. Don't care. Oh, very well. I'll look likes you says." Then that same voice changed to a strangled gulp, then croaked. "Tis a body, not no animal neither. Dunno who. Face is all banged up, but tis a female I reckon."

"Shit," Landry said, kneeling again, while I clung to him with the one hand that still worked.

I heard the indrawn breath as he examined the body. I felt sick again. Speaking was painful, everything was painful, but I tried. Gutteral gasps sounded between every word. "The bastard killed someone else. Did he admit to killing Jessy before you killed him?"

"Not yet." Just a faint murmur.

"Well, he won't now if he's dead," I said. But my voice was too feeble to sound rude.

"I have a form of proof," he told me, "but now there's another murder. The woman left here was clearly killed some time gone." He called Hamward, his voice louder. "Take the rope and tie the corpse, then pull it as we walk. The wretched creature needs identification, and burial. Can you think who she might be?"

Hamward's voice remained reluctant, though I could only see those bulging ankles. "Dunno. I keeps telling you, I don't know nuffin."

I heard the rummaging and scuffling, and presumed the dead female's body was being tied for an easier removal. I still couldn't speak. I thought of Jessy, and knew now that these foul wretches had done perhaps a hundred vile things. I just clutched tight at Landry's shoulder in the hope of stopping my stomach from finding yet more content to expel .

It was a long walk, harder, being uphill. Though I was carried like a baby. It felt such a relief for me, perhaps not for him.

Eventually I could feel the slope had turned flat. We were there. Out of the hole, at least, then through the trees, a dark sky above, between the bare branches. And finally a door.

Landry had dropped the torch he'd been holding, so now the light came only from a smudge of moon. He took me around the edge of the building that looked more like a shed, and I remembered being told I had to sleep in one. Though that could have been one of those dreams.

Then we were inside, and Landry laid me on a small straw bed, whispered about being back soon, and disappeared. I was entirely vague about what was reality. So again, I shut my eyes and I think I dozed. I was aware of things swimming around me. There were bodies, trails of blood, and murmurings. I have no idea how long it was before I woke properly, and tried to sit up, one of my arms screamed at me, and instantly Landry was back at my side. He took my arm gingerly and tested its movement, which hurt like mad.

"I cannot be sure," he said, still soft but louder than a whisper, "if your lower arm is broken just above the wrist, or perhaps only strained. Your shoulder is tender but I'll not risk testing it further until I can find a doctor, so lie back, breathe deeply and listen to me."

All I could do was mumble. "Only one leg works. I lost both knees I think." Nonsense, but he seemed to understand.

"Without undressing you, my dear, I cannot help any further. And as much as I dream of undressing you, I should prefer you to be in one piece, and fully acquiescent. In the meanwhile, I have told Hamward to fetch a medick, and can only hope he doesn't simply run off, but I doubt it, since he is longing to search the house for any hidden money. Now I want to explain several matters of considerable importance"

"More murders?"

"Including that." His face didn't exactly smile down at me, but there was an expression as soft as his voice. Usually, I thought his expression either entirely absent, or threatening. Somehow, as he talked now, I thought he seemed surprisingly sweet.

"Is it night-time?" Another pointless question, but I needed to catch up with reality again.

"It is deep into the evening, and being late in December, the darkness fell some hours past, but you are not at risk, little bird. I am fairly experienced at creating sanctuary." I think I saw a real smile. "Paul Waddington is now dead. He was, without doubt, the one who ordered, and certainly took part in the killing of your friend and her family. Two others helped him, but I am not sure who these were yet. Your young friend described a fat man much like Hamward, who also worked for this creature, but he denies it. He has never worked outside this house, he claims. He believes the man I am looking for may be his brother. I have no proof as yet, but it will come. I will ensure the doctor orders some kind of litter or cart from the village here, and will take you home tonight, whatever the time. You will then sleep in comfort for at least twenty-four hours, though sleeping through Christmas Day may save you being kissed by me beneath the mistletoe, there will be other opportunities." He didn't even try to hide his grin.

"Just twenty-three hours would be enough." I loved the sound of what he'd said, though felt extremely shy saying it.

His eyes lit up for a fleeting moment, but he changed the subject so quickly, I couldn't be sure.

"The body we discovered in the tunnel is of an elderly woman, unknown to me, and has probably been dead for some time. We will investigate that once everything else becomes clear. Her head is badly crushed, but that could have been the means of her murder, or an accident. Until I know who she is, I am interested only in the first matter."

Not feeling the cold now, since the straw in the bed had risen on both sides, due to my weight in the middle and Landry too. I snuggled. He sounded so organised. The pain still smothered my entire body but the joy of Landry's rescue, overcame everything else.

"Did he tell you why?" I croaked.

"Waddington? No. But either tomorrow or the following day, I intend travelling to the quarry where the Waddington governed, and where, Hamward tells me, his brother also works."

A lot was going on in my head and I was piling up a list of far more relevant questions, while trying to ignore all the pain. I wanted sleep most, but I also desperately wanted the doctor. Actually, everything suddenly felt confusing.

Someone outside called to Landry, and he went to the door. "In here," he told whoever it was.

An elderly man bustled in, carrying not the usual hessian sack, but a most impressive leather bag with a buckle at the top. The medic I presumed.

"Mistress Bennet, may I introduce myself," he said, bending over me. "I am a medic and I have worked on battlefields, for barons, and for a duchess. Now, let's see the problem shall we."

"I was attacked," I told him. I was struggling to sit up again, but it wasn't working. I could hear myself groaning. "My wrist is possibly broken." I held up the appropriate arm, and he took it with concentration. "I've got a broken leg too," I said. "or at least, it feels broken." He cringed when he saw the state of my knees, which barely had any skin left on them.

He was slow, studious and friendly. He apologised for his hands on my legs, and twice called Landry to mix something in hot water for him, one he used to bath the cuts and the other he gave me to drink. A drink I really needed, as it seemed to dull the pain. When the doctor did the first clever twist, he grabbed my hand in one of his, and the same arm in his other, then pulled. I dropped back to the pillow, as the intense in pain stunned me. Suddenly the pain in my shoulder absolutely disappeared. There was a fading ache, and a desperate need to sleep, which I prayed would be possible soon.

He bandaged both my knees. "If you have any butter to spare over the next few days," he told me, "wipe a little on these cuts. Now I have put some of my special salve on the worst. Don't wash it off."

There still remained pain on my lower leg, and I half expected him to say it had to be chopped off. Instead he tut tutted and told me the bone was broken. "Down here," he pointed, "you have two bones, luckily only one is broken, but that means you need a brace and a tight bandage. While I work, I think it wise to ask your young man to hold your other hand."

"Will that make a difference?" Now I was expecting the worst. I assumed he meant Landry and not the fat man.

Yes, it was agony again, and this time it lasted, but Landry not only held my hand in an iron grip, he talked about matters that partially diverted me. "It would seem," he told me very softly, "that we are closer to finding all we have been searching for, and in only a few days may find the entire story. If Hamward's brother did indeed help, as Hamward claims, then it seems likely that the reason lies behind some particular situation at the quarry where they both worked. I intend visiting both the quarry and the brother tomorrow morning, once you are settled – at home. Emil Hamward, the man waiting outside this door, seems to feel no particular affection or loyalty for his brother, and once the doctor has left, he agrees to talk with you, if you wish to question him. Not that I intend leaving you alone with him. As yet I have no full trust in his denial of involvement, nor even in the existence of a brother. Meanwhile he claims to have lived simply serving Waddington. He also says the woman who now lies covered elsewhere, is entirely unknown to him. I also find that difficult to believe."

I coughed and spluttered, and tried saying that since the body hadn't been entirely rotten, her death must have happened while Hamward worked here, but I just ended up making strange sounds, unable to ignore the drowsiness of my mind.

"There," said the doctor, looking pleased with himself and wiping his hands on his smart doublet. "Thankfully your skull is not cracked and if you are careful, the swelling will soon desist. You will need support for some weeks," he nodded to me, "but now it's getting late, so I shall be off. I know exactly where to order a cart to take you home, so, in the meantime," he smiled at Landry, "I need to know where to send my bill."

They both walked out, but within minutes Landry came back, followed by the fat man, and while we waited for the cart to roll up, I tried talking. It was half mumble and half croak, but he seemed to understand me.

"So, what do you know of your brother and that other disgusting beast murdering a whole family. They must have talked about it ,so you must have heard something."

"Didn't hear much." Hamward sat on a stool beside the bed where I lay, but the bulk of his body flopped over all sides of the little three-legged stool. For one moment I closed my eyes, knowing that now I only had one working leg, but Landry gave me another drink, previously given by the doctor. It made me feel a so tipsy but the pain relented just a little more.

"Whatever you heard, tell me."

"Said about Fords. Randle Ford. And can't have him telling. That were me brother David. We never got on. He used to clonk me ears when I were little. There were some other fellow I seen over the year a few times. A bit nasty he was too. Talked 'bout blood and screaming and all that, and the fellow laughed and laughed. Used to make funny faces at me and pull me nose. Mean fellow."

"His name?"

"They calls him Benny. Ben. Benjamin, I reckon. Don't know no more. Didn't like him. Don't reckon he liked me. Spat at me once, the bastard. But only worked here a few months."

"And he worked in the quarry?"

"Dunno," said Hamward. "Didn't work much anyways, cos he just talked his head in circles. And they all talks more when I ain't around, so no good asking other stuff. They all calls me a dullard and I just swept floors and did the cooking."

My memory of what had happened was too muddled for me to call him a liar, but I was sure it was his fat fingers which had forced that disgusting rag down my throat. "Just one more question," I managed to ask. "Does your brother look like you?"

"He bloody does," muttered Hamward, "we's twins."

The candlelight, when I managed to sit, showed me the ugliness of my entire body. I was bruised with few pale patches of bandages visible between. So, everything that hurt so very much, had a reason but that did not help. The sickening appearance made it worse, and although utterly exhausted, I was beginning to think I could never sleep again.

CHAPTER THIRTY FOUR

NARRATIVE

The cart, high wheeled, was horse drawn. Landry piled the bedding onto its base, carried Wren outside, and sat her there, back against the cart's wooden side. The horse was an elderly destrier, strong and well trained, past the age of fighting, yet not unable or unwilling to plod the cold miles. But just as any destrier is trained, Dibble, hated strangers, seen as enemies from the battlefield. Snapping as Landry made Wren comfortable, the huge, muscled stallion stamped, while the driver yelled a few curses.

"Peace be, Dibble, you ain't gotta show off no more."

Landry's purse was heavy.

"Tis a long drive," the driver warned Landry.

"Charge whatever seems fair. The payment's not in danger," Landry told him, and turned to Hamward. "You can stay here as you like, search for money as you like. None of this concerns me. However, I may need you soon for further questioning. Will you stay here?"

"Ain't got nowhere else to bloody go, have I."

"You'll probably be safe here. If I send for you and find you've gone, or refuse to come," Landry told him, "I shall immediately order your arrest. And I assure you, I have that power."

"I'll be here, tis free and warm enough."

Although Landry did not seem dressed as a man of authority at the moment, he now spoke like one. "You'll not speak of this to your brother or anyone else. This is simply a warning, but it may lead to your arrest if you disobey."

Emil Hamward nodded fiercely. "You calls – I comes. Might be interesting, and I might have bags o' coin by then. I can buy meself a house in the big city. If I gets arrested, I pay the judge and all's well.'"

"And don't move that body, leave it covered."

"Reckon them badgers and foxes will eat it," the fat man said.

Dragging his focus back from Wren, Landry frowned. "Pull it under cover. You have the small shed where Wren and I were told to sleep. Put the body there and make sure the door is blocked. There's no doubt I'll need you again sometime soon."

"Proper welcome," he said, mentally counting up the stolen money he was eager to find.

No rain or snow, nor even strong winds disturbed the misery of the ride. Neither Wren nor Landry spoke for most of the journey, the driver muttered beneath his breath, which involved lots of curses, the horse let off steam at both ends, and Wren dozed occasionally under the magnificent night sky above them.

The stars seemed to send messages, as if calling for communication. There was sweet moonshine, yet the light did not shine away the sprinkling of a thousand golden pinpricks. The wonder of it washed away Wren's pain. As she nestled on the verge of sleep again, but the freeze kept her waking her.

It was almost morning as she climbed at last into the bed she was looking forward to. Landry had carried her up the grand staircase to her bedchamber, tucked in the blankets and eiderdown around her fully dressed and heavily bandaged body, then whispered a wish of good night and good dreams. Wren heard her door shut, no longer saw the stars but drifted into the warmth.

Not quite twenty-three hours, but she slept for fifteen. The sleep had taken her into worlds of song and sky, but she was delighted when one of the maids woke her by knocking on her door, and brought in a tray laden with hot milk, baked and sliced bacon, bread and a pot of butter.

"May I wish you a healing Christmas, miss?"

Wren had forgotten. She stumbled from bed once the tray held only an empty platter and cup, and bent slowly to smooth down her creased clothes and winced. Deciding she'd ask someone to make a sling for the bandaged wrist, she then attempted to hobble down the stairs, stopped halfway and called for help. The same maid came running, promising a sling, a walking stick, and help with anything else she might need.

Back in the great hall, Wren managed to make it to the chair by the fire, and collapsed there.

Landry was as usual, not present, and she guessed why. He had told her the day before, that he would ride north once more to the quarry, out beyond the moors and marsh. It was a day of celebration, which might be an advantage, although the opposite was equally possible, with nobody present at all.

He did not ride alone, taking two of the earl's guards and his friend, Father Jacob. A bleak two miles took them from Moorgate to the frosted old quarry. They found just two men, sweating in the freezing temperatures, as they smashed and dug, bringing up hillocks of red sandstone.

Neither man appeared large enough to be the twin to Hamward, nor were others visible amongst the pits and caverns. Both guards sat their mounts and watched, taking the reins, as Landry and Jacob dismounted. Climbing across the ledges and rocky dips of the quarry, they went to where the men continued working.

"Do you have a David Hamward working there?"

One man looked up. His boots were solid and strong, but his doublet was thin, and he wore no over-cote. Jacob called, "You don't find it cold?"

The man grinned. "Not likely, we sweat and the walls keep out the wind. Besides, any fellow working on Christmas Day left in peace, and that's what we chose." He rested on the handle of his axe. "You want the Assistant Master Mason, if you wants Hamward. A mile east. The sheds is where he'll likely be."

A mile more to ride, and the horses travelled slowly, careful of their hooves on the sudden cracks, dips and valleys, the surface of sharp rock.

Another hour droned past until they finally came to a patch level stone and the four neat sheds built there. Once again Landry and Jacob dismounted as the guards took the reins and stood waiting. The first shed was the largest, door open to the wind, with one table surrounded by stools stood central, but vacant.

It was the third shed, puffing smoke through a small hole in the timber roof, where they entered, and stopped immediately. Faced with a grossly fat man, wearing the face of Hamward, Landry smiled and said, "David, I believe, assistant to the Quarry-Master. I'm delighted to meet you."

The heavy jowls wavered and the man frowned at Landry's smile. "I'm mighty busy, but yes, David Hamward is me, and I'm in charge here while the master is off. What do you need? I don't deal with trade nor sale, nor building, nor complaints. All that is the business of his lordship, Francis Waddington, Baron Lyle, and you won't find him here, not ever."

"Fortunately," Landry nodded, "it is you that I have come for. It seems you work at an uncomfortable job. Though it is your other work that I've come to discuss."

Hamward's expression changed abruptly. "You'll get out of here, and be quick about it. I've got no other job and I won't be answering any damned questions. So out –. Or I'll call the guard."

"As it happens," said Landry, speaking, as always, politely, "I shall also call the guard, should you cause trouble. Your boss, Paul Waddington, died at my hand yesterday. Your twin brother, as it happens, was rather helpful. And is now searching for whatever sack of coin lies hidden in the old house."

Hamward stared. "I don't believe a pissing word. There's no one able to kill Paul Waddington, and my brother would never be a friend to a fool like you."

It was Jacob, sweeping forwards in his priestly robes, who interrupted. "The good Lord will bare witness," he said, also smiling, "to the truth my friend here is speaking. Your boss died, with his throat cut. Your twin will no doubt become quite rich in the next few hours. And you will be forced to surrender if we call our guards, who are waiting just outside your door. I dislike brutality, but I might enjoy it in this instance, as I know of your disgusting behaviour. You have killed – perhaps many times. It just might therefore be your turn to be die."

Hamward's fat hand was pushing into his doublet opening, and watching him Landry said, "If you're reaching for your knife, don't bother. Mine is most certainly longer, sharper and more practised. I can also call for others to hold you."

The three exceedingly different men stared at each other. Hamward removed his hand and started shouting. "Guards, guards, I need you now."

Both Landry's guards marched in, one raised a pike, the other his sword. The points of both weapons swept to Hamward's neck, and he jerked back, tipping until sitting on the edge of the small table, papers scattering.

Little noise leaked in from the quarry, too distant and too sheltered. The guards did not move. Landry walked to Hamward, his ice grey eyes a hand's width only, from the other man's scared brown gaze.

"It seems your guards are at home for Christmas," smiled Jacob. "but luckily ours are not."

"So, you'll answer my questions or suffer the consequences. I expect you to answer in truthful detail, or I shall immediately order your death. A slow one perhaps. My first question," Landry said softly, "is who helped you with the murder of Randle Ford and his family, and what was the reason for it."

He turned to the guards, lifting one eyebrow. "What do you think, Osbeid? The pike through each leg first, then the groin?"

"No doubt I shall vomit," Jacob said, now leaning back against one wall. "but, I accept the method. This vile creature is capable of worse." He wagged one finger towards Hamward. "And no doubt you deserve far worse still."

"I'll tell you," David Hamward gabbled. "I only did what my orders said. I'd be dead quicker and nastier than you want if I'd disobeyed. I only did what I was told. Benny and me, we do what Waddington tells us, and he obeys his brother." He gasped, inhaled like a man after a race, and gaped at Landry. "I don't know nothing else, honest."

"The reason for killing the wife and two young children?"

"Because Randle would have told 'is family, and since they were all there, they'd know who killed 'im. That's it. The truth, I swear it."

"And the risk for the baron? I presume the knowledge of his crimes, and his methods?"

The fat man shook his head. "I never asked. Those two brothers, they don't answer questions. If you ask one, then you're as good as dead."

Landry accepted his answer and paused. He now held his own knife, a short double-bladed sword, and was looking down as he tapped the knife against the palm of one hand. "And who is Benny?"

"The other fellow. He's no one. I mean, he's just Benny. Only joined with us eight months back." David Hamward slumped against the table, wild eyed. "It's all truth. If Paul Waddington's dead, then you don't go telling the baron on me. You can come and ask me more when you like. But ell him what I told you, and I'll be dead in a day or less."

"Describe what you did," Landry said, waving the knife at Hamward's head. "I need the details."

The two guards remained close, their weapons unmoving. Hamward sighed. "Right, but you can't tell the baron. Swear it to me and I'll tell everything."

"I have every intention of eradicating this world of your vile baron," Landry said. "There would be little point in me telling him anything concerning you."

Hamward clasped his head in both hands. Like his twin, his hands were those of a giant, large fingered and massive. His head disappeared into the clasp, and his shoulders quivered with hidden tears.

"Very well, I'll answer what I know. From what Waddington told me, he was in the big room talking to the baron. The baron don't come here often, too far and too dirty probably, but he owns the quarry, he does. I reckon he makes good money, but he don't need it. He's a spy for some, blackmails others at court, does deals, bribes and threatens, kills if needed. He makes double with that stuff, over what he gets from the quarry. Four times maybe. I dunno. He's gonna tell me about his coin, is he! Anyhow, he comes ere some months back, and was discussing a deal, or some other secret. It was Benny, as said he found Randle Ford standing outside the little window. Listening and shocked wiv his mouth hanging open. So, he heard the lot, Benny said, and how he threatened him to keep it secret, but of course he wouldn't trust that. He knew the fellow would tell his family at least, and then maybe go to the sheriff. So, something had to be done, and done quick. The next morning off we went to the Ford house, knowing where he lived. Not the Baron, he'd not risk being seen, but his brother, the boss here, he went, and called on me and Benny to go with him. So, a' course we did."

CHAPTER THIRTY FIVE

NARRATIVE

"They were stupid enough to drink what we gave them. Silly sods thought it was something special. Dead in minutes they was. Waddington liked his poisons. Almost as good as them Italian folk, he was."

"A skill to admire, it seems." Jacob winced.

"Mixed into a strong Burgundy, it were. Two cups for Randle. Never afforded wine himself a 'course. Now he was being threatened if he told what he knew, so he drank what he was given, to hide his fear, I suppose."

Landry's eyes were fire, though hidden beneath lowered brows and heavy lids. "And the poor wretch, being unaccustomed to wine, wouldn't detect an odd taste. Arsenic has little taste at all, but to accept a drink brought by the man already threatening you?"

Hamward shrugged. "A simpleton he was. The woman maybe had suspicions. Kept looking around. Took ages to drink the one cup. Smallest child upstairs. Older one working at the bakery."

"So no need to kill either child."

"The little one came skidding down the stairs, saw us, and saw his parents on the floor, eyes shut. Little bastard went racing out to fetch his brother. Waddington told us to hang up the two idiots as a warning to anyone else they might have told already." Hamward sighed, but more from his own obvious risk, than from the memory of what had been done. "A mighty warning. Randle said he'd not told a soul, but it was clear he'd told his wife. We couldn't be sure of aught. We were finishing off when the two brats came running back. We grabbed them both and forced the poison down their throats. Died in no time. So we hung them up too. We were leaving when bloody Randle started grunting and the rope swung. Not alive, exactly, but not dead neither."

"And you happily obeyed these orders? You were fine murdering small children, a man you already knew, and his young wife?" Jacob glared, half choking in fury.

"Finish your story," Landry ordered.

"That was it." Hamward was shaking. "We just tightened the rope on Randle Ford's neck and left. We all went in different directions. Done it, and never heard more till you. Months gone and it all seemed safe. The baron, well, he usually makes sure everything stays quiet."

"Your baron doesn't know me," Landry said softly. "but he soon will."

The priest shook his partly shaved head, his eyes half closed. "The king will be informed, and your dear baron will be thrown into the Tower dungeons."

"And me?" Hamward still shivered. "I only did what I had to. No way I could say no, and obeyed you too, didn't I! Told the truth."

Landry turned away, one hand to the door. "You chose to work for Waddington, knowing his business. You were paid to kill."

"I took the job at the quarry. I needed the job."

"And the corpse in the tunnel from the well?" Jacob asked in growing fury. "You did that too, or know of it, at least."

"Waddington – only him," the fat twin grabbed the priest's arm. "I know he did it. I don't know who she was. It was a long time back. Never seen her. My brother says it was Benny asking for a favour. Ben needed that female gone, and joined our group in return."

Hamward slumped down to the ground, onto the dry earth serving as the shed's base. He stayed there shivering in fear and shock, amazed to be left alive, as his two accusers pulled open the door and strode out with no further word.

Back beneath the heavy dark cloud outside, Landry and Father Jacob nodded to the waiting guards, mounted, and rode back to Moorgate and through to London and the earl's grand home. "Another threat," Landry murmured. "before we arrive, no doubt it will pour with rain."

"Or snow," Jacob nodded.

⊁◈⊰

The storm crashed above them as they arrived in the city through the Moorgate, and then rode to the grounds of the great house within the Wall. The earl was still absent, but Wren was wrapped, cosy on the settle, beside the hall's huge hearth, the fire blazing as always.

Both dogs lay stretched at her feet, soaking up the heat before them. No longer recognisable as stray or starving, their stomachs lay plump and fully stuffed against the polished floorboards. They looked up as Landry entered, saw who it was, wagged lethargic tails, and returned cheerfully to sleep.

"So, little bird, our discovery is complete. I now know what I've been looking for, for many months." Landry leaned across the back of the chair by the fire. Wren had also been dozing, but Landry's arrival, and the swift attention of the steward, had woken her. The boredom was over, at least for an hour or so, and she was delighted. As Landry smiled down, he said, "This is a Christmas gift more valuable than any feast. Although now the arrests may not be so easy, and another murder has popped itself into the game."

"You don't mean you killing Paul Waddington. It saved us all."

He shook his head. "I don't kill if I believe it avoidable. Killing Waddington was essential. I mean the body we found in the tunnel to the well."

"Of course. So many dead. Hamward tried to help, but he's probably just as wicked." Wren looked around. "Is that the rattle of wine?"

The steward had brought wine, and everyone relaxed. The earl's underground cellar was well stocked with the wine that cost nearly as much as the wages of his entire household.

Both Landry and Jacob, cups to their mouths, sat opposite Wren and grinned at her. Jacob drank with relish and said, "There's also another Hamward – a twin brother – and another bastard with appalling habits. He must end in Newgate, but the man I have yet to meet, is Baron Lyle. He owns the quarry, but more importantly runs a secret business of crime, corruption and cruelty. He is assuredly vile, and must be removed from our world, but only the king or Lord of the Tower can order such an arrest. Our own earl would complete this for us, if only he was here."

"But since he is not," Landry stared now at the flames dancing close to his feet, "I have no expectation of seeing him soon. Without doubt he is now at his countryside manor with his friend."

Raising his cup, Jacob said, "He'll want to celebrate the Christmas feast with Tim I'm sure."

"Therefore," Landry raised his cup in return salute, "you and I, Jacob, must somehow achieve the improbable."

"You mean, to achieve the impossible." Jacob sighed, leaning back and draining his cup.

"Not in the least," Landry said, face to his own wine, "first we arrange for this twin Hamward to be arrested by tomorrow at the latest. Then the baron's arrest. His majesty knows our names if not our faces, and we will say the earl has sent us."

"We'll have to pay Hastings for an appointment." The priest sighed again and set down his empty cup.

"Perhaps," nodded Landry. "The earl will not object to paying. The matter is urgent, but it will inevitably be another long day." His eyes, bright now, slid to Wren. "Sadly your wounds will mean you cannot accompany us, but I will return and explain every detail.

Unless, of course, I am immediately taken to Newgate by any damned guard that sees me."

"They wouldn't dare," Wren mumbled. "You have the king's protection, and they know it now. They wouldn't dare cross the king."

"No. But they believe we are lying about that particular claim. However, I have no worries concerning Newgate, only concerning an appointment to speak with the king, and the king's decision whether to arrest Lyle, or not."

"We'll start the negotiations tomorrow," Jacob said, peering into his empty cup.

Landry's eyes swept sideways to Wren. "And you, little bird, appear at least to be alive. How do you feel?"

Pleased that he'd asked, she lowered her eyes in false modesty. "Half good, but I still wish I could come with you." Wren's cup was almost full, just two sips gone.

Landry drained his wine. "When you are ready, little bird, I shall carry you upstairs and to bed. Tragically, it will be your own bedchamber, where you will sleep warm and uninterrupted. Hopefully the storm will pass over night, and you'll wake to St. Stephen's Day. We will then say goodbye, as we finish breakfast."

Wren smiling, hid her face in her cup and drank. "Only my leg hurts now, and of course the bruises all over," she mumbled. "but if you don't mind helping – to carry me – which is so kind – I think I shall sleep very well indeed." Wren did not explain that it would be the memory of his warm arms around her, that would fill her dreams.

CHAPTER THIRTY SIX

NARRATIVE

After many hours of shaking window frames, and the whimpering of the dogs, the storm slowly passed. The jagged sparks of lightening, and the slash of hail, faded as the dark hours slithered towards dawn. However, the blackest clouds remained, they dipped low over the city's rooftops and continued to threaten rain.

Well cloaked, Landry and Father Jacob, called for their mounts to be ready saddled and brought to the main doors.

It was Prad who brought Arthur. "My lord, he's a touch tired after his fun on the moors yesterday. You're going to knock the poor boy out entirely today."

"Westminster, and a fair rest once we get there," Landry grinned.

With his hands on Arthur's neck, stroking persistently, Prad mumbled, "I suppose he'll enjoy the palace stables. He'll no doubt get an apple or two."

"Then I have your permission to trot on?" Landry continued with a grin. Prad nodded without smiles, patted Arthur again, and strode off. Jacob was already mounted.

Lord Hastings, bright in scarlet and gold, matching the crimson cheeks of a frequent drinker, kept them waiting for a little over an hour as they stood outside his official chamber of reception, lounging against the corridor walls. They had expected worse. Hastings kept every man waiting.

"I have heard your name, Crawford, but not for some time. I believe you work for his lordship, Earl of Thamesdon."

Standing close to the table where Hastings sat, Landry bowed briefly, his expression cold. "Indeed, My lord, my business is urgent and I act in the name of the Earl of Thamesdon, and at his command. I ask an audience with his majesty, the king."

Hastings sat back, clasping his hands across the golden embroidery of his wide shouldered doublet, and the huge gold chain of authority direct from the king. He smiled. "Without title and without previous notification, this would not be an appointment eagerly accepted by his highness. If you leave this matter with me, I will see what I may arrange. It will take time, naturally, and my time is of considerable value."

"The news I bring is urgent, and of the utmost importance to the royalty of our great country," Landry said, standing so close, unmoving, legs apart and hands clasped behind his back. "My authority is known to his majesty. It is of such consequence that my arrivals are usually kept secret. This time, however, I need immediate licence."

Landry's arrogant confidence angered his host. He was not invited to sit, nor to drink and nor to discuss the matter of such urgency. Hastings said, "It seems we are unlikely to come to an accord," he addressed both men facing him. "My apologies father, but I ask you both to leave."

Neither moved. "The difficulties arising should I fail to meet with his highness this day, are considerable, my lord, and I fear his majesty will be displeased at the slightest delay."

Now Hasting's expression matched Landry's. His face remained coldly unemotional but his eyes were full of fire. "You feign position and importance," Hastings stared. "Yet you are unaware, Master

Crawford, that his royal highness is not at court this day, and has been refusing to give his present direction, being unwell. If you describe matters correctly, you would have known this. You may now consider yourselves dismissed. Good morning." He rang the small bell on the table, calling for the guards who would lead these unwanted beseechers from the palace. "And take this, since it is of no consequence." He held out the scroll devoid of script, but marked with the earl of Thamesdon's coat of arms, and the seal of private recognition.

"My lord," Landry did not move nor retreat in any manner, "I assure your lordship, that once the urgent news I carry is known by those who rule this land, there will be extreme action. It is of considerable importance that I see someone with the authority to speak with me."

The carved door frame shivered as the doors were flung open, and Hasting's four liveried guards entered, standing directly behind Landry and Jacob, as they waited for orders.

Someone else walked in through the open doorway, pushing past the guards. He was dressed in white, the over-sleeves multi-coloured and the clasping's pure gold. The jewelled collar of royal office he wore, was more impressive than the man's casual entrance. He stood a little smaller than the guards, both shorter and slimmer, but at sight of him, Hastings stood and bowed low. The guards immediately stood back beside the wall.

The man nodded at Hastings, ignoring all else. "My Lord Hastings, I intend leaving early tomorrow morning. Whatever appointments you make from this time onwards, I will be unable to take, nor even to oversee. Time, as usual, is against me."

"Indeed, my lord. I thank you." Hastings stood yet kept his head bowed.

Landry, directly behind the man, bent one knee to the floor, head also bent. Yet as the gentleman turned to leave, he spoke immediately. "My lord, Duke of Gloucester, I beg you to consider my request. I am here on the orders of his lordship, the Earl of Thamesdon regarding a matter of great urgency. It concerns the discovery of a baron of this land who has been organising crimes across the country, including the murder of numerous individuals. I can prove that he is a spy against the House of York, and a criminal of appalling cruelty, and yet, he sits free to continue his wickedness."

The Duke of Gloucester stopped, looked down, and reached one beringed hand to Landry's shoulder. "Stand, and come with me. Say no more until we are alone."

"Father Jacob of St. Nicholas's Church by Newgate, is my accompanying witness, sir."

"Bring him," and the king's younger brother, Richard of Gloucester, walked from the room.

Landry and Jacob followed, and neither bothered to look back at Hastings, keeping close to the royal prince. He led them down the wider corridor with its rich murals of mountains, oceans and fields. Further along, they turned abruptly and entered the wide doors of a large chamber, lit with a hundred dazzling candles, both from a chandelier, hanging central and sparkling with reflection, and from carved sconces along each wall. Even greater light heaved from the raging flames on the hearth, the fire echoing the flicker of the many candles.

Richard sat and welcomed his guests to do the same. "Your mission sounds urgent indeed," he said, his hands clasped to one knee, the other leg stretched. "First give me the name of this baron you consider dangerous."

Landry, sitting opposite, briefly bowed his head and began his story. "Baron Lyle, my lord. His brother Paul Waddington carried out the worst of his orders, but for the protection of my workers, I admit to having killed this man when he threatened others and then attacked me just two days past. With the authority of Lord Thamesdon in his royal highness the king's name. Together the brothers organised and carried out the killing of a quarry worker, who had heard of their plans and brutality. His entire family was slaughtered, including his wife and two small sons, the bodies then hung from their own ceiling beams as a warning to others."

Prince Richard leaned forwards. "I heard of that bestial crime," the prince told Landry, "and I have also heard of you and your work, Master Crawford, and much admire it. His Highness, my brother, has spoken of you, with me, and naturally we have known the Earl of Thamesdon for some years. Once you inform me of the full details of this situation, I shall act immediately. I know Baron Lyle only slightly, as he rarely attends court, and nor do I, by choice, but as Lord High Constable of England at this time, I can promise you instant results."

"My lord," Landry bowed his head once more, "I thank you. The details, and in particular finding the culprit of such a vile crime, has been my business for some months, and I confess to having failed to solve the puzzle until this week past. May I also ask that a less urgent warrant be issued for the manager of the quarry, who is the baron's assistant in both cruelty and murder."

Jacob and Landry relaxed a little and related every fact known to them, adding hearsay and rumour in addition. The Hamworth brothers were also explained in detail, including both their villainy and their decisions to help. Ben, or Benny, Landry added, was unknown to them, but was clearly as guilty as the others even though a more recent addition.

After nearly an hour's discussion, Richard rang the bell and called for refreshment. They drank excellent wine and spoke together for another hour. When Richard finally dismissed them, he added a last invitation.

"Speak with me again some time," he told them, "since I find your work both valiant and fascinating. I would wish, some day, to increase the power and range of our sheriffs, ensure their skills, and begin a regulated system of law administration, including the work you already do. It is an ideal basis from which to bring us a healthier and safer country. However, it would be impossible for me at present. I uphold the law in my own lands, but that is unlikely to be extended. We shall see, but within the year I shall send word and speak with you again."

The prince stood, the sign of the meeting now closed, but as they left, Jacob added, "My lord, I thank you and bless you in the name of our lord."

Richard smiled. "Even as the Lord High Constable, my powers are restricted. However, I shall remember both your names. I wish you a good night." And he was gone.

><><

Their ride home was uneventful, and both men remained silent. There was a great deal of information, and possibility they hoped would eventuate, but they knew little of the king's younger brother.

It began to snow. One of the coldest winters in living memory, it seemed almost a fitting background to what else was happening. The fighting with Scotland, finished with agreement by the hand of the Duke of Gloucester, sent to lead both battle and peace by the king himself, was now over. But the mighty quarrels of the nobility, including the erratic Stanley brothers, took advantage of such placidity in the country, and therefore the perfect time, if King Edward would rouse himself, to bring about a more personal peace.

"It won't happen," Jacob said as they strode back into the Thamesdon city manor. "It's not something I'd admit to a single living soul other than yourself, Landry, but the king has grown fat and self-indulgent. He has very little interest any longer, in the rule he once managed so well. Now he sends his little brother, or nothing happens."

"I believe he's unwell," Landry said, pushing open the doors of the great hall.

"With a surfeit of creams, berries, roast meats and cakes."

"But since meeting him, I admire his brother Richard," Landry added. "Created Lord High Constable, the Duke certainly has his brother's trust. If Edward is ill, then Richard will be given more authority, and whatever else happens, the execution of Baron Lyle will help a good deal."

><><

Through the long windows, the snow seemed magical, turning a bleak shivering world into a gentle hushed dance of white. Inside, their own fire was a swell of vivid colour, flames tossed high. As usual, Wren sat close, her face shining. She started to jump up as Landry and Father Jacob marched over, but quickly collapsed back onto the chair.

"Done," Jacob said. "A fine result."

"You saw the king?" Wren was impressed.

"No. His young brother the Duke of Gloucester, which was the best possible result," Landry told her, "and even better," his mouth twitched with a faint smile, "dinner will be served almost immediately. I'll help you to the table, little bird, and have the meat cut for you."

"My wrist's getting better."

"I'm delighted, but you will sit quietly while the serving boy cuts your meat, and I bore you into submission with the details of what we've achieved this morning."

Jacob already stood. "I believe I'm near starving," he grinned, "and desperately in need of food and then I'll drink to the prince and Saint Stephen alike. I'll join the talk afterwards."

CHAPTER THIRTY SEVEN

WREN

L iving freely in the massive comfort of an earl's city home was even more exciting than when I'd moved into Landry's place in the mews. I eat well, my bed is pure luxury, and I'm warmer and more cossetted than I've ever been before in my life. Yes, I'm impatient and bored. These irritating injuries keep me static, while Landry goes dashing off on the most fascinating of business, and this time, perhaps for the first time, the successful result is on its final gallop. I simply wish I'd been there, and meeting the king's little brother would have been the most amazing memory for afterwards.

Knowing who killed poor Jessy, and even knowing why, was a glorious ending. And there was more. I had Landry at my side for more than half my waking hours.

It sometimes now amuses me, sometimes pleases me, and sometimes worries the life out of me, – but whatever my reaction, or whatever I think, doesn't seem to matter. I am strangely attracted to Landry's touch, his tucked away-under the surface humour, – and his natural protection. Not just when searching out the attacker and saving the victim, but actually helping me.

I swear I'm not complaining. His warmth of touch makes me

tingle. My entire body, some parts a little more than others, reacts, although all he touches is my hand, or my shoulder, so, I wasn't sure why I liked what he did, when he was doing very little. I liked him close. I liked his almost disguised smiles. I had even begun to like his pale and cold ice-grey eyes. His eyes should have been very dark like his hair, but as everything else about him, his eyes didn't obey the rules.

Then, three times, he'd carried me. I felt his arms beneath my legs and his hands over my skirts, against my knees. His other arm, almost as glorious, held me close around my shoulders. If he had moved, just a little, he would have touched my breast, but it didn't happen. I suppose he knew just where a woman's body grew.

With no mother, and no nurse throughout my youth, and no courage later, to ask a friend, I had no real idea of what husbands and wives did to each other, when they married and shared a bed. How they had children wasn't easy to understand either. Sometimes the parents were delighted, but occasionally they weren't, so, if they didn't actually want a baby, why did they get it?

It wasn't that rare to know women who had babies without being married. To achieve this totally on her own impressed me, and yet the woman often admitted shame, and was occasionally ostracised. I didn't understand this either. People could be cruel, and this seemed more common each day.

I'd never been a gossiper nor even a chatter. Perhaps knowing so little was simply my own fault. My father's influence kept me dutiful and quiet. When I was very young, my father sometimes touched me in places that I disliked and I became embarrassed and uncomfortable. I hit him once. He hit me back, but after quite a few months of hitting by both of us, he stopped poking at me when I was asleep, or just sitting, curled, staring into the fire, or out of the window. He got the point, and eventually came nowhere near me. I was able to stop feeling all tense and hating what might happen and within the week I had rediscovered relaxed and peaceful happiness. Yet all of this seems to have inspired my courage, and at the same time taught me – what? Cowardice?

Now I remember vaguely what my father had done, and instead of feeling sick as I had originally, I simply wondered – even dreamed – of how it would feel if Landry touched me in the same way.

I was no baby, no young child, not even as young of some women I'd known who had been told to marry an older man. Some of them ended up in terrible pain as they gave birth to babies.

Landry was twenty six, and soon to be older, as he'd once said. I was considerably younger than that, and considered twenty six rather old. Yet sometimes, not often, I actually dreamed the thrill of being married to him myself. Well, that clearly wasn't going to happen, and though dreams never hurt anyone, I knew it stupid and a little improper. Had I told Father Jacob, I think he would have quoted the Bible to me and told me about sin, but since the Bible was only permitted in Latin, I didn't understand any of it anyway. A few words stuck in my memory but very few.

I'd heard plenty of sermons about sinful thoughts in church, but it was sometime since I'd gone to church. Sunday had been the only day off work for a long time, and I grabbed up the habit of crossing myself, whispering aloud for the Lord God to forgive me, then carrying on having a peaceful day. No work. No church. The local priest gave me a sniffy look occasionally, but he never shouted or told me off.

Life was changing in the most remarkable ways now, but that didn't include getting married or having babies.

My father had lost both wife and baby. I still wasn't sure how much of the fault had been his, but it reminded me how long I'd not spoken with him. So he didn't work at the docks any longer and that was a puzzle. I hoped he was back on the carracks and sailing to Italy across a calm sea. Besides, I couldn't walk yet, only hobble with a stick, but I knew I should go and find him sometime fairly soon.

⋈◇⋈

The afternoon of the same day, the one after Landry and Father Jacob had talked with his royal highness Prince Richard, something else happened – with no connection either to church or to marriage.

It seemed blissful at first. Both Landry and Jacob were delighted to talk of meeting Prince Richard, they'd liked him, but there was much more than that. He had evidently been interested in the shocking news and the proof of cruelty. He had promised action, and had taken every detail with serious attention. Immediate arrests were now expected.

Once those arrests took place, I believed the entire country, whether anyone else knew about it or not, would benefit enormously. That vile baron was capable of wickedness which could hurt anyone. Kill anyone, leave weeping relatives and impoverish those who had little enough already.

Heresy and treason were the two worst crimes, and I had no idea if the hideous baron had managed either, but he certainly came close.

Well yes indeed, my father was not a good man and my sense of freedom had seemed magical once I was old enough to leave his home. Yet a man, and a titled gentleman like Baron Lyle, seemed like the devil to me in comparison. Now even his name made me sick, and my stomach, always so well filled these days, would heave and churn.

⋇⬥⋇

We were still discussing everything, laughing, eating, and drinking when the doors opened and the Earl's steward entered

The Earl of Thamesdon's steward, was a man who had spent many years opening the doors to the counts, dukes, earls and barons of the country. Forbidding the entrance of a beautifully dressed gentleman who introduced himself as the Baron Lyle, would never have even occurred to him.

So, when doors to the Grand Hall opened and the steward

announced Baron Lyle, he marched in as the Steward left. I scrambled to stand and just stared, but Landry was more effective, he stood and walked around the table to face the beast.

While staring coldly at the baron, Landry said, "Jacob, please inform the steward of the situation regarding our unexpected visitor, and tell him to inform the staff and arrange for them to arm themselves." He hadn't taken his eyes from the baron, and now addressed him. "You are unwanted here, sir, and I ask you to leave immediately."

The baron was only slightly shorter than Landry, and stood with arrogance, wide shouldered, chin high, eyes cold, and his mouth twisted in fury. That he looked wealthy, was no surprise, however, his clothes were as impressive as I'd ever seen, rich in dark crimson and highly embroidered. His shirt collar, stiff and standing to his ears, was lace. This was something rarely seen, and stunningly beautiful. Ridiculous, of course, to see beauty when gazing at one of the most wicked creatures in the land.

He glared back at Landry as Jacob marched off to inform the steward and the staff as Landry had ordered.

The baron poked his head so close to Landry's, they stood nose to nose. "I do not take orders from the hedge-born riff raff of this city," he spat, "whether they cower in the properties of the titled or not. The earl is absent, and you do not own anything here. You will therefore close your mouth, or I will cut it from your face."

At home and at peace, Landry was unarmed, but I knew some form of blade was always tucked into his belt. The baron also appeared unarmed, or the steward would not have admitted him, but some hidden weapon was there, and we all knew it.

Knowing this, and watching ice facing ice, suddenly the hall wasn't warm anymore, and even the huge fire seemed to crackle once, then fade. I stood, shaking and terrified, wondering if I could help but not knowing how, nor wanting to move. I stood in the baron's direct line of vision. Landry's back was towards me. I tried to look as though simply escaping, crouched a little, carried on shivering, which was genuine enough, and crept along the side of the table until the baron couldn't see me. I only saw his back. I waited there and tried to think like the courageous female that sometimes I was, and now I wasn't.

Face to face and so threateningly close, I blinked at both. I was sure the baron wasn't aware of me. Perhaps even Landry wasn't.

"You, sir," Landry said in that icy silk murmur, "appear sadly unaware of the danger you are facing. The warrant for your arrest has already been drawn up. Your execution will no doubt be public, immediately after your trial. Many of your victims will wish to watch your head removed, I, however, am no victim of yours and never shall be, so leave now or face an even faster execution."

Neither yet held a weapon, which surprised me. They both seemed ready to threaten, rather than act, which I understood, but couldn't approve of the risk. They knew that as soon as one blade appeared, so would another. Each wanted the perfect moment to flash steel first. With that in mind, I could help.

I was biting my tongue as I lifted the larger chair by both its arms, with a struggle held it up above me, kept total silence, and then smashed the baron over the head with the considerable weight of the wood.

He was saying some other pointless nonsense when the weight of the chair smashed onto his flat feathered hat and with a puzzled look, he wobbled, his threat turned to a grunt, and then toppled to the floor boards at Landry's feet.

Within less than a heartbeat, the baron also had a long two edged blade at his neck. He blinked, feeling the first thin cut, staring up as Landry stared down.

Landry actually mumbled, "Thank you, little bird," and as he pressed the steel, the baron squawked, more crow than robin. The door behind me burst open and so many footsteps thundered around us, I was blinded by rushing shadows and deafened by shouts and screams.

Two men grabbed Landry and forced him away from the baron, but the steward and two other large men grabbed the baron. Others milled between and I scurried back to the wall, clutching at the tapestry. I was tempted to hide behind it, but didn't. It was impossible to see who was on which side as more than twenty, perhaps thirty men, ran, dodged and grabbed.

I also knew both dogs were trying to work out which was friend and which enemy. They'd raced in behind the steward and were barking like insane demons.

The steward, one of the few I could recognise, was armed with Landry's principal sword, but others were also raising swords, one had an axe, one had a garden rake and a young page held a carving knife. One of the earl's guards shouted orders. I felt I'd seen him before.

Gradually they moved themselves into separate divisions. Behind Landry, five men held him immovable, as the many crowded together into groups I began to understand. Four of those holding Landry were once again the Newgate guards, and I assumed these had been brought purposefully by the baron, demanding Landry's arrest. Hearing the authority of the baron and the name of Landry himself, they would have been only too delighted.

Another who clearly supported the vile baron was David Hamward, a man I recognised only as identical to his twin brother, whom I'd certainly met, but this twin was better dressed. Others, perhaps the baron's own men, crowded there, stamping and cursing.

The shouting, the swearing and the crash of metal on metal made me turn in confusion. No word was distinct in such a pandemonium, the swirl of cloth against cloth and the moving shadows more like furious ghosts, wanting to lead us all to Hell.

Nearer to me, but just as furious, our staff and guards held the baron, his arms now roped at his back, and his ankles trussed. The Newgate guards might consider themselves the more legal and more powerful, but our guards, the earl's own and long trained, alongside furious grooms, gardeners, kitchen workers and cleaners, were double in number, and had partially understood the truth, whereas the Newgate guards, as usual, thought the truth was entirely the other way around.

The chair I'd swung was now broken on the ground, but several of the grooms and other staff had grabbed the wooden legs as weapons. The rest of our guards were already well armed, but so were the men swearing at us, and holding Landry as if he were a dangerous wolf.

I'd bent down and also grabbed part of the broken chair for my own defence, but I was also in pain, hobbling and tripping, gasping for breath and praying silently for help. Now the dogs, as if answering my prayers, rushed to stand directly in front, my protectors barking and growling too.

Landry stood motionless, but I saw the fury on his face. For perhaps the first time I knew his anger was red hot, not ice cold. He didn't struggle, he waited for both sides to calm themselves into quiet authority.

Finally, it was Father Jacob who shouted loudest. Perhaps he was used to shouting from the pulpit.

"Quiet fools. This is all avoidable. You risk the Lord God's fury with your actions, apart from every angel and angry saint preparing to converge. Now, listen to me, Landry Crawford has Prince Richard's personal word of approval, and it is the baron who is under imminent arrest, to be taken to the Tower by the royal guard. Baron Lyle knows this, and so do his men. Only the Newgate guard are, as usual, utterly confused and believe the wrong argument."

His bellow echoed up into the high beams above, and there was an awed silence for just a few heavy breathing moments. Landry now took advantage. Making no attempt to free himself from his Newgate captors, he spoke considerably softer, saying, "I am prepared to accompany the guards to Newgate, where I can easily prove myself under the king's protection, and will immediately be set free. However, my freedom must not include the baron's release. He must be kept under restraint until the situation is fully understood."

I was waiting to smell fire, blood or even death, but the crowd relaxed slightly, both sides almost silent. Our guards, knowing themselves under order as those upholding the truth, kept the baron tight. The Newgate guards frowned, stared at each other, but wouldn't release Landry. The confusion, fury and fear, mixed like a boiling hot porridge, bubbling backwards and forwards. The great hall had always seemed so vast. Now crammed with the urge to battle, it seemed tiny and squashed. Then I saw Landry nod to Jacob. He said nothing, but the nod was an understood message, and the priest left the hall. No one dared stop a man in the garments of the Holy Church, it being not only blasphemous but illegal to lay angry hands on a priest. I heard a groom open and shut the massive front doors, heard a horse whinny, then suddenly gallop, and almost immediately Prad burst into the hall.

Everyone had started shouting again, and one of the Newgate guards was cursing so loudly, both dogs started to growl once more and abruptly, Shadow leapt. I'd seen him starving, I'd seen him frightened, and I'd seen him well fed and lazy. Now this was different. The large hound leapt at the Newgate guard, barking and snarling, and his canine teeth sank into the guard's wrist, pulling him backwards. The man released Landry at once and the other two Newgate guards did the same, rushing to beat off the dog.

Now I rushed as well. With the old chair's broken leg still in my grasp, I yelled, "How dare you hit my dog," and swung the chair leg against that guard's head. He blinked, snorted, and tumbled over.

Red wasn't prepared to allow Shadow this excitement without joining in, and he leapt at the baron. I tried to call off Shadow but he was shaking the guard's bleeding wrist and the man was almost fainting. The other guards shouted but were frightened to grab at such a dangerous dog.

Meanwhile Landry had freed himself from the one remaining guard, and marched to Shadow, ordering him to release the guard and come to him. Shadow obeyed instantly and sat calmly at Landry's side. His mouth was blood smeared.

The Newgate guards helped their partner to a chair, and demanded bandages. One of the kitchen boys ran off to follow orders. The screaming was now from the baron. Our own men had moved back, watching, while Red gnawed at the baron's bleeding arm and leg, now both on the floorboards, the baron squealing and kicking but unable to release himself.

I watched cheerfully for a moment or two, then copied Landry's behaviour and called Red to me. The baron lay howling. His blood covered the floor.

In the midst of chaos, Jacob reappeared with the sheriff in tow.

Not the best sheriff in London, but Wilson was recognised by the guards on both sides of the hall. The noise once again subsided, and the sheriff stepped between the two clusters of furious movement.

I even wondered if Pansy would turn up.

It was the sheriff who spoke. I was surprised he knew anything about the situation, about Landry, let alone about the baron, but I supposed he hadn't been able to disbelieve a priest's determined story, probably sworn on the Bible as the absolute truth.

"I hereby arrest Lord Francis Waddington, Baron Lyle, in the name of his majesty, King Edward. My guards will escort him to the London Tower, where the royal guard will take him into custody. Meanwhile, Landry Crawford should be immediately released, however, I suggest he kindly accompany the Newgate guard to the office of the High Constable so we can learn the truth of this confusion. It is far too important for repeated and unnecessary misunderstandings."

The sheriff wasn't a tall or impressive man but everyone present, even me, was paying attention.

Landry said, "I have already offered to walk voluntarily beside the guards, for clarification. The High Constable will already have received clear notification." Well, he hoped so.

The baron, although he was still restrained, blood oozing from one thigh and his wrist clearly broken, twisted and face the sheriff, shouting like an animal. "I am an innocent member of the aristocracy. How dare anyone manhandle me in this fashion. That filthy dog's attack was appalling and I demand its immediate destruction. Meanwhile, I need a doctor. Take off these ropes, and I shall ride to the Tower, where when I am in full knowledge of the result, it will end in this lout Landry's arrest, with royal apologies immediately addressed to me and my men."

Landry smiled. "Sheriff Wilson," he said, "I suggest you take two of your own guards and two of those from Newgate, and visit the Tower Constable yourself, for a complete understanding. Royal guards will presumably then accompany you back here to arrest Baron Lyle. I can wait here, with the baron, until you return. I swear not to leave, and the baron will be unable to do so. I shall even offer him a cup of wine, but he will remain here, awaiting the truth.

I'd always thought the sheriff rather banal, although he'd impressed me more while dealing with Bryce. Now I was doubly impressed.

He looked straight at Landry and smiled. "An excellent plan, Master Crawford, and one I shall follow with pleasure. It is not too late to attend the Tower Authorities, and hopefully the Tower Constable will know the full truth by now." He nodded directly at two of the Newgate idiots, and two of our guards, and said, "You, you, and you two will come with me and stand witness to whatever we are then informed."

Then it was Prad who called from the back of the hall. "There are horses ready saddled, Master Sheriff. I had the mounts waiting, knowing what would be needed. It is now full darkness but there is neither storm nor snow to slow your progress. " Personally, I guessed he'd arranged this more for Landry's possible escape, rather than for the sheriff, but it would surely finish the whole business a good deal faster.

Obviously, the idea pleased everybody. Marching the entire length and breadth of the city several times in one day was exhausting as I knew from practise.

It was when the sheriff passed me, very erect and formal, that he whispered sideways, "Your friend Pansy wishes to remain at my side."

So, I whispered back. "I do hope you're both happy. Give her my regards."

His pause was brief, but I saw the fading hope in his eyes as he added very quietly, "I was hoping, ma'am, that you'd visit and persuade her to leave and live with you."

I smiled sympathetically. "But she couldn't come here. It's the earl's house and he's not here to ask permission." I didn't add that I had no desire for Pansy under my feet even more strongly than the sheriff obviously did.

There was no time to add more and the sheriff marched out with a deep audible sigh. Presumably Pansy had sold the shop, but I hadn't bothered checking. I supposed now I'd have to add yet another chore to the list, once the baron was in the Tower, Landry freed, and everyone back at peace.

So - visiting my father, and visiting Pansy. I wasn't sure what I'd hate most, but at least I knew where Pansy was. More importantly, Jessy's murder was solved and the culprits about to face justice.

CHAPTER THIRTY EIGHT

WREN

A commotion so obvious, so loud, and near to the busy roads
beyond the manor, brought the curiosity of everybody
remotely close by. The earl's manor entrance was bushy but small,
the rush of unwanted visitors had left the front gates wide, and so
the street beyond was lined with folk peering over the shrubs, and
even a few cheeky enough to creep in, past the open iron gates.
Noses of all sizes poked in. I could see them from the windows, but
ignored them, having no choice, although I wished I could put back
the wooden shutters.

The sheriff and others had acted on Landry's words and Baron
Lyle was enraged. Staying roped to a chair wouldn't have pleased
me either, but he also knew the danger of imminent arrest. Even
worse, perhaps, he now knew the inevitable end of his enjoyable
and lucrative career. Yet he remained imperious, now only one
wrist loosely tied to the chair, the other still bleeding copiously in
his lap. No more squealing, and with his bleeding hand, he drank
the wine he was brought, watched everyone over the brim of his
cup, eyes oozing with undisguised hatred. I was sure he had plans.

Landry sat at ease, his wine cup in one hand, his other to the
back of my chair. He was under no restraint, but the remainder of

the Newgate guards, and most certainly the baron's six men, all sat close, watching him. He was conversing cheerfully with his own guards, when the Hamward twin stepped forwards, stared and spat, impatient and without any offered drink. Frankly I'd forgotten he was there and perhaps Landry had too. Until the sheriff left, he'd been crouching out of sight and hadn't intervened even when my dogs attacked.

Yes, *my* dogs. Shadow now sat, tongue out, beside Landry, and Red quietly beside me.

The fat man glared, shoulders back and stomach swelling outwards like a threat. The movement seemed to disturb his empty bowels and he farted loudly. Everyone held their noses and quickly turned away. "This is absurd. We wait here, so polite, so placid, not knowing what's going to damn well happen," he said without apology. "I'm off."

Landry looked up. "I'll not order you stopped. There's enough going on and too many confused guards to arrest you as well, but you know the royal guard, perhaps even the Newgate guard, will find you soon enough. If you make any attempt to bring a battle here, either against me, or to release your lord, I shall follow you to the ends of the earth, and kill you myself. Your own freedom will be temporary but the warrant has been issued, so enjoy that without bringing more trouble."

David stood, fat legs stretching out, longing to kick. His chin, sunk into the many folds of his neck, ate his face, but his rage was visible. He mouthed agreement to Landry, but looked not in the slightest as if he meant it. I knew he planned something damned nasty, and if I knew it then certainly Landry knew it too.

I suppose the baron also knew it. He turned, his glare like an alley cat as he spat the words. "You'll never leave me, Bladder-belly, so you'll live and work again, or you'll swing. Meantime, find Ben, but make sure never to be followed."

"You want them all to know?" The twin was aghast.

"Fool. You think they don't already plan to follow and kill you? These are all fools, but not as great an idiot as you, hedge-born hedgehog. I'm warning you, watch where you go, and who goes with you."

David Hamward scrambled out, muttering curses at the legs in his way, and once again the outer doors slammed.

With the sheriff and his assistants, two of the Newgate idiots, and now David, all gone, the great hall was looking less squashed, especially since David took the space of three men. I breathed and was wondering if I should go and talk to Prad, when Landry's sliding grey eyes moved to mine. It was like pale ice tunnels opening. He didn't seem perturbed at David's loud escape.

Although the disgusting murderer was already under arrest, he'd do his best to escape unseen, and I didn't like the idea of him running free. I turned to Landry, but he spoke first.

"What an admirable help you truly are, little bird. I thank you. Your sudden choice of move was a tremendous help."

I felt quite smug. Landry's thanks mattered a great deal, but I just said, "It's nice to know I can be useful."

"Soon, I hope," he said, half under his breath, "you will be a good deal more than that." His smile seemed conspiratorial. Perhaps he was planning on sharing a code. He could say, *'good morning,'* and it would secretly mean *'kick that bastard in the stomach.'*

I was interrupted by the baron. His mouth was permanently pursed sideways. The ugly scowl that seemed to be his perpetual expression, was so fixed, I assumed someone had once split his lip. He had the sort of mouth which suited him. Now he was saying, "Whatever you scum manage to do, it won't serve you. I have friends amongst folk far more important than you dust-riddled rats. And this," he raised his wrist which still dripped scarlet, "will be my proof. I'll be back free within the week, and you'll all be dead within the month."

"I doubt anyone," Landry murmured silkily, "can claim more authority than his royal highness the Prince Richard, Duke of Gloucester. It is the prince, the second most powerful lord in the entire country, who has ordered your arrest and trial. You may also remember that the royal prince is the Lord High Constable of all

England, so no one carries more authority except the king himself. Not any friend of yours, I am more than sure."

Both the remaining Newgate guards frowned, looked impressed, but said nothing.

"Fool and liar," the baron yelled. "The prince lives in Yorkshire and no horse can gallop that distance in a day."

Landry laughed, but it seemed he couldn't be bothered answering, so I answered instead. "Prince Richard lives on the Yorkshire Dales, but he comes to court when required. His majesty is unwell, so Prince Richard has remained at court, and Landry spoke with him for more than an hour. That means you'll never be free, until you're executed, but I suppose death is a sort of freedom."

He shouted over my words, but most of those present would have heard, and hopefully believed enough of what I'd said.

"You, ugly mud-spitting bitch, I'll have you turning on the spit at my kitchen, then slice you for the servant's dinner. I'll not eat your stringy flesh, but I'll watch you roast." Landry was right, there was no point in answering him. Into the partial silence, the baron shouted again. "You ignorant filth have no idea about this land, so let me educate what sliver of brain perhaps exists. My brother is a great warrior, as I was, at Tewkesberry, Towton and more. The king himself knows and loves me, treats me as a loyal brother. I have relatives in high places, and am close with Lord Hastings himself."

"You mean you've bribed him in the past?" Landry turned those ice eyes to stare at him. "Yet powerful as Hastings may be, bought friend or no, he has no authority over the law, nor the orders of Richard, Duke of Gloucester."

Seething, the baron's crooked jaw seemed more serpentine. He was choking on his own threats. I wasn't sure how long we'd have to wait for the sheriff's return, as the Tower wasn't that close, even on horseback, and I had no idea what sort of man the Constable was. I only knew his name as Brackenbury. I'd never even been to the Tower, and never wanted to.

Landry was speaking quietly to his own men, the Baron spat out some sort of insult every now and then, but he couldn't release himself however hard he struggled, and the rest of the guards just stood frowning, silently waiting. Prad had sloped off, probably back to the stables, and would have another saddled mount ready for Landry, if he needed one suddenly.

The earl's steward, Landry's long bladed sword still gripped tight, was both puzzled and a little alarmed, when he heard yet another commotion. None of us had known what was happening, except, as usual, Landry. He stood, but made no attempt to leave the hall, instead he spoke to the steward, loud enough for once so that everyone could hear him.

"It seems that our absent host is absent no longer," Landry smiled. "The Earl of Thamesdon has come home. An unexpected but entirely delightful interruption."

Rushing out to admit his lord and master, the steward flushed bright red, but kept hold of Landry's sword. He then returned, flinging open the hall's carved doors, and announced the earl's entrance. There wasn't only the earl, he had with him his principal secretary, the three leaders of his personal guard, and his best friend, all of whom followed him into the shrinking space, and we were squashed again. However, this time, the shadows were virtually all gloriously on our side.

The earl himself stood amazed and stared around.

"Landry, my dear, what in heaven's name is going on?"

I'd never seen his partner before. The earl was perhaps the prettiest man I'd ever known, but the friend almost surpassed him. Huge brown eyes blinked with golden glimmer, his hair, as he peeled off his extremely regal hat, was curled at both sides of his face, and his cape was a vibrant swirl of gold thread, lined in white fur.

He and the earl were both outstanding, Landry bowed to both, and the baron, who couldn't move anyway, was suddenly silent.

As everyone else was standing, bowing, greeting our host with fervent politeness, a couple of servants ran off to get more wine, as the steward, abruptly realising he still held a dangerous blade, dropped the sword with a loud plonk, and hurried to take their lordships' capes, riding gloves and hats. The rest of us just watched, wondering what would happen next. It was Landry who introduced the baron. It was quite a long introduction.

"As my position demands, with enormous thanks to your lordship," Landry said, sounding very official, "I and my friends in service, recently discovered the man who both ordered and undertook the violent murder of the Ford family. This gentleman sitting under constraint in your manor, sir, is Baron Lyle, the organiser and perpetrator of some of the most heinous crimes committed in this country over past years. I have recently disclosed the facts to his royal highness, Prince Richard, who then swore to issue a warrant for this creature's arrest and confinement in the Tower, and the arrest of his aids, although none of these are here present. Sheriff Wilson and Father Jacob have ridden to confirm the facts and should return reasonably soon. I apologise for bringing such a foul criminal into your premises, my lord."

Everyone listened in silence. Even the earl was somewhat amazed. Then the baron spoke his usual nonsense. "My lord, at long last a gentleman of power and intelligence has arrived. What is more, as you will remember, sir, we are closely related. You will no doubt quickly realise that this foul commoner lies, and it is he who is under arrest. I should be freed immediately."

Of course, Lyle didn't know the situation behind the situation.

The earl's friend knew some of it, but was clearly in shock. He kept turning around staring at anyone and everyone, even me. I was the only female present, so I suppose I stood out, even clutching a walking stick, and dressed in rags. The earl now pulled off his black leather gloves, handed them to the steward, and ignored the baron. He smiled at Landry instead.

"My dear friend, as usual you have achieved the miracle we hoped for. If the Tower guards do not arrive soon, my own guards will escort this vile criminal to the dungeons. Indeed, on our way over the Bridge roughly an hour past, I observed the mounted royal guards galloping towards the Tower, ten of them at least, though too quick to count. This actually delayed us somewhat, as it's a rare sight and I stopped to obtain information, which turned out was pointless, since nobody amongst the watching crowd knew the facts. But now I know, and I'm proud of you as always, Landry. Excellent."

He hardly bothered to look at the baron, and all the guards, from each side, just stared, either alarmed or delighted.

The friend started to smile. His full pink lips puffed up into brilliance. "What an exciting day this is proving to be."

"Dear Thomas," the earl told his friend, "this will be a day to remember, I promise you. Our Christmas feast was a glory, but until we celebrate Twelfth Night, I believe the arrest and imminent execution of the most wicked demon within our land, shall be the most memorable." He turned back to Landry, who was still standing. "Another hero, another courageous act of heroism," he said, adding, "I believe you know my dearest partner, Sir Thomas Chester. Once wined and dined, perhaps tomorrow, we will both attend at Westminster Palace, and hopefully see Prince Richard. By then this rogue will be properly incarcerated.'

The steward, accompanied by several other members of staff, now brought jugs of wine and silver tankards, served the two lords themselves, then Landry, and then, to my astonishment, myself. They made no move towards the baron, and I just stood there sipping the rich red Burgundy while Landry spoke softly to the earl. His friend, Sir Thomas, fascinated me and it was him I was staring at, very impolitely, but without realising it, when the final commotion echoed into the hall and the steward rushed out, leaving the entire room looking surprised once again.

The final commotion of the day, and a gloriously satisfying one. The first to enter, as the steward opened the hall's huge door, was a gentleman fully armoured, with a huge shining silver pike held up in one hand. He strode in and faced us all, banged the base of the pike on the floorboards, lifted his visor with slow deliberation, bowed to the earl and Sir Thomas, turned back to the crowd, and spoked loudly. His voice seemed to carry its own echo.

"In the absence of the Constable of the Tower, I, Sir Gradick

Rollham, Lieutenant of the Tower, hereby arrest Francis Waddington, Baron Lyle, in the name of his royal highness, the Prince Richard, Duke of Gloucester. The warrant demands that the Baron Lyle be taken into custody to the Tower and be contained, while awaiting trial for multiple murder, corruption, fraud, theft and high treason."

His men immediately took the baron's arms, raised him from his chair, and as he dropped his empty cup, they took his wrists, ignoring the injury. Then they dragged him to the doorway and out into the cold grey drizzle. Since his ankles were tightly roped, the baron couldn't walk. I so enjoyed watching as he was hauled out, literally dragged, as he shouted his head off and his hand began to bleed once more.

Those wonderful clothes of his, his proof of grandeur and title, swept across the ground as though a servant's broom. His wounds, however, were clearly serious and added scarlet to his crimson.

The baron's words were hard to decipher, but there was no need to try, since it was only a jumble of insult, threat, and begging interposed with sobs.

The remaining guards, the baron's, and those of Newgate, watched in silence and then gradually followed outside. All kept a dismal silence until they were gone. The earl clapped, Landry smiled, and I almost jumped up and down, but just grinned instead. Space! How remarkable, after so many hours of the stink of sweat on unwashed bodies.

The sheriff, his men, and Father Jacob finally arrived, said all the right things to the right people, after which the sheriff left.

The rest of us, drinking to success with our cups of wine, didn't speak until everyone had gone. Then the earl and his friend sank onto the nearest chairs, even though the largest was now in pieces on the ground, and started to praise themselves and everyone else. Me too!

Asking the steward to arrange for everyone's comfort, including hot bricks for the beds, the earl added that supper, however small and unprepared due to circumstances, should be served within the next half hour. He added that there would be a bonus of one whole sovereign paid to each staff member who had risked their life to help keep Landry safe.

I felt like royalty myself as the earl reached out, took my hand and led me to the table. "Our resourceful Lady," he announced, "you will do me the honour of facing me across the table at supper."

Yes, the great hall now seemed virtually empty, but both Landry and Jacob cheered. That's never going to happen again, I was quite sure.

CHAPTER THIRTY NINE

NARRATIVE

"I consider it a great shame," Sir Thomas was saying, "that our friend Landry, cannot be knighted for the great work he's now achieved."

The earl laughed over his cold pork. "We can address you as Sir Landry. Do you like the idea, my friend?"

"Not in the least," Landry smiled, and then buried his nose in his magnificent tankard. "My various visits to Newgate, I imagine, would be quite difficult to arrange for a knight of the realm."

"The Tower instead, perhaps," said Sir Thomas.

"Even worse," grinned Landry. With little opportunity to question the inmates."

Wren, sitting opposite the earl, across the table, was deliciously aware of feeling relevant, or even somewhat important. The table had been set around her, as though she was central to every conversation. To the earl's right sat Sir Thomas, to his left lounged Landry. Father Jacob sat beyond Sir Thomas, and to that side of the great table was a parade of others. Wren smiled at herself, alone in opposition and so the centre of attention.

She was wishing the dogs had remained as she could have fed them from the table. Prad, however, had hurried them back down to the stables. Now Wren said, ignoring her wine just in case it became too tempting, "I can hardly believe it is all finally solved. Perhaps it may stop haunting me now. I'll go and tell my father, if I can find where he is and walk that far tomorrow, he wasn't a friend of the Ford family, but he did visit them once while he was staying with me. He's disappeared, so it may take a while to find him."

"True, little bird. He no longer works at the docks." Landry looked across the rising steam from the table's remaining platters. "There was some disagreement amongst the other men as to whether he was sacked or left by choice, and no one appeared to know where he'd gone."

"Probably back on the trading caravels," Wren said, sipping the wine, too tempting to ignore any longer. "He sailed to France and Denmark, and even to Italy once. He said he loved it. I'd wager he's back on the Sea."

"That would save you having to look for him," Jacob smiled.

She laughed. "I just think he'd like to know the Fords will be avenged after all. He said such nice things about them when I got upset." The atmosphere and now the wine, merged in a fizz of delight. "Knowing him, he won't care much, but he said what a nice family they were, and how shocking that killing was. If I can't find him, then perhaps I ought to just go and speak with Pansy."

Landry leaned back in his chair, eyes almost closed beneath the heavy lids. "We have another body to identify, once the celebrations are over. First, I intend checking on the fate of Baron Lyle, then I'm chasing the Hamward twins."

"I'd come with you to the Tower, but it may be a week or more before I can walk."

"You can ride," Landry reminded her, "and there is not only Arthur stabled here, but a string of remarkable animals, owned by our gracious host."

The earl raised his cup, then drained it. "The work you've achieved – the king will hear of it from his brother, I promise you. A triumph."

Jacob leaned forwards, elbows to the bright white linen of the tablecloth. "Personally, I suggest we three ride to the Tower tomorrow, take a couple of guards, and leave the earl and Sir Thomas in peace."

Sir Thomas sniggered.

⋈◇⋈

The following day brought a deep grey threat of storm, and the wind howled like wolves. Landry helped Wren up into the saddle and though Arthur first objected to Landry mounting an entirely different horse, he settled, content with Wren's hands stroking between his ears.

The ride to the Tower was a short one, avoiding the bustle of the Cheaps. Father Jacob led them through the gated archway as their accompanying guards told their business to the Tower guards, then rode on to the open door of the lieutenant's business chamber,

Wren sat proud between the mounted guards, as both Landry and Jacob spoke to the assistant of the Tower Constable, whom they had met the previous day.

"As commanded, Master Crawford. The warrant issued by his Royal Highness, was dispatched and immediately put into action. Baron Lyle is in the dungeon beneath the Wakefield Tower, a windowless chamber beneath the level of the river. He is well watched, I assure you. I understand the trial is expected to be held within the following week."

Satisfied, Landry thanked the Lieutenant, Richard Haute, and related the simple facts to Wren, who was sitting snug on Arthur, unable to easily dismount.

"It's done. We'll follow the trial through our friend Thamesdon, who has agreed to attend. In the meantime, you can forget all hauntings, Little bird, and leave the law to do its duty."

Richard Haute's voice interrupted from his doorway. "You wish to visit the baron, while you are here? I have no objection under the circumstances. I shall send two guards to accompany you."

Smiling, Landry turned. "Thank you for the offer, sir, but I've no desire to visit the man. I loathe and distrust a single word he might tell me. I am sure he's guilty of far more than we can prove, but execution will be accepted as punishment, for whatever he may have done. I leave him to your generosity, Sir Richard."

The Lieutenant chuckled. "My generosity is strictly curtailed regarding this particular guest. The Earl of Thamesdon will be informed once the trial date is set."

※◆※

"It's a beautiful building, and so grand," Wren murmured as they rode through the archway and back onto the worn cobbles of Tower Street. Looking to the left and the gloom of the river a little south, the water carried only the reflections of grey on grey and the bursts of spray as the wind swept up from the estuary.

"And now," Jacob added from her other side, "you wish to visit the somewhat less voluptuous building, housing your friend Pansy."

"Yes." Wren nodded. "But she's not really my friend." This reminded her of the statement she had always denied, *'Your dogs are waiting.'* To which she had always answered, *'they're not my dogs.'* She often missed them and though she thought of them as hers, more frequently now, they remained in the kennels beside the stables, and Prad kept them well fed and well loved. They weren't his either, but he had never yet said so.

The storm had been expected for the past hour, and now it thundered its arrival. The sleet angled as the wind pounded, and the sudden flash in the sky echoed between the rooftops. At the narrow door to the sheriff's small office, they stopped. Jacob, his hood already to his nose, dripping torrents to his chin, called a goodbye.

"No point me staying. Too wet. And pointless. I'm back to Saint Nicholas and the sweet perfumes of Newgate." He rode on, keeping to the shelter of the old stone walls.

The two guards waited. Landry dismounted into the puddles and the sluice of water through the gutter. He tethered his horse to the window bar and waved the guard on. "Get back to the stables and tell the earl I'll be back soon. It's good news regarding the baron, but I'll explain more later." Then he helped Wren dismount, put one strong but soaked arm around her shoulders, and half lifted her into the open office.

Sheriff Wilson sat in the guttering light of one small tallow candle and peered at them through the shadows. He recognised Wren as she stumbled onto the single empty stool, the three legs of the stool shaking as violently as both of Wren's.

The sheriff brightened. "Mistress Bennet, you're more than welcome. Have you come – just a small suggestion of course, to invite dear Pansy back into your own dwelling?"

Landry, silently laughing, leaned back against the door, now pushed shut and deep in shadow, as the rain was tossed against it from outside.

Wren hung on to the edge of the sheriff's small table and its pile of scattering scrolls, papers and quills. Even the pot of oak gall seemed in danger of falling, until the door was firmly closed. The dreary shelter resumed, but the noise of the storm continued to shatter the peace.

"I'm sorry," Wren raised her voice, "but as I explained before, I have no home to offer, but I came to visit her, if I can manage the stairs. Meanwhile, Landry wishes to tell you of the baron. So, is Pansy in? She'd be crazy to go out in this weather."

The sheriff ignored the question of whether or not his unwanted guest was crazed, and quickly opened the door to the stairs. "First room up on the left, mistress. She'll be delighted to see you."

Having difficulty with climbing the creaking steps, Pansy heard her long before Wren reached the top, and she flounced from the room to swear at whoever was making the unnecessary noise. She saw the wet hooded shadow and flopped back. Two breaths later, she realised who the visitor was, and dashed down the remaining steps to help Wren up.

"Wonderful, it's my very best and dearest Wren." Pansy appeared on the verge of tears.

Wren stared back, forcing a smile, but feeling more like the tears of a different kind. Never having been Pansy's friend, her words showed how miserable she now was. Evidently the love of the sheriff had been short lived.

Struggling to the small room, Pansy helped Wren to the one chair by the tiny central fire and took the stool next to her.

Wren said, "Aren't you happy here? I thought you'd found the love of your life. First with Bryce, of course, which was so sad. Perhaps you need to know folk for a longer time before falling at their feet."

With a sigh of fatigue, Pansy leaned back and almost fell from the stool. "Please don't mention Bryce again. I thought – I confess – I had a huge tingle for the sheriff. He's – nice," she said eventually. "I cook, and he supplies the food, but I hardly see him except over the table when he eats. He wants privacy and silence. He sits and thinks, eyes shut, almost all day if nothing important calls him. I thought it was – well, you know, romantic, but it isn't. I sit here all day staring at those teeny flames."

"And you've sold the shop?"

That had evidently been recent. "The money can't all be collected until next week, when the lawyer signs the papers." Pansy sniffed. "Until then I can't touch a farthing. I can't even offer you a cup of ale. John won't pay for a thing unless it's urgent. No wine, no clothes, and no visits from his friends as he doesn't have any."

"But weren't you happy at first?"

"Yes." The tears were trickling after all, and Pansy's cheeks were striped with misery. "The first week's always lovely. It was with Bryce. After so long without a man to kiss me, Bryce seemed like a miracle. Then after what happened, the sheriff seemed like another, and he's not nasty, just bossy and incredibly boring."

Wren almost laughed. "Then leave him," she suggested. "I don't think I can invite you with me because it's not my house. But get your money and buy yourself a little cottage somewhere with nice neighbours."

"It's my plan," Pansy clasped her hands as if in prayer. "But then what do I do? I'm bored all day here, but at least John comes in for dinner and supper. I share his bed, and he just rolls away and snores. If I live on my own will I be even more bored?"

"Buy another shop, a clean easy shop. Sell hats, clothes, or go and be a cook at the Tower. They have free rooms there for the staff. There's certainly lots of people there to talk with."

Wren wished she hadn't come.

"But you and Landry are happy?" Sniffing back the tears, Pansy's smile screwed sideways into a wink. "You don't mind living with a thief? I suppose you think yourself in love with him too."

Her back strained as Wren stiffened. "He's no thief." She then remembered that this was precisely what he claimed to be, and was the necessary disguise. "Maybe sometimes, but he works too, and so do I."

"You help him steal? Or you work as a cleaner? You live in Earl Thamesdon's manor, don't you?"

She knew too much already. "Yes," Wren answered, no smiles. "But Landry and I aren't partners. We have separate rooms." Wren gulped slightly. "We're just friends. No love involved."

Pansy brightened. "Then I'll visit tomorrow. If I come to the kitchens, will you be there? I'll pretend I've come to visit you, dear, but of course, I shall see how I can attract Landry. He's so handsome, I'm surprised you haven't snared him. I can wear a low-necked gown if you think it would help, and put blusher on my cheeks and cleavage too. Men always like that."

Wren sighed. "Don't do it, Pansy. He can be dangerous, you know. He killed those brutes when Wyatt was free and gathering some sort of gang. I saw him murder them."

"Not murder. Self-defence," now Pansy scowled. "in fact he was defending you. Don't you like him, saying things like that? I shall be over tomorrow, and give poor Landry someone to smile at."

"He's not like that," Wren said, her own scowl forming. "alright, it wasn't murder, he's a good man. I just thought – and anyway, he won't be in tomorrow."

"I did wonder about your father," Pansy added. "He always has some coin. Not a handsome man but sweet enough. I'd be your step-mother." She giggled. "You'd like that, wouldn't you?"

"Would I?" Wren could imagine the result, being bossed around even more than when Pansy was her boss at the shop. She hurriedly shook her head. "No, he's not an easy man either, he's always a bit rough, and besides, I haven't the slightest idea where to find him. He doesn't work at the docks anymore."

"I know." Pansy's smile returned. "I stopped seeing him when I went to get the eels in the mornings. I've seen him go through Cripplegate a couple of times though. Perhaps he works at Bedlam or one of the farms. I always liked him, you know, when he came to share your room over the shop. He should remember too. He always smiled at me."

"Surely, you'd like a younger man. My father's old. Old and difficult. There are other problems too. He may like sharing beds, but he never seems to fall in love. Actually, I don't think he's capable."

Pansy raised her voice as the wind plummeted against the little window. "Silly girl. Your say things like that about your own father? Obviously, he loved you."

Wren paused as the wind thundered and the little metal frames around thick glass rattled. "I don't think he ever did. Maybe my mother did, but I can't remember her." She swallowed hard. "I can honestly say no one has ever loved me."

"Stupid self-pity, my girl." Pansy's smile was now wildly exaggerated. "I've always loved you as a friend."

Wren doubted it, indeed, knew it was rubbish. "Well, if you find out where he's working, or where he's living, do please let me know. And good luck getting him into your bed, or you into his. He's a bully."

"I can deal with that," Pansy nodded. "after Bryce, I've learned a thing or two, and he'd never be as bad as that."

"Of course he isn't. But he's not gentle either."

"He will be when he falls in love with me." Pansy stood and twirled, holding out her skirts. "A bit old, I suppose but it's him or

Landry." She paused momentarily and the smile faded. "I'm not old. But well, I'm not young either. I thought with Bryce – and then – but I won't go back to loneliness again now."

Landry had already left, so walking home with the wind whipping against her eyes, it was easy to cry. "*And it's true. No one, not one single soul, has ever loved me.*" But Wren wiped her eyes, braced against the bluster, and told herself, "*And I don't think I ever loved Dad. Not once I grew up a bit, so I've never been loved but I've never loved either.*"

A faint thought whistled through her mind, and she heard the word '*Landry*' blow like the wind. Not sure where it came from, while denying that it came from herself, she gritted her teeth and hobbled home, her shoes getting stuck in the mud, and between the cobbles. Her leg burned and stabbed, and the walk took her an absurd two hours. Two aimless and useless visits. She hoped Landry had achieved better.

CHAPTER FORTY

NARRATIVE

"I nearly told her the brothel on the Bridge has a good reputation and pays well. She could go there, or start one of her own." Wren was again close to the fire, but this blaze roared up the chimney and was the biggest and brightest she had ever seen, apart from the destruction of the Mews. "But I didn't, I'm not that mean, besides, I want her to find my father."

"I see no reason why." Landry sat further from the fire, almost lost in shadow. Only the pale glitter of his eyes blinked reflections of flame.

"He just doesn't have friends, at least, I don't think so" explained Wren. "No one does if they move around a lot. I don't think he did on the carracks either, and he doesn't know where I'm living, so it's the same for both of us."

Landry's lips tucked slightly. "So, you plan to search the city for your father, while leaving me to the torture of your lascivious friend."

"She's not my friend."

"But no longer your employer, so why encourage her?"

"I'll never bring her here. Back then she was bossy and demanding," Wren said, memories of regrets and problems quickly pushed away. "but she wasn't that bad. She could be nice, but now she talks about things she would never have mentioned to me when she thought I was just her servant."

It was a warm evening after a long day, and Landry now spoke more to himself, his eyes abruptly closed. "A useful day with the baron in custody and his wretched brother dead. The two leaders gone, leaves their three henchmen less capable. I want the more intelligent of the twins under lock and key, which should be easy enough. The other twin may even be useful to me from time to time. More difficult, will be discovering the killer Ben or Benny, then the name of the dead woman in their well, and the arrest of her killer."

"Who has to be Benny himself, one of the twins, or the baron's dead brother, I presume?"

"That's the assumption." Landry once more opened his eyes. "However, a sensible one, that will hopefully prove accurate. But it means going back to that vile shed and its corpse."

"Though it would mean escaping Pansy's visit."

Landry didn't answer but reached over and took his wine cup from the small table at his side. "The weather is an added difficulty."

Wren grinned. "I don't like being sodden and freezing either, but I didn't think you minded."

Suddenly Landry laughed, as always unexpected. "Discomfort is nature's only answer to humanity's cruel stupidity," he told her softly. The crackle of the flames spat louder, and Landry was back into the shadows. "The horses' shudder at lightening and rear at thunder, the gutter muck slops over to the cobbles, the quarry turns limestone to mud and the folk, I've no doubt, look for excuses to stay indoors under their own shelters."

"I should have known you didn't mean just freezing to death – far too normal." She laughed as well, sounding like the crackle of the fire. "Landry, you're just like the weather yourself. Neither gentleman nor gentle man, no compromise, no placation, you know what to do and you do it. Even if it means you're a criminal too, and then sleeping in Newgate."

His eyes followed her as she stood, moving back from the spitting fire. His murmur was so soft she could barely hear him, but she caught the words that mattered. 'You're tired? Are you going to bed?" She nodded. Then he spoke again. "You know where my bedchamber sits, and the choice is yours."

Wren had heard but pretended deafness, and limped to the stairs beyond the hall. "Golden dreams, Landry. I'll see you at breakfast."

Landry leaned back, legs stretched out, ankles crossed, hands clasped behind his head, adding, "Dream of sunshine, little bird. I shall dream of something far better."

Wren did not dream of sunshine. As the great white feathered owl swooped from stars to ground, catching the mouse in her silent talons, Wren dreamt of Landry.

She woke to the sound of rain against her window. Then she smelled the new baked bread, and imagined the sound of the butter melting on the hot crust and within moments she was once again dressed and attempting to limp down the stairs with one hand on her walking stick and the other grasping the banister. "My skills," Wren told herself, "are improving."

Father Jacob had returned, and he and Landry sat at the breakfast table facing the earl and Sir Thomas. Sir Thomas sat with the placid contentment he invariably wore, while Landry, Jacob and the earl discussed the unknown dead woman in the well.

"The body was partially decomposed. I could not have recognised her, even had I known her. However, I doubt I knew her." Landry looked up, hearing the dramatic arrival behind him. "You saw the body, little bird. Do you remember anything that might help identify her?"

Stopping abruptly and leaning on her stick, Wren knew the memory was easily brought back into her mind. What she had seen was glued to her thoughts, as was the horror of the Fords swinging bodies. "She had fair hair. It wasn't quite white, it was pale though.

Her face was all – in pieces, but her hair was still beautiful. And she wore a very plain green gown, oh – and an apron with lots of big dark stains."

"Her own blood, no doubt."

"No one could have recognised that body. But perhaps could recognise the clothes. I don't think I saw shoes."

"Then," the earl leaned over the table towards her, "what about this other foul killer, Ben someone."

Speaking to an earl was becoming more accepted so Wren shrugged. "My lord, I've no idea about him, nor the woman. I've never travelled. I only saw the Tower for the first time two days back, though I haven't lived far from it for most of my life. I had no reason to go there. So, until I met Landry, I only knew people living close and not all of them. I knew the regular customers at the eel shop, but not where they lived, most of them at least."

Nodding, the earl turned again to the priest. "Whereas you, father, know all the churchgoing folk in the parish. Has a woman you know been missing for some time? Her family would surely be worried."

Jacob was still eating, and his tankard of ale remained clutched in one hand. He shook his head. "I'm not a peaceful preacher, my lord, and my parish is not so close. I deliver sermons at both Newgate gaol, and to those prisoners before the gallows, and I also attend the sad souls held in Bedlam on occasion. A woman missing for such a time – no – I've heard nothing, but later, I'll return to my church and speak with Brother Peter. He is my assistant who stays at the church and he knows the parish far better than I do."

The earl leaned back, smiling at Thomas. Wren noticed both wore loose shirts over hose, the shirts immaculately folded into a hundred neatly sown tucks, bleached linen and high collared, while their hose, identical to each other, were knitted scarlet silk.

Landry's hand grasped his tankard. "Today we separate, though perhaps not you, my lord, who may pass a sweet day by the fire praying for better weather. Meanwhile I intend returning to the country house, where hopefully Hamward remains hunting for hidden coins. There's still a good deal to discover about that wretched body, and there may yet be things remaining in that prison of a well. I'll be questioning whoever I can find. Jacob, can I suggest you speak to your assistant concerning lost parishioners, and then take the pleasure of visiting the Tower dungeons. If that damned baron feels obliged to speak to anyone, it's more likely to be a Holy Father come to bless his confession. Just make sure it's not a confessional you can't then repeat. We need answers, principally this unknown murderer, but there may be past crimes he can admit to also."

"A delightful prospect," Jacob said, wedging butter between two hunks of bread.

Landry turned back to Wren, her eyes fixed on that same new baked bread and the terracotta tub of bright golden butter.

"Little bird, you can walk a little, even attempt the stairs, but if you dislike my suggestion, tell me."

"Climbing London Bridge, or swimming the river?"

He didn't bother to smile. "The western gate. Those damned guards plague us like some hungry dog, but they'll not take a woman into custody who comes with walking stick and bandages, asking about past arrests. There's no warrant issued in your name, little bird, and hopefully at this time of day, they'll not be too ale-sotten to think. You'll ride Arthur, and not dismount if the drop's too arduous."

Wren stared. "It sounds reasonable. That doesn't mean it will be though."

This time Landry smiled. "Jacob might be the safer one to send, but he can't take two jobs, one each end of the city. Newgate could hardly be further from the Tower."

"Unless you send me to Yorkshire." Jacob smiled. "I'll happily travel north and visit Prince Richard instead."

Wren laughed, "I'd sooner do that too. Is it a long ride?"

"A week, with no stopping to sleep." Jacob spoke through his final mouthful, and pushed away the platter as he reached for his tankard. Another joy as a guest of an earl, was not cleaning platters, nor any of the other work needed. "I'll go where you want me, as always," he said, brushing the crumbs from his priestly gown and nodding to Landry. "I'll deliver the news back here, if that's acceptable, my lord."

Both smiling, the earl and Sir Thomas were standing, throwing their napkins from their shoulders, then heading back towards the stairs. "I might not be in," the earl said. "Thomas and I are attending court midday, but you'll be expected by the staff, and they'll let you in and swamp you with wine and anything else you want. Landry will be here, I assume."

"Possibly not," Landry said. "It depends on what I discover waiting at that horror of a shed."

The errand she had been given did not appeal to Wren. She had visited Newgate gaol many times in the past, on her father's behalf. She had even wondered if she would now find him back there. The place was a menacing threat outside, a violent threat inside. She hated the guards who had been determined to take Landry, and throw him back where they thought he belonged, but at one time, even herself as well.

First, she considered the option of taking the sheriff with her, she then changed her mind. It would mean facing Pansy again, and possibly feeling obliged to bring her home afterwards. Nor was Newgate Sheriff Wilson's responsibility. He avoided work that would bring him no reward of coin, nor the glory of reputation.

⚔

Prad stood with Arthur ready saddled, as the steward opened the doors for her, placing her own cloak around her shoulders. Well wrapped, her walking stick strapped upright beside the stirrup, she mounted from the block placed beside the door, and levered herself upwards with Prad's help.

Landry had left an hour since. Jacob had left some minutes later, and the earl and his friend were upstairs dressing for court. It was still dark, although a faint halo of light was peeking over the horizon behind the distant Tower. The city gates were unlocked, gatekeepers kicking the mud from the wet cobbles. Wandering dogs barked, racing to the northern gates for the arrival of the farmers bringing carts of food to market, and the gate keepers, who often threw them dark bread, or the gristle left from breakfast. Doors slammed as folk trudged out for work, for shopping, or the wash house. Smoke began to rise from chimneys, joining the dark clouds above, and as fires were lit, the street ovens were ready for business, shutters brought down with a thump and thud, for opening shops.

The early rain had faded to a grey drizzle, but the clouds hung low and promised more rain before the daybreak. The dark winter mornings were still a long way from surrendering to spring.

The Christmas season had kissed the city and now the final celebration of Twelfth Night was imminent. December had gone back into the shadows.

The city children were back, hopping and running, seeking out fruit they could steal from the markets, and folk paying them to mind a horse. The fun of the chase, before twilight darkened into early winter night.

Wren pulled up her hood, dodged children, pigs, goats and anything else which ran, bent her back against the cold, and clutched tight to her walking stick, as she first limped outside, then quickly turned and headed for the stables. Prad helped her mount, strapped her stick to the saddle and wished her good luck as she rode towards the western gate.

CHAPTER FORTY ONE

WREN

The sun slept so late in winter. Often shops waited for dawn, but that might mean half the day was gone. I hadn't been much earlier than dawn, but arriving at Newgate in absolute darkness, would not gain me an entrance. Even the stars were hidden behind the lowering clouds and the rising smoke. The moon sometimes beat through the darkness, but not that morning.

A pretence of daylight as I arrived at Newgate, meant the gates were open. I had no intention of leaving the city, but if the gatekeeper was up and working, then so were the guards.

Streams of folk were plodding through the gate, so I had to wait for the road to clear. A small flock of geese, feet flap flapping beneath their black tar protection, not knowing they trotted to their deaths. A louder procession trotted in the opposite direction, a stream of some elite household from the court.

Arthur pushed between those arriving, far more than those leaving, and took me to the towering gloom of the prison gates. I didn't dismount, but grabbed up my walking stick, reached out, and used it to knock on the gaolers' doors. One grumpy face appeared, cheeks swelling with breakfast and a dribble of honey on his chin.

Not being one of those who constantly threatened Landry or myself, he swallowed, used his cuff to wipe his chin, and was polite.

"I have a broken ankle and cannot easily dismount," I told him, having to speak loudly over the racket behind. "but I have several questions of importance, and so need to speak with the chief guard or his assistant." I held out the folded paper with the earl's coat of arms stamped on the red sealing wax.

The man actually seemed impressed. "If I can help you dismount, my lady, we can sit in the warm and discuss whatever is the problem."

I didn't bother telling him I was no lady. That would be obvious from my clothes once I dismounted. Landing, even with help, hurt like mad, but I gritted my teeth and followed the gaoler indoors. He had a brazier and four stools, so comfy enough.

I hurried with my questions, not wanting to stay long, nor still be present when other less genial guards arrived for work. First, "Do you have a Haldon Bennet under warrant here now?"

His shook his head but checked on the badly written list smudged with ink gall on the little table. "No, mistress. Though tis a name I know from some time back."

Yes, he'd noticed I was no lady in my scruffy clothes and unravelling hems. I'd taken off my cloak to shake away the attached glimmering of drizzle. "Very well. I hold a legal warrant for the arrests of twin brothers, by the names of David and Emil Hamward. You may know of them already."

Again, the gaoler shook his head. So, the baron had certainly kept his men safely unknown, whatever vile crimes they had helped commit.

"My assistant Ted Smith will be here soon," the guard said. "Has more to do with the inmates on a personal basis than I do, mistress. Feeds them and so forth. Ted is resident here, he's already late, but it's not unusual. No matter, he'll be more help than I am, if you care to wait."

"I'll wait," I told him. "In the meantime, perhaps you know of a man called Ben, Benjamin or Benny? He must have been held here in the past, though not executed, sadly."

It was while the guard denied any such knowledge that the assistant guard arrived, two others following. I knew all of them and they knew me. For a moment they were pleased to see I had been caught and arrested, but they sulked when they realised, I was simply a visitor.

Of course, I might have guessed, it was the assistant chief I disliked the most. I knew his name now, not that it helped anyone. "Master Smith," I said trying to sound like a lady even if I didn't look like one, "I've come here on behalf of Earl Thamesdon, and carry his seal. "I flashed it at his nasty glaring face, "wishing to ask extremely important questions about a criminal named Ben, often called Benny. Since his lordship assumes this man, must have been held under arrest in the past, you may be able to help us with his full name."

Although still glaring, Ted Smith was well aware of the Chief Guard's watchful gaze. "I do," he said at once. "Bernadion du Jules, he is, and a right nasty bugger. French. Ain't no one worked out how to say his name, so called him Ben. Yeh, and Benny if they liked him. I certainly didn't like the bugger."

Well, he didn't like me either, but what he said was extremely helpful. So, I asked, "And he was held here in the past? But not executed?"

"Just being French should have been enough, but no bastard understood him at his trial, and they let him go. Speaks mighty good English, I've heard him, but at trial, the bugger pretended he couldn't understand a word. They got an interpreter, but Ben complained, saying still no way he could understand, t'was the dialect or something. So, he got away with it. A killing, it was, but I've not seen the foreign wretch since. Maybe gone back to that nasty king they got over the water."

I was delighted. That was enough, but an address would help even more. "So, you don't know where he is now?"

"No, but some of the clods downstairs might." Ted pointed. "You been down there before, as well I know. You want another look at our palace?"

I didn't. "I suppose so," I said reluctantly. "But I'm injured and limping. You'll have to go first and then wait for me to get down." I didn't ask for his help. I had no desire to touch the brute. I turned to the chief. "If I don't return shortly," I said with emphasis, "please would you come and get me?"

He said he would, very courteous and smiling and ignoring Ted's scowl. So back I went, downstairs, struggling with every step, but the jagged stone wall actually helped to lean against and grab onto when I stumbled.

So there I was again, in the vile place I had always hated, but remembered well. Nervous of Bryce possibly noticing me, I waited behind the wretched guard, and right in front of me as the door was unlocked and pushed open, was Wyatt.

He stared at me, as if he couldn't remember who I was. Then he remembered. He raised his hands in the air, and shouted, "That's Haldon's little bitch."

I wasn't actually sure whether he was greeting me with delight or hatred. I decided hatred was more likely. I said, "Hello Wyatt. I haven't come for you. I wanted to ask everyone a very quick question about one of the men gaoled here in the past. He was French. You knew him as Ben I believe. He got released at trial. Does anyone know where he might be now?"

Looking around at this disgusting place again, with all these brutal sneering faces, made me feel sick, but I stuck out my chin.

The smell was always the first and the worst. Perhaps that stench had soaked into the stone now too, and so would remain forever. One man had brought his dog with him, poor mangey looking creature, and was asleep on his lap, with a wound on its nose. I immediately thought of how my own dogs had looked when I first started feeding them.

Like everyone else, I avoided the wide gutter running through the earthenware floor, although stone paving slabs lined nearer the entrance. That gutter was piled with muck and faeces, but the stink didn't only come from there. I knew half the men pissed against the walls, and others smelled, simply because of weeks unwashed. The stench alone was enough to make anyone sick, but I'd expected it and refused to retch.

Having arrived in the winter darkness, of early morning, the tiny high barred windows let in no light, but at least I could see it wasn't pouring with rain.

So, I stood there, watching everyone. I expected no help and it seemed I was right, just as I was turning to leave something hit me so hard and so unexpected, I fell, just missing the gutter.

Then through the shadows I saw Wyatt's fist in the air above me. The blood on his knuckles had to be mine.

Rather stupidly, I hadn't expected it, but of course, he'd come to cheat the eel shop while I was there, and Landry had outright killed two of his proud new gang. So, I was the enemy.

At least I wasn't unconscious and would have stood immediately except that I couldn't reach my walking stick, so I only managed to kneel, looking up for the protection of the guard.

He was now, however, halfway across the floor, dragging the huge weight of Wyatt behind him. He'd knocked him out with my walking stick and was now shouting for the other guards. I managed to pull myself backwards and sat there in the black, my back against the wall with my head, my leg and my throat all pounding. My nose that was bleeding, and since I wore a gown absolutely ruined already, I used my sleeve to stop the blood.

Way back in the deeper shadows, I was fairly sure I saw Bryce, quiet but smiling. He was safely out of the way and was unlikely to make a move while Wyatt was the principal interest. I would imagine he was smiling about me being hurt.

Two more guards thundered down the steps and, not even seeing me, rushed over to Ted and the prone body on the stone below. Embarrassed, Ted stormed out and up the stairs.

For only a few moments, the two doors leading to freedom were left open. The wind rushed downwards, and the inmates rushed up. First, the dungeon's solid door was pulled wide, and second, a barred archway halfway along the dark corridor was moved aside, then up the narrow stone steps and into the guard's room. I never discovered how many got away, but perhaps only three or four managed a complete escape. I simply hoped with all my heart that Bryce hadn't been one of them.

Others were dragged back, screaming and shouting, one laughing, all kicked and whacked over their heads and shoulders.

Wyatt remained on the ground. He seemed fatter than I had last seen him, having probably stolen food from others. Not as bulging as the Hamward twins, but his height added to the monster's size. He lay, sprawled and unmoving. Several of the other prisoners still fought as if they enjoyed the game, and both noise and flying blood kept some back, yet called others forward. Perhaps only a cannon would have kept the peace.

I was watching Wyatt. He lay strangely still, but I assumed it was a trick.

One of the guards, kneeling over Wyatt, lifting his head and slapping both cheeks, then looked up and saw me looking back. "The bugger's bloody dead," he said, quite shocked. "Good news if you asks me, but it were only a wallop with a stick. Naught that would kill him. Humph," staring at me, "was it you what did it?"

"Absolutely not," I said primly. "it may have been my walking stick, which I'd appreciate back now, otherwise I can't walk, but it was your chief Ted Smith that swung it. I saw him and so did plenty of others."

"But the stick didn't even break." He brought it back to me, then glared down as I used it to wedge myself up. "Wouldn't kill a child let alone that big bugger, but he crashed back."

Another of the guards was poking at Wyatt's flattened cheek. "Ain't even bleeding."

"Yes, but he fell hard," I said, "taken by surprise. He tumbled flat on his face and smashed himself down onto the stone." I shrugged. "Perhaps he already had something wrong. I don't know, but I'm not sorry."

"Nor me," the guard smiled slowly. "best thing I seen in years."

And then, very carefully unlocking and re-locking every door behind him, he actually helped me back up the stairs to the guard's room. Ted quickly turned his back as he saw me. He was busy clipping his codpiece into place.

"Thank you," I said, staring out at the grey daylight and pulling my cloak tight around me. "did a couple get away? Bryce Judd didn't manage to escape, did he?"

The head guard was as polite as usual. "No, mistress. A fiasco, sadly, but we caught that hedge-born bastard right at the doorway, and dragged him back in. Just as well. His trial's tomorrow."

As I left, I heard the same guard speaking to another. "You did it," he was saying. "That damned beast. We never could get rid of that bastard. Came back and back again, and always avoided the swing. It was you and that lass that finally did it. Reckon you deserve a cup of wine."

CHAPTER FORTY TWO

NARRATIVE

O nly drizzle marked the windows, as Wren sat in the earl's grand hall, waiting, hopefully for someone else to come home. The fire was blazing across the inglenook and brought more light to the room than any window.

"So, one dead, one on trial and about to face the gallows, one in the Tower dungeon knowing he faces execution, two soon to be caught, and only one still unknown." Wren was thinking to herself. It wasn't long that she'd been able to call herself a criminal investigator, and already success whirled like a flag of victory, not that she had too much to do with it, but she had helped a little.

Landry had not yet returned. It was possible that he would not be seen until the following morning. Father Jacob wasn't present, but she did not know whether he had come, and then gone, or had not yet come, in which case, he had spent an unusual time at the Tower. The earl and his friend were not home, but Wren wouldn't have sat and talked to them anyway, she still felt somewhat intimidated.

Sitting alone by the crackling fire, longing to tell her news, but having only her dogs to talk with, was frustrating. Both Red and Shadow, enjoying every soaring flame, were spread, half entwined, their shadows covering Wren's stockinged toes. Her wet boots had been left to dry in the kitchen.

An empty jug, an empty platter and an empty cup, sat on the small table beside her. Soon Wren realised that her head was also empty. The hours dribbled, dark and slow as she was dreaming. It was deep night when finally, Landry returned. He woke her.

"My little bird is sleepy, it seems."

Blinking back the dreams, she smiled. "I expect you have wonderful things to tell me. I've an interesting development to tell you too, so we can talk before I sleep. Is there anything to drink?"

The steward had brought her a cup of wine when she first arrived and had left a full jug on the table. The boredom of waiting had inspired her sleep. Landry saw that the entire jug was empty, and he also noticed that Wren's words were slightly blurred.

"Soon." He sat opposite her, gazing across the blaze of the fire. "When I first met you, you'd hardly ever tasted your favourite drink, little bird. It seems I've taught you more than I intended."

Another jug was brought and soon they both drank, speaking over the silver brims of their cups. Wren leaned forwards. "Wyatt is dead. Killed by a guard in Newgate. He didn't mean it, but he wasn't sorry, though it was my walking stick that killed him. I have to admit."

Now Landry smiled at her, his eyes were warm in the flames' reflections. "I have killed no one today," he told her. "You have out-mastered me. Tell me more."

She giggled. "Bryce is safely in Newgate. His trial's tomorrow. You'll be a witness, won't you?"

"Indeed, as I've been informed. Invariably he manages to bribe the judge, so I have informed the new judge of this, and asked him to sit on this one. I shall be there. And what of your own success, little bird?"

Wren, bright eyed, gulped down the remains of her cup. "No one knows where the creature Benny is, but one of them knew *who* he is.

He's French. Which makes him easier to find as long as he hasn't sailed home. Bernadion, they said. Or maybe Bernhard. No, that sounds wrong." She sniffed and then grinned. "Can't remember but it's Ben something. I think Bernadion Du Jules, but he's definitely French. From France."

"Now that," Landry told her, his smiled hidden, "is an excellent discovery. I know of no one by such a name, nor do many French come to London. They rarely call us friends. So indeed, it should make him easier to find."

"That horrid Duff family always think they know everyone, even if most of it is silly gossip, it still might help."

He agreed. "So back to your favourite family tomorrow, unless you are unwell with a sore head. We now know the name which is the most important step forwards." He paused "So Wyatt is dead in Newgate. Excellent news. My own news is less interesting, but I believe it may bring another step to justice."

"You know the dead woman in the well?" Wren leaned over and helped herself from the wine jug, almost spilling it over the brim of the cup.

Landry regarded her with amusement, but made no move to stop her. "Neither know the woman, nor can be sure of her name, but any step forwards is better than nothing. Whoever she may have been, I know her killer. Twin number two. His arrest, of course, is already authorised." Landry drained his cup, but continued to hold it, turning it between his fingers as though considering what to say, and perhaps how to say it. Finally, "I spoke at length with his brother. He remains at that foul shed, and is ankle deep in rattling coin. It seems he discovered more sovereigns than pence, and offered me one. I snatched up a good deal more, but left him with enough to keep him for years. The rest I gave to Jacob, who will spread it amongst the poor. "

"And you ordered his arrest too? |Did you meet Jacob?"

"He finished early at the Tower, so came to join me. The baron sits insisting loudly of his innocence. He refused to speak of anything else and made no confession, so Jacob left him cursing."

Wren shook her head. "That doesn't surprise me. I hope he'll confess before they put his head to the block, but it'll likely take him an hour. I'm so sure he's been involved in crime for years."

"Undoubtedly," Landry said, soft voiced as he listened to Wren's increasingly eager, but slurred conversation. His own words floated between the spit and flare of the flames. "but as yet I've made no move to arrest the other Hamward. He's been treated as the family fool ever since a child, a wretched upbringing it seems, and whatever he's done has meant little to him except following orders. But if my decision proves wrong, I'll soon know it. In the meantime, I walked through the well tunnel, and found no other evidence except the muck of many years."

"Jacob has arranged the removal of her body to the church, where she'll be cleaned for burial. Hamward didn't know her name. He knew his brother had killed her on orders, and he knew that she was a well-practised – midwife."

Landry watched Wren's face as he spoke. She was frowning and he knew why, but said nothing more.

Wren asked, "From the city? Did he know where?"

"He knew nothing more." Landry stood and refilled both their cups. As he handed the tankard to Wren, he said, "You have blood on your cheek, little bird. Did Wyatt attack you before he died?"

Her look of concentration blurred, and she shook her head, her finger to her cheek. "I thought I'd washed it all off, but I'm not hurt. It was Wyatt of course. He punched me before the guards grabbed him and knocked him over. Then everyone was fighting. That place is horrible. Bryce almost got away, as you did." She paused a moment, frowning. "But of course, that was different. How on earth did you ever manage to sleep there?"

"Cheerfully endowed with curiosity," Landry told her, his mouth once more in his tankard, "and I've slept in worse, under trees and in the cold of a monastery. So where did Wyatt hit you?"

"He made my nose bleed. No matter. My ankle still hurts the most."

The stick she used now lay on the ground, where the dogs also lay unmoving, now considering Landry part of the furniture. "The hounds," he said, "must find this warmer than the stables. I do myself, but Prad has the horses to keep him company, as you have your hounds. I, on the other hand, have no one at all."

Hoping she did not appear flushed at this remark, Wren said, "You have company all the time." She was staring into her lap.

The soft chuckle seemed to respond to something Wren didn't understand. "Not the sort I was hoping for," Landry said through the chuckle, "neither the dogs or Prad would bring the feeling I want."

"Prad's always busy but I don't understand what that's got to do with it." Now the wine had reminded her of what she had been trying to remember. "I want to know more about the woman in the well. Why would that creature kill a midwife? Did he think her a witch?"

"Anything is possible. There is blood on your sleeves."

"That's just where I wiped the blood off my nose when Wyatt – I don't care anyway." Her mind was on something else. "I used to know a midwife, she was nice too. Not a witch. But there's many around, I suppose. No need to think it was her."

"Since the body is too long dead and the face unrecognisable, we may never know who she is," Landry added, "but even as a tired man, I am noticing your gown. Perhaps I should buy you some new clothes."

Wren breathed deeply and smiled wide. "Yes please. If you don't mind. I lost the few extras I had in the fire. I'd like to go back there one day and see if there's anything left. Is that possible? I went past weeks ago but it was just rubble so I didn't search for anything. Is anyone going to rebuild? It was a good house, wasn't it?"

Landry paused before answering. "Yes, the earl has plans. They will include a new home he intends offering to you, I believe. Tomorrow, you can ask him about it. Building has started yet, as the weather makes it too difficult. Naturally it won't be as grand, nor as warm, nor in any manner as luxurious as here, but it will be your own and that should make up for the rest. No doubt he'll take your wishes into consideration. Do you dream of a house, little bird?"

She looked up in amazement, all other thoughts gone. "Mine? I mean, me living there? Though the house will be his, as the Mews was his."

"No. It will be entirely yours." Landry laughed. "The decision is the earl's, and the generosity is his, not mine. I shall also be a homeowner, however, probably close by."

Fainting seemed a reasonable reaction. "Most of my life being stuck with my father," she mumbled, "I went to the Prestwick house by the river, and was cook and cleaner there. Then it was the eel shop. I had my own bedchamber upstairs and I thought that was luxury, but Pansy wasn't easy. Then – it sounds wrong – but I stayed with you."

"In a house I didn't own." He was still smiling. "But the next, we will own ourselves." Above the smile, his eyes watched her.

Wren watched him back. "It's almost too wonderful to believe. I never, ever, thought I'd own my own house. What will it be like, do you know? Will it have a real bedchamber upstairs or just be one room downstairs? Either will be – well – there aren't proper words. Can I paint little birds on the ceiling beams?"

"Your home will be built to the earl's design, depending on what else needs to be fitted within the space. One room or twenty, I have no idea." Landry's gaze remained warm, as the tucks of a smile at the corners of his mouth relentlessly twitched. "But tell him tomorrow, as tonight I doubt he'd understand you."

She sank back in her chair, keeping her feet still, so not kicking the dogs. "I can't think. I can't make sense of anything. Wyatt and that vile place and all the fighting, and my nose gushing and then finding out that killer's name, and then all the things you've told me." She sighed, gazing back at him. "Then possibly knowing the midwife, that's a worry. A house all of my own is a miracle and I can't even imagine such a thing, but, - " and she looked down at Red's twitching ears, "it will be so – nice – having you live close by."

Again, Landry paused, his smile now more visible. "Nice, little bird? Or simply convenient, perhaps?"

"Both." She blushed with a hiccup, and quickly slammed her hand across her mouth.

"A pleasant thought, little bird."

Wren had finished her cup of wine and accepted another. She held out her empty cup quickly as Landry approached the jug. She had entirely lost count of how many she had drunk. "Well, I don't have friends. Pansy thinks she is, but she never was. There was Jessy, but I don't want to talk about her anymore. Can I think of you as a friend, do you mind? I mean, you don't mind lots of things, like snow and storms, and I'm not as bad as a storm surely. Really, you're my boss like Pansy was, but – well, you're a lot nicer than she was."

After a long day the fire now burned low. The great logs were reduced to embers yet still flared, though most now lay in ashes. Wren felt she was melting of a different kind.

"A sweet remark, little bird," Landry told her softly, more murmur than speech. "You have more friends than you realise, it seems, with even an earl on the list. Myself included, naturally."

She looked back into his eyes and now imagined herself hooked on those steel grey arrowheads, pulled then into the tunnels behind. "I can't count the earl, but calling you a friend is –nice."

His smile was now deeper. "You are, I imagine, "just a little cup-shotten. Morgan's wine is a good Burgundy and probably stronger than you're accustomed."

Now she was avoiding the magical arrowheads. "You know, don't you. I'm not used to any sort of wine, but more now than I ever used to be. I hope I'm not drunk," She thought a moment. "But I might be."

Her words were ever more slurred, and her eyes were somehow darker. Landry knew her considerably more than tipsy. He grinned, but she saw nothing, still looking fiercely into her cup. She gulped the wine that was left. Barely hearing his next question, Wren peeped over her shoulder to see if the jug was now empty. It was.

Landry repeated, "I asked you, little one, if you can remember how many cups you've drunk this evening."

"More than one."

"Probably true. More than two, perhaps? And having been here all day – well – the count might be somewhat higher." Then she realised that Landry stood.

"You're tired," she muttered. "Done more than me." She raised her tankard hopefully once more, but sadly it was still empty. She needed courage, having said the unforgiveable and thought of possibilities even more forbidden.

"And your nose is bleeding again, little one," he told her, almost a whisper. Now the fire had fallen silent. Even a fire can sleep.

"It doesn't matter." She sniffed, finally looking up. "There's a bowl of water in my garderobe. There always is at bedtime. It just appears, sort of pops up. Big houses may do that. I'll try and wash. Anyway, like I said, it doesn't hurt. Only my leg does that."

Her words slid together, and Landry's smile widened. "Therefore, rest now, little one, to prepare for tomorrow when you can discuss your new home with the earl. Then I trust you'll accompany me, as I buy you a new wardrobe. First, I must attend the trial at Newgate, but afterwards you may dress as a countess and visit the Duff family, who will hopefully tell you every detail of the Frenchman known as Ben. Finally, you can return here and order a cask of the best wine. It will be a busy day, little one."

"Umm," said Wren. And hiccupped.

"You are undoubtedly correct," now grinning, "two days are more likely." He stood over her, his face no longer glazed with firelight. Looking up, she saw only shadow. Her sight wavered.

With one arm beneath her knees and the other around her shoulders, Landry swept her up, ignored the dogs, and began to carry her towards the corridor beyond the wide doorway. Wren's wavering consciousness dithered, she laid her head against his warm shoulder and wondered whether she should complain or simply kiss him, not that she knew how. Instead of either, she snuggled tight and closed her eyes.

Immediately his hands tightened, and he smiled down at the cheek squashed against his cote. Treading the stairs lightly, Landry made no sound, until once outside her own bedchamber, he kicked open the door, strode in, and laid his captive on the bed. He then sat beside her on the mattress edge, watching as she curled.

"Little bird," he murmured as she half opened her eyes, "I intend washing your face, and checking the splint on your leg."

"Umm," she repeated. Then, words in a rush, "Is this your bedchamber? Or mine?"

"Unfortunately, it is your bedchamber and your bed," he told her. "now lie still while I fetch the water and hopefully a towel." He strode to the tiny garderobe, its door on the other side of her bed, and stood there a moment, lighting the candle which lay beside the bowl of water, the smell of lavender faint, and a curl of steam still rising. Otherwise, the cupboard room was empty. No clothes hung from the pegs along the walls, no shoes lay beneath, and the large wooden chest was bare. On the table beneath the small lead backed mirror, two towels were folded, and the small sponge remained dry. Landry gathered them up, held the bowl of warm water, and returned to the bedside.

"Onto your back, little one," he told her, and as she rolled over, he lay the sponge in the water and lightly washed her face where the blood was dark. He then used the edge of one towel to dry where he had washed. Immediately he bent and took the fragmented drifts of her hems, both of gown and of the shift beneath. Very softly, he told her, "I am not undressing you. I will only unbandage your leg and mend or replace the splint." He was no longer sure she remained awake.

Now she mumbled, although he could barely hear or understand her. "Need – bed. No dresses – in – bed."

His smile drifted. "If I undressed you, I doubt I could stop. It would be dangerous for us both. It is only your lower leg I intend to – touch." He slipped her garter from her foot and rolled down the stocking, and that alone, he knew, would be dangerous enough.

"Umm, hurts," Wren admitted.

"Some of the bruises," he now murmured, "are still dark. You may be in more pain than you admit. Another bruise here by your foot is purple against such pale skin."

"Bruises – all over," she mumbled.

"Thinking of – all over," he whispered, "would be more dangerous still."

CHAPTER FORTY THREE

NARRATIVE

A lthough it still seemed dark, it was a great deal later than she had intended when she woke. Wren struggled to sit up. She had been fully tucked into bed, the covers wrapped up to and over her ear, but she realised that she remained fully dressed. Only one thing seemed odd, and that was the bandage and splint where her leg had been broken in the fall. On that leg, her stocking and garter were missing, and the bandaging replaced. Now it felt noticeably less painful, but she had not yet rolled from the bed, stood, tried to walk, or, usually the most difficult of all, walk down the great staircase.

So, biting her bottom lip with anticipation, she rolled from the soft warmth and tried to stand. Ease and painless relief swamped her.

She began to walk. The pain returned but it was jagged and uneven. As she lifted her foot, in that leg the pain dissolved. Setting it again on the ground, the pain returned. Walking to the doorway, she turned and gazed again at her bedchamber, larger than any room she'd known before, and almost as beautiful as the great hall downstairs.

On the tiny table beside her bed, a carved candle holder stood, and the candle wax sat neat, cold and perfumed. She loved the smell of beeswax instead of the cheap stink of tallow she had always known before when the cost was hers alone. This candle had clearly been used for several hours before dousing, but she did not remember ever seeing it before. The velvet bed curtains had been pulled back. The great wooden chest, empty before, sat open, the elaborate lid up against the wall. Within there were colours, soft fabrics and the promise of wonderful surprises, that could not possibly be hers.

She held tight to the banister and climbed down carefully, one step at a time. She lost balance once, with her leg throbbing. Setting down the foot continued to hurt, but it was at least twenty times, she decided, less painful than before.

Wren swept into the hall where the table was already set. At first, she assumed it was breakfast. Then she realised it was set for midday dinner. The earl, his friend Thomas, and Landry were eating, drinking, talking, and greeted her as she sat down amongst them.

Landry said, "How do you feel little bird?"

"Like a little bird," she told him. "Not yet able to fly."

"Then" continued Landry, "eat everything still on the table, drink your ale, then perhaps we can go to the home of the delightful Duffs, and hope that their gossip will give us those last answers."

She nodded as she reached for the ale cup, already brimming. "Yes, I know exactly what they'll be. Alright, where's Benny? And secondly, who is the missing midwife?"

"Exactly." The earl now leaned over, his large eyes as alight as the beeswax candles. "We are so close, mistress Wren. You and our group of discoverers have almost solved the worst crime yet. Now, before the new year starts, the crime's all but solved."

"Have they found David Hamward? Is he in Newgate already?"

"Sadly, that remains to be done," the earl shook his head. "As of late last night, the guards had not found him. Yet, information to the contrary may still arrive this afternoon. If not, then surely later in the day. We have enough guards, sheriffs and disguised investigators," he grinned at Landry. "no killer in this country can escape for ever. Both the king and his brother are behind us and will send out the royal guard."

❉

As they rode side by side, without guards, Landry spoke, his voice still soft. The wind almost carried each word away, but Wren heard as he told her, "I was able to improve on the doctoring for your leg last evening. I hope you have no unpleasant headache?"

"You mean I was – cup-shotten?"

"Almost as badly as myself."

The freeze, the wind and the clouds promising sleet, kept the streets almost empty. Wren scratched Arthur between his ears, giving herself something else to concentrate on. "Really? Sorry. I mean, well yes, I do have a headache, but food has made some of it go away. I'm just so shocked to have woken so late. So, I suppose I slept – well – what time did we go to bed?"

"*We?*" She could almost hear his silent grin. "*You*, my little bird, were carried to bed at around one of the clock this morning. I, on the other hand spent almost an hour as your doctor, and then discussed with the house keeper, visiting the earl's tailor and creating whatever new clothing might be supplied this morning."

Wren almost fell off the horse. "I haven't looked yet. I just saw colours. I never thought they were mine."

Now his grin turned to chuckle. "All yours, my dear, although some may not fit perfectly. They will be adjusted once Master Colchester can take proper measurements."

He chuckled and she gulped. "I wish I'd looked." She was clutching the reins as though her only grasp of reality.

Landry changed the subject. "The Duffs," his eyes, looking sideways, engulfed her, "will no doubt make your head worse. I should inform you, perhaps, that your condition last night did not stop me from thinking you delicious. I enjoyed carrying you to bed."

Surprise, doubt and worry overtook her shame. "You did? So

that was why –. Can I know what you did? Just because I can't remember doesn't mean I shouldn't know." Now she was staring at him, her voice louder and her breath caught in gasps.

Landry enjoyed laughing at her, but his voice remained unchanged. "Your bedchamber, your own bed, and your ankle to mend. Then I tucked you in and left you to sleep, little one. No licentious intrusion. All temptation, however profound, was sadly denied. Had I kissed you, I would never have found the strength to move away."

She found nothing to say. Every man and every woman she had known, had at some time slipped cup-shotten to their beds, but she had not before included herself amongst them. Finally, she said, "The broken leg feels so much better. Thank you. I mean, for that and everything else."

"You mean for what I did, or for what I did not?"

"Both." It was a whisper. "And the clothes. Really beautiful clothes. Brand new ones. I was wondering about getting some second-hand gowns from the markets."

His voice was almost unheard behind the wind. "No, little one, not an option."

January wind played with the fall of the rain, the chill and wet was London's accustomed state that winter. Beneath the rain and trotting the soaked cobbles, they both slowed even more, recognising where they were.

Wren stopped abruptly, and even Arthur, recognising the earl's old property, stood staring, shook his mane, and turned away. The stink of the burnt mews still hovered, although the frequent rain had washed out most of the smell, and the gentle perfumes of the happiness as well. The blackened stumps, the bedraggled piles of broken wood, the thick dark mess across the cobbles, blew back the misery of the devastation and the heaving sense of loss she felt seeing it again.

But a new sense of excitement swept over her like a shiver of sunshine. "When spring comes," she mumbled, "all that will be cleared away, and I'll live in a brand-new house. Will it take months?"

"I doubt it," Landry answered her. "Three perhaps, no more, unless the weather worsens. Remember to talk with Morgan tonight."

The Duff house was not far. The building next door still empty. No one wished to live where four wretched ghosts would surely haunt for many years.

Dismounting, Landry took the reins, attached them to the boot scrubber outside the door, and lifted Wren to the ground. Wren knocked, though since the door was unlocked, as always, they walked in, calling softly. The Duff's roof was leaking. A slow drip showed on the plaster ceiling, and the dark damp circle enlarged as they watched.

"Your thatch needs repair," Landry said. "but I assure you, that is not why we're here."

Of the dismal family, only Belinda stood as their visitors arrived. From cross legged boredom on the bare floor, she bounded up and hugged Wren. "You said as how you'd come again."

Doria peered up from her knitting. "Poor Will is at work, and long hours they are too. Another week and we can fix the thatch. He tried to do it hisself but he made it worse. It ain't an easy job. We just needs the money."

Mary, crouching in the corner on a crooked legged stool, also smiled. "That's not what you come for, is it."

"No." Wren took the stool where Doria pointed. "I just hoped, since you know so much of what's around us, that you might know of a Frenchman who lived somewhere near here a couple of years back, and may still be here."

Doria grunted. "Yeah, I knew one, Bernard, he was. Never had a nice word to say, nor me for him. Typical French, the bugger, though he spoke English nigh almost as good as me. They took him off to Newgate. Reckon he swung, for I've heard nothing of him since."

Disappointed, Wren added, looking around, "Have none of the rest of you heard of the Frenchman?" Her voice faded.

The family looked around at each other. The young boy also sat on the floor since the weather was too wet for him to work. The three girls shook their heads, even Lyanna politely silent. "Not that I can think on," Mary said. "You can always tell a Frenchman cos they don't know how to talk proper."

"Just like that wretched Pansy," Doria said, her knitting now laying in her lap. "Came here, she did, just yesterday threatening to arrest us for noise and for kicking a boy chucking stones at our door. Silly bitch. Just cos she lives with a sheriff now, it don't give her the right to pretend she's one too. I pushed her out and went to the sheriff this morning. Don't you let that stupid whore pretend she can cart folk off to gaol, I told him. I hope they had a good fight about that after I left."

Wren thought that more than likely, but shook her head. She asked her last question. "We heard a local midwife was found dead. Not sure who she was though. Have you heard of anyone gone missing?"

"Yes, indeed I have." Now Lyanna raised her voice. "A good woman too, Sara. You must have knowed her since she birthed your little sister what died. She's a load older than me, but I thought maybe I'd learn off her, and maybe be a midwife meself. Then I never saw hide nor hair of her. Not for months."

"Sara!" Wren had dreaded that answer, though half expected it. Her father had killed his young wife for killing her baby, but there had never been tales of him attacking the midwife. It would mean that her father might be involved after all. "Do you know where my father went. You know him, I think. Haldon."

"I know him," Doria nodded. "He stayed with you at the eel shop back when you worked there with Pansy. Course I know him. Knew him before too, and he didn't live that far off, till he went working at the docks. Everyone knew him."

"Do you know where he is now? Have you seen him recently?" Landry was leaning, his shoulder to the doorway, not having fully entered the room. He had left the talking to Wren. Now he knew her upset, so spoke for her. "It's important. Have you any idea?"

Once again, they turned in their seats, looking around.

"Reckon I seen him," Belinda said from the centre of the floor. Everyone turned their heads, staring down at her. Another opportunity for enjoying attention had tipped from the clouds, now she grinned in delight. "I seen him in that burnt out mews. I was going to say hello but he went off. Turned opposite."

"Lime Lane?"

"I think tis that one. But I ain't saying he lives there. He just walked, and I ain't seen him since."

"When was it? How many days ago?" It was still Landry who spoke.

"Not sure. Not yesterday. Reckon it were the day before that. Or might have been the one before that." Belinda seemed pleased with herself and flushed slightly pink.

Nodding, Landry stopped, dropping a handful of rattling pennies into her lap. Belinda was ecstatic, having rarely seen money at all, let alone holding it herself. She did not hold it for long. Doria leaned over, took the girl's hand and emptied it into her own, counting furiously.

"Twenty-six and a ha'penny, mister. That's proper kind. You wants to know anything more, you come again."

He smiled, gave another two pennies, two halfpennies and a farthing to the child. "These are for you," he told her. Then one day next week, should crime give me a rest, I'll buy you that warm cloak I promised."

Outside in the slash of wind and rain, Landry bent and untied the horse's reins. Both animals stood heads down, tails limp. "They look so miserable," Wren muttered, "We should take them home." She was sure she noticed Arthur nodding his head. "After all, Pansy said she saw him at Cripplegate. He might live there, and we could go to both another day."

Landry helped Wren mount, "As for his having travelled to York. In this weather even Cripplegate is a drag too far. Let us try the closest."

"You mean now?" She clenched her teeth as though resisting the urge to run away.

"Tomorrow," Landry nodded. "Now I'm expected to attend the trial at Newgate. Bryce must hang. Then tomorrow morning, we can search for the delights of speaking with your father."

With a brief grin, he turned the horse instantly and headed due west. Wren pulled up her hood and sighed, headed northwest herself. Prad, as she knew, would help her dismount, but there was no one who would help her pass the remainder of the day without hours of boredom. No wine this time, she told herself. Cupshotten two nights in a row would be shameful. Instead, she could hobble up the stairs and explore her new chest of clothes.

In bed that night, she closed her eyes against the moon's pernicious peep between the shutters. She turned away, thought of her father, and wondered who he really was. She realised that she'd rather not meet with him ever again.

CHAPTER FORTY FOUR

LANDRY

I gnorance, they say, can be a saviour. My ignorance in some directions has been that indeed. Not understanding love, and never experiencing such a thing, permitted me the peace I needed to do the work – which now I do love.

Whether that dark and terrifying emotion has now captured me in another way, I cannot be sure.

Having ridden to Newgate, the iced wind in my face and the sweeter memories in my mind's sight, I settled myself for a trial of more wretched memories, and Bryce's furious denials. He was accused of theft and the extreme abuse of a woman who was not his wife, but his landlady.

Watching Bryce, I could see neither fear nor remorse. I had expected neither. He, I imagine, expected release, as he had previously arranged at every trial in the past. Whether by bribery, or by somehow convincing the jury, I cannot be sure. I assumed the former. He now ranted, denied all wrongs, explained how Pansy had thrown hot pies and living eels at him, kicked him from her bed to the floor.

The jury had gasped, although two of the twelve had snickered.

Pansy, as a witness, was polite and believable until, as he swore at her, she threw her grubby kerchief in his face.

"See," the creature screeched, "the bitch is violent. Her. Not me."

Despite my work, I have rarely stood witness, and do not enjoy the effort of convincing strangers of all I've seen, but I'm good at my job. Having suffered and seen the most appalling crimes, it would be ludicrous if I was unable to describe each detail.

It took the jury less than one minute to announce Bryce guilty. For the first time he would pay for his crimes, and the judge roared, "Get that bugger off to Tyburn now."

Bryce threw up his arms pleading for mercy, yet no person in the court, including his own advocate, appeared interested. As the fool was literally dragged out, he snarled in my face and spat. "It's your fault, stinking turd, tis you I should have beaten."

While he screamed his head off, pulled by a guard on each side, I could see Pansy hurrying towards me. I also hurried, into the blistering wind, grabbed Arthur and rode towards Tyburn.

Jacob stood close to the high wooden gibbet, awaiting the criminal's confession, which he knew Bryce would never offer. I had never intended to be present at Bryce's execution. The hurried approach of Wren's acquaintance, Pansy, was motive enough. She might have followed, but I doubted she would wish to watch. I sat astride at the back of a very small and disinterested crowd.

Reading briefly from his Bible, Jacob did not look up. Bryce cursed and attempted to kick out. He had been pushed up a five step ladder, hands chained behind his back. The kick reminded Bryce that his stance was precarious, and he might cause the ladder to fall, and thus kill himself, and so, for one moment his expression changed. He stood very still as the miserable realisation swallowed him.

The rope was secured around his neck and the ladder was suddenly pulled away. He was neither masked nor gagged, and clearly vomited. He choked, then hung limp.

Yet the man was not dead. The marks of strangulation around his neck were purple and seeping blood. His eyes were huge and staring. The face puffed up, first streaked in a bold crimson, then dark purple. The piss trickled slowly down his hose to his shoeless feet.

I had no particular reason to look away, but as his legs managed their last futile kicks, I felt a sense of absurd pity. The man had been utterly cruel. Yet his death was both putrid and piteous.

Having once been the thief I still claimed to be, I reminded myself that genuine arrest and conviction must certainly be avoided.

Above, two hawks flew, wings bristled against the wind, waiting for the crowd to disperse, so they might safely land on the dead shoulders and scavenge what flesh they could tear from the corpse. The eyes were often the first to be eaten. Bryce, whatever remained, would be left on the gibbet to rot until some other prisoner was brought to hang.

I stared once more before turning Arthur, and returning home.

⋈◈⋈

Cruelty was a horror of my childhood. I feared my mother when I was a child. My father was my saviour, but a reluctant one. The wretched soul knew as much misery as I did, living with that woman, though finally he helped me kill her. I learned courage, a more useful emotion in so many ways.

Since then, I have met so many who have a need to be cruel. It brings power, where they frequently felt powerless.

Yet cruelty brings the of powerlessness to others – who may then grow their own need for cruelty. I bless my own strength, and perhaps for my father's help, for bringing me a disgust for cruelty and no desire for power.

Now love, if that is what it is, seems to have arrived to complicate both what I do, and what I am.

She is, of course, a complication.

Loving Wren is both pleasure and difficulty. Perhaps she thinks she loves me in return, but I am rarely trusting of my own feelings, let alone those of another.

The wounds she has suffered remain still, and a doctor should again be called with salve and cream. I could act the medick, but undressing the woman I already imagine in my bed, would be a cruelty and not a kindness.

As with most men my age, I've taken many women to my bed and enjoyed while giving enjoyment, but never one I've loved, nor one who has loved me.

My own mind calls me fool, yet I relax in her company, and feel myself cocooned.

Morgan and Jacob laugh. Jacob loves life and his God. Morgan loves his partner, so understands the same feelings within me, whether I deny it or not.

Although I speak of my hatred for the cruelty of others, I can be violent, and feel no guilt because of it. When I kill, it is as a solution and not for provocation. If a man attacks me then I retaliate, and when I kill him, as I do, it will no doubt be quicker and less painful than the noose.

Riding the muddy cobbles from Tyburn, to the earl's city manor, these thoughts concern only myself.

CHAPTER FORTY FIVE

NARRATIVE

The morning brought Wren and Landry sitting opposite each other, once again, at the breakfast table. She asked him about Bryce. He seemed unwilling to describe it in detail.

He said, "Guilty. Hanged. A delightful experience for both of us, no doubt."

"No bribery then?" she smiled.

He smiled back. "Talking of which, we need to find your father."

She looked down at the uneaten bacon on her platter, and did not admit how much she wished she might avoid her father.

Within one sodden hour, they were riding the beaten earth of Lime Lane, not so far, but far enough for both to be soaked. They dismounted, and led the horses, which also dripped. No person welcomed then. "How can we know if he's here?" wondered Wren, shaking rain from her hood.

"We ask," Landry said, and he did.

Knocking on the second door within the lane, he received no answer and so knocked on the next. A woman looked down from a tiny window above. "Who do you want? Haldon Bennet. I know him. He lives over there, though he's not much at home."

The house opposite lay in deeper shadows, yet avoided the slant of the rain. It was Wren who knocked this time, standing close to the door, and preparing to shout if no one answered. But the door opened, and it was a young woman who peeped out. She appeared just a little older than Wren herself, was pretty, neat and polite.

This surprised Wren as she asked for her father. She hoped the woman was perhaps the owner, and was renting out rooms.

"You're his daughter? Yes, come in, both of you. He never told me he had a daughter."

Wren was neither alarmed nor insulted. Surely after Maggs, he had not so soon found a lover. But she reversed her guess almost immediately. She knew her father. He was older, unattractive, and swayed between friendly and brutal, but would have searched out a woman, perhaps a young widow, with her own home , since now, sacked from the job at the docks, he was homeless.

He sat snoring on the long bench against one wall, a cushion beneath his head. His mouth lay open, and the snores echoed. The woman sat on unused edge of the settle, leaned over and kissed Haldon's forehead. Then she called his name. "Haldon dearest, your daughter and her friend have come to see you."

Haldon woke, gazing around. Landry again leaned one shoulder against the wall close to the doorway. A strategic foot to the door ensuring any escape would be blocked, was a useful habit. Wren stood over the bench where her father lay, and stared down at him, neither smiling nor frowning. She said, "You didn't tell me you were leaving."

Sitting up, his own frown was immediate. "And how the bloody hell could I, girl, when I didn't know where you went."

"True I suppose, but you could have left a message after you got sacked. You could have gone to the eel shop."

"You'd gone, Miss high and mighty, don't you keep blethering at me. I won't have it. How'd you find me, anyhow?"

"Luck," Wren said. "and it doesn't matter, I just wanted to see you, and talk with you." The young woman had moved, now sitting on a small wooden chair nearby. Wren turned and smiled at her. "I'm sorry, I don't know your name."

"Tilda. I'll soon be Tilda Bennet. I'll be your stepmother. I'm mighty pleased to know you."

Wren winced. "You intend marrying?" In shock, she collapsed onto the nearby stool, gazing at her father. "Well, I wish you both great happiness, but it's a bit soon, isn't it?"

"Mind your business," Haldon said.

Tilda raised an eyebrow. "Soon -?"

Wren was aware of Landry's eyes watching her and felt protected. "I know I never really got to know Maggs, it was all so quick," she said. "I wondered if you could tell me the whole story again. Tilda should know about the past, shouldn't she?"

On his feet immediately and without warning Haldon grabbed his daughter. "You just want to cause trouble, bitch?"

Wren pulled away, scowling. Aware of Landry's quiet step forwards, Haldon let Wren go, and relaxed. Wren quickly asked, "Dad, have you seen Sara lately? You know, the midwife who delivered Magg's baby?"

"And let it die."

"But have you seen her?" Wren insisted.

Haldon sighed and sank back on the wooden settle "Yes, often enough. Two days ago was the last." He smiled across at Tilda, but Wren knew his eyes were as watchful as Landry's, waiting and suspicious.

"You can't have," Wren said at once. "She's disappeared. Missing. Maybe dead, and gone, long before you're telling me you saw her."

Snorting and shaking his head, Haldon looked back at the three pairs of eyes staring through the gloom. "Well, I never knew her that well. Maybe it weren't her. Someone a bit like maybe."

Landry abruptly stepped closer. His voice was neither low, nor soft. He demanded, looking down, almost bending over Haldon. "I was not at court, and nor did I know your daughter, Haldon, when I first knew you. We were both in Newgate and I heard you brag of getting a young girl with child, then changing your mind, and arranging to be rid of them. So now tell us the real story."

Tilda's intake of breath now faded into silence. Haldon shook his head. The last few wisps of grey hair fell to his eyes, but he didn't bother brushing them back. His anger showed only in his eyes and the trembling of his fingers. "You speak of Newgate, but you know I was found to be an innocent man. Don't you make trouble now, since it was you found guilty and escaped. You're the bugger, lad, not me. That chat in Newgate, just showing off a bit. I wanted no risk of being thought feeble, or would've been beaten, maybe knifed. The others would have taken my food."

"So, tell me the true story."

Haldon sighed. "I was on the high seas, being a sailor and trader, that was me. I had to leave the new wife at home, and when I got back, I found her giggling and our baby dead. She told her story, but it was all lies. We had a mighty row and – I admit it – I killed the girl, but I never meant it. She'd starved the baby and I was too angry to stop and think till I looked down and saw her dead. Not my fault, as the court said."

"Dad, did you – I beg you to tell me the truth – get someone to kill the midwife for revenge?"

"Never, and I swear it," Haldon said. "She were a – good woman, and I was sorry for what I'd done to Maggs. Mighty sorry about it all."

She wished it was true and had once trusted it. Now she looked into her father's eyes and knew differently. The tickle of hope died. Wren stared, angry. "Dad, you're lying." Then she turned, looking back at Tilda over her shoulder. Knowing she might fall if she stood suddenly, she controlled the fury. "Did you know anything about his first wife, my mother? Then his second wife, Maggs, the one he killed?"

Tilda stared back, biting her lip. "I didn't know anything about any of it. I mean, I feel sorry for the baby and the mother, but I feel sorry for Haldon too."

"That's exactly what I thought at first," Now Wren stared again into her wet lap, "but now I know I was wrong."

Now afraid to catch Haldon's gaze, Tilda looked down. "Someone tell me the truth."

Haldon glared and stayed silent. Wren fisted both hands but did not look up. It was therefore Landry who replied.

CHAPTER FORTY SIX

WREN

When Landry spoke, his voice so cold, I stared again at my father.

Landry was saying, "Your story is all lies, Haldon, as I have known for some time. For some months I watched you, suspicious of your motives." He looked aside to me, and for a moment. He had already told me in part, but was hoping to learn more. Landry carried on, "asking for your help, little bird, had a double purpose at first, as I distrusted your father."

That made perfect sense to me. Distrusting of me too, I suppose, but I wasn't going to complain. "I hope I've proved my innocence. I was stupid believing Dad when I knew he was rotten anyway."

"Few children really know the worst of their parents," Landry said, and looked back at my father. "Those deaths were also gruesome, and so I had been asked to investigate. I admitted myself to Newgate at that time, in order to know you and prove your guilt. In only two days in that cell, I learned the truth. Then after leaving, I heard of your trial, which was a travesty."

Dad was muttering and snorting as Landry spoke, and shouted out, "I was found innocent, you stupid arse. You call it what you like, if the trial calls me innocent, then innocent I am."

"The truth is quite different," Landry continued, almost placid in contrast to my father's yelling. "You returned from the cog I know you sailed earlier in the year, and arrived to find the midwife, Sara, protecting your daughter. She told you that Maggs had been forced away as since her mother was sick and dying. You told the midwife you would care for the child until your wife returned, and so sent Sara away. Then you, personally, and by choice, left the child to starve. You shut the infant away, and only when Maggs came home did you produce the corpse, and blame her absence. You then purposefully killed your wife accusing her of something you had done yourself. You then needed to hide the truth by disposing of the midwife too, and so paid someone to kill her I presume, no doubt at a distance which would save you from any risk of blame. We discovered the body only a few days ago. Three vile deaths and all your choice, and your doing."

He looked back to me. Dad stared too. "Go on," I whispered, more to myself than to him, "prove that wrong." The horrifying picture of the starved baby in my mind and I jumped up, the stool clattering back. "But you can't. It's the truth, isn't it." I was swallowing back tears of sick fury. "How could you watch your own tiny daughter slowly starve?" I stood over him and shouted down into his lying eyes. "Admit it."

My father sat there rigid, like a burned-out candle. In that moment, I hated him so furiously, I had to drag back the rickety old stool where I'd been sitting before. I wanted to kill the man then and there. The tears streaming down my face made my eyes sore, but I couldn't stop. I hadn't wanted to truly believe it before, but now, there was no doubt left in my mind.

Dad's response was as nasty as everything else. He didn't even bother to claim innocence in front of me and Tilda, he just seemed to think the result of the trial was enough. "I've bin proved bloody innocent, you bastard. You can't drag me back to court again. Just you try."

Landry didn't bother answering. He bent even further over my father and talked with disgust, his teeth gritted. I watched him spit out the words. "Nothing is as evil as to purposefully starve your new born child to death."

Watching Landry's fury was terrifying, but watching my father was even worse. He really didn't care at all. "I never killed the stupid midwife, and you can't prove none of it."

Then I thought of something, I knew I'd have to run outside and vomit on the cobbles. But I needed to say it first, though my throat half stuck in my mouth, I managed it. "Dad, did you pay someone to kill dear Sara? You'd not be paid by the ship-owners until the trading coin came through. How did you pay the price for a woman to be killed? You couldn't have afforded it, and a killer wouldn't have just accepted a promise, so you must have promised a service in return."

As Dad stared back at me, I knew the truth. It hung there, staring at me. Landry had known and thought I'd break down if he told me. But he was wrong, I'd always hated my father in my thoughts, and now I knew he'd never deserved even the love I'd tried feebly to give.

I managed to stand, leaned on my stick, and looked past Landry at that beast on the settle. "You are a sick, vile, disgusting brute!" I leaned right into his face. I hope he felt my spit as I yelled, then I heaved, and struggled outside, puking into the wet streaming gutter.

As I crept back in, I heard Landry's voice. I stopped, listening outside the half open door. Without me there, I thought the disgusting man would possibly speak more honestly.

Landry had said, "If that is accurate regarding your lack of money, and knowing that it was not you who killed the woman, there is one obvious answer of how you paid."

Then the other voice. "I'm telling you, I stole it. I paid up. I stayed out the way after that. I stayed with Wren first, then got that job on the docks."

"And how did you steal so much?"

I knew my father's delaying tactics. First, he coughed, spluttered, proclaimed his innocence all over again, and finally said he'd got the money from the traders. "Good coin," he said. "and I stole some from the eel shop." I think I actually heard him snigger. "And don't you judge me, you're a thief worse n' I ever been. And I guess you killed more lost souls than I ever have."

So that was when I walked back in. "It's true about stealing from the shop," I told Landry. "but not enough to pay for a murder and then still have enough to pay for a new home at the docks."

I waited for him to think up an answer, but I didn't expect what happened next. It was Tilda. I wasn't looking at her as she sat behind me, but now she swooped, grabbed the iron trivet and crashed it down on my damned father's head. Blood spurted as he fell back against the wall behind the settle. Tilda was shouting now, though I don't think my father heard any of it. He was unconscious. "Horrid, horrid man. What lies you've told me. I'll have no more to do with you and you'll leave my home immediately."

Well, he couldn't. He couldn't even open his eyes. "We'll have to wait until he's conscious," I pointed out. She shrugged and flopped back to her chair, her head now in her hands, and tears in her eyes.

I suppose I felt sorry for her. Most of all I pitied my tiny sister and couldn't stop picturing her slow agony of starvation, almost the only experience the poor little thing had ever known.

Landry looked around silently. He seemed to be searching my face for something. Finally, in his voice of cold silk, "Are you prepared, little bird? There may be more to hear, and it will not be sweet."

"I hate the man," I said, practically shaking as I glared down at my disgusting unconscious father. "I never loved him really. I loathed him most of the time, even though I pretended not to. So, it won't upset me more than it has already."

"Or what your father says?"

I told Landry, "Tell me the worst. I'm already guessing what he might say."

Dad was waking up, blurry and sniffing. He glared at us all. Then at Landry, he swore. "Bastard – you tried to kill me."

"I did," Tilda interrupted. "I wish I'd managed more. Now I'm going to get all your rubbish from my rooms, then you're leaving."

Landry again took control, "I don't believe anything you say, Haldon. I have a suspicion of what you offered in return for the death of the midwife."

My ankle was weak still, so I had to sit down. I interrupted as it came to me, "It's true. Ben. We've tried to find him. But it's not a Bernard or Bereth, is it! This monster's name's Bennet. Haldon Bennett. He did it, didn't he. All of it. Not a French Barnardo, it was him?"

It wasn't a question, and Landry nodded, still staring at my father, with a threat like a loosed arrow. I was trying to wipe away my heaving, tears. I kept trying to stop, but even as I spoke, those wretched tears were streaming down my face like rain. I wasn't sad, these were tears of disgust and absolute fury.

Landry told him, "Yes indeed, you are Ben. You lived with the others, including the baron's brother, out at that shed. When we went there, you saw Wren, and quickly disappeared. Then once we'd left, you told Waddington he'd hired your daughter, and so fallen into a trap. Once again you intended causing your daughter's death."

"Waddington wanted to kill me." I muttered, and didn't doubt a word. "You wanted me dead as you did with poor Hannah. It would have been quicker if you'd suffocated her with a pillow, but you wanted to use the baby as an excuse to get rid of Maggs. Then me. You're the devil."

Watching him watch me, I really did heave. I was standing again, and holding the stool, ready to crash it onto his head. But I felt the damned stool fall apart in my hands, and had to drop it. Then I had to look away.

"So now your daughter knows what you did," Landry said, almost in a whisper.

I watched the vile creature's little sneaky smile through my tears. "My fool of a daughter knows me too well, yet she never guessed until now."

I stared at the brute with disgust. "What did you do to my

mother? She didn't die at my birth, did she? You – did something. I'd wager you murdered her too."

"Your mother was a bore. She went pious. I'd thought her a good prospect. She was pretty, and I imagined what I could do with her. Then we married, and I found she was a damned prude. Then I got her with child. She was probably a good mother. But I kept out of the way. Purposefully got work on the ships."

"How old was I," I whispered, "when you killed her?"

He shook his head. "Dunno," he said, pulling a face. "can't remember. I suppose you'd have been about five or six. I didn't want you left for me to look after so I waited until you could look after yourself."

"At five or six?"

"More or less. I got a few things done before, telling your mother to teach you to cook and the like. You could clean up and be useful."

"And how," a real pathetic shivering whisper, "did you kill her?"

"She was my first, so I was careful. Chucked her on the floor, put a bolster over her face, then sat on it. Stayed there getting bored for a while, just to make sure. Then I told everyone she'd had a weak heart and pretended to sob my heart out. I even got her a proper funeral and sat crying. I was quicker with the next ones"

All my feelings were running round in circles. I wanted to spit in his face. All I managed was throwing one of those stool legs at him, which missed entirely.

I stood there trembling. "You aren't my father. You're a demon."

"I bloody am, chit." His cackle was foul. "You want the truth, then you'll have it all. I enjoyed killing after that."

I flinched as someone came from behind, then realised it was Landry pulling me into his arms, and holding me tight, embracing me in tender comfort, I almost smiled. But I laid my cheek against his warm doublet and quietly wept and tried to forget the words from my father, knowing I'd been a fool to ask. I should have crept outside at the start and learned nothing new.

Instead, Landry was asking him over my head, "So once past the initial experience, you enjoyed the killing?"

"I did by then." I knew he'd be smiling, although I had my eyes shut and my face encased in dark wool.

"Now," Landry spoke again, this time looking at Tilda. "Can you go to the sheriff, and tell him to bring guards?"

I heard her whisper and quickly skuttle out. Haldon couldn't follow her, as Landry and I stood directly against the tight shut door. So no one was going to get out until the sheriff arrived. I could guess my vile father would try to get away, after all his confessions, and certainly wouldn't sit quietly waiting for his arrest.

Then Landry said what I was thinking. "No doubt you enjoyed hanging up the family from their own beams. Did you help with the poisoning too?"

"How did you know that?" He sounded alert again.

Landry told him, "Haven't you guessed yet? I've been investigating crime and tossing culprits into Newgate for some years. You know Waddington is dead by my hand. The baron is in the Tower, awaiting execution."

"I didn't have anything to do with the poisoning," my beast of a father said, all smug now. "Not my thing. I just encouraged them to drink up that wine. But I helped hang them. Half-starved idiots, they were." He pointed one plump finger at Landry. "And you'll send for no sheriff, fool. He'd arrest you before getting to me."

"No one is as sick as you." I'd moved a step back from Landry now and was looking around the little room for something else to throw at him.

"I'd visited them you know, when I stayed at the eel shop. I met the woman while serving her some cheap muck for supper. So, I went there, only ten steps down the road and not so cold back then, took a wine jug, and had the task of asking them if they knew about the baron's secret. He owned the quarry, and the fellow, I can't remember his name, worked there of course, so he knew his boss was a real crook. They were shocked. So, then I told the fool of a baron. Told him the Ford family had known all along and now they were planning to tell the sheriff. So naturally they had to be got rid of."

Without a moment's thought, I pulled away from Landry and dashed at my father. I probably was as much of an idiot as he kept calling me, but I should have done this before. I punched his face as hard as I could manage, right on the nose. Then I grabbed his throat, my fingernails in his skin. I don't suppose it even bothered him, but he was fast and grabbed my wrist, twisting it. I was just crying out when Landry came behind me, thrust his knife, snatched from his boot, at dad's face.

Because I was in the way, the thrust was weak and my pig of a father actually laughed, let me go, and brushed the knife away with his covered arm. He and Landry faced each other, both furious in their very different ways. "You touch her again," Landry spat, "and I'll kill you."

Dad pushed past towards the door, kicking and punching at both of us. I could see the hope in his eyes. After all, he thought no one else knew the truth except Landry and me, and no one would ever believe us. He had no idea who Landry really was.

Landry proved him wrong in the same instant. He swung, punched him on the nose, and with his other hand, slashed the knife right across that his face from cheek to cheek, then grabbed both my father's frantically waving arms and twisted them behind him with a grip too strong for him to break free. The blood was dripping down his chin, and so was the slime from his nose.

It was so fast and utterly inescapable. Now instead of crying, I was laughing. My relief was enormous.

"You pin prick, let me go." Dad shouted through the blood.

Then his arms jerk upwards behind his back. Landry could have broken them both, but he just wrenched so hard and fast that the nasty pig was bent over double, his bloody nose to the floorboards. Now his wail was half smothered.

The footsteps stamped loudly outside, as Haldon groaned, as the sheriff and four guards arrived, pushing through the doorway, grabbing my disgusting father. The sheriff nodded to Landry. "He'll stand trial without a witness this time, Master Crawford. You'll not see him again until he's on the swing."

I hadn't expected it, but Pansy was with them, and tried to smile at me as she held onto Tilda. Tilda had evidently explained the whole story and the sheriff was convinced. This would be a big help for his reputation. She shouldn't have been there, but Pansy hugged poor Tilda, who obviously needed it. I was watching as the four guards dragged my father away.

He fought to get away of course, but the guards kicked and punched him in the belly until he wheezed and doubled over once more and disappeared into the rain. I could still hear his shouts of innocence. I was busy thinking that it was possible I'd never hear my father's voice again. I smiled at the thought.

CHAPTER FORTY SEVEN

NARRATIVE

L andry mounted Arthur and drew Wren up to sit side saddle
before him. Leaning against him, she closed her eyes. The
drying tears striping her face, now turned icy in the bitter wind.

He rode quickly back to the earl's manor by the Wall. Prad took
the horses off to the stables, feed and groom them.

"The same I intend doing with you, little bird," Landry told Wren
as he carried her through the great doors, ignoring the entrance to
the Hall, then strode immediately to the staircase. He paused, then
whispered, more to himself than to her, "Your bedchamber – or
mine, little one? Sadly, once again I believe it must be yours."

Wren had not heard the last words. In her mind she saw only the
final struggle between the sheriff, her father, and the guards. His
hands had been roped together, but he wasn't gagged, and had
continued to curse, drowning out the pelting rain and sudden
thunder. Her pity was not for him but for those he'd killed, for the
loss of her mother, for Jessy, Sara, and her baby sister.

Kicking open the bedchamber door, Landry called to the
steward for wine, and laid Wren gently onto her own bed. He sat
beside her, looking down, one hand to the side of her face. She was
wet from the rain, her tears now washed away.

She whispered up at Landry, "I hate him, so much more than I ever thought possible."

"You could never have realised how evil he really was, nor that he was capable of such horror." Landry's silver-grey eyes seemed darker in the shadows. "You've shown such courage, but this is the betrayal that took place over years."

Her face was turned, buried into the pillows, her cheeks now dried by linen and feathers. She stayed hidden as she heard the steward, the clank of jugs and metal cups, the fizz of flaring candles, and Landry's voice ordering towels, his own bedrobe, and some light form of food.

Hearing the steward leave, she peeped up. Six candles blazed high, shimmering light now vivid across the room. The unshuttered window was dark and the pounding of the rain against the small panes of glass was heavy. Landry, again reaching over, held the cup of wine, his arm slipping beneath her shoulders to help her sit, take the cup and drink. Wren found that the rich liquid helped her to feel both more alive and awake. She started to speak, but the sound of the steward's return urged her to pull up one of the bedcovers, and disappear beneath.

After those brief moments, the door shut once more. "Come out, little bird," Landry grinned. "Towels first, I think, and then we can talk." Her cup was now half empty on the bedside tabletop, and Landry took Wren into his arms and first wrapped her within the large white cloth, rubbing her hair, more carefully wiping her face, down to her neck, and smiled as she popped free from the towel and sniffed.

"But you won't – I mean –?"

"I've no intention of undressing you," he told her softly. "That would bring complications." He was grinning now. "But if you agree, I believe your outer garments should come off. The gown, the belt, perhaps will be enough."

Her boots and cloak had already been left downstairs, but the skirts of her gown were soaked, and no towel would dry them. Wren nodded. "I can do that. Honestly. I don't mind."

Landry had thrown the towel to the rugs, and ignored her words, taking her once more into his arms, reaching below her arm to unlace the cotton ties. He removed the high sash, and again tossed the wet materials to the floor. No fire had been lit, but now, with the wet clothes gone, Landry tucked Wren into her bed, pulling the warmth to her chin. In only her shift, he had watched the rise of her body, the push of her cold breasts. Temptation lessened as she curled beneath the covers.

He stood. "I'm calling a page. You'll be warm now, little bird, but I we need a fire."

Wood was already stacked beside the grate, and it took the page, who scampered at the call, only moments to set the flames to crackle and rise higher. Landry stood before the hearth. His outer clothes still dripped. He shrugged off his cote, then the doublet, and stood like a silhouette in the white pleated shirt which came well below the waist, and beneath this remained the dark hose. He pulled on his bedrobe, and came to sit once more on the bed.

Peeping up beyond the bedcovers, Wren tried to hide her interest. The curl of his thigh outlined the upper muscles of his leg as the hose enclosed them so tightly, being soaked, and so slightly transparent. She forced herself to look away. "Your legs are still wet," Wren admitted her interest.

"Taking off my hose now, would not be a good idea," he smiled. "We have other matters to discuss." She wasn't able to stop the blush that rushed into her cheeks, which made Landry smile.

"Now your father is in Newgate and his trial, for the multiple crimes he is accused of, is likely to come quickly. I have no doubt he'll be found guilty and taken immediately to the gallows. Although this is what must happen, it may be very difficult for you, little one. I need you to consider, and decide for yourself if you want to be there to witness. I'll not argue with whatever you choose, though I suggest you take your time to consider."

The tousled mess of her hair, still damp, was spread beneath her over the pillow. In the firelight her cheeks were flushed and her eyes bright. "Perhaps I'll get cup-shotten again." She suggested, her smile a little forced.

Landry did not smile in return. "You seem less troubled now. Can you accept what will happen, or you prefer not to think about it?"

She lifted herself on both elbows and gazed up at him. She had never seen him wear only a shirt before, and it intrigued her as much the clinging outline of his thigh.

Now speaking to her own shadow stretched over the bed before her, rather than look at him. "He's not my father any more. I don't think he ever *liked* me," she said, shaking the tousles of her hair. "He only liked killing it seems."

Taking one of the small shaking fists in her lap as she sat, he began to rub warmth into her fingers one by one. "Not knowing your mother, little bird, it may mean he was not your true father."

"A lovely thought but thinking of my mother makes me sad too. Finding out what he's done was a horrible shock, and I suppose knowing his blood runs in me is enough to make cringe. So, perhaps I'll pretend he's no relation at all."

"No pretending, little one." He watched her fingers curl, lit by the rising flames beyond the bed. "The truth is rarely easy, but yet it remains, and you can find the sweeter side. This man who might – or might not – be your father will never be able to hurt you again."

Wren seemed on the verge of more tears, so Landry smiled, squeezing her fingers once more. "No misery now, little bird. The women of this city can live a little easier now."

"There's others, I suppose. That we won't ever know about"

Landry took her between his arms, resting her against him. The pressure of her breasts through the torn shift was a pleasure he made no attempt to ignore. His voice was again soft. "He enjoyed killing, and was close to ensuring your own death, little one. Don't think of more nightmares."

With her voice muffled against his shirt, she sniffed, still talking. "I just can't stop thinking about it. There's so much I never even suspected before. Heaven only knows how many others died at his hand. I'd almost like to watch him hung – kicking and screaming in pain until he chokes to death, but I know it would haunt me, so I don't want to go. I just want to know that he's gone."

It was Landry who then asked, "Will you attend the trial? I shall be called as a witness, but I'd prefer you not to watch."

"No – I won't come."

"I'm glad. I'll tell you afterwards, as little or as much as you want to hear." He paused, enjoying the feel of her against only his shirt. "And there's another in two days, one you might wish to attend, or perhaps not, as you wish. Yet it's another duty of mine, and I must attend."

She looked up at once. "Hamward?"

"No, although Hamward will be captured soon, perhaps already. I was present recently at the baron's trial, and again stood witness. A dull collection of lie after lie. But I'd found other witnesses to his corruption. I was tempted to name your little friend Belinda, but considered her too young to face that crowd. He was found guilty."

"You didn't tell me." But she felt no animosity.

"It was far from interesting, my dear. Indeed, once the jury stated their decision, the judge admitted he'd also faced the baron's bribery and had been waiting only for the chance to announce the execution."

"He sounds as dreadful as my father." Wren swallowed hard.

Landry pulled her closer. "There's no other outstanding millstone for us to investigate as yet, just Haldon." His fingers were in her hair. "I'll attend the execution. Alone, I believe."

"I won't come with you. I've seen enough horror these last months." She snuggled against his chest, loving his touch in her wet hair.

"Instead, you can disappear into the comfort of your bed, sweep downstairs for meals, sit in peace by the fire, and do as you wish while enjoying the luxury of the incoming spring. Comfort and good food will heal your leg further and fade all those cuts and bruises."

"The cuts have gone already."

He nodded down at her. "Then I doubt you'll need much more of the doctoring I enjoy giving you." He laughed, partially releasing her and looking down as she stayed snuggled against his shirt.

As if it was not her own voice, Wren spoke aloud. "Kiss me?" she whispered. Landry stared. "I meant it."

He bent over her immediately, his eyes like another candle flame. Then he pulled back. "One day perhaps, my love, but if I do that now, I will be unable to stop, and this night is a dark one. I want our first touch to begin a night dreams."

She watched him leave. Wren felt a tingle in her stomach which she'd never experienced before. Now she wanted that again. Realising what she felt, and what it could mean.

Wren curled again beneath the covers. The room was warm now, shadows flickering only in the varied reflections of rising flame, the hiss of the fire and the flicker from every candle. She had admitted that she wanted Landry, she had watched the delight and hunger in his eyes, then the kindness as he moved away. Since she had no idea what would happen, which brought excitement in itself.

Her misery fled back behind the new thoughts swirling in her head. Bryce was dead. The baron would soon be beheaded. Her father would be hanged. Even Pansy wasn't a problem anymore. She wasn't quite sure what she felt about Landry, but was fairly sure she knew what he felt about her. Very soon, she'd hopefully find out more.

CHAPTER FORTY EIGHT

NARRATIVE

The huge stone battlements stared down at their own shadows. A light drizzle had replaced the previous day's storms, and that dull greyness hung across the land. Beyond the far walls, the Thames slumped in grey reflection. The tide was out.

A crush of men and not as many women crowded the space allotted. This was a death welcomed by many. Those who had suffered through the baron's plots of brutality and corruption were numerous and although too frightened of the beast's position of power to have whispered their knowledge to sheriff, they now relished the death of the man who had brought them such misery.

Many of the crowd were well dressed, their fur lined hoods protecting their velvets and embroidered trimmings, but Landry, plain and dark clothed, stood alone at the back. The rain continued.

The execution block stood cold. Surrounded by the thick straw that lay over the grass, thick enough to absorb the blood about to be spilled, it sat under the sheen of drizzle's mist. It was the blood that the crowd hoped for, yet the continuous drizzle had dissuaded some from the wait required. The scooped centre at the block's surface, roughly at the height of a kneeling man's shoulders, had been many times blood soaked. Yet years of heavy rain dutifully washed it clean, and there remained little visible history of its past.

Indeed, the previous execution was some four years gone, and had been private, only the priest and the executioner present as Prince George, Duke of Clarence, bent his neck to the block. Yet gossip from the Tower staff claimed that the prince, by order of his brother the king, had been offered five cups of Malmsey before the axe was swung, and was therefore almost mentally absent. Indeed, afterwards the executioner had chuckled, and wagered that the duke had well-nigh drowned in the wine before the axe even fell.

No wine was offered to Baron Lyle, condemned by a jury of his peers. He was now led from the tower, a swarthy black bundle invisible beneath his cape. His wrists were roped behind his back as he was led from the Keep to the grassy slope where the priest and the executioner, leaning on the handle of his axe, stood silently waiting. The baron sniffled.

"The bastard's arrived," someone whispered, and the crowd began to shift, abruptly alert, peering over the heads of others, of those most eager to see the death of the man they despised and loathed. Some pushed forwards, yet the line of Tower guards stood at the front, immovable.

The cape was taken from the baron's shoulders and the weeping rain began to soak into his hair and remaining clothes. Yet refusing to shiver or huddle, the baron stood as though proud. Landry smiled to himself, then nodded to one of the guards, and was led to the front of the crowd. The surrounding audience looked in faint surprise or disapproval, yet said nothing since a Tower guard had initiated the move.

Walking straight, with a scowl of fury, Baron Lyle was led to stand on the damp straw while the restraint was removed from his wrists. The priest, the bible open between his hands, began to murmur the prayers most expected.

But Lyle turned, facing the crowd, his scowl intact. He yelled his message.

"I've nothing to confess and nothing to regret. I'll not apologise to our fool of a king."

The priest stared down at his bible, mutters unheard. One of the guards chuckled beneath his breath. The executioner stepped forward, but did not lift his axe.

Now most of those in the crowd were cursing and one woman stooped, then threw a handful of wet mud at Lyle's face. It landed well after a good aim, splattering against the baron's nose. Most of the crowd cheered as he wiped off the mud and attempted to throw it back. Yet now too thinly spread, he failed, and stood fierce eyed, snarling his words. With fingers dripping mud, his fury accelerated.

"That's enough," said the chief guard standing beside the baron, "Now kneel, and you can discover exactly what's waiting for you beyond without confession." He hauled the baron, grabbing his arm. "And I think we'll not bother with a blindfold," and he pushed Lyle to his knees.

The baron's scrawny neck emerged from the shirt's open collar and without hesitation, the muscles of his neck relaxed as he laid over the block, chin down beyond the wet stone. Then his arms, outstretched to either side, signified the moment. Without blindfold or holy blessing with the priest's words of redemption, the baron awaited his death.

His behaviour had disgusted most, and so they waited, breath withheld. The executioner stepped forwards again, this time with the axe blade lifted, and positioned himself, until comfortable. Then, staring down, he swung.

The squelch of parting flesh was audible. The baron's eyes were wide in bloodshot horror. The audience gazed. One man bit his lip until it also bled. Landry leaned against the post beside him.

Smiling slightly to himself, the executioner raised his axe for the second time, swinging it high over his head. It smashed downwards, slicing through the remaining artery, veins and tendons. The baron's head rolled from its body, blood streaming from both head and the gruesome ravaged neck which had once supported it. Baron

Lyle was dead, his blood draining as his body crumpled, collapsing on the sticky soaked straw at his knees.

The executioner, his smile as wide as his strategy, stared down at the white and scarlet mess around the block, his axe blade still buried in the old oak. Although he was heavily masked, his pleasure was obvious. The executioner clutched the baron's thinning hair and held up the dripping head to his audience. "I announce the successful execution of the Baron Lyle, traitor and murderer."

The head swung a little, blood still trickling, the eyes staring and the mouth gaping. The dark blotch of tongue emerged. The crowd cheered. Landry nodded, turned away, and retraced his steps to the stables where Arthur, unperturbed, waited while munching carrots, turnips and clover.

The crowd dispersed gradually, breathing deeply and determined to remember the scene they had just witnessed, while forgetting their own pain.

Neither Wren nor the earl had chosen to hear the baron's final words, but Landry found a crowd almost as large awaiting him in the earl's grand hall.

A late breakfast lay cooling across the table, for the execution, as usual, had been held immediately after late winter's desultory dawn.

Landry sat, and raised his brimming cup.

"It is done. The younger Hamworth is in Newgate I am told, the third man is already there and incarcerated until his own execution, and the most heinous, the baron, lies dead in a pauper's grave, his head impaled high over the archway at the southern end of the Bridge."

It was several hours later, having discussed every detail, "Too depressing, no matter that he deserved it," he had said, "and not an event I hope to watch again," that Landry took Wren's arm and walked with her in the grounds, avoiding the wet cobbles and keeping to the shade of the willow trees beside the paths. Rain drops still lining her lashes, she gazed up at him as they strolled, her eyes peeping from beneath their hood, now pulled forwards against renewed drizzle.

"I wanted you next to me," Landry said as though speaking to the clouds, barely audible. "Your presence would have been a cruelty for you, and a comfort to me. Now I wonder what you might have said had I only pleased myself by dragging you along."

"I'm not easily dragged anywhere anymore," she told him. "And it's you who gave me that confidence."

"Good." His voice drifted on the chilly wind. "A lesson well taught and well learned then."

Wren was already laughing. "But I might come willingly if there's ever another time." She nodded and her hood bounced. "Will we work together from now on?"

She had chosen to dress very differently that morning. With the the excitement of choosing something new from the chest in her bedchamber. Landry would arrive home, she had decided, to see her in a way he had never seen before.

A new shift was pleated, bleached white linen and ruffled at the ankles. Then the gown, helped by the maid, covered her in light green damask, tied beneath one arm, the neck not too low and then caught below her breasts by the wide green sash. The light material swirled out below the hips, almost hiding the soft shoes. The top sleeves fell wide at her wrists, their embroidered cuffs drifting downwards to join the golden flowers embroidered along the hem.

He had stared at her even while speaking with others. Jacob had cackled while the earl and his friend had turned to gaze at each other. Now those clothes had disappeared under the copious crimson and fur lined cape. Landry still found it difficult to look elsewhere. Wren knew that he watched her.

He watched as he answered, "Yes, little bird. Now we work together, yet the choices remain yours." His arm was already around her shoulders. "And, perhaps there may arise other situations we might enjoy together, other than simply work."

Having opened her mouth to laugh or complain, yet without

knowing which suited her mood, instead she relished the warmth of his closeness. So she murmured, instead, "I'm not exactly sure what you mean."

"I think you do, little one, but I'll not press it." He stopped walking, brushed away the dripping leaves above his head, and looked down at her. "This has been the most arduous of criminal situations for many years. But now it ends. All have met their fate and died, except for two."

"Including my father. But both of them are in Newgate."

"And await the rope. Our work is done, and we have some freedom before some other monstrosity falls. I doubt work will ever finish since greed for both coin and power will surely never end. This has been the worst I've known, but some other nightmare is bound to threaten sooner or later. While we can, we should enjoy the peace."

CHAPTER FORTY NINE

NARRATIVE

H aldon Bennet, heavily shackled by the chains around his ankles, sprawled silently on the stone floor, his clothes filthy now and blood stained. He said nothing while watching David Hamward being dragged in, kicking and cursing. They stared at each other and denied any acquaintance. Each rolled over, shivering cold, with anger and regret.

"Your trial's the day after tomorrow," the guard told Haldon, kicking at his legs, waking him from an uneasy sleep. "Tomorrow'll be your last day alive, but I doubt you'll enjoy it," and the guard threw down the share of dark rye bread.

"Well," sighing, but contemplating the possible escape already made by some others, and in particular the man he now hated the most, "reckon my damned daughter won't come visiting this time."

The only visitor was the plague.

Haldon was the first to feel unwell, and lay silently fuming, wondering if the Lord God was seeking revenge, even though the noose waited on the gibbet outside. He felt feverish and his body ached. The fault of being dragged, and the cold damp in the dungeon he decided, with the expectation of greater pain to come.

Hamward watched him from a distance, stuffing the bread into his mouth. "You not eating that?" He pointed at Haldon's untouched chunk of the same.

"Bugger off, David. I feel shitting foul." He left the bread rolling on the stone.

David Hamward grabbed it, shouting back. "You look as foul as you sound,"

Haldon did not answer. His head hammered, burning hot, beating him into silence. He lay still. His body hurt too much for him to move. Then he started to cough, coughed sputum and then blood.

Other prisoners moved away. Haldon accepted it, preferring to be left alone. The pain increased. Eventually, although sweating and coughing, he slept.

The morning woke him with the violence of the pounding against his skull, and the freeze fighting the sweats. When forcing up the energy to climb to his knees and crawl to the wide central gutter, he was too late to pull apart his hose and twist off the codpiece. The stench mattered little enough since the dungeons stank with more than a hundred years of filth never cleaned.

Haldon lay back, but the ooze of black slime coated the floor around him, with streaks of crimson blood amongst it. "You got some foul muck in you," Hamward called, scuttling quickly from the touch of him. "Reckon you got gaol fever."

"No," someone called back. "Reckon tis worse. You look at the bugger's chest." Another inmate called the guard.

"Well, I told you this be your last day alive," the guard said, stamping to his side and staring down at Haldon. "Reckon your trial won't be needed. So, you'll escape one death, but another got you first."

What Haldon felt, hurt like the hell he was expecting, but the pain grew worse, swelling into his throat as he coughed, into his groin as he bled from every opening, and across his chest where pinpricks of blood beneath the skin massed like a black rash. The agony spread across his body, joining each pain with another. He felt himself dying, and ate nothing, but he drank, when able, both ale and water, even when the water was dirty and came directly from the river. A desperate thirst raged deep inside him. He slept from exhaustion.

The following day he was told that his trial was indeed cancelled. No one would touch him, and his pain had grown into a torture he could never have imagined existed.

A scuttling fear drenched the other inmates, each imagining a death more vile than the noose, recognising the symptoms and muttering that it might spread to any man sitting too close. One prisoner had kicked Haldon into a corner where none needed to watch his slow yet inevitable death, though they couldn't block out the sound.

By the afternoon, Haldon was no longer alone. Two others were sweating, coughing blood, and saw blood leaking in their urine. The guards were called again, stared, then shouted, racing from the dungeon and locking it behind them.

"Tis the Black Death. It'll be all of us if we go in there."

"Not me," one guard said. I'm off."

"Call for the doctor."

"Why bother. There ain't no doctor able to keep the plague away. Besides, sick or not, these are bastards going to die one way or another."

Haldon's body now terrified him, yet without the energy for comprehension. Sleeping again, Haldon expected, and desired, die so the pain would fade. Yet he woke still living, and when he opened his eyes, they were bloody.

The pain would not allow Haldon to sleep, and he felt the grinding within his body, as though leaving him as a shell of twitching torture.

The days were impossible to count. He could see nothing except his own death, but the desperate hours crawled ever onwards.

Haldon heard others dying, his own inevitable death seeping closer. He no longer had thoughts except the flailing terror of what he felt now, and what he would feel faced with hellfire. He could neither move nor speak and the humanity leaked from his body.

It was finally as his heart shrank and so lost the strength to beat, that the torment left, and he knew nothing at all. His breath was a reek of decay as it gurgled from his throat and his chest fell flat. He did not move again.

※◇※

She had been dozing when Landry returned to the same bed, removed his bedrobe, and joined his fiancé beneath the embroidered eiderdown. Wren asked in a half mumble, "Where did you go? Did the steward bring a message?"

He paused, then pressed his thumb beneath her eyes, wiping the shadow of sleep from her sight, then nestled her head against him. "A message, considered of some importance."

"Not more work from the earl? Is it urgent?" She hated the thought of having to immediately jump up, get dressed and while still half asleep, dash out after some hideous criminal.

Landry paused waiting. Then he spoke softly, unsure of her response. "They say your father is dead," Landry finally told her, barely more than a whisper.

Wren looked up. She was naked in the bed, but cossetted both by the blankets and by the muscled warmth of Landry's arms. She breathed, "But you haven't been even called to the trial."

"He needed no trial," Landry told her as he kissed her forehead, his breath hot. "He died of the Black Plague which infested the dungeon. He was the first to be ill."

Now wide awake, she seemed more puzzled than surprised. "No hanging, then, and don't start expecting me to sob my eyes out," she said, her cheek to his heartbeat. "He had to die for all he did. I want him dead too. I want to forget all about him though I suppose I won't."

"I have some talent at making you forget."

She giggled, half catching her breath, while proving she'd not mourn her father's death.

They were in Landry's bedchamber, so often mentioned and always ignored. But now life had changed. Haldon Bennet was dead, soon to be thrown to the pits of Newgate graves, however, other changes had come before. It had been a week past when Landry had carried Wren up the earl's staircase, and had taken her to a room she had never entered before.

She had whispered. "I'm not stupid and I'm not cup-shotten. What do you want?"

"What I intend," he had whispered to her, closing his door behind them, "is to very slowly help you to love me as much as I love you." Then he had laid her gently on the bed.

"I do. Already. I do, so much. You must have guessed, but I won't do that, I mean, – you haven't even asked."

He murmured, "I have a different question first. "Do you love me, and trust me, enough to marry me?"

She no longer had the nightmares and no longer remembered she had never been loved.

"A quiet wedding on the church porch," he had continued, "with Jacob as our priest?"

"Oh yes please," she had said, bouncing upright against his pillows, her eyes brighter than the candles.

More than a week later, Landry's intended wife smiled and kissed his chest. "And you have no worries about your father's death," he asked her.

"Should I?" although she knew the answer.

"No, my love." Landry leaned back, his own naked leg curling across hers. "That creature's death saves others from misery and pain, even the worry of the trial and then the gallows."

"I'll never cry over that man again," she wriggled up, facing Landry. "If I ever feel like crying, I'll run and find you and kiss you instead." Wren leaned forwards and kissed Landry's ear, then laughed. "I only wish he could look down and see how little I want him. Not a single tear."

"I doubt he'll care about that," Landry told her, pulling her hard back into his embrace. The candle was guttering, and the last shivers of flame pitched the bedchamber into shadow. "but it's me, little bird, who cares, though only for you."

ABOUT THE AUTHOR

My passion is for late English medieval history and this forms the background for my historical fiction. I also have a love of fantasy and the wild freedom of the imagination, with its haunting threads of sadness and the exploration of evil. Although all my books have romantic undertones, I would not class them purely as romances. We all wish to enjoy some romance in our lives, there is also a yearning for adventure, mystery, suspense, friendship and spontaneous experience. My books include all of this and more, but my greatest loves are the beauty of the written word, and the utter fascination of good characterisation. Bringing my characters to life is my principal aim.

For more information on my other books please visit **barbaragaskelldenvil.com**

Printed in Great Britain
by Amazon